About the Authors

Kate Hewitt has worked at a number of jobs, from drama teacher to church worker, but writing romance is the best one yet. She also writes women's fiction and all her stories celebrate the healing and redemptive power of love. Kate lives in a tiny village in the English Cotswolds with her husband, five children, and an overly affectionate Golden Retriever.

Tara Pammi can't remember a moment when she wasn't lost in a book, especially a romance which, as a teenager, was much more exciting than a mathematics textbook. Years later Tara's wild imagination and love for the written word revealed what she really wanted to do: write! She lives in Colorado with the most co-operative man on the planet and two daughters. Tara loves to hear from readers and can be reached at tara.pammi@gmail.com or her website www.tarapammi.com

Melissa James is a former nurse, waitress, shop assistant and history student at university. Falling into writing through her husband (who thought it would be a good way to keep her out of trouble while the kids were little) Melissa was soon hooked. A native Australian, she now lives in Switzerland which is fabulous inspiration for new stories.

Royal Rebels

Royal Rebels: His Passionate Duty

KATE HEWITT

TARA PAMMI

MELISSA JAMES

MILLS & BOON

First Published in Great Britain 2021
By Mills & Boon, an imprint of HarperCollins*Publishers* Ltd
1 London Bridge Street, London, SE1 9GF

www.harpercollins.co.uk

HarperCollins*Publishers*
1st Floor, Watermarque Building,
Ringsend Road, Dublin 4, Ireland

ROYAL REBELS: HIS PASSIONATE DUTY
© 2021 Harlequin Books S.A.

A Queen for the Taking? © 2014 Kate Hewitt
Married for the Sheikh's Duty © 2016 Harlequin Books S.A.
The Rebel King © 2009 Lisa Chaplin

Special thanks and acknowledgement are given to Tara Pammi for her contribution to the *Brides for Billionaires* series.

ISBN: 978-0-263-30037-6

MIX
Paper from
responsible sources
FSC™ C007454

This book is produced from independently certified FSC™ paper to ensure responsible forest management.

For more information visit: www.harpercollins.co.uk/green

Printed and bound in Spain
by CPI, Barcelona

A QUEEN FOR THE TAKING?

KATE HEWITT

CHAPTER ONE

ALESSANDRO DIOMEDI, KING of Maldinia, opened the door to the opulent reception room and gazed resolutely upon the woman intended to be his bride. Liana Aterno, the daughter of the duke of Abruzzo, stood in the centre of the room, her body elegant and straight, her gaze clear and steady and even cold. She looked remarkably composed, considering the situation.

Carefully Sandro closed the door, the final click seeming to sound the end of his freedom. But no, that was being fanciful, for his freedom had surely ended six months ago, when he'd left his life in California to return to Maldinia and accept his place as first in line to the throne. Any tattered remnant of it had gone when he'd buried his father and taken his place as king.

'Good afternoon.' His voice seemed to echo through the large room with its gilt walls and frescoed ceilings, the only furniture a few ornate tables of gold and marble set against the walls. Not exactly the most welcoming of spaces, and for a moment Sandro wished he'd specified to put Lady Liana into a more comfortable chamber.

Although, he acknowledged cynically, considering the nature of their imminent discussion—and probable relationship—perhaps this room was appropriate.

'Good afternoon, Your Highness.' She didn't curtsey,

which he was glad of, because he hated all the osten-
tatious trappings of royalty and obeisance, but she did
bend her head in a gesture of respect so for a moment he
could see the bare, vulnerable nape of her neck. It almost
made him soften. Then she lifted her head and pinned
him with that cold, clear-eyed gaze and he felt his heart
harden once more. He didn't want this. He never would.
But she obviously did.

'You had a pleasant journey?'

'Yes, thank you.'

He took a step into the room, studying her. He supposed she was pretty, if you liked women who were colourless. Her hair was so blonde it appeared almost white,
and she wore it pulled back in a tight chignon, a few
wispy tendrils coming to curl about her small, pearl-
studded ears.

She was slight, petite, and yet she carried herself with
both pride and grace, and wore a modest, high-necked,
long-sleeved dress of pale blue silk belted tightly at the
waist, an understated strand of pearls at her throat. She
had folded her hands at her waist like some pious nun
and stood calmly under his obvious scrutiny, accepting
his inspection with a cool and even haughty confidence.
All of it made him angry.

'You know why you're here.'

'Yes, Your Highness.'

'You can dispense with the titles. Since we are considering marriage, you may call me Alessandro, or Sandro,
whichever you prefer.'

'And which do you prefer?'

'You may call me Sandro.' Her composed compliance
annoyed him, although he knew such a reaction was un-
reasonable, even unjust. Yet he still felt it, felt the deep-
seated desire to wipe that cool little smile off her face

and replace it with something real. To feel something real himself.

But he'd left real emotions—honesty, understanding, all of it—behind in California. There was no place for them here, even when discussing his marriage.

'Very well,' she answered evenly, yet she didn't call him anything; she simply waited. Annoyance warred with reluctant amusement and even admiration. Did she have more personality than he'd initially assumed, or was she simply that assured of their possible nuptials?

Their marriage was virtually a sealed deal. He'd invited her to Maldinia to begin negotiations, and she'd agreed with an alacrity he'd found far too telling. So the duke's daughter wanted to be a queen. What a surprise. Another woman on a cold-hearted quest for money, power, and fame.

Love, of course, wouldn't enter into it. It never did; he'd learned that lesson too many times already.

Sandro strode farther into the room, his hands shoved into the pockets of his suit trousers. He walked to the window that looked out on the palace's front courtyard, the gold-tipped spikes of the twelve-foot-high fence that surrounded the entire grounds making his throat tighten. *Such a prison.* And one he'd reentered willingly. One he'd returned to with a faint, frail hope in his heart that had blown to so much cold ash when he'd actually seen his father again, after fifteen years.

I had no choice. If I could have, I'd have left you to rot in California, or, better yet, in hell.

Sandro swallowed and turned away.

'Tell me why you're here, Lady Liana.' He wanted to hear it from her own mouth, those tightly pursed lips.

A slight pause, and then she answered, her voice low

and steady. 'To discuss the possibility of a marriage between us.'

'Such a possibility does not distress or concern you, considering we have never even met before?'

Another pause, even slighter, but Sandro still felt it. 'We have met before, Your Highness. When I was twelve.'

'Twelve.' He turned around to inspect her once again, but her cold blonde beauty didn't trigger any memories. Had she possessed such icy composure, as well as a resolute determination to be queen, at twelve years old? It seemed likely. 'You are to call me Sandro, remember.'

'Of course.'

He almost smiled at that. Was she provoking him on purpose? He'd rather that than the icy, emotionless composure. Any emotion was better than none.

'Where did we meet?'

'At a birthday party for my father in Milan.'

He didn't remember the event, but that didn't really surprise him. If she'd been twelve, he would have been twenty, and about to walk away from his inheritance, his very self, only to return six months ago, when duty demanded he reclaim his soul—or sell it. He still wasn't sure which he'd done. 'And you remembered me?'

For a second, no more, she looked…not disconcerted, but something close to it. Something distressing. Shadows flickered in her eyes, which, now that he'd taken a step closer to her, he saw were a rather startling shade of lavender. She wasn't so colourless, after all. Then she blinked it back and nodded. 'Yes, I did.'

'I'm sorry to say I don't remember you.'

She shrugged, her shoulders barely twitching. 'I wouldn't have expected you to. I was little more than a child.'

He nodded, his gaze still sweeping over her, wondering what thoughts and feelings lurked behind that careful, blank mask of a face. What emotion had shadowed her eyes for just a moment?

Or was he being fanciful, sentimental? He had been before. He'd thought he'd learned the lessons, but perhaps he hadn't.

Liana Aterno had been one of the first names to come up in diplomatic discussions after his father had died, and he'd accepted that he must marry and provide an heir—and soon.

She was related to royalty, had devoted her life to charity work, and her father was prominent in finance and had held various important positions in the European Union—all of which Sandro had to consider, for the sake of his country. She was eminently and irritatingly suitable in every way. The perfect queen consort—and she looked as if she knew it.

'You have not considered other alliances in the meantime?' he asked. 'Other…relationships?' He watched her pale, heart-shaped face, no emotion visible in her eyes, no tightening of her mouth, no tension apparent in her lithe body. The woman reminded him of a statue, something made of cold, lifeless marble.

No, he realised, what she really reminded him of was his mother. An icy, beautiful bitch: emotionless, soulless, caring only about wealth and status and fame. About being queen.

Was that who this woman really was? Or was he being stupidly judgmental and entirely unfair, based on his own sorry experience? It was impossible to tell what she felt from her carefully blank expression, yet he felt a gut-deep revulsion to the fact that she was here at all, that she'd accepted his summons and was prepared to marry a stranger.

Just as he was.

'No,' she said after a moment. 'I have not...' She gave a slight shrug of her shoulders. 'I have devoted myself to charity work.'

Queen or nun. It was a choice women in her elevated position had had to make centuries before, but it seemed archaic now. Absurd.

And yet it was her reality, and very close to his. King or CEO of his own company. Slave or free.

'No one else?' he pressed. 'I have to admit, I am surprised. You're— What? Twenty-eight years old?' She gave a slight nod. 'Surely you've had other offers. Other relationships.'

Her mouth tightened, eyes narrowing slightly. 'As I said, I have devoted myself to charity work.'

'You can devote yourself to charity work and still be in a relationship,' he pointed out. 'Still marry.'

'Indeed, I hope so, Your Highness.'

A noble sentiment, he supposed, but one he didn't trust. Clearly only queen would do for this icy, ambitious woman.

Sandro shook his head slowly. Once he'd dreamed of a marriage, a relationship built on love, filled with passion and humour and joy. Once.

Gazing at her now, he knew she would make an able queen, a wonderful queen—clearly she'd been grooming herself for such a role. And the decision of his marriage was not about desire or choice. It was about duty, a duty he'd wilfully and shamefully ignored for far too long already.

He gave a brisk nod. 'I have obligations in the palace for the rest of this afternoon, but I would like us to have dinner together tonight, if you are amenable.'

She nodded, accepting, unsmiling. 'Of course, Your Highness.'

'We can get to know each other a bit better, perhaps, as well as discuss the practical aspects of this union.'

Another nod, just as swift and emotionless. 'Of course.'

He stared at her hard, wanting her to show some kind of emotion, whether it was uncertainty or hope or simple human interest. He saw nothing in her clear violet gaze, nothing but cool purpose, hard-hearted determination. Suppressing a stab of disappointment, he turned from the room. 'I'll send one of my staff in to see to your needs. Enjoy your stay in the palace of Averne, Lady Liana.'

'Thank you, Your Highness.'

It wasn't until he'd closed the door behind him that he realised she'd never called him Sandro.

Liana let out a long, slow breath and pressed her hands to her middle, relieved that the fluttering had stopped. She felt reassuringly calm now, comfortingly numb. So she'd met Alessandro Diomedi, king of Maldinia. Her future husband.

She crossed to the window and gazed out at the palace courtyard and the ancient buildings of Averne beyond the ornate fence, all framed by a cloudless blue sky. The snow-capped peaks of the Alps were just visible if she craned her neck.

She let out another breath and willed the tension to dissipate from her body. That whole conversation with King Alessandro had been surreal; she'd almost felt as if she'd been floating somewhere up by the ceiling, looking down at these two people, strangers who had never met before, at least not properly. And now they intended to marry each other.

She shook her head slowly, the realisation of what her future would hold still possessing the power to surprise and even unnerve her although it had been several weeks since her parents had suggested she consider Alessandro's suit.

He's a king, Liana, and you should marry. Have children of your own.

She'd never thought to marry, have children. The responsibility and risk were both too great. But she knew it was what her parents wanted, and a convenient marriage, at least, meant a loveless one. A riskless one.

So marry she would, if King Alessandro would have her. She took a deep breath as the flutters started again, reminded herself of the advantages of such a union.

As queen she could continue to devote herself to her charity work, and raise the profile of Hands To Help. Her position would benefit it so much, and she could not turn away from that, just as she could not turn away from her parents' wishes for her life.

She owed them too much.

Really, she told herself, it was perfect. It would give her everything she wanted—everything she would let herself want.

Except it didn't seem the king wanted it. *Her.* She recalled the slightly sneering, incredulous tone, the way he'd looked at her with a kind of weary derision. She didn't please him. Or was it simply marriage that didn't please him?

With a wary unease she recalled his sense of raw, restless power, as if this palace could not contain him, as if his emotions and ideas would bubble over, spill forth.

She wasn't used to that. Her parents were quiet, reserved people, and she had learned to be even more quiet and reserved than they were. To be invisible.

The only time she let herself be heard was when she was giving a public address for Hands To Help. On stage, talking about what the charity did, she had the words to say and the confidence to say them.

But with King Alessandro? With him looking at her as if... Almost as if he didn't even *like* her?

Words had deserted her. She'd cloaked herself in the cool, numbing calm she'd developed over the years, her only way of staying sane. Of surviving, because giving into emotion meant giving into the grief and guilt, and if she did that she knew she'd be lost. She'd drown in the feelings she'd never let herself acknowledge, much less express.

And King Alessandro, of all people, wasn't meant to call them up. This marriage was meant to be *convenient*. Cold. She wouldn't have agreed to it otherwise.

And yet the questions he'd asked her hadn't been either. And the doubt his voicing of them stirred up in her made her insides lurch with panic.

Tell me why you're here, Lady Liana.... Such a possibility does not distress or concern you, considering we have never even met before?

He'd almost sounded as if he *wanted* her to be distressed by the prospect of their marriage.

Perhaps she should have told him that she was.

Except, of course, she wasn't. Wouldn't be. Marriage to King Alessandro made sense. Her parents wanted it. She wanted the visibility for Hands To Help. It was the right choice. It had to be.

And yet just the memory of the king's imposing figure, all restless, rangy muscle and sinewy grace, made her insides quiver and jump. He wore his hair a little too long, ink-black and streaked with silver at the temples, carelessly rumpled as if he'd driven his fingers through it.

His eyes were iron-grey, hard and yet compelling. She'd had to work not to quell under that steely gaze, especially when his mouth had twisted with what had looked—and felt—like derision.

What about her displeased him?

What did he want from her, if not a practical and accepting approach to this marriage?

Liana didn't want to answer that question. She didn't even want to ask it. She had hoped they would be in agreement about this marriage, or as much as they could considering she hadn't wanted to marry at all.

But then perhaps King Alessandro didn't either. Perhaps his seeming resentment was at the situation, rather than his intended bride. Liana's lips formed a grim smile. Two people who had no desire to be married and yet would soon be saying their vows. Well, hopefully they wouldn't actually be seeing all that much of each other.

'Lady Liana?'

She turned to see one of the palace's liveried staff, his face carefully neutral, standing in the doorway. 'Yes?'

'The king requested that I show you to your room, so you may refresh yourself.'

'Thank you.' With a brisk nod she followed the man out of the ornate receiving room and down a long, marble-floored corridor to the east wing of the palace. He took her up a curving marble staircase with an impressive gold bannister, and then down yet another marble corridor until he finally arrived at a suite of rooms.

During the entire journey she'd only seen more staff, liveried and stony faced, giving her the uneasy sense that she was alone in this vast building save for the countless nameless employees. She wondered where the king had gone, or, for that matter, the queen dowager. Surely Sandro's mother, Sophia, intended to receive her?

Although, Liana acknowledged, she couldn't assume anything. The summons to Maldinia's royal palace had come so quickly and suddenly, a letter with Alessandro's royal insignia on top, its few pithy sentences comprising the request for Lady Liana Aterno of Abruzzo to discuss the possibility of marriage. Liana had been in shock; her mother, full of expectation.

This would be so good for you, Liana. You should marry. Why not Alessandro? Why not a king?

Why not, indeed? Her parents were traditional, even old-fashioned. Daughters married, produced heirs. It was perhaps an archaic idea in this modern world, but they clung to it.

And she couldn't let them down in their hopes for her. She owed them that much at least. She owed them so much more.

'These will be your rooms for your stay here, my lady. If you need anything, simply press the bell by the door and someone will come to your attention.'

'Thank you,' Liana murmured, and stepped into the sumptuous set of rooms. After ensuring she had no further requirements, the staff member left with a quiet click of the door. Liana gazed around the huge bedroom, its opulence a far cry from her modest apartment in Milan.

Acres of plush carpet stretched in every direction, and in the centre of the room, on its own dais, stood a magnificent canopied four-poster bed, piled high with silk pillows. The bed faced a huge stone fireplace with elaborate scrollwork, and several deep armchairs in blue patterned silk flanked it. It was a chilly March day and a fire had already been laid and lit, and now crackled cheerfully in the huge hearth.

Slowly Liana walked towards the fireplace and stretched her hands out to the flames. Her hands were icy; they always went cold when she was nervous. And despite her every attempt to convey the opposite to King Alessandro, she *had* been nervous.

She hadn't expected to be, had assumed a marriage such as theirs would be conducted like a corporate merger, their introduction no more than a business meeting. She wasn't naive; she knew what marriage would entail. Alessandro needed an heir.

But she hadn't expected his energy, his emotion. He'd been the opposite of her in every way: restless, quick-tempered, seething with something she didn't understand.

She closed her eyes, wished briefly that she could return to the simple life she'd made for herself working at the foundation, living in Milan, going out on occasion with friends. It probably didn't look like much to most people, but she'd found a soothing enjoyment in those small things. That was all she'd ever wanted, all she'd ever asked for. The safety of routines had calmed and comforted her, and just one meeting with Sandro Diomedi had ruffled up everything inside her.

Swallowing hard, she opened her eyes. *Enough.* Her life was not her own, and hadn't been since she was eight years old. She accepted that as the price she must pay, *should* pay.

But she wouldn't think anymore about that. It was as if there were a door in Liana's mind, and it clanged shut by sheer force of will. She wouldn't think about Chiara.

She turned away from the fire, crossing to the window to gaze out at the bare gardens still caught in the chill of late winter. Strange to think this view would become familiar when she was wed. This palace, this life, would all become part of her normal existence.

As would the king. *Sandro.*

She suppressed a shiver. What would marriage to King

Alessandro look like? She had a feeling it wouldn't look or feel like she'd assumed. Convenient. Safe.

She'd never even had a proper boyfriend, never been kissed except for a few quick, sloppy attempts on a couple dates she'd gone on over the years, pressured by her parents to meet a boy, fall in love, even though she hadn't been interested in either.

But Alessandro would want more than a kiss, and with him she felt it would be neither sloppy nor quick.

She let out a soft huff of laughter, shaking her head at herself. How on earth would she know how Alessandro would kiss?

But you'll find out soon enough.

She swallowed hard, the thought alone enough to make her palms go icy again. She didn't want to think about that, not yet.

She gazed around the bedroom, the afternoon stretching emptily in front of her. She couldn't bear to simply sit and wait in her room; she preferred being busy and active. She'd take a walk through the palace gardens, she decided. The fresh air would be welcome.

She dressed casually but carefully in wool trousers of pale grey and a twin set in mauve cashmere, the kind of bland, conservative clothes she'd chosen for ever.

She styled her hair, leaving it down, and did her discreet make-up and jewellery—pearls, as she always wore. It took her nearly an hour before she was ready, and then as soon as she left her room one of the staff standing to attention in the endless corridor hurried towards her.

'My lady?'

'I'd like to go outside, please. To have a stroll around the gardens if I may.'

'Very good, my lady.'

She followed the man in his blue-and-gold-tasselled

uniform down the corridor and then down several others and finally to a pair of French windows that led to a wide terrace with shallow steps leading to the gardens.

'Would you like an escort—?' he began, but Liana shook her head.

'No, thank you. I'll just walk around by myself.'

She breathed in the fresh, pine-scented mountain air as she took the first twisting path through the carefully clipped box hedges. Even though the palace was in the centre of Maldinia's capital city of Averne, it was very quiet in the gardens, the only sound the rustle of the wind through the still-bare branches of the trees and shrubs.

Liana dug her hands into the pockets of her coat, the chilly wind stinging her cheeks, glad for an afternoon's respite from the tension of meeting with the king. As she walked she examined the flowerbeds, trying to identify certain species although it was difficult with everything barely in blossom.

The sun was starting to sink behind the snow-capped peaks on the horizon when Liana finally turned back to the palace. She needed to get ready for her dinner with the king, and already she felt her brief enjoyment of the gardens replaced by a wary concern over the coming evening.

She could not afford to make a single misstep, and yet as she walked back towards the French windows glinting in the late afternoon sun she realised how little information King Alessandro had given her. Was this dinner a formal occasion with members of state, or something smaller and more casual? Would the queen be dining with them, or other members of the royal family? Liana knew that Alessandro's brother, Leo, and his wife, Alyse, lived in Averne, as did his sister, the princess Alexa.

Her steps slowed as she came up to the terrace; she

found herself approaching the evening with both dread and a tiny, treacherous flicker of anticipation. Sandro's raw, restless energy might disturb her, but it also fascinated her. It was, she knew, a dangerous fascination, and one she needed to get under control if she was going to go ahead with this marriage.

Which she was.

Anything else, at this point, was impossible, involved too much disappointment for too many people.

She forced her worries back along with that fascination as she opened the French windows. As she came inside she stopped short, her breath coming out in a rush, for Alessandro had just emerged from a gilt-panelled door, a frown settled between his dark, straight brows. He glanced up, stilling when he saw her, just as Liana was still.

'Good evening. You've been out for a walk in the gardens?'

She nodded, her mind seeming to have snagged on the sight of him, his rumpled hair, his silvery eyes, his impossibly hard jaw. 'Yes, Your Highness.'

'You're cold.' To her complete shock Alessandro touched her cheek with his fingertips. The touch was so very slight and yet so much more than she'd expected or ever known. Instinctively she jerked back, and she watched as his mouth, which had been curving into a faint smile, thinned into a hard line.

'I'll see you at dinner,' he said flatly. He turned away and strode down the hall.

Drawing a deep breath, she threw back her shoulders, forced herself to turn towards her own suite of rooms and walk with a firm step even as inside she wondered just what would happen tonight—and how she would handle it.

CHAPTER TWO

ALESSANDRO GAZED DISPASSIONATELY at his reflection as he twitched his black tie into place. This afternoon's meeting with Lady Liana had gone about as well as he could have expected, and yet it still left him dissatisfied. Restless, as everything about his royal life did.

This palace held too many painful memories, too many hard lessons. *Don't trust. Don't love. Don't believe that anyone loves you back.*

Every one drilled into him over years of neglect, indifference, and anger.

Sighing, he thrust the thought aside. He might hate returning to the palace, but he'd done it of his own free will. Returned to face his father and take up his kingship because he'd known it was the right thing to do. It was his duty.

And because you, ever naive, thought your father might actually forgive you. Finally love you.

What a blind fool he was.

He wouldn't, Sandro thought as he fastened his cufflinks, be blind about his wife. He knew exactly what he was getting into, just what he was getting from the lovely Lady Liana.

Yet for a moment, when he'd seen Liana coming through the French windows, her hair streaming over her shoulders like pale satin, the fading sunlight touching it with gold, he'd felt his heart lighten rather ridiculously.

She'd looked so different from the coldly composed woman he'd encountered in the formal receiving room. She'd looked alive and vibrant and beautiful, her lavender eyes sparkling, her cheeks pink from the wind.

He'd felt a leap of hope then that she might not be the cold, ambitious queen-in-waiting she'd seemed just hours ago, but then he'd seen that icy self-possession enter her eyes, she'd jerked back when he had, unthinkingly, touched her, and disappointment had settled in him once more, a leaden weight.

It was too late to wish for something else for his marriage, Sandro knew. For his life. When he'd received the phone call from his father—after fifteen years of stony silence on both sides—he'd given up his right to strive or even wish for anything different. He'd been living for himself, freely, selfishly, for too long already. He'd always known, even if he'd acted as if he hadn't, that it couldn't last. Shouldn't.

And so he'd returned and taken up his kingship and all it required…such as a wife. An ambitious, appropriate, perfect wife.

His expression hardening, he turned from his reflection and went in search of the woman who fitted all those soulless requirements.

He found her already waiting in the private dining room he'd requested be prepared for their meal. She stood by the window, straight and proud, dressed in an evening gown of champagne-coloured silk.

Her face went blank as she caught sight of him, and after a second's pause she nodded regally as he closed the door behind him.

Sandro let his gaze sweep over her; the dress was by

no means immodest and yet it still clung to her slight curves. It had a vaguely Grecian style, with pearl-and-diamond clips at each shoulder and a matching pearl-and-diamond pendant nestled in the V between her breasts.

The dress clung to those small yet shapely breasts, nipping in at her waist before swirling out around her legs and ending in a silken puddle at her feet. She looked both innocent and made of ivory, everything about her so cold and perfect, making Sandro want to add a streak of colour to her cheeks or her lips—would her cheeks turn pink as they'd been before if he touched her again?

What if he kissed her?

Was she aware of his thoughts? Did she feel that sudden tension inside her as well? He couldn't tell anything from her blank face, her veiled eyes.

She'd pulled her hair back in a tight coil, emphasising her high cheekbones and delicate bone structure, and he had a mad impulse to jerk the diamond-tipped pins from her hair and see it spill over her shoulders in all of its moon-coloured glory. What would she do, he wondered, if he acted on that urge? How would this ice princess in all her white, silken haughtiness respond if he pulled her into his arms and kissed her quite senseless?

Almost as if she could sense the nature of his thoughts she lifted her chin, her eyes sparking violet challenge. *Good.* Sandro wanted to see emotion crack that icy demeanour; he wanted to sense something real from her, whether it was uncertainty or nervousness, humour or passion.

Passion.

It had been a while since he'd been with a woman, a lot longer since he'd been in a relationship. He felt a kick of lust and was glad for it. Perhaps he would act on it tonight. Perhaps *that* would melt the ice, and he would find the real woman underneath all that haughtiness... if she existed at all. He hoped, for both of their sakes, that she did.

'Did you have a pleasant afternoon?' he asked politely. He moved to the table that was set for two in front of the huge fireplace and took the bottle of wine that had been left open to breathe on the side.

'Yes, thank you.' She remained by the window, utterly still, watching him.

Sandro lifted the bottle. 'May I pour you a glass?'

A hesitation, and then she nodded. 'Yes, thank you.'

Yes, thank you. He wondered if he could get her to say it a third time. The woman had perfect manners, perfect everything, but he didn't want perfection. He wanted something real and raw and passionate—something he'd never had with any woman, any *person*, even though he'd long been looking for it. Searching and striving for it. He suspected Lady Liana was the last person who could satisfy him in that regard.

He poured them both glasses of red wine, the ruby liquid glinting in the dancing light thrown from the flames of the fire. He crossed the room to where she still stood by the window and handed her the glass, letting his fingers brush hers.

He felt her awareness of that little act, her eyes widening slightly before she took the glass with a murmured thanks. So far they'd been alone for five minutes and she'd said thank you three times, and nothing else.

He walked back to the fire, taking a long swallow of his wine, enjoying the way the velvety liquid coated his throat and fired his belly. Needing that warmth. 'What did you think of the gardens? Were they to your liking?' he asked, turning around to face her. She held the wine glass in front of her, both hands clasped around it, although she had yet to take a sip.

'Yes, thank you—'

'Yes, thank you,' he mimicked, a sneering, almost cruel tone to his voice. He was reacting out of a deep-seated revulsion to this kind of shallow conversation, this *fakery*. It reminded him of too much disappointment, too much pain. Too many lies. 'Do you say anything else?'

She blinked, but otherwise showed no discomfiture. 'Are you irritated by my manners, Your Highness?'

'You are meant to call me Sandro, but you have yet to do so.'

'I apologise. Your first name does not come easily to me.'

He arched an eyebrow, curious yet also still filled with that edgy restlessness that he knew would lead him to say—or do—things they both might regret.

'And why is that?' he asked, and she lifted her shoulders in a tiny shrug.

'You are the king of Maldinia.'

'It's nothing more than a title.'

Her mouth tightened, eyes flashing before she carefully ironed out her expression, her face smoothing like a blank piece of paper. 'Is that what you truly think?'

No, it wasn't. The crown upon his head—the title before his name—was a leaden weight inside him, dragging him down. It always had been, rife with expectations and disappointment. He'd seen how his father had treated that title, and he had no desire to emulate him. No desire to spiral down that destructive path, and yet he did not know if he possessed the strength to do otherwise. 'What do you think?' he asked.

'I think it is an honour and a privilege.'

'And one you are eager to share.' He heard the sardonic

edge to his words and he knew she did too, even though her expression didn't change, didn't even flicker. Funny, how he knew. How he'd somehow become attuned to this ice princess without even trying.

Or maybe he just knew her type, the kind of woman who would do anything to be queen, who didn't care about love or friendship or any softer emotion. Hadn't he encountered such women before, starting with his own mother? And Teresa had been the same, interested only in his wealth and status. He'd yet to find a woman who didn't care about such things, and he no longer had the freedom to search.

'Of course,' she answered calmly.

'Even though you don't know me.'

She hesitated, and he took another sip of wine, watching her over the rim of his glass. He wondered how far he would have to push her to evoke some response—*any* response. Further than that, clearly, for she didn't answer, merely sipped her own wine, her expression coolly serene.

'It doesn't bother you,' he pressed, 'that we barely know each other? That you are going to pledge your life to a stranger? Your body?'

Awareness flared in her eyes at his provocative remark, and he took a step towards her. He wanted her to admit it did, longed for her to say something real, something about how strange or uncertain or fearful this arrangement was. Something. Anything.

She regarded him for a moment, her expression thoughtful and yet still so shuttered. 'So you asked me earlier,' she remarked. 'And yet I thought that was the point of this evening. To get to know one another.'

'Yet you came to Maldinia prepared to marry me without such a luxury.'

'A fact which seems to provoke you, yet I assume you have been prepared to marry me under the same circumstances?' She was as coolly challenging as he had been, and he felt a flicker of respect, a frisson of interest. At least she'd stopped with her milky thank yous. At least she was being honest, even if he despised such truth.

'I was and still am,' he answered. 'I have a duty to provide an heir.'

The faintest blush touched her cheeks at the mention of heirs and she glanced away. 'So you are acting out of duty, and I am not?'

'What duty insists you marry a king?'

'One it appears you wouldn't understand.'

'Oh, I understand,' he answered, and she pressed her lips together, lifted her chin.

'Do you? Why don't you tell me, then, what you understand?'

He stared at her for a moment, and then decided to answer her with honesty. He doubted he'd get even a flicker of response from her. 'You want a title,' he stated flatly. 'A crown. Wealth and power—'

'And in exchange I will give you my allegiance and service,' she answered back, as unruffled as he'd suspected. 'Children and heirs, God willing. Is it not a fair trade?'

He paused, amazed at her plain speaking, even a little admiring of it. At least she wasn't pretending to him, the way so many others would. He could be thankful for that, at least. 'I suppose it is,' he answered slowly. 'But I would prefer my marriage not to be a trade.'

'And yet it must be, because you are king. That is not my fault.'

'No,' he agreed quietly. 'But even so—'

'You think my reasons for this marriage are less than yours,' Liana finished flatly. 'Less worthy.'

Her astuteness unnerved him. 'I suppose I do. You've admitted what you want, Lady Liana. Money. Power. Fame. Such things seem shallow to me.'

'If I wanted them for my own gratification, I suppose they would be.'

He frowned. 'What else could you possibly want them for?'

She just shook her head. 'What has made you so cynical?'

'Life, Lady Liana. Life.' He glanced away, not wanting to think about what had made him this suspicious, this sure that everyone was just out for something, that people were simply to be manipulated and used. Even your own children.

'In any case, you clearly don't relish the prospect of marriage to me,' she said quietly.

'No, I don't,' he answered after a pause. He turned to meet her clear gaze directly. 'I'm sorry if that offends you.'

'It doesn't offend me,' she answered. 'Surprises me, perhaps.'

'And why is that?'

'Because I had assumed we were in agreement about the nature of this marriage.'

'Which is?' he asked, wanting to hear more despite hating her answers, the reality of their situation.

She blinked, a hint of discomfiture, even uncertainty, in the way she shifted her weight, clutched her wine glass a little more tightly. 'Convenience.'

'Ah, yes. Convenience.' And he supposed it was convenient for her to have a crown. A title. And all the trappings that came with them. 'At least you're honest about it.'

'Why shouldn't I be?'

'Most women who have wanted my title or my money have been a bit more coy about what they really want,' he answered. 'More conniving.'

'You'll find I am neither.'

'How refreshing.'

She simply raised her eyebrows at his caustic tone and Sandro suppressed a sigh. He certainly couldn't fault her honesty. 'Tell me about yourself,' he finally said, and she lifted her shoulders in a tiny shrug.

'What is it you wish to know?'

'Anything. Everything. Where have you been living?'

'In Milan.'

'Ah, yes. Your charity work.'

Ire flashed in her eyes. 'Yes, my charity work.'

'What charity do you support again?'

'Hands To Help.'

'Which is?'

'A foundation that offers support to families with disabled children.'

'What kind of support?'

'Counselling, grants to families in need, practical assistance with the day-to-day.' She spoke confidently, clearly on familiar ground. He saw how her eyes lit up and everything in her suddenly seemed full of energy and determination.

'This charity,' he observed. 'It means a lot to you.'

She nodded, her lips pressed together in a firm line. 'Everything.'

Everything? Her zeal was admirable, yet also surprising, even strange. 'Why is that, Lady Liana?'

She jerked back slightly, as if the question offended her. 'Why shouldn't it?'

'As admirable as it is, I am intrigued. Most people

don't live for their philanthropic causes. I would have thought you simply helped out with various charities as a way to bide your time.'

'Bide my time?'

'Until you married.'

She let out an abrupt laugh, the sound hard and humourless. 'You are as traditional as my parents.'

'Yet you are here.'

'Meaning?'

He spread his hands. 'Not many women, not even the daughters of dukes, would enter a loveless marriage, having barely met the man in question, in this day and age.'

She regarded him coolly. 'Unless, of course, there was something in it for them. Money. Status. A title.'

'Exactly.'

She shook her head. 'And what do you see as being in it for you, Your Highness? I'm curious, considering how reluctant you are to marry.'

His lips curved in a humourless smile. 'Why, all the things you told me, of course. You've detailed your own attributes admirably, Lady Liana. I get a wife who will be the perfect queen. Who will stand by my side and serve my country. And of course, God willing, give me an heir. Preferably two.'

A faint blush touched those porcelain cheeks again, intriguing him. She was twenty-eight years old and yet she blushed like an untouched virgin. Surely she'd had relationships before. Lovers.

And yet in their conversation this afternoon, she'd intimated that she hadn't.

'That still doesn't answer my question,' she said after a moment. 'I understand your need to marry. But why me in particular?'

Sandro shrugged. 'You're a duke's daughter, you have

shown yourself to be philanthropic, your father is an important member of the European Union. You're fertile, I assume?'

The pink in her cheeks deepened. 'There is no reason to think otherwise.'

'I suppose that aspect of unions such as these is always a bit of a risk.'

'And if I couldn't have children?' she asked after a moment. 'Would we divorce?'

Would they? Everything in him railed against that as much as the actual marriage. It was all so expedient, so cold. 'We'll cross that bridge when we come to it.'

'How comforting.'

'I can't pretend to like any of this, Lady Liana. I'd rather have a normal relationship, with a woman who—' He stopped suddenly, realising he was revealing too much. *A woman who chose me. Who loved me for myself, and not because of my money or my crown.* No, he wasn't about to tell this cold-blooded woman any of that.

'A woman who?' she prompted.

'A woman who wasn't interested in my title.'

'Why don't you find one, then?' she asked, and she didn't sound hurt or even peeved, just curious. 'There must be a woman out there who would marry you for your own sake, Your Highness.'

And she clearly wasn't one of them, a fact that he'd known and accepted yet still, when so baldly stated, made him inwardly flinch. 'I have yet to find one,' he answered shortly. 'And you are meant to call me Sandro.'

'Then you must call me Liana.'

'Very well, Liana. It's rather difficult to find a woman who isn't interested in my title. The very fact that I have it attracts the kind of woman who is interested in it.'

'Yet you renounced your inheritance for fifteen years,'

Liana observed. 'Couldn't you have found a woman in California?'

He felt a flash of something close to rage, or perhaps just humiliation. She made it sound as if he was pathetic, unable to find a woman to love him for himself.

And maybe he was—but he didn't like this ice princess knowing about it. Remarking on it.

'The women I met in California were interested in my wealth and status,' he said shortly. He thought of Teresa, then pushed the thought away. He'd tumbled into love with her like a foolish puppy; he wouldn't make that mistake again. He wouldn't have the choice, he acknowledged. His attempt at relationships ended in this room, with this woman, and love had no place in what was between them.

'I'm not interested in your wealth,' Liana said after a moment. 'I have no desire to drape myself with jewels or prance about in designer dresses—or whatever it is these grasping women do.'

There was a surprising hint of humour in her voice, and his interested snagged on it. 'These grasping women?'

'You seem to have met so many, Your— Sandro. I had no idea there were so many cold, ambitious women about, circling like hawks.'

His lips twitched at the image even as a cynical scepticism took its familiar hold. 'So you do not count yourself among the hawks, Liana?'

'I do not, but you might. I am interested in being your queen, Sandro. Not for the wealth or the fame, but for the opportunity it avails me.'

'And what opportunity is that?'

'To promote the charity I've been working for. Hands To Help.'

He stared at her, not bothering to mask his incredulity. Was he really expected to believe such nonsense? 'I know you said that the charity meant everything to you, but, even so, you are willing to marry a complete stranger in order to give it greater visibility?'

She pursed her lips. 'Clearly you find that notion incredible.'

'I do. You are throwing your life away on a good cause.'

'That's what marriage to you will be? Throwing my life away?' She raised her eyebrows, her eyes glinting with violet sparks. 'You don't rate yourself highly, then.'

'I will never love you.' Even if he had once longed for a loving relationship, he knew he would never find it with this woman. Even if she wanted to be queen for the sake of some charity—a notion that still seemed ridiculous— she still wanted to be queen. Wanted his title, not him. Did the reason why really matter?

'I'm not interested in love,' she answered, seeming completely unfazed by his bald statement. 'And since it appears you aren't either, I don't know why our arrangement can't suit us both. You might not want to marry, Your Highness—'

'Sandro.'

'Sandro,' she amended with a brief nod, 'but obviously you have to. I have my own reasons for agreeing to this marriage, as you know. Why can we not come to an amicable arrangement instead of festering with resentment over what neither of us can change?'

'You could change, if you wanted to,' Sandro pointed out. 'As much as you might wish to help this charity of yours, you are not bound by duty in quite the same way as I am.'

Her expression shuttered, and he felt instinctively that

she was hiding something, some secret sorrow. 'No,' she agreed quietly, 'not in quite the same way.'

She held his gaze for a moment that felt suspended, stretching into something else. All of a sudden, with an intensity that caught him by surprise, he felt his body tighten with both awareness and desire. He wanted to know what the shadows in her eyes hid and he wanted to chase them away. He wanted to see them replaced with the light of desire, the blaze of need.

His gaze swept over her elegant form, her slight yet tempting curves draped in champagne-coloured silk, and desire coiled tighter inside him.

An amicable arrangement, indeed. Why not?

She broke the gaze first, taking a sip of wine, and he forced his mind back to more immediate concerns…such as actually getting to know this woman.

'So you live in Milan. Your parents have an apartment there?'

'They do, but I have my own as well.'

'You enjoy city life?'

She shrugged. 'It has proved convenient for my work.'

Her charity work, for which she didn't even get paid. Could she possibly be speaking the truth when she said she was marrying him to promote the charity she supported? It seemed absurd and extreme, yet he had seen the blazing, determined light in her eyes when she spoke of it.

'What has made you so devoted to that particular charity?' he asked and everything in her went tense and still.

'It's a good cause,' she answered after a moment, her expression decidedly wary.

'There are plenty of good causes. What did you say Hands To Help did? Support families with disabled children?'

'Yes.'

A few moments ago she'd been blazing with confidence as she'd spoken about it, but now every word she spoke was offered reluctantly, every movement repressive. She was hiding something, Sandro thought, but he had no idea what it could be.

'And did anything in particular draw you to this charity?' he asked patiently. Getting answers from her now felt akin to drawing blood from a stone.

For a second, no more, she looked conflicted, almost tormented. Her features twisted and her eyes appealed to him with an agony he didn't understand. Then her expression shuttered once more, like a veil being drawn across her face, and she looked away. 'Like I said, it's a good cause.'

And that, Sandro thought bemusedly, was that. Very well. He had plenty of time to discover the secrets his bride-to-be was hiding, should he want to know them. 'And what about before you moved to Milan? You went to university?'

'No. I started working with Hands To Help when I was eighteen.' She shifted restlessly, then pinned a bright smile on her face that Sandro could see straight through.

'What about you, Sandro?' she asked, stumbling only slightly over his name. 'Did you enjoy your university days?'

He thought of those four years at Cambridge, the heady freedom and the bitter disillusionment. Had he enjoyed them? In some respects, yes, but in others he had been too angry and hurt to enjoy anything.

'They served a purpose,' he said after a moment, and she cocked her head.

'Which was?'

'To educate myself.'

'You renounced your title upon your graduation, did you not?'

Tension coiled inside him. That much at least was common knowledge, but he still didn't like talking about it, had no desire for her to dig. They both had secrets, it seemed.

'I did.'

'Why?'

Such a bald question. Who had ever asked him that? No one had dared, and yet this slip of a woman with her violet eyes and carefully blank expression did, and without a tremor. 'It felt necessary at the time.' He spoke repressively, just as she had, and she accepted it, just as he had. Truce.

Yet stupidly, he felt almost disappointed. She wasn't interested in him; of course she wasn't. She'd already said as much. And he didn't want to talk about it, so why did he care?

He didn't. He was just being contrary because even as he accepted the necessity of this marriage, everything in him rebelled against it. Rebelled against entering this prison of a palace, with its hateful memories and endless expectations. Rebelled against marrying a woman he would never love, who would never love him. Would their convenient marriage become as bitter and acrimonious as his parents'? He hoped not, but he didn't know how they would keep themselves from it.

'We should eat,' he said, his voice becoming a bit brusque, and he went to pull out her chair, gesturing for her to come forward.

She did, her dress whispering about her legs as she moved, her head held high, her bearing as straight and proud as always. As she sat down, Sandro breathed in the perfumed scent of her, something subtle and floral, perhaps rosewater.

He glanced down at the back of her neck as she sat, the skin so pale with a sprinkling of fine golden hairs. He had the sudden urge to touch that soft bit of skin, to press his lips to it. He imagined how she would react and his mouth curved in a mocking smile. He wondered again if the ice princess was ice all the way through. He would, he decided, find out before too long. Perhaps they could enjoy that aspect of their marriage, if nothing else.

'What have you been doing in California?' she asked as one of the palace staff came in with their first course, plates of mussels nestled in their shells and steamed in white wine and butter.

'I ran my own IT firm.'

'Did you enjoy it?'

'Very much so.'

'Yet you gave it up to return to Maldinia.'

It had been the most agonising decision he'd ever made, and yet it had been no decision at all. 'I did,' he answered shortly.

She cocked her head, her lavender gaze sweeping thoughtfully over him. 'Are you glad you did?'

'Glad doesn't come into it,' he replied. 'It was simply what I needed to do.'

'Your duty.'

'Yes.'

Sandro pried a mussel from its shell and ate the succulent meat, draining the shell of its juices. Liana, he noticed, had not touched her meal; her mouth was drawn into a prim little line. He arched an eyebrow.

'Are mussels not to your liking?'

'They're delicious, I'm sure.' With dainty precision she pierced a mussel with her fork and attempted, delicately, to wrest it from its shell. Sandro watched, amused, as she wrangled with the mussel and failed. This was a food that required greasy fingers and smacking lips, a wholehearted and messy commitment to the endeavour. He sat back in his chair and waited to see what his bride-to-be would do next.

She took a deep breath, pressed her lips together, and tried again. She stabbed the mussel a bit harder this time, and then pulled her fork back. The utensil came away empty and the mussel flew across her plate, the shell clattering against the porcelain. Sandro's lips twitched.

Liana glanced up, her eyes narrowing. 'You're laughing at me.'

'You need to hold the mussel with your fingers,' he explained, leaning forward, his mouth curving into a mocking smile. 'And that means you might actually get them dirty.'

Her gaze was all cool challenge. 'Or you could provide a knife.'

'But this is so much more interesting.' He took another mussel, holding the shell between his fingers, and prised the meat from inside, then slurped the juice and tossed the empty shell into a bowl provided for that purpose. 'See?' He lounged back in his chair, licking his fingers with deliberate relish. He enjoyed discomfiting Liana. He'd enjoy seeing her getting her fingers dirty and her mouth smeared with butter even more, actually living life inside of merely observing it, but he trusted she would find a way to eat her dinner without putting a single hair out of place. That was the kind of woman she was.

Liana didn't respond, just watched him in that chilly way of hers, as if he was a specimen she was meant to examine. And what conclusions would she draw? He doubted whether she could understand what drove him, just as he found her so impossibly cold and distant. They were simply too far apart in their experience of and desire for life to ever see eye to eye on anything, even a plate of mussels.

'Do you think you'll manage any of them?' he asked, nodding towards her still-full plate, and her mouth firmed.

Without replying she reached down and held one shell with the tips of her fingers, stabbing the meat with her fork. With some effort she managed to wrench the mussel from its shell and put it in her mouth, chewing resolutely. She left the juice.

'Is that what we call compromise?' Sandro asked softly and she lifted her chin.

'I call it necessity.'

'We'll have to employ both in our marriage.'

'As you would in any marriage, I imagine,' she answered evenly, and he acknowledged the point with a terse nod.

Liana laid down her fork; clearly she wasn't going to attempt another mussel. 'What exactly is it you dislike about me, Your Highness?'

'*Sandro*. My name is Sandro.' She didn't respond and he drew a breath, decided for honesty. 'You ask what I dislike about you? Very well. The fact that you decided on this marriage without even meeting me—save an unremarkable acquaintance fifteen years ago—tells me everything I need to know about you. And I like none of it.'

'So you have summed me up and dismissed me, all because of one decision I have made? The same decision you have made?'

'I admit it sounds hypocritical, but I had no choice. You did.'

'And did it not occur to you,' she answered back, her voice still so irritatingly calm, 'that any woman you approached regarding this marriage, any woman who accepted, would do so out of similar purpose? Your wife can't win, Sandro, whether it's me or someone else. You are determined to hate your bride, simply because she agreed to marry you.'

Her logic surprised and discomfited him, because he knew she was right. He was acting shamefully, *stupidly*, taking out his frustration on a woman who was only doing what he'd expected and even requested. 'I'm sorry,' he said after a moment. 'I realise I am making this more difficult for both of us, and to no purpose. We must marry.'

'You could choose someone else,' she answered quietly. 'Someone more to your liking.'

He raised an eyebrow, wearily amused. 'Are you suggesting I do?'

'No, but…' She shrugged, spreading her hands. 'I do not wish to be your life sentence.'

'And will I be yours?'

'I have accepted the limitations of this marriage in a way it appears you have not.'

Which made him sound like a hopeless romantic. No, he'd accepted the limitations. He was simply railing against them, which as she'd pointed out was to no purpose. And he'd stop right now.

'Forgive me, Liana. I have been taking out my frustrations on you, and I will not do so any longer. I wish to marry you and no other. You are, as I mentioned before, so very suitable, and I apologise for seeming to hold it against you.' This little speech sounded stiltedly formal, but he did mean it. He'd made his choices. He needed to live with them.

'Apology accepted,' she answered quietly, but with no

real warmth. Could he even blame her? He'd hardly en-
deared himself to her. He wasn't sure he could.

He reached for his wine glass. 'In any case, after the
debacle of my brother's marriage, not to mention my
parents', our country needs the stability of a shock-free
monarchy.'

'Your brother? Prince Leo?'

'You know him?'

'I've met him on several occasions. He's married to
Alyse Barras now.'

'The wedding of the century, apparently. The love
story of the century….' He shook his head, knowing
how his brother must have hated the pretence. 'And it
was all a lie.'

'But they are still together?'

Sandro nodded. 'The irony is, they actually do love
each other. But they didn't fall in love until after their
marriage.'

'So their six-year engagement was—?'

'A sham. And the public isn't likely to forgive that
very easily.'

'It hardly matters, since Leo will no longer be king.'

God, she was cold. 'I suppose not.'

'I only meant,' she clarified, as if she could read his
thoughts, 'that the publicity isn't an issue for them anymore.'

'But it will be for us,' he filled in, 'which is why I have
chosen to be honest about the convenience of our marriage. No one will ever think we're in love.'

'Instead of a fairy tale,' she said, 'we will have a business partnership.'

'I suppose that is as good a way of looking at it as any
other.' Even if the thought of having a marriage like his
parents'—one born of convenience and rooted in little

more than tolerance—made everything in him revolt. If a marriage had no love and perhaps not even any sympathy between the two people involved, how could it not sour? Turn into something despicable and hate-filled?

How could *he* not?

He had no other example.

Taking a deep breath, he pressed a discreet button to summon the wait staff. It was time for the next course. Time to move on. Instead of fighting his fate, like the unhappy, defiant boy he'd once been, he needed to accept it—and that meant deciding just how he could survive a marriage to Lady Liana Aterno.

CHAPTER THREE

LIANA STUDIED SANDRO'S face and wondered what he was thinking. Her husband-to-be was, so far, an unsettling enigma. She didn't understand why everything she did, from being polite to trying to eat mussels without splattering herself with butter, seemed to irritate him, but she knew it did. She saw the way his silvery eyes darkened to storm-grey, his mobile mouth tightening into a firm line.

So he didn't want to marry her. That undeniable truth lodged inside her like a cold, hard stone. She hadn't expected that, but could she really be surprised? He'd spent fifteen years escaping his royal duty. Just because he'd decided finally to honour his commitments didn't mean, as he'd admitted himself, that he relished the prospect.

And yet it was hard not to take his annoyance personally. Not to let it hurt—which was foolish, because this marriage wasn't personal. She didn't want his love or even his affection, but she had, she realised, hoped for agreement. Understanding.

A footman came in and cleared their plates, and Liana was glad to see the last of the mussels. She felt resentment stir inside her at the memory of Sandro's mocking smile. He'd enjoyed seeing her discomfited, would have probably laughed aloud if she'd dropped a mussel in her lap or sent it spinning across the table.

Perhaps she should have dived in and smeared her face and fingers with butter; perhaps he would have liked her better then. But a lifetime of careful, quiet choices had kept her from making a mess of anything, even a plate of mussels. She couldn't change now, not even over something so trivial.

The footman laid their plates down, a main course of lamb garnished with fresh mint.

'At least this shouldn't present you with too much trouble,' Sandro said softly as the door clicked shut. Liana glanced up at him.

She felt irritation flare once more, surprising her, because she usually didn't let herself feel irritated or angry...or anything. Yet this man called feelings up from deep within her, and she didn't even know why or how. She definitely didn't like it. 'You seem to enjoy amusing yourself at my expense.'

'I meant only to tease,' he said quietly. 'I apologise if I've offended you. But you are so very perfect, Lady Liana—and I'd like to see you a little less so.'

Perfect? If only he knew the truth. 'No one is perfect.'

'You come close.'

'That is not, I believe, a compliment.'

His lips twitched, drawing her attention to them. He had such sculpted lips, almost as if they belonged on a statue. She yanked her gaze upwards, but his eyes were no better. Silvery grey and glinting with amusement.

She felt as if a fist had taken hold of her heart, plunged into her belly. Everything quivered, and the sensation was not particularly pleasant. Or perhaps it was *too* pleasant; she felt that same thrill of fascination that had taken hold of her when she'd first met him.

'I would like to see you,' Sandro said, his voice lowering to a husky murmur, 'with your hair cascading over your shoulders. Your lips rosy and parted, your face flushed.'

And as if he could command it by royal decree, she felt herself begin to blush. The image he painted was so suggestive. And it made that fist inside her squeeze her heart once more, made awareness tauten muscles she'd never even known she had.

'Why do you wish to see me like that?' she asked, relieved her voice sounded as calm as always. Almost.

'Because I think you would look even more beautiful then than you already are. You'd look warm and real and alive.'

She drew back, strangely hurt by his words. 'I am quite real already. And alive, thank you very much.'

Sandro's gaze swept over her, assessing, knowing. 'You remind me of a statue.'

A statue? A statue was cold and lifeless, without blood or bone, thought or feeling. And he thought that was what she was?

Wasn't it what she'd been for the past twenty years? The thought was like a hammer blow to the heart. She blinked, tried to keep her face expressionless. Blank, just like the statue he accused her of being. 'Are you trying to be offensive?' she answered, striving to keep her voice mild and not quite managing it.

His honesty shouldn't hurt her, she knew. There was certainly truth in it, and yet… She didn't want to be a statue. Not to this man.

A thought that alarmed her more than anything else.

'Not trying, no,' Sandro answered. 'I suppose it comes naturally.'

'I suppose it does.'

He shook his head slowly. 'Do you ever lose your temper? Shout? Curse?'

'Would you prefer to be marrying a shrew?' she answered evenly and his mouth quirked in a small smile.

'Does anything make you angry?' he asked, and before she could think better of it, she snapped, 'Right now, you do.'

He laughed, a rich chuckle of amusement, the sound spreading over her like chocolate, warming her in a way she didn't even understand. This man was frustrating and even hurting her and yet...

She liked his laugh.

'I am glad for it,' he told her. 'Anger is better than indifference.'

'I have never said I was indifferent.'

'You have shown it in everything you've said or done,' Sandro replied. 'Almost.'

'Almost?'

'You are not quite,' he told her in that murmur of a voice, 'as indifferent as you'd like me to believe—or even to believe yourself.'

She felt her breath bottle in her lungs, catch in her throat. 'I don't know what you mean, Your Highness.'

'Don't you?' He leaned forward, his eyes glinting silver in the candlelight. 'And must I remind you yet again that you are to call me Sandro?'

She felt her blush deepen, every nerve and sinew and sense so agonisingly aware. Feeling this much *hurt*. She was angry and scared and, most of all, she wanted him... just as he knew she did. 'I am not inclined,' she told him, her voice shaking, 'to call you by your first name just now, *Your Highness*.'

'I wonder, under what circumstances would you call me Sandro?'

Her nails dug into her palms. 'I cannot think of any at the moment.'

Sandro's silvery gaze swept over her in lingering assessment. 'I can think of one or two,' he answered lazily, and everything in her lurched at the sudden predatory intentness in his gaze. She felt her heart beat hard in response, her palms go cold and her mouth dry. 'Yes, definitely, one or two,' he murmured, and, throwing his napkin on the table, he rose from the chair.

She looked, Sandro thought, like a trapped rabbit, although perhaps not quite so frightened a creature. Even in her obvious and wary surprise she clung to her control, to her coldness. He had a fierce urge to strip it away from her and see what lay beneath it. An urge he intended to act on now.

Her eyes had widened and she gazed at him unblinkingly, her hands frozen over her plate, the knife and fork clenched between her slender, white-knuckled fingers.

Sandro moved towards her chair with a loose-limbed, predatory intent; he was acting on instinct now, wanting—needing—to strip away her cold haughtiness, chip away at that damned ice until it shattered all around them. She would call him Sandro. She would melt in his arms.

Gently, yet with firm purpose, he uncurled her clenched fingers from around her cutlery, and the knife and fork clattered onto her plate. She didn't resist. Her violet gaze was still fastened on him, her lips slightly parted. Her pulse thundered under his thumb as he took her by the wrist and drew her from the chair to stand before him.

Still she didn't resist, not even as he moved closer to her, nudging his thigh in between her own legs as he lifted his hands to frame her face.

Her skin was cool and unbearably soft, and he brushed his thumb over the fullness of her parted lips, heard her tiny, indrawn grasp, and smiled. He rested his thumb on the soft pad of her lower lip before he slid his hands down to her bare shoulders, her skin like silk under his palms.

He gazed into her eyes, the colour of a bruise, framed by moon-coloured lashes, wide and waiting. Then he bent his head and brushed his mouth across hers, a first kiss that was soft and questioning, and yet she gave no answer.

She remained utterly still, her lips unmoving under his, her hands clenched by her sides. The only movement was the hard beating of her heart that he could feel from where he stood, and Sandro's determination to make her respond crystallised inside him, diamond hard. He deepened the kiss, sliding his tongue into her luscious mouth, the question turning into a demand.

For a woman who was so coldly determined, her mouth tasted incredibly warm and sweet. He wanted more, any sense of purpose be damned, and as he explored the contours of her mouth with his tongue he moved his hands from her shoulders down the silk of her dress to cup the surprising fullness of her breasts. They fitted his hands perfectly, and he brushed his thumbs lightly over the taut peaks. Still she didn't move.

She was like the statue he'd accused her of being, frozen into place, rigid and unyielding. A shaft of both sexual and emotional frustration blazed through him. He wanted—*needed*—her to respond. Physically. Emotionally. He needed something from her, something real and alive, and he would do whatever it took to get it.

Sandro tore his mouth from hers and kissed his way along her jawline, revelling in the silkiness of her skin even as a furious determination took hold of him once more.

Yet as his mouth hovered over the sweet hollow where her jaw met her throat he hesitated, unwilling to continue when she was so unresponsive despite the insistence pulsing through him. He had never forced a woman, not for so much as a kiss, and he wasn't about to start now. Not with his bride. Submission, he thought grimly, was not the same as acceptance. As want.

Then she let out a little gasping shudder and her hand, as if of its own accord, clasped his arm, her nails digging into his skin as she pulled him infinitesimally closer. She tilted her head back just a little to allow him greater access to her throat, her breasts, and triumph surged through him. She wanted this. *Him.*

He moved lower, kissing his way to the V between her breasts where the diamond-and-pearl pendant nestled. He lifted the jewel and licked the warm skin underneath, tasted salt on his tongue and heard her gasp again, her knees buckling as she sat down hard on the table amidst the detritus of their dinner.

Triumph mixed with pure lust and he fastened his hands on her hips, sliding them down to her thighs so he could spread her legs wider. He stood between them, the silken folds of her dress whispering around him as he kissed her like a starving man feasting at a banquet.

He felt her shy response, her tongue touching his before darting away again, and he was utterly enflamed. He slid the straps of her dress from her shoulders, freeing her breasts from their silken prison.

She wore no bra, and desire ripped through him at the sight of her, her head thrown back, her breath coming in gasps as she surrendered herself to his touch, her face flushed and rosy, her lips parted, her body so wonderfully open to him. *This* was how he'd wanted to see her. He bent his head, kissing his way down her throat, his hand cupping her bared breast—

And then the door opened and a waitress gasped an

apology before closing it again quickly, but the moment, Sandro knew, had broken. Shattered into shock and awkwardness and regret.

Liana wrenched herself from his grasp, holding her dress up to her bare front, her lips swollen, her eyes huge and dazed as she stared at him.

He stared back in both challenge and desire, because as much as she might want to deny what had just happened between them, her response had said otherwise. Her response had told him she really was alive and warm and real beneath all that ice, and he was glad.

'Don't—' she finally managed, the single word choked, and Sandro arched an eyebrow.

'It's a little late for that. But obviously, I've stopped.'

'You shouldn't have—'

'Stopped?'

'Started—'

'And why not? We are to be married, aren't we?'

She just shook her head, fumbling as she attempted to slide her arms back into the dress, but she couldn't manage it without ripping the fragile fabric. Sandro came to stand behind her, unzipping the back with one quick tug.

'Don't touch me—'

'I'm helping you dress,' he answered shortly. 'You can't get your arms through the straps otherwise.'

Wordlessly she slid her arms through the straps, and he felt her tremble as he zipped her back up, barely resisting the urge to press his lips to the bared nape of her neck and feel her respond to him again.

Her hair had come undone a bit, a few tousled curls lying against her neck. The back of her dress, he saw, was crumpled and stained from where she'd sat on the table. Just remembering made hot, hard desire surge through him again. She might, for the sake of pride or modesty, play the ice maiden now, but he knew better. He wanted to make her melt again, even as he watched her return to her cold composure, assembling it like armour.

'Thank you,' she muttered and stepped quickly away from him.

'You're welcome.' He surveyed her, noticing the faint pink to her cheeks, the swollen rosiness of her mouth. She would not look at him. 'I'm afraid our meal is quite ruined.'

'I'm not hungry.'

He couldn't resist quipping, 'Not for food, perhaps.'

'*Don't.*' She dragged her gaze to his, and he was surprised—and slightly discomfited—to see not simple embarrassment in her stormy gaze, but a tortured recrimination that ate at the satisfaction he'd felt at her physical response. He'd seduced her quite ruthlessly, he knew. His kisses and caresses had been a calculated attack against her senses. Her coldness.

But she *had* responded. That had been real. Even if she regretted it now.

He folded his arms. 'Our marriage might be one of convenience, Liana, but that doesn't mean we can't—or shouldn't—desire one another. Frankly I find it a relief.' She shook her head wordlessly, and a different kind of frustration spiked through him. 'What do you see our marriage looking like, then? I need an heir—'

'I *know* that.' She lifted her hands to her hair, fussing with some of the diamond-tipped pins. A few, he saw, had fallen to the floor and silently he bent to scoop them up and then handed them to her. She still wouldn't look at him, just shoved pins into the tangled mass of silvery hair that he now realised was really quite a remarkable colour. Quite beautiful.

'Are you a virgin?' he asked abruptly, and her startled gaze finally met his. She looked almost affronted.

'Of course I am.'

'Of course? You're twenty-eight years old. I'd hardly expect, at that age, for you to save yourself for marriage.'

Colour deepened in her cheeks. 'Well, I did. I'm sorry if that is yet another disappointment for you.' She didn't sound sorry at all, and he almost smiled.

'Hardly a disappointment.' Her response to him hadn't been disappointing at all. 'But I can understand why you might feel awkward or afraid about what happened between—'

'I'm not *afraid*.' Her lips tightened and her eyes flashed. She dropped her hands from her hair and busied herself with straightening her rather ruined dress.

'What, then?' Sandro asked quietly.

Her hands shook briefly before she stilled them, mindlessly smoothing the crumpled silk of her dress. 'I simply wasn't... This isn't...' She took a breath. 'I wasn't expecting this.'

'It should be a happy surprise, then,' Sandro answered. 'At least we desire each other.' She shook her head, the movement violent. 'I still fail to see the problem.'

She drew a breath into her lungs, pressed her hands against her still crumpled dress. 'This marriage was— is—meant to be convenient.'

'Not that convenient,' Sandro answered sharply. 'We were always going to consummate it.'

'I know that!' She took another breath; her cheeks were now bright pink. 'I simply don't... I don't want to *feel*...' She broke off, misery swamping her eyes, her whole body. Sandro had the sudden urge to comfort her, to offer her a hug of affection rather than the calculated caress of moments before.

What on earth was causing her such torment?

Liana felt as if Sandro had taken a hammer to her heart, to her very self, with that kiss. She'd very nearly shattered into a million pieces, and it was only by sheer strength of will that she'd kept herself together.

She'd never been touched like that before, never felt such an overwhelming, aching need for even more. More touches, more kisses, more of Sandro. It had called to a craving inside her she hadn't even known she had. Didn't want.

Because if she opened herself up to wanting anything from Sandro—even *that*—she'd open herself up to pain. To disappointment. To feeling, and she'd cut herself off from all of it for too long to want it now. To risk the fragile security she'd built around her heart, her self.

The point of this marriage, she thought helplessly, was that it wouldn't demand such things of her. It would be safe.

Yet nothing felt safe now. And how could she explain any of it to Sandro without sounding as if she was a freak? A frigid freak?

I'm sorry, Sandro, but I have no desire to enjoy sex with you.

She sounded ridiculous even to herself.

'What is it you don't want to feel, Liana?' he asked and she just stared at him.

This. Him. All of it. What could she tell him? He was clearly waiting for an answer. 'I...I don't want to desire you,' she said, and watched his eyebrows raise, his mouth thin.

'And why is that?'

Because it scares me. You scare me. She'd sound like such a pathetic little mouse, and maybe she was, but she didn't want him knowing it. Knowing how weak and frightened she was, when she'd been trying to seem strong and secure and safe.

Clearly it was nothing more than a facade.

Sandro was still staring at her, his expression narrowed and assessing. He probably couldn't imagine why any woman wouldn't desire him, wouldn't *want* to desire him. She'd read enough gossip websites and trashy tabloids to know Sandro Diomedi, whether he was king of Maldinia or IT billionaire, had plenty of women falling at his feet.

She didn't want to be one of them.

Oh, she'd always known she'd have to do her duty in bed as well as out of it. She might be inexperienced, but she understood that much.

She also knew most people didn't think of it as a duty. She'd read enough novels, seen enough romantic movies to know many people—*most* people—found the physical side of things to be quite pleasurable.

As she just had.

She felt her face heat once more as she remembered how shameless she had been. How good Sandro's mouth had felt on hers, his hands on her body, waking up every deadened nerve and sense inside her—

She looked away from him now, willing the memories to recede. She didn't *want* to wake up. Not like that.

'Liana?' he prompted, and she searched for an answer, something believable. Something that would hurt him, as she'd been hurt first by his derision and incredulity, and then by his desire. A Sandro who reached her with his kiss and caress was far more frightening than one who merely offended her with his scorn.

'Because I don't respect you,' she said, and she felt the electric jolt of shock go through him as if they were connected by a wire.

'Don't *respect*?' He looked shocked, almost winded, and Liana felt a vicious stab of petty satisfaction. He'd shaken up everything inside her, her sense of security and even her sense of self. Let him be the one to look and feel shaken.

Then his expression veiled and he pursed his lips. 'Why don't you respect me?'

'You've shirked your duty for fifteen years, and you need to ask that?'

Colour touched his cheekbones, and she knew she'd touched a nerve, one she hadn't even considered before. But there was truth in what she'd said, what she'd felt. He'd walked away from all he was meant to do, while she'd spent a lifetime trying to earn back her parents' respect for one moment's terrible lapse.

'I didn't realise you were so concerned about my duty.'

'I'm not, but then neither are you,' Liana snapped, amazed at the words—the feeling—coming out of her mouth. Who was this woman who lost her temper, who melted in a man's arms? She felt like a stranger to herself, and she couldn't believe how reckless she'd been with this man…in so many ways. How much he made her feel. Physically. Emotionally. So in the space of a single evening she'd said and done things she never had allowed herself to before.

'You're very honest,' Sandro said softly, his voice a dangerous drawl. 'I appreciate that, if not the sentiment.'

Liana dropped her hand from her mouth, where it had flown at his response. She knew she should apologise, yet somehow she could not find the words, or even the emotion. She wasn't sorry. This man had humiliated and

she'd worn around her neck. The diamond he'd lifted when he'd licked the skin underneath....

Remembering made lust beat along with his fury, and hell if that wasn't an unwholesome mix. Sighing, he pushed away from the window. 'I didn't realise you knew her.'

Leo's smile was wry. 'Father considered an alliance between us, briefly.'

'An alliance? You mean *marriage*?' Sandro turned around to stare at his brother in surprise. Yet how could he really be shocked? Leo had been the future king. And hadn't Liana already shown him just how much she wanted to be queen? For fifteen years—over half her life—he'd been essentially out of the picture. Of course she'd looked at other options.

As had his own brother, his own father.

'So what happened?' he asked Leo, and his brother's smile was crooked and yet clearly full of happiness. Of joy.

'Alyse happened.'

Of course. Sandro had seen the iconic photo himself, when it had been taken over six years ago. Leo had been twenty-four, Alyse eighteen. A single, simple kiss that had rocked the world and changed their lives for ever. And for the better now, thank God.

'Although to be honest,' Leo continued, 'I don't think Liana was ever really interested. It seemed as if she was humouring me, or maybe her parents, who wanted the match.'

Or hedging her bets, perhaps, Sandro thought, just in case the black-sheep heir made a reappearance. 'I'm happy for you, you know,' he said abruptly. 'For you and Alyse.'

'I know you are.'

Yet he heard a coolness in his brother's voice, and he could guess at its source. For fifteen years they hadn't spoken, seen each other, or been in touch in even the paltriest of ways. And this after their childhood, when they'd banded together, two young boys who had had only each other for companionship.

Sandro knew he needed to say something of all that had gone before—and all that hadn't. The silence and separation that had endured for so long was, he knew, his fault. He was the older brother, and the one who had left. Yet the words he knew he should say burned in his chest and tangled in his throat. He couldn't get them out. He didn't know how.

This was what happened when you grew up in a family that had never shown love or emotion or anything real at all. You didn't know how to be real yourself, as much as you craved it—and you feared that which you craved.

And yet Leo had found love. He was real with Alyse. Why, Sandro wondered in frustration, couldn't he be the same?

And in the leaden weight of his heart he knew the answer. Because he was king…and he had a duty that precluded such things.

CHAPTER FOUR

LIANA GAZED AT her reflection in the gold-framed mirror of one of the royal palace's many guest suites. She was in a different one from the last time she'd been here six weeks ago, yet it was just as sumptuous. Then she'd come to Maldinia to discuss marriage; this time she was here for a wedding. Hers.

'You're too thin.' Her mother Gabriella's voice came out sharp with anxiety as she entered the room, closing the door behind her.

'I have lost a little weight in the past few weeks,' Liana said, and heard the instinctive note of apology in her voice. Everything with her parents felt like an apology, a way to say sorry over and over again. Yet she could never say it enough, and her parents never seemed to hear it anyway.

They certainly never talked about it.

'I suppose things have been a bit stressful,' Gabriella allowed. She twitched Liana's short veil over her shoulders and smoothed the satin fabric of the simple white sheath dress she wore.

Her wedding to Sandro was to be a quiet affair in the palace's private chapel, with only family in attendance. After the fairy-tale proportions of Leo and Alyse's ceremony, and the resulting fallout, something quiet and dignified was needed. It suited Liana fine.

She wondered what Sandro thought about it. She hadn't seen him since she'd arrived two days ago, beyond a formal dinner where she'd been introduced to a variety of diplomats and dignitaries. She'd chatted with everyone, curtsied to the queen, who had eyed her coldly, and met Sandro's sister, Alexa, as well as his brother, Leo, and sister-in-law, Alyse.

Everyone—save the queen—had been friendly enough, but it had been Sandro's rather stony silence that had unnerved her. It had occurred to her then in an entirely new and unwelcome way that this man was going to be her *husband*. She would live with him for the rest of her days, bear his children, serve by his side. Stupid of her not to think it all through before, but suddenly it seemed overwhelming, her decision reckless. Was she really going to say vows based on a desire to please her parents? To somehow atone for the past?

No wonder Sandro had been incredulous. And it was too late to change her mind now.

Gabriella put her hands on Liana's shoulders, met her gaze in the mirror. 'You do want this marriage, Liana, don't you?' Liana opened her mouth to say of course she did, because she knew she couldn't say anything else. Not when her mother wanted it so much. Even now, with all the doubts swirling through her mind, she felt that. Believed it.

'Because I know we might seem old-fashioned to you,' Gabriella continued in a rush. 'Asking you to marry a man you've barely met.' Now Liana closed her mouth. It was old-fashioned, but she wasn't going to fight it. Wasn't going to wish for something else.

What was the point? Her parents wanted it, and it was

too late anyway. And in any case, a real marriage, a marriage based on intimacy and love, held no appeal for her.

Neither did a husband who seemed as if he hated her.

And wasn't that her fault? For telling him she didn't respect him? For pushing him away out of her own hurt pride and fear? But perhaps it was better for Sandro to hate her than call up all those feelings and needs. Perhaps antipathy would actually be easier.

'I just want you to be happy,' Gabriella said quietly. 'As your father does.'

And they thought marrying a stranger would make her happy?

No, Liana thought tiredly, they didn't want her to be happy, not really. They wanted to feel as if she had been taken care of, dealt with. Tidied away. They wanted to forget her, because she knew soul deep that every time her parents looked at her they were reminded of Chiara. Of Chiara's death.

Just as she was.

If she married Sandro, at least she'd be out of the way. Easier to forget.

Better for everyone, really.

She drew a breath into her lungs, forced her expression into a smile. 'I am happy, Mother. I will be.'

Her mother nodded, not questioning that statement. Not wanting to know. 'Good,' she said, and kissed Liana's cold cheek.

A few minutes later her mother left for the chapel, leaving Liana alone to face the walk down the aisle by herself. Maldinian tradition dictated that the bride walk by herself, and the groom keep his back to her until she reached his side.

A stupid tradition, probably meant to terrify brides into submission, she thought with a grimace. And would it terrify her? What would the expression on Sandro's face be when he did turn around? Contempt? Disgust? Hatred? *Desire?* She knew she shouldn't even care, but she did.

Ever since she'd first met Sandro, she'd started caring. Feeling. And that alarmed her more than anything.

She closed her eyes, fought against the nerves churning in her stomach and threatening to revolt up her throat. Why had this man woken something inside her she'd thought was not just asleep, but dead? How had he resurrected it?

She longed to go back to the numb safety she'd lived in for so long. For twenty years, since she was eight. Eight years old, pale faced and trembling, staring at the grief-stricken expressions on her parents' faces as she told them the truth.

I was there. It was my fault.

And they had, in their silence, agreed. Of course they had, because it *was* the truth. Chiara's death had been entirely her fault, and that was a truth she could never, ever escape.

This marriage was, in its own way, meant to be more penance. But it wasn't meant to make her *feel*. Want. Need.

Yet in the six weeks since she'd returned from Maldinia, it had. She felt the shift inside herself, an inexorable moving of the tectonic plates of her soul, and it was one she didn't welcome. Ever since Sandro's scathing indictment of her, his assault on her convictions, her body, her whole self, she'd started to feel more. Want more. And she was desperate to stop, to snatch back the numbness, the safety.

'Lady Liana? It's time.'

Woodenly Liana nodded and then followed Paula, the

palace's press secretary, to the small chapel where the service would take place.

'This will be a very quiet affair,' Paula said. 'No cameras or publicity, like before.'

Before, when Alyse and Leo's charade had blown up in their faces, Liana knew, and they'd been exposed as having faked their fairy-tale love story for the entirety of their engagement. This time there was no charade, yet Liana still felt as if everything could explode around her. As if it already had.

'All right, then.' Paula touched her briefly on her shoulder. 'You look lovely. Don't forget to smile.'

Somehow Liana managed to make the corners of her mouth turn up. Paula didn't look all that satisfied by this expression of expectant marital joy, but she nodded and left Liana alone to face the double doors that led to the chapel, the small crowd, and Sandro.

Drawing a deep breath, she straightened her shoulders, lifted her chin. She was doing this for a good reason. Forget her own feelings, which she'd tried to forget for so long anyway. There was a good reason, the best reason, to marry Sandro, to make her life worth something. Her sister.

For a second, no more, she allowed herself to think of Chiara. *Chi-Chi.* Her button eyes, her impish smile, her sudden laugh.

I'm doing this for you, Chi-Chi, she thought, and tears, tears she hadn't let herself cry for twenty years, rose in her eyes. She blinked them back furiously.

Forward.

'Lady Liana?'

Liana turned to see Alyse Barras—now Diomedi— walking towards her, a warm smile on her pretty face. She wore an understated dress of rose silk, with a matching coat and hat. Silk gloves reached up to the elbow on each slender arm. She looked every inch the elegant, confident royal.

Liana had met Alyse briefly at the dinner last night, but they hadn't spoken beyond a few pleasantries.

'I'm sorry we haven't had a chance to talk properly,' Alyse said, extending one hand that Liana took stiffly, still conscious of the tears crowding under her lids. 'I just wanted to tell you I know how you feel. Walking down an aisle alone can be a little frightening. A little lonely.' Her gaze swept over Liana's pale figure in obvious sympathy, and she instinctively stiffened, afraid those treacherous tears would spill right over. If they did, she feared there would be no coming back from it.

'Thank you,' she said, and she knew her voice sounded too cool. It was her only defence against losing it completely in this moment. 'I'm sure I'll manage.'

Alyse blinked, her mouth turning down slightly before she nodded. 'Of course you will. I just wanted to say... I hope we have a chance to get to know one another now that we're both part of this family.' Her smile returned. 'For better or for worse.'

And right now felt like worse. Liana nodded, too wretchedly emotional to respond any further to Alyse's friendly overture.

'Thank you,' she finally managed. 'I should go.'

'Of course.' Alyse nodded and stepped back. 'Of course.'

Two footmen came forward to throw open the doors of the chapel, and with that icy numbness now hastily re-assembled, her chin lifted and her head held high, Liana stepped into her future.

The chapel was as quiet and sombre as if a funeral were taking place rather than a wedding. A handful of guests she didn't know, her parents in the left front row. Sandro's back, broad and resolute, turned towards her. She felt the tears sting her eyes again, her throat tighten and she willed the emotion away.

This was the right thing to do. The only thing she could do. This was her duty to her parents, to the memory of her sister. She was doing it for them, not for herself. *For Chiara....*

She repeated the words inside her head, a desperate chant, an appeal to everything she'd done and been in the twenty years since Chiara's death.

This was her duty. Her atonement. Her absolution. She had no other choice, no other need but to serve her parents and the memory of her sister as best she could.

And as she came down the aisle she finally made herself believe it once more.

Sandro had heard the doors to the chapel open, knew Liana was walking towards him. He fought an urge to turn around, knowing that tradition had Maldinian grooms—royal ones, at least—facing the front until the bride was at their side.

When she was halfway down he gave in and turned around, tradition be damned. He wanted to see Liana, wanted to catch a glimpse of the woman he was about to promise to love, honour, and cherish before he made those binding vows. For the past six weeks he'd been trying *not* to think of her, of the proud contempt he'd seen on her face the last time they'd spoken, when she'd told him with a sneer in her voice that she didn't respect him.

And as shocked as her contemptuous indictment had been, how could he actually be surprised? Hurt? She'd been speaking the truth, after all.

Now as she came down the aisle, her bearing regal

and straight, her chin tilted proudly and her eyes flashing violet ice, he felt the hopes he hadn't even realised he still had plummet.

She was just as he remembered. Just as composed, just as soulless and scornful as he'd first feared. And in about three minutes she would become his wife.

As she joined him at the altar, her dress whispering against his legs, she lifted her chin another notch, all haughty pride and cool purpose.

Sandro turned away without so much as a smile and listened to the archbishop begin with a leaden heart.

An hour later they were man and wife, circulating through one of the palace's many receiving rooms among the few dozen guests. They still hadn't spoken to each other, although Sandro had brushed his lips against Liana's cold ones at the end of the ceremony before she'd stepped quickly away.

They'd walked down the aisle together, her hand lying rigidly on his arm, and gone directly to one of the palace's salons for a champagne reception.

Liana, Sandro couldn't help notice, seemed to take to the role of queen with instant, icy poise. She smiled and chatted with a reserved dignity that he supposed fitted her station. She was friendly without being gregarious or warm or real.

She wasn't, he thought, anything he wanted. But he had to live with it, with her, and he was determined to put such thoughts behind him.

He moved through the crowds, chatting with various people, conscious of Liana by his side, smiling and yet so still and straight, so proud. She seemed untouchable and completely indifferent to him, yet even so he found his mind—and other parts of his body—leaping ahead to a few hours from now, when they would leave the reception and all the guests behind and retire upstairs to the tower room that was the traditional honeymoon suite.

There wouldn't actually be a honeymoon; he saw no point, and he doubted Liana did either. But tonight... Tonight they would consummate their marriage. The prospect filled him with desire and distaste, hunger and loathing.

He wanted her, he knew, but he didn't want to want her, not when she didn't even respect him. And she obviously didn't want to want him.

Sandro took a long swallow of champagne, and it tasted bitter in his mouth. What a mess.

Liana felt tension thrum through her body as she made a valiant effort to listen to another dignitary talk about Maldinia's growing industry, and how Prince Leo was helping to raise funds for technological improvements.

But her real focus was on the man next to her. Her husband. He listened and chatted and smiled just as she did, but she felt the tension in his body, had seen the chilly expression in his eyes when he'd turned to her, and in the moment before she'd said her vows she had felt panic bubble up inside her. She'd wanted to rip off her veil and run back down the aisle, away from everything. The anxiety and hope in her parents' eyes. The ice in her groom's. And the churning fear and guilt inside herself that she could never escape, no matter how far or fast she ran.

And so she'd stayed and repeated the vows that would bind her to this man for life. She'd promised to love and honour and obey him, traditional vows for a traditional marriage, and she'd wished she'd considered how different it would feel, to fill her mouth full of lies.

She didn't love this man. She hadn't honoured him. And as for obedience...

Sandro placed a hand on her elbow, and despite every intention not to feel anything for him, just that simple touch set sparks racing up her arm, exploding in her heart. She hated how much he affected her. Hated how weak and vulnerable he made her feel, how he made her want things she knew he would never give her.

'We will say our goodbyes in a few minutes,' he said in a low voice, and Liana stiffened.

'Goodbyes? But we're not going anywhere.'

Sandro's mouth curved in a humourless smile. His eyes were as hard as metal. 'We're going to our honeymoon suite, Liana. To go to bed.'

She pulled her arm away from his light touch, realisation icing her veins. Of course. Their wedding night. They would have to consummate their marriage now. It was a duty she'd known she would have to perform, even if she hadn't let herself think too much about it. Now it loomed large and incredibly immediate, incredibly *intimate*, and even as dread pooled in her stomach she couldn't keep a contrary excitement from leaping low in her belly—fear and fascination, desire and dread all mixed together. She hated the maelstrom this man created within her.

'You aren't going to steal away yet, are you?' Alyse approached them, Leo by her side. 'I haven't even had a chance to talk with Liana yet, not properly.'

Liana offered a sick smile, her mind still on the night ahead, alone with Sandro.

'You'll have plenty of opportunity later,' Sandro answered, his fingers closing once more over Liana's elbow. 'But for now I want my bride to myself.' He smiled as he said it, but to Liana it felt like the smile of a predator, intent on devouring its prey.

And that was how intimacy with Sandro felt. Like

being devoured. Like losing herself, everything she'd ever clung to.

Alyse glanced uncertainly at Sandro before turning back to Liana. 'We'll have to have a proper chat soon,' she said, and Liana nodded jerkily.

'Yes, I look forward to getting to know both of you,' she said with as much warmth as she could inject into her voice, although she feared it wasn't all that much. 'You both seem very happy in your marriage.'

'And you will be in yours, Queen Liana,' Leo said quietly, 'if you just give Sandro some time to get used to the idea.'

Liana watched as he slipped his hand into his wife's, his fingers squeezing hers gently. Something in her ached at the sight of that small yet meaningful touch. When had she last been touched like that?

It had been years. Decades. She'd found it so hard to give and receive affection after Chiara's death. For a second she could almost feel her sister's skinny arms hook around her neck as she pressed her cheek next to hers. She could feel her silky hair, her warm breath as she whispered in her ear. She'd always had secrets, Chiara, silly secrets. She'd whisper her nonsense in Liana's ear and then giggle, squeezing her tight.

Liana swallowed and looked away. She couldn't think of Chiara now or she'd fall apart completely. And she didn't want to think about the yearning that had opened up inside her, an overwhelming desire for the kind of intimacy she'd closed herself off from for so long. To give and receive. To know and be known. To love and be loved.

None of it possible, not with this man. Her husband.

She might be leaving this room for her wedding night, but that kind of intimacy, with love as its sure foundation, was not something she was about to experience. Something she didn't *want* to experience, even if everything in her protested otherwise.

Love opened you up to all sorts of pain. It *hurt*.

But she didn't even need to worry about that, because right now she and Sandro were just going to have sex. Emotionless sex.

They spent the next few minutes saying their goodbyes; her mother hugged her tightly and whispered that she hoped she would be happy. Liana murmured back nonsense about how she already was and saw the tension that bracketed her mother's eyes lessen just a little. Her father didn't hug her; he never had, not since Chiara had died. She didn't blame him.

A quarter of an hour later she left the reception with Sandro; neither of them spoke as they walked down several long, opulent corridors and then up the wide front staircase of the palace, down another corridor, up another staircase, and finally to the turret room that was kept for newlyweds.

Sandro opened the door first, ushering her in, and Liana didn't look at him as she walked into the room. She took in the huge stone fireplace, the windows open to the early evening sky, the enormous four-poster bed piled high with silken pillows and seeming almost to pulse with expectation.

She resisted the urge to wipe her damp palms against the narrow skirt of her wedding gown and walked to the window instead, taking in several needed lungfuls of mountain air. The sun was just starting to sink behind the timbered houses of Averne's Old Town, the Alps fringing the horizon, their snowy peaks thrusting towards a violet sky. It was all incredibly beautiful, and yet also chilly and remote. As chilly and remote as she felt, shrinking further and further into herself, away from the reality—the intimacy—of what was about to happen between them.

Behind her she heard the door click shut.

'Would you like to change?' Sandro asked. He sounded formal and surprisingly polite. Liana didn't turn from the window.

'I don't believe I have anything to change into.'

'There's a nightdress on the bed.'

She turned then and saw the silk-and-lace confection spread out on the coverlet. It looked horribly revealing, ridiculously romantic. 'I don't see much point in that.'

Sandro huffed a hard laugh. 'I didn't think you would.'

She finally forced herself to look at him. 'There's no point in pretending, is there?'

'Is that what it would be?' He lounged against the doorway; while she'd been gazing out of the window he'd shed his formal coat and undone his white tie. His hair was ruffled, his eyes sleepy, and she could see the dark glint of a five o'clock shadow on his chiselled jaw, the hint of chest hair from the top opened buttons of his shirt. He looked dissolute and dangerous and...*sexy*.

The word popped into her head of its own accord. She didn't want to think of her husband as sexy. She didn't want to feel that irresistible magnetic pull towards him that already had her swaying slightly where she stood. She didn't want to feel so *much*. If she felt this, she'd feel so much more. She would drown in all the feelings she'd suppressed for so long.

'You weren't pretending the last time I kissed you,' Sandro said softly, and to Liana it sounded like a taunt.

'You're as proud as a polecat about that,' she answered. Sandro began to stroll towards her.

'Why fight me, Liana? Why resist me? We're married. We must consummate our marriage. Why don't we at least let this aspect of our union bring us pleasure?'

'Because nothing else about it will?' she filled in, her tone sharp, and Sandro just shrugged.

'We've both admitted as much, haven't we?'

Yes, she supposed they had, so there was no reason for her to feel so insulted. So *hurt*. Yet as Sandro kept moving towards her with a predator's prowl, she knew she did.

He stopped in front of her, close enough so she could feel the heat of him, and he could see her tremble. She stared blindly ahead, unable to look at him, to see what emotion flickered in his eyes. Pity? Contempt? Desire? She wanted none of it, even as her body still ached and yearned.

Sandro lifted one hand and laid it on her shoulder; she could feel the warmth of his palm from underneath the thin silk of her gown. He smoothed his hand down the length of her arm, the movement studied, almost clinical, as if he was touching a statue. And she felt like a statue just as he'd accused her of being: lifeless, unmoving, even as her blood heated and her heart lurched. Sandro sighed.

'Why don't you take a bath?' he said, turning away. 'Relax for a little while. If you don't want to wear that nightgown, there are robes in the bathroom that will cover you from chin to toe.'

She watched out of the corner of her eye as he moved to the fireplace, his fingers deftly undoing the remaining studs of his shirt. He shrugged out of it, the firelight burnishing the bronzed skin of his sculpted shoulders, and Liana yanked her gaze away.

On shaky, jelly-like legs she walked to the bathroom, her dress whispering around her as she moved, and closed the door. Locked it. And let out a shuddering breath that ended on something halfway to a sob.

CHAPTER FIVE

SANDRO LEANED BACK in the chair by the fire and gazed moodily at the flames flickering in the huge hearth. Resentment warred with guilt inside him as he listened to Liana move in the bathroom, turning on taps. Taking off her clothes. Would she be able to get that slinky dress off by herself? He knew she wouldn't ask for help.

Ever since they'd entered this room with all of its sensual expectation she'd become icier than ever. It angered him, her purposeful coldness, as if she couldn't stand even to be near him and wanted him to know it, but he still couldn't keep a small stab of pity from piercing his resentment. She was a virgin; even if she would never admit it, she had to be a little nervous. He needed to make allowances.

The desire he'd felt for her still coiled low in his belly but even so he didn't relish the prospect of making love to his wife. Of course there would be no love about it, which was neither new nor a surprise. He shouldn't even want it, not when he knew what kind of woman Liana really was.

He had no illusions about how she would handle their wedding night. Lie stiff and straight as a board on that sumptuous bed, scrunch her eyes tight, and think of her marital duty. Just the thought of it—of her like that—was enough to turn his flickering desire into ash.

Distantly Sandro realised the sounds from the bathroom had stopped, and he knew she must be stuck in that dress. He rose from the chair, dressed only in his trousers, and rapped on the bathroom door.

'Liana? Do you need help getting out of your gown?' Silence. He almost smiled, imagining how she was wrestling with admitting she did, and yet not wanting to accept anything from him. Certainly not wanting him to unzip her. 'I'll close my eyes,' he said dryly, half joking, 'if you want me to help you unzip it.'

'It's not a zipper.' Her voice sounded muffled, subdued. 'It's about a hundred tiny buttons.'

And before he could stop himself, Sandro was envisioning all those little buttons following the elegant length of her spine, picturing his fingers popping them open one by one and revealing the ivory skin of her back underneath. Desire leapt to life once more.

'Then you most certainly need help,' he said, and after a second's pause he heard the sound of the door unlocking and she opened it, her head bowed, a few tendrils of hair falling forward and hiding her face.

Wordlessly she turned around and presented him with her narrow, rigid back, the buttons going from her neck to her tailbone, each one a tiny pearl.

Sandro didn't speak as he started at the top and began to unbutton the gown. The buttons were tiny, and it wasn't easy. It wasn't a matter of a moment either, and he didn't close his eyes as he undid each one, the tender skin of her neck and shoulders appearing slowly underneath his fingers as the silk fell away in a sensual slide.

His fingers brushed her skin—she felt both icy and soft—and he felt her give a tiny shudder, although whether she was reacting out of desire or disgust he didn't know. He sensed she felt both, that she was as conflicted as he was—probably more—about wanting him. The realisation sent a sudden shaft of sympathy through him and he stilled, his fingers splayed on her bared back. He felt her stiffen beneath him.

'If you'd rather,' he said softly, 'we can wait.'

'Wait?' Her voice was no more than a breath, her back still rigid, her head bowed.

'To consummate our marriage.'

'Until when?'

'Until we're both more comfortable with each other.'

She let out a little huff of laughter, the sound as cynical as anything he'd ever heard. 'And when will that be, do you think, Your Highness? I'd rather just get it over with.'

What a delightful turn of phrase, he thought sardonically. Her skin had warmed under his palm but when he spread his fingers a little wider he felt how cold she still was. Cold all the way through. 'You're right, of course,' he answered flatly. 'We might as well get it over with.'

She didn't answer, and he finished unbuttoning the dress in silence. She held her hands up to her front to keep it in place, and Sandro could see the top curve of her bottom, encased enticingly in sheer tights, as she stepped back into the bathroom. She closed the door, and with a grim smile he listened to her lock it once more.

Liana lay in the bath until the water grew cold and the insistent throb of her body's response to Sandro started to subside—except it didn't.

She'd never been touched so intimately as when he'd unbuttoned her dress. She realised this probably made her seem pathetic to a man like him, a man who was so sensual and passionate, who had probably had a dozen—a hundred—lovers. As for her? She'd had so little physical affection in her life that even a casual brush of a hand had everything in her jolting with shocked awareness.

And now the feeling of his fingers on her back, the whisper of skin on skin, so intimate, so *tender*, an assault so much softer and gentler than that life-altering kiss they'd had six weeks ago and yet still so unbearably powerful, had made that awakened need inside her blaze hotter, harder, its demand one she was afraid she could not ignore.

The water was chilly now, and reluctantly she rose from the tub, and swathed herself in the robe that covered her just as Sandro had promised but which she knew he could peel away in seconds.

She took time brushing and blow-drying her hair, stared at her pale face and wide eyes, and then pinched her cheeks for colour. No more reasons to stay in here, to stall.

Taking a deep breath, she opened the bathroom door.

Sandro was facing the window, one arm braced against its frame, wearing only a pair of black silk pyjama bottoms, and the breath rushed from Liana's lungs as she gazed at him, the firelight flickering over his powerful shoulders and trim hips, his hair as dark as ink and his skin like bronze. He looked darkly powerful and almost frightening in his latent sensuality, his blatant masculinity. Just his presence seemed to steal all the breath from her body, all the thoughts from her head.

She straightened her spine, took a deep breath. 'I'm ready.'

'Are you?' His voice was a low, sardonic drawl as he turned around, swept her from head to toe in one swiftly assessing gaze. 'You look terrified.'

'Well, I can't say I'm looking forward to this,' Liana

answered, keeping her voice tart even though her words were, at least in part, no more than lies. 'But I'll do my duty.'

'I thought you'd say something like that.'

'Then perhaps you're getting to know me, after all.'

'Unfortunately, I think I am.'

She flinched, unable to keep herself from it, and Sandro shook his head. 'I'm sorry. That was uncalled for.'

'But you meant it.'

'I only meant…' He let out a long, low breath. 'I just wish things could be different.'

That she was different, he meant. Well, sometimes she wished she were different too. She wished being close to someone—being vulnerable, intimate, *exposed*—wasn't scary. Terrifying.

Was that what Sandro wanted? That kind of…closeness? The thought caused a blaze of yearning to set her senses afire. Because part of her wanted that too, but she had no idea how to go about it. How to overcome her fear.

'Well, then,' she finally said, every muscle tensed and expectant. A smile twitched at his lips even though she still sensed that restless, rangy energy from him.

'Do you actually think I'm going to pounce on you right this second? Deflower you like some debauched lord and his maiden?'

'I hope you'll have a bit more finesse than that.'

'Thank you for that vote of confidence.' He strolled towards her with graceful, loose-limbed purpose that had Liana tensing all the more.

He stood in front of her, his gaze sweeping over her so that already she felt ridiculously exposed, even though she wore the bathrobe that covered her completely.

'You're as tense as a bow.' Sandro touched the back

of her neck, his fingers massaging the muscles knotted there. 'Why don't you relax, just a little?'

Her fingers clenched convulsively on the sash of her robe. Relaxation felt like an impossibility. 'And how am I supposed to do that when I know—' She stopped abruptly, not wanting to admit so much, or really anything at all.

Sandro's dark eyebrows drew together in a frown as he searched her face. 'When you know what?'

'That you don't like me,' she forced out, her voice small and suffocated, her face averted from his. 'That you don't even respect me or hold me in any regard at all.'

Sandro didn't answer, just let his gaze rove over her, searching for something he didn't seem to find because he finally sighed, shrugged his powerful shoulders. 'And you feel the same way about me.'

'I—' She stopped, licked her lips. She should tell him that she'd only told him she didn't respect him to hurt him and hide herself, because she'd hated how vulnerable she'd felt. And yet somehow the words wouldn't come.

'I think it's best,' Sandro said quietly, 'if we put our personal feelings aside. The last time we were alone together, I kissed you.' He spoke calmly, rationally, and yet just that simple statement of fact caused Liana's heart to thud even harder and a treacherous, hectic flush to spread over her whole body. 'You responded,' he continued, and she closed her eyes, the memory of his kiss washing over her in a hot tide. 'And I responded to you. Regardless of how different we are, and how little regard we have for each other's personal priorities or convictions, we are physically attracted to one another, Liana.'

He rested his hands lightly on her shoulders, and she felt the warmth of his palms even through the thick terry cloth of her robe. 'It might seem repellent to you, to be attracted to someone you don't respect, but *this* is the only point of sympathy it appears we have between us.'

And with his hands still on her shoulders he bent his head and brushed his lips across hers. That first taste of him was like a cool drink of water in the middle of a burning desert. And her life *had* been a desert, a barren wasteland of loneliness and yearning for something she hadn't realised she'd missed until he'd first touched her.

Her mouth opened instinctively under his, her hands coming up to clutch the warm, bare skin of his shoulders, needing the contact and the comfort, the closeness. Needing him.

His lips hovered over hers for a moment, almost as if he was surprised by the suddenness of her response, the silent *yes* she couldn't keep her body from saying. Then he deepened the kiss, his tongue sweeping into the softness of her mouth, claiming and exploring her with a staggering intimacy that felt strangely, unbearably sweet.

It felt *important*, to be touched like this. To feel warm hands on her body, gentle, caressing, accepting her in a way she'd never felt accepted before. Not since she'd lost Chiara, since she'd let her go.

She'd never understood how much she needed this in the years since then, the touch of a human being, the reminder that she was real and alive, flesh and blood and bone, emotion and want and need. She was so much more than what she'd ever let herself be, and she felt it all now in an overwhelming, endless rush as Sandro kissed her.

And then he stopped, pulling back just a little to smile down at her with what seemed terribly like smugness. 'Well, then,' he said softly, and she heard satisfaction and perhaps even triumph in his voice, and with humiliation scorching through her she pulled away.

Of course he didn't accept her. Didn't like her, didn't

respect her. Didn't even know her. And she didn't want him to, not really, so with all that between them, how could she respond to him this way? How could she crave the exposing intimacy she hated and feared?

Numbness was so much easier. So much safer. She might have lived her life in a vacuum, but at least it had been safe.

She tried to pull back from Sandro's light grasp and he frowned.

'What's wrong?'

'I don't—'

'Want to want me?' he filled in, his voice hardening, and Liana didn't answer, just focused on keeping some last shred of control, of dignity, intact. *Blink. Breathe. Don't cry.*

'But you do want me, Liana,' Sandro said softly. 'You want me very much. And even if you try to deny it, I'll know. I'll feel your response in your lips that open to mine, in your hands that reach for me, in your body that responds to me.' He brushed his hand against her breast, his thumb finding the revealingly taut peak even underneath her heavy robe. 'You see? I'll always know.'

'I know that,' she choked. 'I'm not denying anything.' She turned her face with all of its naked emotion away from him.

'No,' he agreed, his voice as hard as iron now, as hard as his gunmetal-grey eyes. 'You're not denying it. You're just resisting it with every fibre of your being. Resisting me.' She let out a shudder, and he shook his head. 'Why, Liana? You agreed to this marriage, as I did. Why can't we find this pleasurable at least?'

'Because…' Because she wasn't strong enough. She'd open herself up to him just a little and a tidal wave of emotion would rush through her. She wouldn't be able to hold it back and it would devastate her. She knew it instinctively, knew that giving in just a little to Sandro would crack her right open, shatter her into pieces. She'd never come together again.

How could she explain all of that?

And yet even so, she knew she had to stop fighting him, stop this futile resistance, because what purpose did it really serve? She was married to this man. She had known they would consummate this marriage. She just hadn't expected to feel so much.

'Liana,' Sandro said, and he sounded so tired. Weary of this, of her.

'I'm sorry,' she said quietly. 'I'll…I'll try better.'

'Try better?' He raised his eyebrows. 'You don't need to prove yourself to me, Liana.'

Didn't she? Hadn't she been proving herself to her parents, to everyone, for so long she didn't know how to do anything else? How to just *be*?

She dragged in a deep breath. 'Let's…start over.' She forced herself to meet his narrowed gaze, even to smile although she felt her lips tremble, and the tears she'd kept at bay for so long threatened once more to spill.

When had she become so emotionally fragile? Why did this man call up such feelings in her? She wanted to be strong again. She wanted to be safe.

She wanted to get this awful, exposing encounter over with.

'Start over,' Sandro repeated. 'I'm wondering just how far we need to go back.'

'Not that far.' She made her smile brighter, more determined. She could do this. They'd get over this, and life would be safe again. 'You're right. I…I do want you.' The words were like rocks in her mouth; she nearly choked on them. Willing her hands to be steady, she undid the sash of her robe, shrugged it off, and stood before him naked.

Sandro's gaze widened, and Liana felt herself flush, a rosy stain covering her whole body that could not be hidden. And she longed to hide it, hide her whole self, mind and body and heart, yet she forced herself to stand there, chin tilted proudly, back straight. Proud and yet accepting.

Sandro shook his head, and her heart swooped inside her. 'This isn't starting over,' he said quietly. 'This is you just gritting your teeth a bit more and putting a game face on.'

'No—' she said, and with desperation driving her, a desperate need to get this all finished with so she could hide once more, she crossed to him and, pressing her naked body against his, she kissed him.

Sandro felt the softness of her breasts brush his bare chest, her lips hard and demanding on his, a supplication his libido responded to with instant acceptance. Instinctively his arms came up and he pulled her closer, fitted her against the throb of his arousal and claimed the kiss as his own.

She tasted so sweet, and her body was so soft and pliant against his. Too pliant. He inwardly cursed.

He didn't want this. Liana might be submitting to him, but it was an awful, insulting submission. He wanted her want, needed her not just to acknowledge her desire of him, but to embrace it, *him*, even if just physically. Emotionally they might be poles apart, but couldn't they at least have this?

Almost roughly, his own hands shaking, he pushed her away from him and shook his head.

'No. Not like this.'

Her eyes widened. 'Why not?'

He stared at her for a moment, wondering just what was going on behind that beautiful, blank face. Except she wasn't quite so blank right now. Her eyes were filled with panic, and her breath came in uneven, frantic gasps.

This wasn't the understandable shy reticence of a virgin, or even the haughty acceptance of the ice queen he'd thought she was. This was, he realised with a sudden jolt of shock, pure *fear*.

'Liana…' He put his hands on her shoulders and felt a shudder rack her body. 'Did you have a bad experience?' he asked quietly. 'With a man? Is that why you're afraid of me? Of physical intimacy?'

She whirled away, snatched up her robe, and pushed her arms into the billowing sleeves. 'I'm not afraid.'

'You're certainly giving a good impression, then.' He folded his arms, a cold certainty settling inside him. Something had happened to her. It all made sense: her extreme devotion to her charity work, her lack of relationships, her fear of natural desire. 'Were you…abused? Raped?'

She whirled back round to face him, a look of shocked disbelief on her face. *'No!'*

'Most women wouldn't fight a natural, healthy desire for a man, Liana. A man who has admitted he wants you. Why do you?'

'Because…' She licked her lips. 'Because I wasn't expecting it,' she finally said and he raised his eyebrows.

'You weren't expecting us to find the physical side of things pleasant? Why not?'

She shrugged. 'Nothing about this marriage or our meeting suggested we would.'

'The kiss we shared six weeks ago didn't clue you in?'

he asked, a gentle hint of humour entering his voice, surprising even him.

She blushed. He liked it when she blushed, liked how it lit up her face and her eyes, her whole self. It gave him hope. 'Before that, I mean,' she muttered.

'All right, fine. You weren't expecting it. But now it's here between us, and you're still fighting it. Why?'

She hesitated, her gaze lowered, before she lifted her face and pinned him with a clear, violet stare. 'Because I agreed to this marriage because it was convenient, and I didn't want anything else. I didn't want love or even affection. I didn't want to get to know you beyond a...a friendly kind of agreement. I thought that's how you would think of this marriage too, and so far nothing—' her breath hitched, her face now fiery '—nothing has been like I expected!'

He didn't know whether to laugh or groan. 'But you're still not telling me why you don't want those things,' Sandro finally said quietly. 'Why you don't want love or affection.' And while her admission didn't surprise him, he suspected the reason for it was different from what he'd thought. She wasn't cold. She was hiding.

She stared at him mutinously, and then her lower lip trembled. It made him, suddenly and fiercely, want to take her in his arms and kiss that wobbling lip. Kiss the tears that shimmered in her eyes, tears he knew instinctively she wouldn't let fall. Then the moment passed and her expression became remote once more. 'I just don't.'

'Still not an answer, Liana.'

'Well, it's the only one I have to give you.'

'So you don't want to tell me.'

'Why should I?' she demanded. 'We barely know each other. You don't—'

'Like you?' he filled in. 'That might have been true

initially, but how can I ever get to like you, or even know you, if you hide yourself from me? Because that's what the whole ice-princess act is, isn't it? A way to hide yourself.' He'd never felt more sure of anything. Her coldness was an act, a mask, and he felt more determined than ever to make it slip, to have it drop away completely.

'Oh, this is ridiculous.' She bit her lip and looked away. 'I don't know why you can't just toss me on the bed and have your wicked way with me.'

He let out a choked laugh of disbelief. Liana, it seemed, had read a few romance novels. 'You'd really prefer that?'

'Yes.' Her eyes turned the colour of a stormy sea and she shook her head. 'I want to want that,' she said, her voice filled with frustration, and he thought he understood.

She wanted something different now. Well, so did he. He wanted to know this contrary bride of his, understand her in a way he certainly didn't now. But he was getting a glimpse of the woman underneath the ice, a woman with pain and secrets and a surprising humour and warmth. A woman he could live with, maybe even love.

Unless of course he was being fanciful. Unless he was fooling himself just as he had with Teresa, with his father, believing the best of everyone because he so wanted to love and be loved.

But surely he'd developed a little discernment over the years?

'I'm not going to throw you on that bed, Liana,' he said, 'and have my way with you, wicked or otherwise. When we have sex—and it won't be tonight—it will be pleasurable for both of us. It will involve a level of give and take, of vulnerability and acceptance I don't think you're capable of right now.'

She didn't answer, just flashed those stormy eyes at

him, so Sandro smiled and took a step closer to her. 'But I will sleep with you in that bed. I'll lie next to you and put my arms around you and feel your softness against me. I think that will be enough for tonight.' He watched her eyes widen with alarm. 'More than enough,' he said, and he tugged on the sash of her robe so it fell open and she walked unwillingly towards him.

'What are you doing—?'

'You can't sleep in that bulky thing.' He slid it from her shoulders, smoothing the silk of her skin under his palms. 'But if you want to wear that frothy nightgown, go ahead.'

Her chin jutting out in determination, she yanked the nightgown from the bed and put it on. It was made mostly of lace, clinging to her body, and Sandro's palms itched to touch her again.

'Now what?' she demanded, crossing her arms over her breasts.

'Now to bed,' Sandro said, and he pulled her to the bed, lay down, and drew her into his arms. She went unresistingly, yet he felt the tension in every muscle of her body. She was lying there like a wooden board.

He stroked her hair, her shoulder, her hip, keeping his touch gentle yet sure, staying away from the places he longed to touch. The fullness of her breasts, the juncture of her thighs.

If he was trying to relax her, it wasn't working. Liana quivered under his touch, but it was a quiver of tension rather than desire. Again, Sandro wondered just what had made his wife this way.

And he knew he wanted to find out. It would, he suspected, be a long, patient process.

He continued to slide his fingers along her skin even as his groin ached with unfulfilled desire. He wanted her, wanted her in a way he hadn't let himself before. He'd fought against this marriage, against this woman, because he'd assumed she was the same as the other conniving women he'd known. His mother. Teresa.

But he suspected now—hell, knew—that his wife wasn't like that. There was too much fear and vulnerability in that violet gaze, too much sorrow in her resistance. She fought against feeling because she was afraid, and he wanted to know why. He wanted to know what fears she hid, and he wanted to help her overcome them. He wanted, he realised with a certainty born not of anger or rebellion but of warmth and fledgling affection, to melt his icy wife.

CHAPTER SIX

LIANA STIRRED SLOWLY to wakefulness as morning sunshine poured into the room like liquid gold. It had taken her hours to get to sleep last night, hours of lying tense and angry and afraid, because this was so not what she'd expected from her marriage. What she'd wanted.

Yet it seemed it was what she'd wanted, after all, for with every gentle stroke of Sandro's fingers she felt something in her soften. Yearn. And even though her body still thrummed with tension, the desire to curl into the heat and strength of him, to feel safe in an entirely new way, grew steadily like a flame at her core.

And yet she resisted. She fought, because fear was a powerful thing. And her mind raced, recalling their conversations, Sandro's awful questions.

Were you abused? Raped?

He wasn't even close, and yet she was hiding something. Too many things. Guilt and grief and what felt like the loss of her own soul, all in the matter of a moment when she'd failed to act. When she'd shown just what kind of person she really was. He'd seen that, even if he didn't understand the source, and she could never tell him.

Could she? Could she change that much? She didn't know if she could, or how she would begin. With each stroke of Sandro's fingers she felt the answer. *Slowly. Slowly.*

And eventually she felt her body relax of its own accord, and her breath came out in a slow sigh of surrender. She didn't curl into him or move at all, but she did sleep.

And she woke with Sandro's hand curved round her waist, his fingers splayed across her belly. Nothing sexual about the touch, but it still felt unbearably intimate. She still felt a plunging desire for him to move his hand, higher or lower, it didn't matter which, just *touch* her.

And then Sandro stirred, and everything in her tensed once more. He rose on one elbow, brushed the hair from her eyes, his fingers lingering on her cheek.

'Good morning.'

She nodded, unable to speak past the sudden tightness in her throat. 'Sleep well?' Sandro asked, and she heard that hint of humour in his voice that had surprised her last night. She'd seen this man cold and angry and resentful, but she hadn't seen him smile too much. Had only heard him laugh once.

And when he softened like this, it made her soften too, and she didn't know what would happen then.

'Yes.' She cleared her throat, inched away from him. 'Eventually.'

'I slept remarkably well.' He brushed another tendril of hair away from her cheek, tucked it behind her ear, his fingers lingering.

Liana resisted the urge to lean into that little caress. 'What are we going to do today?'

'We have a few engagements.' Smiling, Sandro sat up in bed, raking his hair with his hands, so even though she was trying to avoid looking at him Liana found her gaze drawn irresistibly to his perfectly sculpted pectoral muscles, the taut curve of his biceps. Her husband was beautiful—and fit.

'What engagements?' she asked, forcing her brain back into gear.

'A brunch with my delightful mother as well as my sister and my brother and his wife. An appearance on the balcony for the adoring crowds.'

He spoke with a cynicism she didn't really understand, although she could probably guess at. 'You don't like being royal,' she said, 'do you?'

He sighed and dropped his hands. 'Not particularly. But hadn't you already figured that out, since I shirked my royal duty for fifteen years?' His gaze met hers then, and instead of anger she saw recrimination. She recognised it, because she'd felt it so often herself.

'I shouldn't have said that,' she said quietly. 'I'm sorry.'

'Why, Liana.' He touched her chin with his fingers, tilting her face so their gazes met once more. 'I don't think you've ever apologised to me before. Not sincerely.'

'I am sorry,' she answered. Her chin tingled where he touched her. 'I was just trying to hurt you, so I said the first thing that came to mind.'

'Well, there was truth in it, wasn't there?' His voice came out bitter and he dropped his hand from her face. 'I did shirk my duty. I ran away.'

And she knew all too well how guilt over a mistake, a wrong choice, ate and ate at you until there was nothing left. Until your only recourse was to cut yourself off from everything because numbness was better than pain. Was that how Sandro felt? Did they actually have something—something so fundamental to their selves—in common?

'But you came back,' she said quietly. 'You've made it better.'

'Trying to.' He threw off the covers and rose from

the bed. 'But we should get ready. We have a full day ahead of us.'

He was pulling away from her, she knew. They'd had a surprising moment of closeness there, a closeness that had intrigued her rather than frightened her. And now it was Sandro was who shuttering his expression, and she felt a frustration that was foreign to her because she was usually the one who was pulling away. Hiding herself.

So maybe this was why Sandro had been feeling so frustrated. It was hard to be on the receiving end of someone's reticence—especially when you actually wanted something else. Something more.

'Where are we meant to get ready?' she asked. 'I've only got my wedding dress or this nightgown here.'

Sandro pushed a discreet button hidden in the woodwork of the wall. 'One of your staff will show you to your room,' he said and turned away.

A few minutes later a shy young woman named Maria came to the honeymoon suite and showed Liana her own bedroom, a room, judging from its frilly, feminine décor, Sandro clearly wouldn't share.

So this was what a marriage of convenience looked like, Liana thought, and wondered why she didn't feel happier. Safer. She'd have her own space. Sandro would leave her alone. All things she'd wanted.

Yet in that moment, standing amidst the fussy little tables and pink canopied bed, she wasn't quite so sure she wanted them anymore. They didn't feel as comforting as she'd expected.

Maybe she was just tired. Feeling more vulnerable from everything she and Sandro had said and shared last night. The memory of his hands gently stroking her from shoulder to thigh still had the power to make her quiver.

Enough. It was time to do the work she'd come here

to do, to be queen. To remember her duty to her parents, to her sister, to everything she'd made her life about.

And not think about Sandro, and the confusion of her marriage.

An hour later she was showered and dressed in a modest dress of lavender silk, high necked and belted at the waist. She'd pulled her hair back into its usual tight chignon and then frowned at her reflection, remembering what Sandro had said.

I would like to see you with your hair cascading over your shoulders. Your lips rosy and parted, your face flushed.

For a second she thought about undoing her hair. Putting some blusher on her cheeks. Then her frown deepened and she turned away from the mirror. She looked fine.

Downstairs, the royal family had assembled in an opulent dining room for the official brunch. And it felt official, far from a family meal. A dozen footmen were stationed around the room, and the dishes were all gold plate.

The queen dowager glided into the room, her eyes narrowed, her mouth pursed, everything about her haughty and distant.

Was that how Sandro saw her? Icy and remote, even arrogant? Liana felt herself inwardly cringe. She'd never considered how others saw her; she'd just not wanted to be seen. Really seen. The woman underneath the ice. The girl still trying to make herself invisible, to apologise for her existence.

Sophia went to the head of the table and Sandro moved to the other end. A footman showed Liana her place, on the side, and for a second she hesitated.

As queen, her place was where Sophia now sat, eyeing everyone coldly. Clearly the queen dowager did not want to give up her rights and privileges as monarch, and Liana wasn't about to make a fuss about where she sat at the table. She never made a fuss.

And yet somehow it hurt, because she realised she wanted Sandro to notice where she sat. Notice her, and put her in her rightful place.

He didn't even look at her, and Liana didn't think she was imagining the triumph glittering in her mother-in-law's eyes as she sat down.

Sandro excused himself directly after the brunch, and Liana hadn't had so much as two words of conversation with him. They were meant to appear on the palace balcony at four o'clock, and she had a meeting with her secretary—someone already appointed and whom she hadn't met—at three.

And until then? She'd wander around the palace and wonder yet again just what she was doing here. What had brought her to this place.

Most of the palace's ground floor was made up of formal receiving rooms much like the one she'd first met Sandro in. Liana wandered through them, sunlight dappling the marble floors. As she stood in the centre of one room, feeling as lost and lonely as she ever had and annoyed that she did, she heard a voice from behind her.

'Hello.'

She turned to see Alyse standing in the doorway, looking lovely and vibrant and full of purpose. She'd changed from her more formal outfit for brunch, and now wore a pair of jeans and a cashmere sweater in bright pink. Liana suddenly felt absurd and matronly in her high-necked dress and tightly coiled hair. She fiddled with the pearls at her throat, managed a smile.

'Hello.'

'Did you have a good night?' A blush touched Alyse's cheeks. 'Sorry. I didn't mean that— Well.' She laughed and stepped into the room. 'I was only asking if you'd slept well.'

'Very well, thank you,' Liana answered automatically, and Alyse cocked her head.

'You look tired,' she said, her voice filled with sympathy. 'It's so overwhelming, isn't it—marrying into royalty?'

'It's been a lot to take in,' Liana answered carefully. She didn't want to admit just how overwhelming it had been, and how uncertain and unfulfilled she felt now.

'At least you don't have the press to deal with,' Alyse said with a little laugh. 'That was the hardest part for me. All those cameras, all those reporters looking for a hole in our story, and of course they found one.'

'Was that very hard?'

Alyse made a face. 'Well, I certainly didn't like facing down all those sneering reporters, but the hardest part was how it affected Leo and me.'

Curious now, Liana took an inadvertent step towards her sister-in-law. 'And how did it?'

'Not well. Everything was so fragile between us then. It wasn't ready to be tested in such a way.' She gave Liana a smile. 'Fortunately we survived it.'

'And you love each other now.' Alyse's smile was radiant, the joy in her voice audible, and Liana felt a sharp shaft of jealousy. She'd never wanted what Alyse and Leo had before, never let herself want it. Yet now the yearning that had been skirting her soul seemed to swamp it completely.

She swallowed past the huge lump that had formed in her throat and forced a smile. 'I'm so happy for you.' And she was, even if she was also jealous. Even if she was realising she wanted something more than she could ever expect from Sandro, or even herself.

'It might not be for me to say this,' Alyse said quietly, laying a hand on Liana's arm, 'but Leo and Sandro—they haven't had easy lives, royal though they may be.'

'What do you mean?'

'Their relationship with their parents...' Alyse sighed and shook her head. 'It wasn't healthy or loving. Far from it.'

Liana just nodded. She couldn't exactly say her relationship with her parents was healthy, even if she loved them. She wasn't sure if they loved her. If they could, anymore, and she could hardly blame them.

'Sophia doesn't seem like the most cuddly person I've ever met,' she said, and Alyse gave a wry smile back.

'No, and neither was the king. And yet I think both Leo and Sandro wanted their love, even if they wouldn't admit it. They might not trust love, they might even be afraid of it, but they want it.'

'Leo did,' Liana corrected.

'And I think Sandro does too. Give him a chance, Liana. That's all I'm really saying.'

And again Liana could just nod. Sandro might want love, but he didn't want *her* love. Did he? Or could he change? Could *she*?

She still didn't know if she wanted to change, much less whether she had the courage to try. She'd entered this marriage for a lot of reasons, and none of them had been love. She'd never even let herself think about love.

She'd been skating on the surface of her life, and now the ice below was starting to crack—and what was beneath it? What would happen when it shattered and she fell? She couldn't bear to find out, and yet she had a horrible feeling she would whether she wanted to or not.

But would Sandro be there to catch her? Would he even want to?

'Thank you for telling me all this,' she said, turning back to Alyse. 'It's very helpful.'

'Of course. And you must come have dinner with us one night, you and Sandro. Escape from the palace for a bit.'

After Alyse had gone she went to meet her private secretary, an efficient young woman named Christina. Liana sat and listened while Christina outlined all her potential engagements: cutting ribbons at openings of hospitals and schools, attending events and galas, choosing a wardrobe created by Maldinian fashion designers.

'Are there many?' she asked. 'Maldinia is a small country, after all.'

'A few,' Christina said confidently. 'But of course, your stylist will go over that with you.'

'All right.' Already Liana felt overwhelmed. She hadn't considered any of this. 'I'd like to support a charity I've been working with for many years,' she began, and Christina nodded quickly.

'Of course, Hands To Help. Perhaps a fundraiser in the palace?'

'Oh, yes, that would be wonderful.' She felt her heart lighten at the thought. 'I can contact them—'

'I believe they've already been contacted by King Alessandro,' Christina said. 'It was his idea.'

'It…was?' Liana blinked in surprise. Sandro had seemed sceptical and even mystified about her charity work, yet he'd thought to arrange a fundraiser? Her heart lightened all the more, so it felt like a balloon on a string, soaring straight up. 'Where is the king? Do you know?'

Christina glanced at her watch. 'I imagine he's getting ready for your appearance together in twenty minutes.'

She pulled out a pager and pressed a few numbers. 'I'll page your stylist.'

Just minutes later Liana was primped and made up for the appearance on the balcony. Sandro strode into the room, looking as handsome as ever in his royal dress, but also hassled. Liana's heart, so light moments ago, began a free fall. She hated that her mood might hinge on his look, that such a small thing—the lack of a greeting or a glance—could affect it.

And yet it did. Despite all her attempts to remain removed, remote, here she was, yearning. Disappointed.

'Ready?' he said, barely looking at her, and then with his hand on her lower back they stepped out onto the ornate balcony overlooking the palace courtyard, now filled with joyous Maldinians.

The cheer that rose from the crowd reverberated right through her, made her blink in surprise. She'd never felt so much…*approval*.

'I think they want us to kiss,' Sandro murmured, and belatedly Liana realised they were chanting *'Baccialo!'*

Sandro slid his hand along her jaw, turned her to face him. His fingers wrapped around the nape of her neck, warm and sure, as he drew her unresistingly towards him. His lips brushed hers, soft, hard, warm, cool—she felt it all in that moment as her head fell back and her hands came up to press against his chest.

The roar of the crowd thundered in her ears, matching her galloping pulse as Sandro's mouth moved over hers and everything inside her cracked open.

She wanted to be kissed like this. Loved like this. She was tired of hiding away, of staying safe.

Sandro stepped away with a smile. 'That ought to do it.'

Liana blinked the world back into focus and felt everything in her that had cracked open scuttle for shelter. That kiss had been for the crowds, not for her. It hadn't meant anything.

Their marriage was still as convenient as it ever had been…and she wished it weren't.

As soon as they left the balcony Sandro disappeared again and Liana went to meet with her stylist and go over her wardrobe choices.

'A queen should have a certain modest style,' the stylist explained as she flipped through pages of designs, 'but also be contemporary. The public should feel you can relate to them.'

Liana glanced down at her chaste, high-necked dress. 'So what I'm wearing…?'

'Is beautiful,' the stylist, Demi, said quickly. 'So elegant and classic. But perhaps something a little…fresher?'

'Yes, I suppose I could update my look a little bit,' Liana said slowly. She'd been dressing, for the most part, like a businesswoman facing menopause, not a young woman in her twenties. A young woman with everything ahead of her.

But she'd never actually felt as if she had anything ahead of her before, and she didn't know if she did now.

She had a quiet supper in her bedroom, as Sophia was dining out and Alyse and Leo had gone back to their town house. Sandro was working through dinner, and it wasn't until it was coming on ten o'clock that she finally went to find him.

She had no idea what she'd say, what she wanted to say. He was leaving her alone, just as she'd hoped and wanted. How could she tell him she actually wanted something different now, especially when she wasn't sure herself what that was?

She wandered through the downstairs, directed by footmen to his private study in the back of the palace. With nerves fluttering in her tummy and her heart starting to thud, she knocked on the door.

'Come in.'

Liana pushed open the door and stepped into a wood-panelled room with deep leather club chairs and a huge mahogany desk. Sandro sat behind it, one hand driven through his hair as he glanced up from the papers scattered on his desk.

'Liana—' Surprise flared silver in his eyes and he straightened, dropping his hand. 'I'm sorry. It's late. I've been trying to clear my desk but it never seems to happen.'

'A king has a lot of work to do, I suppose,' she answered with a small smile. Sandro might have avoided his royal duty for most of his adult life, but he was certainly attending to it now.

'What have you been doing today? You had some appointments?'

She nodded. 'With my private secretary and stylist. I've never had a staff before.'

'And is it to your liking?'

'I don't know whether it is or not. It's overwhelming, I suppose. My style is meant to be fresher, apparently.'

'Fresher? It makes you sound like a lettuce.'

'It does, doesn't it?' She smiled, enjoying this little banter. 'I know I've dressed a bit—conservatively.'

He glanced at the lavender dress she still wore. 'And why do you think that is?'

'I suppose I've never wanted to draw attention to myself.'

He nodded slowly, accepting, and Liana fiddled with

the belt at her waist, uncomfortable with even this little honesty. 'Are you—are you coming to bed?'

He gazed at her seriously. 'Do you want me to?'

Yes. And no. She didn't know what she wanted anymore. She'd had such clear purpose in her life...until now. Until she suddenly wanted more, more of him, more of feeling, more of life. Yet she couldn't articulate all that now to Sandro.

He sat back, his hands laced over his middle as he let his gaze sweep over her. 'You're still scared. Of me.'

'Not of you—'

'Of marriage. Of—intimacy.'

She swallowed hard, the sound audible. 'Yes.' It was more than she'd ever admitted before.

'Well, you can breathe easy, Liana. We won't make love tonight.'

Make love. And didn't that conjure all sorts of images in her head? Images that made her dizzy, desires that dried her throat and made everything inside her ache. 'When—?' she asked, her voice only a little shaky, and he smiled.

'Soon, I think. Perhaps on our honeymoon.'

'Honeymoon?' They weren't meant to have a honeymoon. What was the point, when your marriage was about convenience?

'Well, honeymoon might be overstating it a bit. I have to go to California, wrap up some business. I want you to go with me.'

Her cheeks warmed, her blood heated. Everything inside her melted. *He wanted her.* Was it foolish to feel so gratified? So...thrilled?

'Is that all right?' Sandro asked quietly. 'Do you want to go with me, Liana?'

A week ago, a day ago, she would have prevaricated.

Protected herself. She'd never admitted want to herself, much less to another person. Now she nodded. 'Yes,' she said. 'I want to go with you.'

CHAPTER SEVEN

SANDRO SAT ACROSS from Liana on the royal jet and picked a strawberry dipped in chocolate from the silver platter between them. He held it out to her, a mischievous smile playing about his mouth. They were halfway across the Atlantic and he was determined to begin what he suspected would be the very enjoyable process of melting his wife.

It was already working; last night she'd lain in his arms and it had only taken her an hour to relax. He'd watched her face soften in sleep, those tightly pursed lips part on a sigh. Her lashes had fluttered and brushed against her porcelain-pale cheeks. He'd stroked her cheek, amazed at its softness, at the softness he felt in himself towards this woman he'd thought was so hard. So icy and cold.

Yet even as he'd held her and stroked her cheek, he'd wondered. Doubted, because God only knew his judgment had been off before. He'd thought the best of his parents, of the one woman he'd let into his heart. He'd insisted on it, even when everything said otherwise.

Was he doing the same now? Desperate, even now, to love and be loved? Because Liana might lie in his arms, but she didn't always look as if she wanted to be there. One minute she was kissing him with a sudden, sweet passion that had taken him by surprise on the balcony and the next she was cool and remote, all chilly indifference.

Which was the real woman?

Now Liana eyed the chocolate strawberry askance. 'You have a thing about messy food.'

'They tend to be aphrodisiacal.'

'Aphro— *Oh.*' Her cheeks pinked, and he grinned.

'Try one.'

'I don't—'

'You don't like strawberries? Or chocolate? I can't believe it.'

'I've never had one before.'

'A strawberry?'

'Not one dipped in chocolate.' Her blush deepened and she looked away. 'Sometimes I think I must seem ridiculous to you.'

Surprise made him falter. He dropped his hand, still holding the strawberry, the chocolate smearing his fingers. 'Nothing about you is ridiculous, Liana.'

'I know I haven't experienced much of life.'

'And why is that?'

She paused, pressed her lips together. 'I don't know.'

But he thought she did. She must at least have a good guess. No need to press her now, though. Instead he held out the strawberry once more. 'Try it.'

She hesitated, her lips still pursed, everything in her resisting. Then he saw the moment when she made the decision to be different, and with a little shrug and a smile she reached for it. He drew back, his eyes glinting challenge. 'Open your mouth.'

Her eyes widened and for a second he thought he'd pushed too far. Too hard. But she did as he said, parting her lips so he could hold the strawberry out to her. He felt his groin harden and ache as she touched the tip of her pink tongue to the chocolate and licked.

'Mmm.' She sounded so sweetly innocent and yet as seductive as a siren as she gazed at him with eyes as wide and clear as lakes. He could drown in them. He was drowning, lost in this moment as she licked the chocolate again. 'I don't think I knew what I've been missing,' she said huskily, and he knew she wasn't just talking about a single, simple strawberry.

'Liana…' His voice was a groan as she bit into the strawberry, juice trickling down her chin, chocolate smearing her lush lips.

She ate it in two bites, and then Sandro could hold back no longer. He reached for her, dragging his hands through her hair as he brought her face to his and kissed her strawberry-sweet lips.

She tasted better, sweeter than any strawberry. And he wanted her more than he'd wanted anything or anyone before in his life. He kissed her deeply, as if he was drawing the essence of her right out of her mouth and into himself. Wanting and needing to feel her closer than a kiss, with his hands spanning her waist he drew her onto his lap, fitted her legs around him so she pressed snugly against his arousal and he flexed his hips against hers, craving that exquisite friction.

'Now, that's better,' he murmured and she let out a choked laugh.

'Sandro—' She broke off, her head buried in his neck, and Sandro stilled.

He was moving too fast. He'd forgotten, in the sweet spell of that kiss, that she was a virgin. Untouched. Inexperienced.

Sandro closed his eyes and willed the tide of his desire

back. Even so it misted his mind with a red haze. Gently he eased her off his lap.

'Sorry. Lost my head a bit there.'

'It's okay,' she murmured, but her face was still buried in his neck.

Sandro leaned back against the sofa cushions and tried, without success, to will away the ache in his groin.

'Sex doesn't scare me, you know,' she said suddenly, and he suppressed a smile.

'I'm very glad to hear it.'

'It's just…' She licked her lips, sending a shaft of lust burrowing deep into him. *Painful.* 'Everything else does. About…being with someone.'

'What do you mean?'

'Intimacy. Like you said. Sharing things. Being—vulnerable.'

He smiled, tried to draw her into that smile, into something shared. 'None of it is a walk in the park, is it?'

'You mean it scares you too?'

'Sometimes.' He was the one to glance away now. 'I'm not exactly an expert in all this myself, you know, Liana.'

'But you've had loads of relationships, according to the media anyway.'

'Don't believe everything you read.'

Her eyebrows rose, two pale arcs. 'It's not true?'

He shifted in his seat, uncomfortable to impart so much, yet knowing he could only be honest with this woman. His wife. 'I've had quite a few…sexual relationships, I admit. They didn't mean anything to me.'

'That's more than I've had,' she said with a soft laugh that wobbled at the end, a telling note.

He felt a sudden stab of surprising regret for all the pointless encounters he'd had, all attempts to stave off the loneliness and need he'd felt deep inside. The need that was, amazingly, starting to be met by this woman.

'Have you ever...loved anyone?' Liana asked softly. 'I mean, a woman? A romantic... Well, you know.'

'Yes.' Sandro paused, pictured Teresa. What had drawn him to her originally? She'd been so different from everything about his former life, he supposed. A California girl, with sun-kissed hair and bright blue eyes, always ready to laugh, always up for a good time. It had taken him nearly a year to realise Teresa only wanted a good time. With his money. His status. She wasn't interested in the man he really was, didn't want to do the whole 'for better or for worse' thing. At least, not for worse.

'Sandro?' Liana's soft voice interrupted the bleakness of his thoughts. 'You must have loved her very much.'

'Why do you say that?'

'Because your face is like a thundercloud.'

He shook his head. 'I thought I loved her.'

'Is there really a difference?'

He sighed. 'Maybe not. Sometimes disillusionment is worse than heartbreak.'

'How were you disillusioned?'

He shrugged, half amazed he was telling her all of this. 'I thought she loved me for me. But I discovered she was really only interested in my money and status, and not so much me, or being faithful to me.' He'd caught her in bed with the landscaping guy, of all people. She hadn't even been sorry.

Liana pressed her lips together. 'So that's why you're so suspicious.'

'Suspicious?'

'Of me.'

He hesitated then, because as much as he'd been enjoying their conversation and this new, startling intimacy, her words reminded him that she had agreed to marry him for exactly those reasons. Money. Power. A title.

Nothing had really changed, except maybe in his own sentimental mind.

He pushed the thought away; he wanted, for once, to enjoy the simple pleasure of being with a woman. With his wife. 'Have another strawberry,' he said, and held another one out to her parted lips.

Liana licked the last of the chocolate from her lips, every sense on impossible overload. She'd never felt so much— the sweetness of the strawberry, the seductive promise of his kiss, the alarming honesty of their conversation that left her feeling bare and yet bizarrely, beautifully light, as if she'd slipped the first tiny bit of a burden she'd been carrying so long she'd forgotten it was weighing her down. Crippling her.

This was why people fell in love, she supposed. This was what the magazines and romance novels hinted at— and yet she didn't even love Sandro. How could she, when she barely knew him?

And yet he was her husband, and he'd held her all night long and kissed her as if he couldn't get enough. She'd had more with him already than she'd ever had before, and if that made her pathetic, fine. She was pathetic. But for the first time in her life she could almost glimpse happiness.

But could he? Could they have something other than a marriage of convenience, even if they wanted it? Her own emotions and desires were a confused tangle, and she had no idea what Sandro's were. What he thought. What he felt. She didn't want to ask.

'What are you thinking about?' Sandro asked as he popped a strawberry into his own mouth.

'Lots of things.'

'You're all sunlight and shadows, smiling one minute, frowning the next.'

'Am I?' She laughed a little, tried for some more of this hard honesty. 'I guess I'm trying to figure out what I think. What I feel.'

'Maybe,' Sandro suggested softly, 'you should stop thinking so much. Just run with it.'

She nodded. Yes, that seemed like a good idea. Stop analysing. Stop worrying. Just…feel.

She'd spent half a lifetime trying not to feel, and now that was all she wanted to do. She laughed aloud, the sound soft and trembling, and Sandro smiled.

'Good idea?' he asked and she nodded again.

'Yes,' she answered with a smile. 'Good idea.'

They arrived in Los Angeles tired and jet-lagged, but Liana was still euphoric. This was a new place, a new day. A new life.

A limo was waiting for them at the airport, and Liana kept her nose nearly pressed on the glass as they drove through the city to Sandro's beachside villa in Santa Monica.

'I've never been to the US before, you know,' she said as she took in the impressive elegance of Rodeo Drive, the iconic Hollywood sign high above them.

'Consider yourself a tourist. I have some work to do, but we can do the sights.'

'What are the sights?'

'The usual museums and theme parks. The beach. I'd like to take you to a spa resort out in Palm Desert and pamper you to death.'

She let out a little laugh as a thrill ran through her. 'That sounds like a pretty good way to go.'

'I don't think you've ever been pampered,' Sandro said quietly. 'Spoiled.'

'Who would want to be spoiled?'

'I mean...' He shrugged, spread his hands. 'Treated. Indulged. Given an experience just to enjoy and savour.'

No, she'd never had any of those things, not remotely. 'Well, good thing I'm with you, then,' she said lightly. 'Pamper away.'

Sandro smiled and let it drop; she knew he knew there were things she wasn't saying, things she was afraid to say. And would she ever tell him? She thought of his fingers stroking her back, her hip, softening her. *Slowly, slowly.*

The limo pulled up to Sandro's gated mansion and they spent the next hour walking through it. He showed her the voice-controlled plasma-screen television, the shower stall big enough for two people that was activated by simply placing your palm on the wall.

'This place is like something out of James Bond,' she said with a laugh. 'I had no idea you were a gadget guy.'

'I worked in IT.'

'And Leo does too, doesn't he? I remember someone saying at our reception that he's drafting an IT bill.'

'He is.' Sandro's expression seemed to still, everything in him turn wary. 'He's worked hard in my absence.'

She heard the note of recrimination in his voice that she'd sensed before and she wanted to ask him about it. Wanted to know if he struggled with guilt the way she did. But the sun was so bright and they'd been having so much fun exploring his house that she didn't want to weigh down the lightness of the moment.

And, she knew, she was a coward.

They had lunch out on the private beach in front of the house, although Liana's body clock was insisting it

was some impossible, other time. She stretched her legs
out on the sun-warmed sand and gazed out at the Pacific,
started to fall halfway asleep.

Or maybe it was all the way asleep, because she startled to wakefulness when Sandro scooped her up in his
arms.

'Time for bed, I think,' he murmured, and carried her
across the sand and into the house. She sank onto the silk
sheets of his king-size bed and felt the mattress dip as
Sandro lay next to her, his arm still around her.

He drew her against him so her head rested on his
shoulder, the steady thud of his heart under her cheek.
Liana let out a little breathy sigh of contentment. How
had she gone without this all of her life?

She must have fallen asleep, because she awoke in
the middle of the night, the room drenched in darkness
save for a sliver of moonlight that bisected the floor. The
space in the bed next to her yawned emptily.

Liana shook her hair out of her face and glanced
around the bedroom, but Sandro was nowhere to be seen.
On bare feet she padded through the upstairs looking for
him, wondering where he'd gone—and why he'd left her
in the middle of the night.

She finally found him downstairs in his study, dressed
only in a pair of black silk pyjama bottoms, just as he had
been on their wedding night. He had his laptop in front
of him and papers were scattered across his desk. He
worked so hard, she thought with a twist of guilty regret.
She'd accused him of neglecting his royal duty, of being
someone she couldn't respect, but she was beginning to
see just how far from the truth that accusation had been.

'Can't sleep?' she asked softly and he glanced up, the
frown that had settled between his brows smoothed away
for a moment.

'My body clock is completely out of sync. I thought I might as well get some work done.'

'What are you working on?'

'Just tying up some loose ends with DT.'

'DT?'

'Diomedi Technology.'

She came into the room, driven by a new and deeper curiosity to know this man. To understand him. 'You founded it, didn't you? When you…moved?'

The smile he gave her was twisted, a little bitter. 'You mean when I abandoned my royal duty to pursue my own pleasures?'

She winced. 'Don't, Sandro.'

'It's true, though.'

'I'm not sure it is.'

'And how do you figure that, Liana?' His voice held a hard edge but she had a feeling for once it wasn't for her. He was angry with himself for leaving, for somehow failing. She knew because she understood that feeling too well. The churning guilt and regret for doing the wrong thing or, in her case, nothing at all.

Briefly she closed her eyes, willed the memory of Chiara's desperate gaze away, at least for this moment. Her sister's face, she knew, would haunt her for the rest of her life.

'I think there's always more to the story than there first appears,' she said quietly, coming to perch on the edge of his desk. 'You told me leaving felt necessary at the time, but you didn't tell me why.'

He glanced down at the papers on his desk. 'I didn't think we had that sort of relationship.'

Her breath hitched and she willed it to even out again. 'We didn't. But—but maybe we do now. Or at least, we're trying to.'

He glanced up at her then, everything about him inscrutable. Fathomless. 'Are we?'

Liana stared back at him, words on her lips and fear in her heart. This was the moment when she should show her hand, she knew. Her heart. Tell him that in the few days since they'd been married she'd started to change. He'd changed her, and now she wanted things she'd never let herself want. Affection. Friendship. *Love.*

The words were there and they trembled on her lips but then the fear of exposing so much want and need made her swallow them and offer a rather watery smile instead.

'You tell me.'

Wrong answer, she knew. A coward's answer. Sandro looked away. 'I don't know, Liana. I don't know what secrets you're hiding, or why you've, as you said yourself, experienced so little of life. It's almost as if you've kept yourself from it, from enjoying or feeling anything, and I won't know why or understand you until you tell me.' He glanced back at her then, his expression settled into resolute lines. 'But I'm not even sure you really want that. You told me you married me because of the opportunities being queen would give this charity of yours. Has that changed?'

She swallowed. 'No, not exactly.' Sandro's expression tightened and he started shuffling his papers into piles. 'But I've changed, Sandro, at least a little. I want to get to know you. And I hope you want to know me.' And that, Liana thought with a weary wryness, was about as honest as she could make herself be right now.

Sandro gazed at her thoughtfully. 'And how do you propose we do that?'

'Get to know one another, you mean?' She licked her lips, saw Sandro's gaze drop to her mouth, and felt warmth curling low in her belly. 'Well…as we have been doing. Talking. Spending time with one another.'

'We can talk all you like, but until you tell me whatever it is you're keeping from me, I don't think much is going to change.'

'But I told you I've already changed,' she said quietly. 'A little, at least. You've changed me.'

'Have I?' Sandro asked softly. He was still staring at her mouth and Liana felt a heavy languor begin to steal through her veins, making her feel almost drunk, reckless in a way she so rarely was. 'I can think of another way we could get to know one another,' she whispered.

He arched an eyebrow, heat flaring in his eyes, turning them to molten silver. 'And what would that be?'

'This.' She leaned forward, her heart thudding hard, and brushed her lips across his.

His mouth was cool and soft, his lips only barely parted, and he didn't respond as she'd expected him to, pulling her in his arms and taking control. No, he was waiting to see what she would do. How far she would go.

Emboldened, Liana touched her tongue to the corner of Sandro's mouth, heard his groan, felt it in the soft rush of breath against her own lips. Desire bit deeper, and she brought her hands up to his shoulders, steadying herself on the edge of his desk as she kissed him again, slid her tongue into his mouth with a surge of pure sexual excitement she thrilled to feel.

'Liana…' Sandro's hands tangled in her hair as he fastened his mouth more securely on hers, taking the kiss from her and making it his. Theirs.

And what a kiss it was. Liana could easily count the number of times she'd been kissed, half of them by Sandro, but this kiss was something else entirely. This kiss was shared, a giving and a taking and most of all an admission. A spilling of secrets, a confession of desire.

It felt like the most honest thing she'd ever done.

And then it was more than a kiss as Sandro swept all his papers aside and hauled her across the desk. She came willingly, sliding onto his lap, her legs on either side of him as she felt the hard, insistent press of his arousal against her and pleasure spiked deep inside.

Sandro deepened the kiss, his hands moving over her, cupping her breasts, the thin cotton of her sundress already too much between them. In that moment she wasn't afraid of her own feelings, the strength of her own desire—and his. She just wanted more.

Recklessly Liana pulled the dress over her head and tossed it to the floor. Sandro's gaze darkened with heat and then she unclasped her bra and sent it flying too. She was wearing only her panties, and even that felt like too much clothing.

'You're so beautiful,' he whispered huskily as his hands roved over her. 'Your skin is like marble.'

A small smile twitched her lips. 'Like a statue?'

He glanced up at her, his hands now cupping her breasts, his thumbs brushing over their taut peaks. 'Like Venus de Milo.' And then he put his mouth to her breasts and if she were a statue she came alive under him, writhing and gasping as he teased her with his tongue and lips.

She tangled her hands in his hair, arching her back and pressing against him, gasping aloud when he flexed his hips upwards and she felt the promise of what was to come, of what it would feel like to have him inside her, to be part of him. She wanted it now.

Sandro let out a shaky groan. 'Not here, Liana. Let me take you to bed—'

'Why do we need a bed?' she murmured and she slid

his hands up his bare chest, fingers spreading across hot skin and hard muscle.

'Your first time—'

'Are there rules about a woman's first time? Does it have to be on a bed, with roses and violins?'

He let out a shaky laugh. 'I don't have any roses at the moment—'

'I don't actually like roses.' She pressed against him, muscles she hadn't known she had tightening, quivering. 'Or violins.'

'Even so—'

'I want this.' She might not be able to be honest about everything yet, but she could be honest about this. About this real, rushing desire she felt. 'I want you. And I want you here, now, just like this.'

He eased away from her, but only to hold her face in his palms and search her expression. She stared back, firm in her purpose, clear-headed even in the midst of the haze of sexual desire. 'You want me,' he said slowly, almost wonderingly, and she leaned forward so her breasts brushed his chest and her lips touched his.

'I want you,' she whispered against his mouth, and then she kissed him again, another honest kiss, deeper this time, drawing everything from him even as she gave it back.

She'd never grow tired of this, she thought hazily as Sandro kissed his way down her body and her head fell back. She'd never have enough of this, of him. Her breath came out in short gasps as his fingers skimmed the waistband of her panties and then with one swift tug tore the thin cotton and tossed them aside, along with his own pyjama bottoms.

The sudden feel of his fingers against her most sensitive flesh made her let out a surprised cry, and all her muscles clenched as Sandro slid his fingers inside her.

She dropped her head on his shoulder, her fingernails biting into his back as he moved his hand with such delicious certainty and a wave of pleasure so intense and fierce it almost hurt crashed over her.

'*Sandro.*' Her breath came out in a shudder. 'Why didn't I know about this?'

'Because you didn't let yourself,' he murmured, and as his hand kept moving her hips moved of their own accord, her body falling into a rhythm as natural as breathing.

'I—I want you,' she gasped, each word coming out on a pant. 'I want you inside me.'

'It could hurt a little, your first—'

'Shut up about my first time,' she cut him off on a gasp, angling her hips so she was poised over him. She met his hot gaze as she sank slowly onto him, her eyes widening as she felt herself open and stretch. Her hands gripped his shoulders, and his hands were fastened to her hips, their bodies joined in every way. 'Nothing about this hurts.'

That wasn't quite true. Nothing hurt, but the feel of him inside her was certainly eye-opening. *Intense.* And wonderful. Intimate in a way she'd always been afraid to be. To feel.

She never wanted to go back to numbness again.

Sandro's gaze stayed on hers as he began to move, his hands on her hips guiding her to match his rhythm.

'Okay?' he murmured and she laughed, throwing her head back as pleasure began shooting sparks deep inside her, jolts of sensation that made speech almost impossible.

'More than okay,' she answered when she trusted her voice. 'Wonderful.'

And then words failed her as sensation took over, and Sandro's body moved so deeply inside hers she felt as if he touched her soul.

Maybe he did, because when the feelings finally took over, swamping her completely so her voice split the still air with one jagged cry of pleasure, she knew she'd never felt as close to a human being before, or ever.

And it felt more than wonderful. It felt as if he'd brought her back to life.

CHAPTER EIGHT

THEY HAD FIVE days in California, five days of seeing the sights and enjoying each other's company and each other's bodies. Making love.

That was what it felt like to Sandro, what it *was*. He was falling in love with his wife, with the warm woman who had broken through the coldness and the ice.

Looking at her as they strolled down the pier in Santa Monica, Sandro could hardly believe Liana was the same coolly composed woman he'd met two months ago. She wore a sundress in daffodil yellow, her pale hair streaming about her shoulders, her eyes sparkling and her cheeks flushed. She looked incandescent.

Her step slowed as she glanced at him, her brow wrinkling. 'You're giving me a funny look.'

'Am I?'

'Do I have ice cream on my face or something?' She'd been eating a chocolate ice cream with the relish usually exhibited by a small child, and every long lick had desire arrowing inside him and making him long to drag her back to his house and make love to her in yet another room. So far they'd christened his study, his bedroom, the shower, the beach, and the front hall when they'd been in too much of a rush to get any farther inside. At this rate, Santa Monica pier would be next, and damn the crowds.

'I'm just enjoying watching you eat your ice cream.'

'Is it really that fascinating?' She laughed and Sandro felt himself go hard as she took another lick, her pink tongue swiping at the chocolate with a beguiling innocence.

'Trust me, it is.'

She faltered midlick as she took in the hotness of his gaze, and then with an impish little smile she leaned forward and gave him a chocolatey kiss. 'That's to tide you over till later.'

'How much later?'

'I want to walk to the end of the pier.'

Sandro groaned and took her arm. 'You're going to kill me, woman.'

'You'll die with a smile on your face, though.'

'Or else a grimace of agony because you're too busy enjoying your ice cream to satisfy your husband.'

She arched her eyebrows in mock innocence. 'I believe I satisfied my husband twice today already, and it's not even noon. I think you might need to talk to a doctor.'

'I might,' he agreed. 'Or maybe you just need to stop eating ice cream in front of me.' And then because he couldn't keep himself from it any longer, he pulled her towards him and kissed her again, deeper this time, more than just something to tide him over until he could get her alone.

The ice-cream cone dangled from Liana's fingers and then fell to the pier with a splat as she kissed him back, looping her arms around his neck to draw his body against her pliant softness, and he very nearly lost his head as everything in him ached to finish what they'd started right there, amidst the rollerbladers and sun-worshippers.

And Liana must have agreed with him, because she

kept kissing him, with all the enthusiasm he could ever want from a woman.

A woman he was falling in love with, and damn if he didn't want to stop.

A flashbulb going off made him ease back. The paparazzi hadn't bothered them too much since they'd arrived in LA; there were enough famous people in this town to make Sandro, thankfully, just another celebrity. But having his hands all over his wife in public was front-page fodder for sure.

'Sorry,' he said, and eased back. 'That's going to be in the papers, I'm afraid.'

'I don't care,' Liana answered blithely. 'We're married, after all.' She glanced down at their feet. 'But you'd better buy me another ice cream.'

'Not a chance.' Sandro tugged her by the hand back down the pier. 'I won't be answerable for my actions if I do.'

Several hours later they were lying in his bed—they'd made it there eventually, after christening another room of his beach house, this time the kitchen—legs and hands entwined, the mellow afternoon sunlight slanting over them.

And as much as Sandro never wanted any of it to end, he knew it had to.

'I've finished up with DT,' he said, sliding a hand along the smooth tautness of Liana's belly. 'We should return to Maldinia tomorrow.'

'Tomorrow?' He heard the dismay in her voice and then she sighed in acceptance, putting her hand over his and lacing her fingers through his. 'It went by so fast. I don't think I've ever enjoyed myself so much.'

'Me neither. But duty calls.' He heard the slightly sardonic note enter his voice, as it always did when he talked about his royal life, and he knew Liana heard it too.

She twisted towards him, her expression intent and earnest, her bare breasts brushing his chest. An interesting combination, and one that made Sandro want to kiss her again. And more.

'Why do you hate being king?' she asked, and he felt as if she'd just touched him with a branding iron. Pain, white-hot, lanced through him. Desire fled.

'Why do you think I hate being king?' he answered, glad his voice stayed even.

'Maybe hate is too strong a word. But whenever you talk about it—about Maldinia and the monarchy—you get this...*tone* to your voice. As if you can't stand it.'

He started to shift away from her, sliding his fingers from her own, but she tugged him back, or at least stayed him for a moment. 'Don't, Sandro,' she said quietly. 'I'm not trying to offend you or make you angry. I just want to know you.'

'I think you've known me pretty well this week, wouldn't you say?'

Her expression clouded, her eyes the colour of bruises. 'But that's just sex.'

'Just sex? I'm offended.'

'All right, fine. Amazing sex, but still, I want to know more than your body, as fantastic as that is.'

He stared at her then, saw the shadows in her eyes, the uncertain curve of her mouth. 'Do you really, Liana?' he asked quietly. 'We've had a wonderful time this past week, I'll be the first to admit it. But we haven't talked about anything really personal and I think you've liked it that way.'

Her lips trembled before she firmed them into a line and nodded. 'Maybe I do. I'm a private person, Sandro, I admit that. There are—things I don't like talking about. But I still want to get to know you. Understand you.'

'So I bare my soul while you get to keep yours hidden? Doesn't sound like much of a fair trade to me.'

'No, it doesn't.' She was silent for a moment, nibbling her lip, clearly wrestling with herself. Sandro just waited. He had no idea what she was going to say or suggest, and he felt a wariness leap to life inside him because he might accuse her of keeping things back, but he knew he was too.

About his family. His father. Himself.

'How about this,' she finally said, and she managed to sound both resolute and wavering at the same time. It made Sandro want to gather her up in his arms and kiss her worries away, as well as his own. That would be far more enjoyable than talking. 'We ask each other questions.'

He frowned, still wary. 'Questions?'

'Sounds simple, doesn't it?' she agreed with a wry smile that tugged at his heart. And other places. 'What I mean is we take turns. You ask me a question and I have to answer it. Then I get to ask you a question and you have to answer it.' She eyed him mischievously, although he could still tell this was big for her. And for him. Honesty, intimacy? He might crave it but that didn't make it easy. 'I'll even,' she added, 'let you go first.'

Sandro took a deep breath, let it out slowly. He nodded. 'Okay.'

'Okay. Ask me the first question.' Liana scrambled into a seated position, her legs crossed, her expression alert. She was completely naked and Sandro didn't know whether he wanted to ask her a question or haul her into his arms. No, actually he did.

Sex would be easier. Safer. And far more pleasurable.

But he'd accused Liana of holding things back and he'd be both a coward and a hypocrite now if he was the one to pull away. He drew another deep breath and sifted through all the things he'd wondered about his wife. 'Why have you devoted your life to Hands To Help?'

She inhaled sharply, just once, and then let it out slowly. 'Because my sister had epilepsy.'

Surprise flashed through him. 'You've never mentioned—'

She held up one slender palm. 'Nope, sorry. My turn now.'

'Okay.' He braced himself for the question he knew she would ask, the question she'd asked before. *Why do you hate being king?* And how would he answer that? Nothing about that answer was simple. Nothing about it was something he wanted to say.

'Why did you choose California?' she asked, and his jaw nearly dropped. She was gazing at him steadily and he knew with a sudden certainty that she was going easy on him. Because she knew how hard he'd found her first question. And yet he'd cut right to the quick with his own. He felt a surge of feeling for this woman who had shown him in so many ways just how strong and deep and wonderful she was.

'I chose California because I wanted to go into IT and it was a good place for start-up businesses. Also, for the weather.'

She smiled, just slightly, and he felt herself tense for his next question. 'What's your sister's name?' he asked, and to his surprise and recrimination her eyes filled with tears. He'd meant it to be an easy question, but obviously it wasn't.

'Chiara.' She drew a clogged breath. 'I called her Chi-Chi.'

The past tense jumped out at him and he realised what

a moron he was. He should have realised her sister was no longer alive. 'What—?'

She shook her head. 'My turn.' She blinked rapidly until the tears receded, although Sandro would have rather they'd fallen. When, he wondered, had Liana last cried? He had a feeling it had been a long, long time ago.

'What made you renounce your inheritance?'

It felt necessary at the time. That was what he'd told her before. He could say the same now, but it wasn't really much of an answer. He gazed at her steadily, saw the remnant of old sorrow in her eyes even as she gazed unblinkingly back. 'Because I thought I'd lose myself— my soul—if I stayed.'

'Why—?'

'Fair's fair. My turn now.'

'All right.'

He saw her brace herself, everything in her tensing for his next question. 'How did your sister die?' he asked softly.

For a second, no more, her features twisted in a torment that made him want to lean forward to embrace her, comfort her, but then her expression blanked again and she said quietly, 'She choked during an epileptic fit when she was four years old.'

This time he didn't keep himself from reaching for her. 'God, Liana. I'm sorry.' No wonder she devoted herself to her damned charity, to supporting the families of children like Chiara. She remained in his arms, stiff and unyielding as he stroked her hair, her shoulder. 'How old were you when it happened?'

'Eight.' She drew a shuddering breath. 'But that's two questions from you, so I get two now.'

'We could stop—'

'Not a chance.' She eased back, dabbed at her eyes with one hand before she stiffened her shoulders, gave him a look of stony determination.

'Why did you feel as if you'd lose yourself, your soul, if you stayed in Maldinia?'

They were drawing the big guns now, Sandro thought wryly. Asking and admitting things that made them both very uncomfortable. Terribly vulnerable. 'Because I couldn't stand all the hypocrisy.'

'What hypocrisy?'

'It's my turn now—'

'No.' She shook her head, her pale hair flying over her shoulders. 'I get two questions in a row, remember.'

'Damn.' He smiled wryly, sighed. 'The hypocrisy of my parents as well as myself.'

'What—?'

'Nope.' He shook his head now. 'My turn.'

She closed her eyes, and he felt as if she was summoning strength. 'Go ahead.'

'What was your favourite subject in school?'

Her eyes flew open and she stared at him in surprise, before a small smile tugged at her mouth. 'Art. What was yours?'

'Computers.'

They stared at each other for a long moment, the only sound their breathing, the rustle of covers underneath their naked bodies. 'Do you want to stop?' Liana asked softly, and he realised he didn't. He wanted to tell everything to this woman, bare his soul and his heart along with his body. And he wanted her to do it too, and, more importantly, to want to. He wanted that intimacy. That vulnerability. That trust, that love.

And he hoped to God that Liana wanted it too.

* * *

Liana held her breath while Sandro's gaze roved over her and then he smiled and shook his head.

'No, let's keep going. My turn to ask now.'

She nodded, steeling herself. It was almost a relief to answer his questions, like lancing a wound or easing an intense pressure. But it also hurt, and while he might have given her a break with the last question she didn't think he would now.

'Why didn't you go to university?'

'Because I wanted to start working with Hands To Help as soon as I could.' That one, at least, was easy, even if it most likely made him think she was a bit obsessive about her charity. That was because he didn't know the whole truth about Chiara; he hadn't asked. And she wasn't, she acknowledged, going to admit it unless he did.

Now her turn. She eyed him, his body relaxed and so incredibly beautiful as he lay stretched out across from her, unashamedly naked, the late afternoon sunlight glinting off his burnished skin, the perfect tautness of his muscled body. 'How were your parents hypocrites?'

He didn't say anything for a long moment, his gaze drawn and thoughtful, and finally Liana prompted him softly. 'Sandro?'

'It's not just a one-sentence answer.'

'We didn't make a rule about answers having to only be one sentence.'

'But it's easier, isn't it?' He glanced up at her, eyes glinting even as his mouth twisted with something like bitterness. 'We're both revealing as little information as we can.'

She couldn't deny that. 'So we start small,' she said with a shrug. 'No one said this had to be a complete confessional.'

'My parents were hypocrites because they only pretended that they loved us when there was a camera or reporter around. When it mattered.'

'Why—?'

'Nope. My turn.' So he was sticking with a one-sentence answer. She gave a little shrug of assent and waited, wondering just what he would ask her next. 'What do you fantasise about doing with me that we haven't done already?'

Shock had her jaw dropping even as heat blazed through her at his heavy-lidded look. 'Umm…' Her mind was blank, spinning. 'Going to the cinema?'

He let out a low, throaty chuckle. 'I see I'm going to have to rephrase that question.'

Her cheeks warmed. She might have been unabashed with him in the bedroom—or whatever room it happened to be—but talking about it felt different. More revealing somehow. 'My turn,' she said, her voice nearly a croak as she willed her blush to fade. She was suddenly, achingly conscious that they were both naked. That they'd just made love but already she wanted to again. And so, it seemed, judging from his words as well as the proud evidence of his body, did Sandro.

'What's your question, Liana?' Sandro asked in a growl. 'Because the way you're looking at me, I'm not going to give you the time to ask me.'

'Sorry.' She jerked her gaze up to his face, tried to order her dazed thoughts. 'Umm… How were you a hypocrite?'

'Because I bought into their lies and when I realised that's what they were I kept it going.' He tossed the words away carelessly, but they made Liana want to ask more. Understand more.

'My turn now,' Sandro said, his voice a growl of sexual

intent. 'Now I'll rephrase my last question. What do you fantasise about doing with me *sexually* that we haven't already done?'

Just the question, in that husky murmur of his, made her breasts ache and her core throb. 'We've already done a lot....'

'Are you saying there isn't something?' Sandro asked silkily, his tone suggesting that he knew otherwise.

'No, not exactly....'

'Then what? Play by the rules, Liana. Answer the question.'

She pressed her hands to her face. 'This is embarrassing.'

'Why?'

'I—I don't know.'

'I think you do.'

'Fine, if you know so much, you tell me what I fantasise about.'

He laughed softly. 'I don't think so. You're not going to get off that easily.' His mouth curved in a wicked smile. 'No pun intended. But I will tell you what I fantasise about.'

'Okay,' she breathed, and Sandro leaned forward, all predatory power and sexual intent.

'I fantasise about tasting you.' Liana inhaled sharply and felt her insides turn liquid. 'And I don't mean your mouth.'

She let out a wobbly laugh. 'I might be inexperienced, but I didn't think that's what you meant.'

'I want to taste you, Liana. I want to feel you tremble against me while I do.'

She closed her eyes, images, amazing, explicit images, blitzing through her brain, making it impossible to think. To respond. And yet the words came of themselves and with her eyes still closed she heard herself whisper, 'I want that too.'

And then Sandro was reaching for her and kissing her, his mouth hard and hot and yet so very sweet. His hands slid down her body as his tongue delved deep and Liana tangled her fingers in his hair, drawing him closer, needing him more.

But then he began to move his mouth down her body and she knew where he was going, knew what he wanted—and what she wanted. Everything in her seemed to still and hang suspended, waiting, yearning—

And then her breath came out in a sudden gasp of pleasure as he spread her thighs and put his mouth to her, his tongue flicking against the sensitive folds, everything in her exposed and open and vulnerable.

It was exquisite. Unbearable. *Too much.* Too much pleasure, too much openness, too much feeling. She felt his breath against her heated, tender skin and she let out a choked gasp, felt tears start in her eyes. Tears that felt like the overflow of emotion in her soul.

'Sandro...'

He lifted his head slightly. 'Do you want me to stop?'

'No—'

And then he tasted her again, deeper still, his mouth moving over her so surely, and her thighs clenched, her hands fisting in his hair as she cried out her climax and tears trickled down her cheeks. She felt as if she'd been broken and put together again; as if Sandro had reconstructed her.

He rested his cheek against her tummy as her heart rate slowed and she wiped the tears from her face with trembling fingers.

Gently he reached up and took her hands from her face, wiping the remaining tears away with his thumbs.

'I'm sorry,' she whispered.

'Sorry? What on earth for?'

'For crying—'

'I don't mind your tears, Liana.' He kissed her navel. 'You're amazing,' he said softly and she let out a shaky laugh.

'I feel as weak as a kitten.'

'Amazing,' he repeated, and Liana had a sudden, overwhelming urge to tell him she loved him, but she kept the words back. Despite what they'd just done, it felt like too much too soon.

So instead she decided to admit to her fantasy and pay him in kind.

Gently she pushed at his shoulder and he lifted his head, his chin resting on her tummy, to gaze at her, his expression sleepy and hooded. 'It's your turn now,' she said, and that sleepy gaze became suddenly alert.

'My turn?'

She pushed him again and with a smile he rolled over onto his back, everything about him masculine, magnificent, *hers*. 'Fair's fair,' she said and, with a blaze of sensual anticipation and ancient, feminine power, she straddled his thighs, bent her head so her mouth brushed his navel—and then moved lower.

CHAPTER NINE

LIANA GAZED AT her reflection and tried to still the nervous fluttering in her stomach. They'd been back in Maldinia for a week, and tonight was the fundraiser for Hands To Help.

In the week since they'd returned from California, they'd continued exploring the sexual side of their relationship with joyous abandon. The nights were pleasure-filled, and the days…?

Liana wasn't so sure about the days. They'd both been busy with royal duties, but there had still been time to spend just with each other—if they had wanted to. Sandro, however, hadn't sought her out. They certainly hadn't had any more question-and-answer sessions, and the most honest either of them seemed to be was with their bodies. Not their words. Not their hearts.

It was ironic, really, that she wanted that now. She'd entered this marriage because she'd believed it would be convenient, that it *wouldn't* involve her heart. She hadn't wanted love or intimacy or any of it—and now she did.

Now she did so much, and Sandro was the one pulling away. She'd felt his emotional withdrawal from the moment they'd stepped off the royal jet. At first she'd thought he was just preoccupied with work; he'd spent the entire fourteen-hour flight from LA working in his study on the plane. But after a week of incredible sex and virtually no conversation, she knew work couldn't be the only reason.

She'd gone over what Sandro had told her about himself many times, yet those few terse sentences hardly gave anything away.

My parents were hypocrites because they only pretended that they loved us when there was a camera or reporter around. When it mattered.

Because I bought into their lies and when I realised that's what they were I kept it going.

What did it mean, he kept it going? And what, really, did his parents' lack of love have to do with being king? Unless he simply found the whole atmosphere of the palace too toxic to endure. Liana had to admit she always felt herself tense when the queen dowager was around. But to walk away from everything he'd known and been for fifteen whole years? There had to be more to his story, just as there was more to hers.

And even if she wanted to admit more to Sandro, he didn't seem willing or interested to hear it. He'd been perfectly polite, of course, even friendly, and at night he made her body sing. But they'd been teetering on the edge of a far deeper intimacy and since returning here Sandro had taken a few definite, determined steps back.

Which shouldn't, Liana told herself, make her feel restless. Anxious. Why couldn't she accept what they had and deem it enough? It was more than she'd ever had before, more than she'd ever let herself want.

And yet it wasn't enough. Not when she'd had a glimpse—a taste—of just how much more they could have.

Taking a deep breath, she forced her thoughts away from such pointless musings and inspected her reflection once more. She wore an emerald-green evening gown, a bold choice for her, and she'd selected it with the help of Demi, her stylist. She wondered what Sandro would think of the asymmetrical cut, with one shoulder left bare. She worn her hair up, but loosely, unlike the more severe chignons she used to favour. To finish the outfit she'd chosen diamond chandelier earrings and a matching necklace that had belonged to her mother.

She took a deep breath and turned away from the mirror. The maid, Rosa, who had helped her dress, smiled encouragingly. 'You look lovely, Your Highness.'

'Thank you, Rosa.'

Rosa handed her a matching wrap of emerald satin and Liana draped it over one arm before leaving her suite of rooms. The dress whispered against her legs as she walked down the corridor, her heart thudding harder with every step that took her towards Sandro. What would he think of her gown? And what would he think of *her*? Tonight was such an important night for her, finally bringing more visibility to Hands To Help, and yet in this moment she cared more about what Sandro thought than anything else. She wanted that intimacy back again, that closeness that didn't come from sex—as amazing as that was—but from simply being with one another. Talking and laughing in a way they hadn't since returning from California.

Sandro was waiting at the bottom of the palace's sweeping staircase as Liana came down. He looked dark and dangerous and utterly devastating in black tie, his hair brushed back, his eyes glittering like shards of silver.

He stilled as she approached, his expression going utterly blank as his gaze swept her from head to toe, making Liana wonder just what he thought. It was the first time she'd worn a formal gown since their marriage.

'You look beautiful,' he said quietly, and pleasure flared through her at the obvious sincerity of those simple words. 'That colour suits you.'

'Thank you,' she murmured. 'You do amazing things to a tuxedo.'

His mouth quirked in a smile and his eyes lightened to the colour of a dawn mist as he took her arm. 'I'd like to do amazing things to you,' he whispered as he drew her down the last few steps.

'And I'd like you to do them,' she answered back. 'I have a few amazing things up my sleeve as well.'

Sandro grinned, and even as familiar heat flared inside her Liana knew it wasn't enough. Sex wasn't enough, never would be. But now was surely not the time for a heart-to-heart. Perhaps later tonight they would talk again. Learn each other again.

Sandro's grin faded and Liana stilled, wondering what had changed, when he addressed a member of the palace staff, who came hurrying forward.

'Your Highness?'

'Please bring the crown jewels to my study. The emerald parure, I think.'

'Very good, Your Highness.'

'The crown jewels?' Liana repeated, and touched the chandelier necklace around her throat. 'But—'

'What you're wearing is very lovely,' Sandro said as he led her towards his study, one hand warm and firm on the small of her back. 'But there is a piece from the royal collection that would suit you—and that dress—perfectly. Do you mind?'

'Mind?' She shook her head. 'No, of course not.'

'Here you are, Your Highness.' The footman brought in a mahogany case inlaid with ivory, and placed it on the desk before handing Sandro the keys.

'Thank you,' Sandro murmured, and the man left as he unlocked the case and lifted the lid. Liana gasped at the sight of the glittering jewels within, and Sandro turned to her with a glint in his eye. 'Lovely, aren't they?' he murmured. 'Supposedly once owned by Napoleon.'

'For Josephine?'

'His empress. And you are my queen.'

His queen. Liana thrilled to the words, to their implication. She was his, heart and soul, whether he knew it or not. Whether he wanted it or not. Yet in this moment she felt only happiness as he lifted the heavy necklace from its velvet bed, the diamond-encrusted emeralds catching the light and twinkling as if lit with a fire from within. 'May I?' Sandro asked softly, and wordlessly she nodded, holding her breath as she felt his fingers, warm and sure, on the back of her neck.

Goosebumps rose on her flesh as he unclasped her diamond necklace and slid it from her, his fingers brushing the tender skin of her neck, the hollow of her throat. Liana bit her lip to keep a shudder of pure longing from escaping her. He reduced her to want so effortlessly, and yet she felt his own response, the strength of his own need as his fingers rested against her throat, his breath hitching slightly as it fanned the nape of her neck. She eased back against him, leaning against his chest, and his hands came around her shoulders, cradling her. For a perfect moment she felt completely at peace, wonderfully loved. He brushed his lips against her neck and then he steadied her again, before putting the emerald-and-diamond necklace around her throat, the stones heavy against her skin and warm from his hands.

He clasped the necklace and then rested his hands on her shoulders again, his fingers curling around her, seeming to reach right inside. 'Liana…' he began, his voice an ache, a caress, and everything in her longed to know what he was thinking. Feeling. And what he was going to say.

But he didn't say anything, just slid his hands from her shoulders and reached for the other pieces of the parure: earrings, bracelet, and a tiara.

'I've never actually worn a tiara,' Liana said as he placed it on her loose updo. 'Does it look ridiculous? As if…as if I'm trying to be a princess?'

'You're not a princess,' Sandro reminded her. 'You are a queen.'

Liana touched the stones, wanting once again to tell him she loved him. Had he been about to tell her the same thing? She didn't know whether she dared to hope, and she didn't say anything, just put on the earrings and bracelet.

'Thank you,' she said, when she was wearing all of the jewels. 'They're amazing.'

'You're amazing. They look beautiful on you. A true queen.'

She met his eyes, smiling, only to have her smile wobble and then slip completely from her face as she saw the frown settle between Sandro's brows, the darkness steal into his eyes. He might call her a true queen, but she didn't know then whether he wanted to be her king.

Sandro watched Liana from across the crowded ballroom where the fundraiser for Hands To Help was being held; she was talking to several dignitaries, a flute of champagne in one slender hand, her body resplendent, like an emerald flame, in that amazing dress, the light from the crystal chandeliers catching the strands of gold and silver in her moon-coloured hair. She looked beautiful, captivating, and every inch the consummate queen.

Sandro saw several men cast her covert, admiring

glances, and he felt his insides clench with a potent mix of jealousy, desire, and love.

He loved her. He hadn't told her, hadn't even wanted to tell her, not just because he didn't know if she loved him, but because he didn't trust his own feelings. His own self.

Hadn't he been wrong before? And while their time in California had been sweet, and their nights together since then even sweeter, he still didn't know if it was real.

Well, sex was real. Real and raw and powerful. But love? Could he love her after so short a time? What had happened to the icy, reserved woman he'd first met? Had she really changed—and had he?

Restlessly, Sandro shifted and took a sip of champagne. Watching Liana now, he felt a new and unwelcome realisation sweep over him. Here she was in her element; she was queen. He saw the sparkle in her eyes as she talked about Hands To Help, the regal bearing of her beautiful body. This, he thought, made her come alive in a way he hadn't seen before, even when she'd been in his arms. This was why she'd agreed to marry him in the first place, what gave her her whole reason for being.

To be queen.

And while that shouldn't bother him, he knew it did. Because while Liana made a beautiful and perfect queen, he didn't feel like her match.

He didn't deserve to be king.

If I could have, I'd have left you to rot in California, or, better yet, in hell.

So many months after his father's death, his savage nearly last words still had the power to hurt him. To make him question himself, just as he had so many years before. His father hadn't called him back from California because he'd wanted a reconciliation, as Sandro had so naively believed.

No, his father had asked him because he was desperate. Because the media mess of Leo and Alyse's marriage had seemed irredeemable. Sandro was the second choice.

He hadn't realised any of that until his father had died, three weeks after he'd called him in California. The former king had known he was terminally ill, had wanted to get the succession sorted out before his death.

Had really wanted Leo.

Sandro's gaze moved from his wife to his brother, chatting with a group of IT businessmen, Alyse by his side. Would Leo make a better king than him?

Sandro was sure of it.

And yet from the moment he'd returned Leo hadn't offered a single word of protest. He'd stepped aside gracefully, had accepted his position as cabinet minister with a nod and a smile. Leo, Sandro had to assume, was relieved. And why shouldn't he be?

Neither of them had wanted to follow in their father's footsteps. Neither of them had wanted the awful burden of royal duty.

And yet here they were.

One of the footmen flanking the room rang a bell, and Sandro watched as the crowd fell silent and with a shyly assured smile Liana went to the front of the room. Sandro watched her, felt a surge of admiration and love, and yet washed over it all was desperation. Because she was too good for him. Because he didn't believe she could really love him, a man who had shirked his duty for so long. A man who was second best.

'Thank you all so much for coming,' Liana said, her voice clear and musical. Sandro felt as if he could listen to her for ever. And everyone else must have too because the room went utterly silent as she spoke about Hands To Help's mission and what it meant to her.

She didn't, Sandro realised with a flicker of surprise, talk about her sister.

But he could hear the passion in her voice, the utter sincerity, and he knew everyone else could too. And when she was done the room broke out into an applause that was not merely polite, but spontaneous and sincere.

Sandro's gut twisted. How could this amazing woman love him?

She moved through the crowd, chatting with various guests, but he saw her gaze rove restlessly over the clusters of people and knew she was looking for him.

He came forward, smiling as he took her by the hand. 'Well done. You spoke beautifully, Liana.'

Pink touched her cheeks and her eyes sparkled. How had he ever thought she was a statue? Or icy and cold? In this moment she looked real, warm, vibrant, and glorious. He almost told her he loved her right then.

Almost.

But he didn't, because along with his other sins he was a coward. He didn't want to hear the silence he feared would be the answer back…just as it had been before.

Liana felt Sandro's preoccupation as they left the fundraiser and headed for their suite in the private family wing of the palace. It was past midnight and all around them the palace was dark and hushed, only a few sleepy footmen on duty.

'I think it went well tonight, don't you?' Liana said as they turned down the corridor that housed their suite of rooms.

'Very well.' His lips curved in a smile but his voice was toneless, and she had no idea what he was thinking. Feeling.

'Thank you for organising it,' she said, hating that she felt awkward, even if just a little. 'It was very thoughtful.'

'It was the least I could do.'

Sandro opened the door to his bedroom, the bedroom they'd shared since returning from California even though Liana had her own adjoining room.

Uncertainly she stepped in behind him, because she couldn't decipher his mood at all and she was getting so very tired of wondering. Worrying.

'Sandro—'

Before she could say another word she was in his arms, her back pressed against the door as he kissed her with a raw, rough intensity she hadn't felt before. It was a kiss of passion but it felt like grief. Even so it ignited everything inside her and she kissed him back, matching him even though part of her cried out that whatever was wrong between them, it couldn't be solved by sex.

Maybe Sandro disagreed. Or maybe sex was all he wanted, for he slid his hands down her satin-clad legs before sliding the material up to her hips. Heat flared as he pressed his hand against her, the thin silk of her panties the only barrier between them.

She put her hands on either side of his face, tried to get him to look at her. 'Sandro, what is it?' she whispered even as an insistent, pleasurable ache had started between her thighs, urged on by the press of his hand. 'What's wrong?'

'Nothing's wrong,' he answered, his voice thick with desire. 'I just need you, Liana. I want you. Now.' He hoisted her leg up and wrapped it around his hip, and as he kissed her again Liana closed her eyes, let the sensation wash over her.

She wanted him too, and while she wanted his honesty

more, she understood he needed this. Needed her. And maybe that could be enough, at least for now.

He buried his head in the curve of his neck, a shudder racking his body as he moved against her. Liana put her arms around him, drawing him even closer, and then he was inside her, and it felt as deep and overwhelming and as wonderful as always.

She met him thrust for thrust, gasping out his name, her head thrown back against the door, and afterwards as their hearts raced against each other and the sweat cooled on their skin Sandro whispered against her throat.

'I love you.'

Everything in Liana stilled, and she felt a fragile happiness emerge from the tumult of her emotions like the first bloom of spring, tender and new.

She smoothed his hair away from his face and kissed his lips. 'I love you too.'

Neither of them spoke, and even as they remained in each other's arms Liana wondered why that confession of love—something she'd longed for—made her feel sadder than ever.

CHAPTER TEN

SANDRO STARED UNSEEINGLY down at the various letters he'd been given by his secretary to sign. The words blurred in front of him and wearily he rubbed his eyes. He'd been working in his study all day, reviewing fiscal plans and budget cuts in preparation for a meeting with his cabinet tomorrow.

He could see Leo's mark on everything he read, from the proposal to extend broadband to most of the country—something his brother felt passionately about, just as he did—to the necessary budget cuts in the palace. Leo clearly would rather go without a few luxuries than cut anything that affected his people.

He would have made a good king, Sandro thought, not for the first time. If the press hadn't uncovered the whole marriage masquerade debacle, his brother would have been a great king. And he *would* have been king, because Sandro would have stayed in California. He wouldn't have come back. Wouldn't have married Liana.

Wouldn't have had any of it.

Sighing, he rubbed his temples, felt the beginnings of a headache.

A quick knock sounded and then Leo opened the door, closing it behind him.

'I'm heading home, but I just wanted to make sure you didn't need me for anything?'

'No, I think I'm ready for tomorrow.' He tapped the papers in front of him. 'I can see you've done a lot of good work here, Leo.'

Leo shrugged. 'Just doing my job.'

Sandro nodded, even as he felt that tension and awful uncertainty ratchet up inside him. And it had been Leo's job, for fifteen years. A hell of a long time. 'You did it well.'

'Thank you,' Leo answered, and Sandro heard the repressive note in his brother's voice, felt a pang of sorrow. Once, they'd been close, two small boys banding together. Now he felt a distance yawn between them and he had no idea how to close it.

He stared down at the papers again, wished he knew the words to say, and had the courage to say.

'Sandro?' Leo asked for a moment. 'Is everything all right…between you and Liana?'

'Between me and Liana?' Sandro's voice came out sharp. 'Why do you ask?'

Leo shrugged. 'Because I know you married for convenience, and yet I've seen the way you look at each other. Something's going on.'

'We're married, Leo. Of course something is going on.'

'Do you love her?'

Sandro felt his throat go tight. 'That's between Liana and me, isn't it?'

'Sorry. I don't mean to be nosy.' Leo sighed. 'I just want you to be happy.'

'And since you've just fallen in love you want everyone else to as well.'

'Something like that, I suppose.'

'Don't worry about Liana and me, Leo. We're fine.' Sandro spoke with a firmness he didn't really feel, because they weren't fine. Not exactly. Ever since returning to Maldinia, he'd felt the emotional distance yawn between them. Physically things were amazing, exciting. But emotionally? He might have been honest and vulnerable and all that in California, but here? Where the memories mocked him? When the fear that he didn't deserve any of this, couldn't live up to it, suffocated him?

No, not so emotionally available now. Here. Even if, in a moment of weakness, he'd told her he loved her.

'Okay,' Leo said after a moment. 'Well. Goodnight.'

'Goodnight.'

It was early evening and a purple twilight was settling over the palace and its gardens as Sandro left his study a few minutes after Leo. He and Liana had a dinner engagement that evening, something official and most likely boring at the Italian embassy.

But before he got ready for it, he wanted to see Liana. Talk to her…although he had no idea what he was going to say.

He found her in the pretty, feminine little room she used as her own study, going over her schedule with her private secretary. Sandro watched them for a moment, two heads bent together, smiling and chatting as they reviewed certain points.

Liana was in her element, and that was brought home to him no more so than when she looked up and smiled her welcome.

'I've just been going over my schedule—it looks like a very busy week!'

'Does it?' The secretary, Christina, excused herself, and Sandro closed the door, leaning against it. 'So what are you doing?'

'Well…' Liana glanced down at the typewritten sheet. 'On Monday I'm visiting the paediatric ward of the hospital here in Averne. Tuesday is a lunch for primary caregivers of disabled and elderly. Wednesday I'm meeting with a primary school, and Thursday I'm officially opening a new playground in the city's public gardens.' She looked up, eyes sparkling. 'I know I'm not inventing a cure for cancer or anything, but I like feeling so useful.'

'Surely you felt useful before, when you worked for Hands To Help.'

'Yes, I did,' Liana answered after a moment. 'Of course I did. But sometimes…' She trailed off, and, intrigued, Sandro stepped closer.

'Sometimes?'

Liana gave a little shrug. 'Sometimes it hurt, working there. It reminded me of—of my sister.'

'Do you miss her?' he asked quietly and she blinked rapidly, needlessly straightening the papers in front of her.

'Every day.'

'It must be hard. I didn't think many people actually died from epilepsy.'

'They don't.'

'So Chiara was just one of the unlucky ones?'

And for some reason this remark made her stiffen as if she'd suddenly turned to wood. 'Yes,' she said, and her voice was toneless. 'She was unlucky.'

Sandro stared at her, saw how the happiness and excitement had drained from her, and felt guilt needle him. Damn it, he'd done that. He shouldn't have asked those questions, and yet he'd just been trying to get to know her all over again. Get closer.

Yet you keep your secrets to yourself.

'I'm sorry I've been a bit—distant lately,' he said abruptly, and Liana looked up, startled.

'At least you noticed.'

'And you have too, I assume?'

'Yes.' Her voice was soft, sad. 'I know we've been— Well, the nights have been—' She laughed a little, shook her head. 'You know what I mean.'

'I certainly do.'

'But we haven't talked, really. Not since California.'

Not since they'd sat across from each other on his bed, naked not just with their bodies but with their souls. He sighed. 'Returning to this palace always brings back some bad memories for me. It's hard to combat them.'

'What memories, Sandro?'

He dragged his hand across his eyes as words burned in his chest, caught in his throat. How much to admit? To confess? 'A lot of memories.' She just waited, and he dropped his hand. 'Memories of my father always telling me how he was counting on me,' he said, his voice expressionless now. 'Counting on me to be a good king. Just like him.'

'Just like him?' Liana repeated softly, a slight frown curving her mouth downwards. She knew, just as the whole world did, that his father hadn't been a good king at all. He'd been dissolute, uninterested in his people, a spendthrift, a scoundrel, an arrogant and adulterous *ass*.

And Sandro had idolised him.

'He was my hero, growing up,' he said, and then laughed. 'Which sounds ridiculous, because you know as well as I do there was nothing heroic about him.'

'But you were a child.'

'I believed that until I was eighteen.' He winced just saying it aloud. 'I insisted on believing it, even when boys at boarding school taunted me with the truth, even when

I saw the newspaper headlines blaring about his affairs, his reckless spending.' He shook his head. 'I convinced myself they were jealous or just stirring up trouble. I insisted on believing he was a good man, even when everything showed me otherwise.'

'That's not something to be ashamed of, Sandro,' Liana said quietly. 'Believing the best of someone, someone you love.'

'But that's it, isn't it? Because I was so desperate to love him, and believe he loved me back. I wanted to impress him with how good I could be—as good as he was. I wanted to believe the reason I hardly ever saw him was because he was so busy with his important duties, not because he didn't give a damn. Not because he'd rather screw and spend his way through Europe than spend one unnecessary moment with his son.' He broke off, nearly panting, the old rage and hurt coursing through him so hard and fast he felt as if he couldn't breathe.

And he felt so ashamed—ashamed that it still made him angry, still hurt. Ashamed that Liana knew.

She rose from her desk and he stiffened as she put her arms around him, drew his head to her shoulder as if he was still that desperate, deluded, and disappointed child.

And maybe he was.

'Oh, Sandro.' She was silent for a moment, stroking his hair, and he closed his eyes, revelling in her acceptance, her comfort even as he acknowledged that he didn't deserve it. 'What was the final straw, then?' she asked and he stiffened.

'The final—'

'What was the thing that made you leave?'

He drew a shuddering breath. 'I found out the truth about him when I was eighteen, at university. It was the first time I'd really had any freedom, and everything about it made me start to wonder. Doubt.'

She nodded slowly. 'I know how that feels.'

'And then one afternoon my father's private secretary called me up and asked me to issue a statement that he'd been visiting me that week when he hadn't. It didn't make any sense to me, but I did it. I started really doubting then, though, and the next time I was home I asked my father why he'd wanted me to do that.' He was silent for a moment, recalling the look of impatience on his father's face. 'He'd been with a mistress, some pretty young thing my mother was annoyed about, and he knew there would be a big media fuss if the tabloids got wind of it. He told me all of this so matter-of-factly, without so much as a flicker of guilt or remorse, and I suppose that's when the scales really fell from my eyes.' Sandro let out a long, weary sigh. 'But I didn't actually leave until three years later. Three years of going along with it all, corroborating his stupid stories, lying to the press, to him, to myself, about everything.'

Liana's gaze was wide and dark. 'And then?'

'And then…' He'd told more to this woman than he had to anyone else, and yet he still felt reluctant to reveal all. Reveal himself, and his own weaknesses. 'And then I just couldn't take it anymore. I hated who I'd become. So I told him I was renouncing my inheritance, that I wanted to start my own business and live my own life.' It sounded so selfish, even now, after all these years. 'The funny thing is,' Sandro made himself continue, 'I didn't really mean it.'

He saw surprise flash across Liana's face. 'You didn't?'

'No, I was just—testing him, I suppose. Pushing him. Because I expected him to beg me to stay, admit he loved me and it was all a mistake and— I don't even know.'

He let out a ragged huff of laughter as he raked his hand through his hair. 'How stupid can you be, eh?'

'I don't call that stupid,' Liana said quietly. 'Desperate, maybe.'

'Fine. I was desperate. Desperate and deluded right to the end, because of course he didn't do any of that. He just laughed in my face and told me to go right ahead. He had another son who would do just as well.'

And so he'd gone, proud and defiant and so desperately hurting. He'd gone, and he'd stayed away for fifteen years, only to come back because he'd thought his father had finally seen the light. Would finally admit he was sorry, he'd been wrong, he really did love him.

Blah. Blah. Blah. None of that, of course, had happened. But he'd told Liana enough, and he didn't feel like admitting to that.

'I'm sorry,' Liana whispered, and brushed a kiss across his lips. 'For all of it.'

'So am I.' He kissed her back, needing her touch, her sweetness. Needing to forget all the hurt and anger and disappointment he'd just raked up with his words.

And she did make him forget it; in Liana's arms he didn't feel like the sad, needy boy desperate for love. He didn't feel like a man racked by remorse and guilt for turning his back on his duty. He didn't feel like a king who didn't deserve his crown.

He just felt like a man, a man this amazing, wonderful, vibrant woman loved.

And that was all he wanted to be.

That night Liana lay in bed with Sandro's arm stretched out across her stomach and felt as if the first of the past's ghosts had been banished.

But what about hers?

She recalled Sandro's innocent question, so gently posed. *So Chiara was just one of the unlucky ones?*

She hadn't told Sandro the truth about that. About her. Chiara had been unlucky because she'd had a sister who had gone blank and still and unmoving when she'd needed her most. She'd had Liana.

And while part of her craved to tell Sandro the truth, to have him know and accept her wholeheartedly, the rest of her was too afraid because there were no guarantees. No promises that Sandro would accept her, would love her, if he knew how badly she'd failed someone she'd loved.

Her parents hadn't. Her father hadn't spoken to her for months after Chiara's death; even now he never quite looked at her when they talked. And he never showed her any affection. They'd never been the most demonstrative family—Chiara had cornered the market on that—but since her little sister's death her father hadn't touched her at all. Not one kiss or hug or even brush of the hand.

And could she really blame him?

She was a hypocrite, Liana knew, for wanting Sandro's secrets, his pain and shame and fear, and keeping all of hers back. If she'd been able to accept and love him, why couldn't he do the same for her?

Because your secrets are worse, your sins greater.

And yet not telling him—keeping that essential part of her back—felt like a cancer gnawing at all of her certainties, eating her heart.

How could she keep something so crucial from him?

CHAPTER ELEVEN

SANDRO ATTEMPTED TO listen as one of his cabinet ministers talked, his voice reminding him of the buzzing of a bumblebee that flung itself against the window of one of the palace's meeting rooms. He'd been closeted in here with his cabinet for nearly three hours and he'd barely been able to hear a word that had been said.

All because of Liana.

Ever since he'd unburdened himself to her he'd felt as if they were closer than ever. He loved her more than ever, for simply loving him. And that fact—that they actually loved each other—felt like an incredible blessing, a miracle.

A wonder and a joy.

And yet occasionally, when he glimpsed the shadows in her eyes, the way she'd suddenly turn away, he'd still feel as if she was keeping something from him. Hiding part of herself, but he didn't want to press. Demand answers she might not be ready to give. They had time, after all. Their love was new, perhaps fragile. He wasn't ready to test it in that way.

They had time.

'Your Highness?'

With effort Sandro jerked his gaze back to his expectant cabinet and attempted to focus on the discussion of domestic policy that had been taking up the better part of the afternoon.

'Yes?'

The minister of economic policy cleared his throat. 'We were just going to take a look at the budget Prince Leo proposed....'

Sandro glanced down at the painstakingly and laboriously made list of figures he'd assumed his ministers had put together. Not just Leo.

'Leo drafted this budget?' he asked, heard how sharp his voice sounded. 'When?'

He saw several ministers glance at Leo sitting on the other end of the table and an unease that had been skirting the fringes of his mind for months now suddenly swooped down and grabbed him by the throat. He felt as if he couldn't breathe.

'A few years back, when—' one of the ministers began, glancing uncertainly at Leo, whose face was expressionless, his body still.

'Years,' Sandro repeated, his mind spinning. Years ago, when Leo had thought he would be king.

He turned to stare at his brother, who gazed evenly back. 'I didn't realise you had taken such an interest, Leo,' he murmured. His father would have been alive, of course, and reigning as king. Leo would have been waiting, no more than a reluctant placeholder. Or so Sandro had thought.

But perhaps his brother hadn't been so reluctant, after all.

'I took an interest in all government policy,' Leo answered, and Sandro couldn't tell a thing from his tone. 'Naturally I wanted to be prepared.'

'For when you would become king,' Sandro clarified,

and he felt a silent tension ripple its way around the room, felt it in Leo's body as well as his own.

'Yes.'

The air felt charged, electric. Why hadn't Leo told him this before? Why had he kept it from him, like some damn secret he was the only one who didn't know?

'Perhaps we ought to review your proposals,' Sandro said after a moment. 'I'd be interested in knowing just what they are.'

Something flickered across Leo's face, something sad, almost like grief. 'Of course,' he said. 'I'll have my assistant put all the relevant paperwork in your study.'

They held each other's gaze for a moment longer, a moment that felt taut with tension, almost hostile. Then Sandro broke first, reaching for another sheaf of papers as the meeting went on.

Three hours later Sandro sat in his father's study, dazed by what he had learned and read. What he had never known, even if he should have. Guessed, or at least wondered about.

For fifteen years Leo had thought he would be king. Sandro had been utterly out of the picture, disinherited, as good as forgotten, and Leo would have been preparing for his own kingship, planning on it. And then Sandro had swept in and taken it away without so much as a passing thought for his brother.

He sank onto a chair in his study, his head in his hands. He'd spent the past few hours reading all of Leo's proposals, well-thought-out multi-year plans for industry, economic policy, energy efficiency. After his father's outdated and uninterested reign, Leo had been poised to take Maldinia in a whole new and exciting direction.

Until Sandro had returned and taken it all away from him.

Sandro's mind spun with realisations, with new understanding about the nature of the coolness between him and the brother he'd once loved more than any other person. The brother who had hero-worshipped him as a child. The brother who he had left because he'd been so angry and hurt by his father's contempt and rejection.

The brother, he thought hollowly, who would make an excellent king.

Better than he would.

Why had Leo never told him of his ambitions, his plans? When Sandro had returned, Leo had not made a single protest. He'd stepped aside so quickly Sandro had assumed he'd been relieved to be done of his duty. He'd projected his own feelings onto Leo without ever really considering how his brother might have changed over the past decade and a half.

Yet the uncertainty had always been there, lingering. The fear that Leo would make a better king than he would—deserved to be king more than he did—had always taunted him from the dark corners of his heart and mind.

And now?

Now, Sandro thought numbly, he should step aside and let his brother rule as he'd been intending to for so long. As he deserved to. The cabinet would surely approve; their respect and admiration for Leo and his proposals had been evident in every word they'd spoken this afternoon.

And if Leo were king…Sandro would be free, as he'd claimed he always wanted. He could return to California, take up the reins of his IT firm once more. Be his own man. Live his own life.

Why did the thought make his stomach sour and his fists clench?

He knew why; of course he did. Because of Liana. Liana had married him to become queen. No matter what feelings had since grown between them since then, he could not escape that truth. He couldn't escape the hard reality that their marriage was that of a king and queen, based on convenience and duty. Not a man and woman deeply in love, as much as he might still wish for it. As much as it had felt like that, for the past few weeks.

Weeks. They'd only had weeks together, little more than a handful of days. Put that against fifteen years of Leo working for the monarchy and there was no question. No contest.

A knock sounded on the door and Sandro jerked his head up, blinking the room back into focus. 'Come in.'

'Sandro?' Leo stood in the doorway.

Sandro stared at his brother and felt a pressure build in his chest. Everything inside him felt so tight and aching he could barely force the words out. 'Why didn't you tell me?'

Quietly Leo closed the door, leaned against it. 'Tell you what, exactly?'

'How hard you've been working these past fifteen years—'

Leo raised an eyebrow. 'Did you think I'd been slacking off?'

'No, but—' Sandro raked his hands through his hair, shook his head. 'I thought— I thought— I don't know what I thought.'

'Exactly,' Leo answered, and with a jolt Sandro realised that underneath his brother's unruffled attitude was a deep, latent anger—an anger he was now giving voice to, even as his tone remained steady. 'You didn't think. You haven't thought about me or what I've been doing when you were away for fifteen years, Sandro, and you didn't think about me when you returned.'

Sandro stared at Leo, felt a hot rush of shame sweep over him. 'That's not true, Leo. I did think of you.'

'In passing?' The cynicism in his brother's voice tore at him. 'A moment here or there? You didn't even say goodbye.'

Sandro glanced down. No more excuses. 'I'm sorry,' he said quietly. 'I should have. I should have done it all differently.'

'So why did you leave, out of curiosity?' Leo asked after a moment. 'Did it all just get a bit much for you?'

'I suppose you could say that. I felt— I honestly felt as if I'd lose my soul if I stayed another minute. All the lies, Leo, all the pretending. I couldn't stand it.'

'Neither could I.'

'I know.' Sandro dragged in a breath. 'And I'm sorry if it felt as if I were dumping you in it. But when Father disinherited me— Well, I had no choice then. I had no place here.'

Leo's expression tightened. 'He only disinherited you because you told him you were leaving.'

'I was bluffing,' Sandro confessed flatly. He felt that familiar ache in his chest. 'I was trying to make him admit— Oh, God, I don't even know what. That he needed me. Loved me.' He blinked hard and set his jaw. 'Stupid, I know.'

He couldn't look at Leo, didn't want to see the pity or scorn on his brother's face. 'Not stupid,' Leo said after a moment. 'Naive, maybe, in believing there was anything good in him. He was the most selfish man I ever knew.'

'And I can't believe I didn't see that until I was eighteen years old. You saw through him from the first, didn't you? And I insisted on believing he was a good man. That he loved me.'

Leo shrugged. 'I was always more cynical than you.'

'I am sorry,' Sandro said again, and he felt his regret and remorse with every fibre of his being. He hoped his brother did too. 'I should have reached out to you. Explained. And when I came back I should have asked if you still wanted to be king—'

'It's not a game of pass the parcel, Sandro. Father chose you to be king. He never really wanted me.'

Sandro shook his head. 'That's not true. It was me he didn't want.'

Leo let out a hard bark of laughter. 'Oh? How do you reckon that?'

'He told me. When I threatened to leave. He said he didn't care, I should go right ahead, because he had another son who would do just as well.'

Leo stared at him for a long moment. 'He never acted as if he thought I would,' he finally said. 'He was always telling me how I was second choice, second best, and he only put up with me at all because you were out of the picture.'

Sandro shook his head slowly. 'What a bastard.'

'I know.'

They sat in silence for a moment, but it lacked the tension and hostility of a few moments before. It felt more like grief.

'Even when I came back,' Sandro finally said, the words painful to admit even though he knew Leo needed to hear them, 'he said he'd still rather have you as his heir. It was only because of the media fallout with Alyse that he summoned me.'

'He was just looking for an excuse to get you back.'

'I don't know.' Sandro sat back in his chair, weary and

heartsick at the thought of how their father had manipulated them for so long. Hurt them with his casual cruelty. 'It's all so pointless. Why did he want us both to feel like a second choice? What good would it do?'

'Because he was a weak man and he wanted us to be weak. Strength scared him. If one of us was actually a decent king, his own legacy would look even worse.'

'Maybe so.' They were both silent for a moment, and then, a new heaviness inside him, Sandro spoke again. 'And you would be a good king, Leo, no matter what our father thought.'

Leo just shrugged. 'I would have done my duty, just as you will.'

'I wish I'd known—'

'Do you, really?' There was no anger in Leo's voice, just a certain shrewdness. 'Because you never asked.'

'I know.' His own weakness shamed him. He hadn't asked because he hadn't really wanted to know, no matter what he said now. Hadn't wanted to consider that not only did he not deserve his title, but his brother did. 'I've been ashamed of myself, Leo. For running away all those years ago. For not being strong enough to stay. What kind of king acts like that?'

Leo was silent for a long moment. 'Sometimes it's stronger to go.'

'It didn't feel like strength to me.'

'You did what you needed to do, Sandro. There's no point raking yourself over the coals now. The past is finished.'

'It's not finished,' Sandro said quietly. 'Not yet.'

Leo frowned. 'What do you mean?'

He met his brother's gaze squarely. 'You should be king.'

Leo narrowed his eyes. 'Sandro—'

'I shouldn't have come back,' he continued steadily, as if Leo hadn't even spoken. 'If I hadn't, you'd be king now. All those plans, all those proposals—you'd have put them into place.'

Leo just shrugged again, but Sandro saw a certain tautness to his brother's mouth, a hardness in his eyes. He was right; his brother still wanted to be king. Still *should* be king. 'Tell me, Leo, that there isn't at least a part of you that wants what you deserve. What you'd been preparing for, for half of your life. It's only natural—'

'Fine. Yes.' Leo bit off the words and spat them out. 'I'll admit it. A *part*. It's hard to let go of certain expectations of what you think your life is going to look like. I thought I'd be king, and I wanted to be a damn good one after Father. Then in the matter of a moment it was snatched away from me. I won't pretend that didn't sting a little, Sandro.'

'More than a little.'

'Fine. Yes. What does it matter now?'

'It matters now,' Sandro said quietly, 'because I should abdicate. Let you take the throne as planned.'

Leo's eyebrows shot up. 'Don't be ridiculous—'

'I've only been king for six months. A blip on the radar. The people here don't even know me, except as the brother who ran away.' His smile twisted. 'The prodigal son. I don't know why I didn't see it before. I suppose I was too blinded by my own misery. But it makes sense, Leo. You know it does.'

'I don't know anything of the sort.' Leo's jaw bunched. 'Stop talking nonsense, Sandro.'

'It isn't nonsense—'

'Do you *want* to abdicate?'

He heard curiosity in his brother's voice, but also a certain eagerness, even if Leo would insist otherwise with every breath in his body. Sandro knew better, and he kept his face blank, his voice toneless, as he gave the only answer he could. 'Of course I do. It's the right thing to do. You'd make a better king, and I never wanted to be king anyway. You know that, Leo.' He felt as if the words were tearing great strips off his soul, pieces from his heart, and yet he knew it was the only thing he could say. Could do, even if it meant losing Liana. His brother deserved his rightful place.

And he deserved his.

Woodenly he rose from the desk. 'It shouldn't take long to put it into motion.'

'Sandro, wait. Don't do anything rash—'

'It's not rash. It's obvious to me, Leo. And to you, I think.'

He turned, saw his brother shaking his head, but there was a light in his eyes neither of them could deny. He wanted this. Of course he did.

Smiling, Sandro put a hand on Leo's shoulder. 'I'm happy for you,' he said, and then he left the room.

Liana gazed in the mirror, smoothed a strand of hair away from her forehead and checked that her dress—a full-skirted evening gown in a silvery pink—looked all right.

She heard the door to her bedroom open and saw with a light heart that it was Sandro.

'I was wondering where you were. We're due at the Museum of Fine Art in an hour for the opening of the new wing.' Sandro didn't answer, and she smoothed the skirt of her evening gown. 'I don't know about this dress. Do I look too much like Cinderella?'

'An apt comparison.'

She laughed lightly and shook her head. 'How's that?'

'She found her prince, didn't she? At the ball. And then she lost him again.'

For the first time since he'd entered the room Liana registered his tone: cool and flat. She turned to face him with a frown. 'What's wrong, Sandro?'

He lifted one shoulder in a shrug. 'Nothing's wrong.'

Confusion deepened into unease. Alarm. 'You're acting rather strange.'

'I had an eye-opening cabinet meeting today.'

'Oh?' Liana eyed him warily, noting the almost eerie stillness of his body, the blankness of his face. She hadn't seen him look like this in weeks...since they'd first been strangers to one another, talking marriage. 'Eye-opening?' she repeated cautiously. 'Why don't you tell me about it?'

'The details don't matter,' he dismissed. 'But it's made me realise—' He stopped suddenly, and for a moment the blankness of his face was broken by a look of such anguish that Liana started forward, her hands outstretched.

'Sandro, what is it? What's wrong?'

'I'm planning to abdicate, Liana.'

Sandro watched the shock rush over Liana, making her eyes widen, her face go pale. She looked, he thought heavily, horrified.

'Abdicating?' she finally repeated, her voice little more than a whisper. 'But...why?'

He felt emotions catch in his chest, words lodge in his throat and tangle on his tongue. So far her reaction was far from hopeful. She looked shell-shocked. Devastated. And all because she wouldn't be queen. 'Does it really matter?'

'Of course it matters.'

'Why?' The one word was raw, torn from him. He

stared at her, willing her expression to clear, for her to say it didn't matter, after all. She'd follow him anywhere. She'd love him without a throne or a title or a crown. But why should she say that? She obviously didn't feel it.

She didn't say anything. She just stared at him helplessly, her face pale and shocked as she shook her head slowly. 'Because, Sandro, you're *king*. And I'm your wife.'

'My queen.'

'Yes, your queen! You can't just leave that behind—'

'But I did before, as you've reminded me—'

'I've reminded you? When was the last time I've mentioned that?'

'You haven't forgotten.'

'I don't have amnesia! It's not something you can just forget.'

'Exactly.'

'Why are you thinking of this?' Liana asked, her voice wavering, her expression still dazed. 'It seems so sudden—'

'And unwelcome, obviously.' There could be no mistaking her disappointment, her distress at learning he might no longer be king. And she would no longer be queen.

'Of course it's unwelcome,' Liana said, and Sandro's last frail hope withered to ash. 'We were just starting to build a life here, a life I thought you were happy with—'

'Being king is not my life. It's not *me*.' The words, he knew, had been in his heart, burning in his chest for his whole life. Hadn't he wanted his parents, his friends, *anyone* to see that he was more than this title, this role? Hadn't he wanted just one person in his life to see him as something other than future king, heir apparent?

And obviously Liana didn't. He hated that he'd put

himself out there again. 'But obviously,' he continued, his voice cold and lifeless now, 'you don't feel the same.'

Liana went even paler, even stiller. 'What do you mean?'

'Our marriage doesn't have much point now, does it?' he asked, his mouth forming a horrible parody of a smile. 'If I'm not king, you're not queen.'

Something flashed across her face but he couldn't tell what it was. 'True,' she said, her voice expressionless. She'd assembled her features into a mask, the Madonna face he recognised from when they'd first met, icy and composed. Sandro hated seeing her like that again, when he'd seen her so vibrant and beautiful and alive. So real with him...except perhaps none of it had been real, after all, or at least not real enough.

'And if our marriage has no point,' he forced himself to continue, 'then there's no point to being married.'

He didn't see so much as a flicker on her face. *Damn it,* he thought, *say something. Fight for me. For us.* Here he was, pushing as he always did, practically begging. *Accept me. Love me.* And of course she didn't.

She just remained silent, staring and still. No response at all. Even so Sandro ached to go to her, take her in his arms. Kiss her into responding to him, just as he had when they'd first met. He wanted to demand that she admit the days they had were real, and they could have more. That she could love him even if he weren't king.

Still Liana didn't speak, and with a sound that was somewhere between a sneer and a sob Sandro stalked out of the room.

Liana stood there, unmoving and silent as the door clicked shut. He'd left. In a matter of moments—not much more than a minute—her entire life, all her hope and happiness, had been destroyed.

Just as before.

Just as when Chiara had choked to death and she'd watched and done nothing. Been unable to do anything, and that appalling lack of action would haunt her for all of her days.

And had she learned nothing in the past twenty years? Once again she'd let her own stunned silence damn her. She had seen from Sandro's expression that he wanted something from her—but what? As she'd stared at him, his expression so horribly blank, she'd had no idea what it was. And while her mind spun and her body remained still, he walked out of her room.

Out of her life.

As if the realisation had kick-started her, she suddenly jerked to life, strode to the door, and wrenched it open. Sandro was halfway down the hallway, his bearing straight and proud as he walked away from her.

'Stop right there, Sandro.'

He stiffened, stilled, then slowly turned around. 'I don't think we have anything more to say to each other.'

'You don't *think*?' Liana repeated in disbelief. She grabbed handfuls of her frothy dress as she strode towards him, full of sudden, consuming rage. 'You just drop that bombshell on me and walk out of my life with hardly a word, and you think that's *it*?' Her voice shook and tears started in her eyes, although she didn't know whether they were of anger or grief. 'You told me you *loved* me, Sandro. Was that a lie?'

'You told me the same,' he answered coolly.

She stared at him for a moment, trying to fathom what had brought him to this decision. 'I think I get it,' she finally said slowly. 'This is another ultimatum.'

'Another—'

'Just like with your father.'

'Don't—'

'Don't what? Don't tell the truth? You threatened to leave once before, Sandro, with your father all those years ago. You wanted him to admit he loved you and he didn't. He disappointed you and so you left, and now you're doing the same to me, threatening me—'

'It wasn't a *threat*.'

'Maybe you don't think it was. Maybe you are seriously considering abdicating. But you didn't come to me as a husband, Sandro. As a—a lover and a friend. You didn't sit me down and tell me what was on your mind, in your heart, and what I might think about it. No, you just walk in and drop your damned bomb and then leave before the debris has even cleared.'

'Your response was obvious—'

'Oh, really? Because as I recall I didn't say much of anything. I was still processing it all and you decided that meant I couldn't love you if you weren't king. You jumped to so many damn conclusions you made my head spin.' And her heart break.

Sandro folded his arms. 'You made your reasons for our marriage clear, Liana. You wanted to be queen—'

'You're going to throw that at me? After everything we've said and done and felt?' She shook her head, her throat too thick with tears to speak. Finally she got some words out. 'Damn you, Sandro. Damn you for only thinking about your feelings and not mine.'

A muscle flickered in his jaw. 'So you're denying it?'

'Denying what?'

'That you married me to become queen—'

'No, of course not. That is why I chose to marry you. There were a lot of messed-up reasons behind that choice, but what I am trying to say—what I thought you knew—is that I've *changed*. As I thought you had changed, except maybe you didn't because I thought you were a cold-hearted bastard when I met you, and you certainly seem like one now.' He blinked, said nothing, and the floodgates of Liana's soul burst open. She drew in a wet, revealing breath.

'I never told you about Chiara's death.'

He blinked again, clearly surprised, maybe discomfited. 'You told me she choked—'

'Yes, she had a seizure and she choked on her own vomit. But what I didn't tell you was that I was there. The only one there. My parents were away and our nanny was busy. I was alone in the room with her and I watched her choke and I couldn't move to help her. Couldn't even speak. I panicked, Sandro, so badly that it caused my sister's death. I could have run to her, could have called for help, and instead I was frozen to the floor with shock and fear.' She felt her chest go tight and her vision tunnel as in her mind's eye Chiara's desperate face stared up at her in mute appeal. And she'd simply stood there, wringing her hands. 'By the time I finally got myself to move, it was too late.' She'd run to her, turned her over. Cleared out her mouth with her own scrabbling fingers, sobbing her sister's name. And Chiara had just stared lifelessly back. *Too late.*

Liana drew in another ragged breath. 'I as good as killed her, Sandro, and I'll live with that for my whole life.' She realised, distantly, that tears were running down her face but she didn't care. Didn't wipe them away. 'And when you delivered your awful ultimatum, I froze again. Didn't speak. Didn't move. But damn if I'm going to lose my soul again, Sandro, because I didn't have the courage or the presence of mind to do something.'

She stepped closer to him, close enough to poke him in the chest. 'I love you. You love me. At least I hope you do, after what I just told you—'

He shook his head, his own eyes bright. 'Do you really think something like that would make me change my mind?'

'I don't know. It changed my parents' minds. At least, it felt like that. We've never recovered. I never recovered, because I spent the past twenty years living my life as an apology and cloaking myself in numbness because feeling meant feeling all the guilt and shame and fear, and I couldn't do that and survive.'

'Liana—' Sandro's face was twisted with anguish, but she wasn't done.

'So we love each other, then, and I might not know much about love but I do know that when you love someone, you believe the best of them. You don't wait for them to let you down. You don't set up situations so they fail. Maybe you've been looking for love for most of your life, Sandro, since you didn't get it from your parents. Guess what? I didn't get it either. My father has barely looked at me since Chiara died. But even I know enough to realise that you don't find love when you act like it's going to disappoint you. When you don't trust it or the person who is meant to love you for five minutes of honest conversation.' She shook her head, empty now, so terribly empty. 'You think I disappointed you by not saying something when you wanted me to. Well, you know what, Sandro? *You* disappointed *me.*'

And with another hopeless shake of her head, she turned and walked back down the hall, away from him.

CHAPTER TWELVE

HE'D SCREWED UP. Big time. It was nearing midnight and Sandro sat in his study, gazing broodingly into space.

Every word Liana had spoken was true.

He had given her an ultimatum, been testing her and the truth of her feelings. It had been an arrogant and appalling thing to do, and, worst of all, he'd been so self-righteous about it.

And while he hadn't had the courage to be honest with her, she'd possessed more than enough to be honest with him. He thought of what she'd admitted about her sister and felt tears sting his eyes.

He was such a bastard.

It had taken him all of ten seconds to realise just how wrong he was, but ten seconds was too long because Liana had already locked her bedroom door, and she wouldn't answer it when he hammered on it and asked her—begged her—to let him in.

He'd hated feeling as if he was begging for love or just simple affection from his parents, hated how as a child he'd always tried to get his father to notice him. But he didn't care now how desperate or foolish or pathetic he looked. He'd go down on his knees to beg his wife to forgive him. He just wanted to be given the chance.

He heard the door to his study open and lurched forwards, hoping against all the odds that it was Liana.

It wasn't. It was Leo.

'Sandro,' he said, unsmiling. 'What the hell did you do?'

'What do you mean?'

'Half the palace could hear Liana shouting at you. And she doesn't shout.'

'I told her I was abdicating.'

Leo stared at him for a long moment. 'Sandro,' he finally said, 'you are a damned idiot.'

Sandro tried to smile, but it felt as if his face were cracking apart. 'I know.'

Leo stepped forward. 'And so am I.'

'What do you mean?'

'I don't want you to abdicate, Sandro. I don't want to be king.'

Sandro shook his head. 'I saw it in your eyes—'

Leo shook his head impatiently. 'Oh, screw that. Yes, as I told you before, there is a part of me that feels hard done by. Disappointed. I'll get over it, Sandro. I'm a big boy. So are you. And you have spent the past six months working yourself to the bloody bone to prove what a good king you are. A great king. You're the only one who doesn't think so.'

'No, I don't,' Sandro said in a low voice. He closed his eyes briefly. It was the first time he'd admitted it out loud.

'And why is that? Why don't you think you'll make—*you are*—a good king?'

Sandro didn't answer for a long moment. Admitting so much to anyone, especially Leo, who had once idolised him, was painful. 'Because,' he finally said in a low voice, 'I shirked my duty, didn't I? I ran away.'

'And you came back.'

'After fifteen years—'

'So? Is there a time limit? And running away—if you really want to call it that—seemed like your only choice back then.' Leo's voice roughened with emotion. 'I believe that, Sandro, even if I've acted like I didn't because I was hurt. I know you wouldn't have left me like that unless you felt you had to.'

Sandro felt his eyes fill. 'I wouldn't have,' he said, his voice choked as he blinked hard. 'I swear to you, Leo, I wouldn't have.'

They stared at each other, faces full of emotion, the air thick with both regret and forgiveness.

Finally Leo smiled, and Sandro did too. 'Well, then,' he said. 'You see?'

Sandro dragged a hand over his eyes. 'I'm not sure I see anything.'

'Leave behind the bitterness and anger, Sandro. Forget about how Mother and Father raised us, how they treated the monarchy. Usher in a new kingdom, begin a new era. You can do it.'

'And what about you?'

'Like I said, I'll get over it. And to be honest, I'm a little relieved. I admit, when you first came back, I was shocked. Hurt too, if I'm honest, because after fifteen years of working myself to the bone to prove myself to our father, he cast me aside at the first opportunity. But I've already promised myself not to live steeped in bitterness or regret, Sandro, and in their own way things have worked out for the best. I'm happy not to be in the spotlight. So is Alyse. We've spent a hell of a long time there, and it wasn't very pleasant.'

'And what of your ambitions? Your plans?'

With a wry smile Leo gestured to the papers scattered

across the desk. 'Feel free to use them. And consult me anytime. My fees are quite reasonable.'

Sandro felt something unfurl inside him, a kind of fragile, incredulous hope. 'I don't know,' he said and Leo just smiled.

'No one does, do they? No one knows what's going to work, what's going to happen. But you have my support, and Alyse's, and the cabinet's.' He paused. 'And you have Liana's, but you might have to grovel a bit to get it back.'

To his amazement Sandro felt a small smile quirk his mouth. 'There's no might about it,' he answered. 'That's a definite.'

'So what are you waiting for?'

'She won't see me.'

'She's angry and hurt. Give her a little time.'

Sandro nodded, even though he didn't want to give her time. Didn't want to wait. He wanted to break her door down and demand that she listen to him. Tell her what an ass he'd been and how much he loved her.

He just needed to find a way to make her listen.

Liana stood in her bedroom with its spindly chairs and feminine décor and stared out of the window at the gardens now in full, glorious spring. The roses were just beginning to unfurl, their petals silky and fragrant. Everything was coming to life, and she felt as if she was dead inside.

She had barely slept last night, had tossed and turned and tormented herself with all the what-ifs. What if she'd said something when Sandro had wanted her to? What if she'd let him back in when he'd knocked on her door and asked her to talk to him?

But she couldn't talk; she felt too empty and grief-stricken for words. She'd given Sandro everything. *Ev-*

erything. And he hadn't loved her enough to wait five minutes—five *seconds*—to explain. Say something. Do something.

And what had he done but judge her and jump to conclusions? Was that what love was?

If so, she was better off without it. Without him.

Even if her heart felt like some raw, wounded thing, pulsing painfully inside her. It would heal. She would. She didn't want to go back to numbness, but maybe she'd go back a *little*. Feel a little less. Eventually.

And as for her marriage? Sandro was right; if he wasn't king, she didn't need to be queen. They certainly didn't need to stay married for convenience's sake. He didn't need an heir, after all, and maybe he wanted to return to his life in California. Maybe he didn't want her anymore. Maybe her confession about Chiara had made him despise her.

Yet the thought of actually divorcing was too awful to contemplate. Maybe they would simply live as strangers, seeing as little of each other as possible, just as she'd envisioned a lifetime ago. Just as she'd *wanted*.

The thought was almost laughable, ridiculous; she certainly didn't want it now. But after the debacle of their confrontation last night, she wasn't sure how they could go on.

Behind her she heard the door open and she drew a shuddering breath. She'd asked Rosa to bring her breakfast to her room because she couldn't face seeing everyone—much less Sandro—in the dining room.

'Liana.'

Everything in her tensed at the sound of Sandro's voice. She turned, saw he was carrying her breakfast tray. She shook her head.

'Don't, Sandro.' Although she wasn't sure what she

was asking him not to do. *Don't break my heart, fragile thing that it is, again.*

'Don't what?' he asked quietly. 'Don't say I'm sorry?'

She drew a shuddering breath. 'Are you?'

'Unbelievably so. More than I've ever been, for anything, in my life.'

She shook her head. It wasn't that simple, that easy. 'Why did you do that to me?'

'Because I'm a stupid, selfish idiot.'

'I'm serious, Sandro.'

'So am I.' With a sad smile he put the breakfast tray down on the table by her bed. He gestured at one of the silver dishes on the tray. 'Strawberries. No chocolate, though.'

Liana just folded her arms. 'I want answers, Sandro.'

'And I'll tell you. You know how you thought you looked like Cinderella last night?'

She eyed him warily; she had no idea where he was going with this. 'Yes….'

'You are Cinderella, Liana. You came to the castle to marry a prince, except in this case the said prince was a king and he wasn't all that charming. He was kind of an ass, actually.'

A smile twitched at her mouth even though she still felt heavy inside. 'Was he? Why?'

'Because he was so consumed with how frustrated he felt and all the things he wanted out of life that he didn't have and how no one loved him. Pathetic, whingy little so-and-so, really.'

'I think you might be being a little hard on him.'

'No, he definitely was. He never thought about what other people might be feeling, especially his Cinderella.'

Her mouth curved again in a tremulous smile, almost

of its own volition. 'I wouldn't say he was *quite* that self-absorbed.'

'He was worse,' Sandro answered. 'Cinderella couldn't find that pointy glass slipper because it was stuck up his ass.'

She let out a sudden, startled laugh. *'Sandro—'*

'He had no idea what he was doing or how much he was hurting people.' He took a step towards her, a sad, whimsical smile on his face. 'Seriously, Liana, he was a mess.'

'And what happened?'

'Cinderella woke him up with a good old slap. Yanked her shoe out and made him realise just how self-important and stupid he was being—about a lot of things. Her. His family. His past. Himself.'

'And?' she asked softly.

'And he only hopes he can still make it right.' He took another step towards her, and he was close enough to touch. She almost did. 'I hope I can make it right, Liana, by telling you how wrong I've been. How unbelievably, unbearably stupid and selfish.' The smile he gave her was shaky, vulnerable, and it made her yearn. She shook her head, not ready to surrender even though another part of her ached to.

'You hurt me, Sandro.'

'I know. I was so afraid of being pushed away again. Rejected. And instead I did exactly what you said. I set up a situation where I'd force you to fail, because it was better than feeling like a failure myself. I'm so sorry.'

Liana felt the burn of tears beneath her lids. 'I forgive you.'

'Enough to take me back?'

She wanted him back. Wanted his arms around her,

her head on his shoulder, the steady thud of his heart against her cheek. 'You can't ever do that again.'

'I won't.'

'I know we'll argue, Sandro, I'm not saying we can't disagree or get angry or annoyed or what have you. But you can't—you can't set me up like that. Make me feel like a failure.' Her throat clogged and she blinked hard. 'Because I've felt like that before, and I don't ever want to feel it again.'

'Oh, Liana. Sweetheart.' He took her in his arms then, and she went, pressing her cheek against his shoulder just as she'd longed to. 'I'm sorry for what you endured with your sister,' he whispered, and the first tears started to spill.

'It was my fault.'

'No, it wasn't.'

'Didn't you listen—?'

'I listened, Liana. And I heard a woman who has been torturing herself for two decades about something that was an accident. You were eight years old, Liana, and you were in shock. Where was that nanny anyway?'

'I don't know.'

'If anyone should feel guilty—'

'But I should have done something. I could have—'

'Did you love your sister?'

'More than anything—'

'Then how can you blame yourself for something that was out of your control? If you could have saved her, you would have. The fact that you didn't meant you weren't able to. You didn't know how. You panicked, you froze, yes, but you were *eight*, Liana, a child. And someone else should have been there.'

She shook her head, her tears falling freely now. 'It's not that easy.'

'No, it isn't. But if you can forgive me, then you can forgive yourself. For your own sake, Liana, as well as mine. Because I love you so very much and I can't stand the thought of this guilt eating away at you until there's nothing left.' He eased back from her, gazed down at her with eyes that shone silver. 'I love you. I love your strength and your grace and even your composure that terrified and annoyed me in turns when we first met. I love how you've stepped so beautifully into being a queen my country—our country—is starting to love, just as I love you.'

His words dazed her so much she could hardly speak. Finally she fastened on to the one thing that seemed least important, least overwhelming. 'But I'm not queen anymore.'

'Yes, you are.' The smile he gave her now was crooked and he reached out to brush at her damp cheeks. 'I'm not going to abdicate. I spoke to Leo, and he talked some sense into me. I realised I was thinking of it because I've felt so much guilt and regret about leaving. Running away. And then I was about to do it again.' He shook his head, his thumbs tracing the lines of her cheekbones, wiping away her tears. 'Do you think you're willing to stay married to such a slow learner? A slow learner who loves you quite desperately?'

'Of course I am.' Liana's lips trembled as she tried to smile. 'I'm a bit of a slow learner, myself. I love you, Sandro, but it scared me for a long time, to feel that much, never mind admitting it. But I do love you. So very much.'

He framed her face with his hands, brought her closer to him so her forehead rested against his. They stayed that way for a moment, neither of them speaking, everything in Liana aching with emotion and a new, deeper happiness than she'd ever felt before. A happiness based on total honesty, deep and abiding love.

'We're quite a pair, aren't we?' he murmured. 'Wanting love and being afraid of it at the same time.'

She pressed one hand to his cheek, revelling in the feel of him, and the fact that he was here, that he'd come back and he loved her. 'Love *is* pretty scary,' she said, a smile in her voice, and Sandro nodded, his forehead bumping against hers.

'Terrifying, frankly.'

She let out a shaky laugh and put her arms around him. 'Definitely terrifying. But I do love you, Sandro.'

'And I love you.' He kissed her gently on the lips, a promise and a seal. 'And since it seems that we're both slow learners, it will take us a long time to figure this love out. I think,' he continued as he drew her closer and deepened the kiss, 'it will take the rest of our lives.'

EPILOGUE

One year later

LIANA SMOOTHED THE satin skirt of the gown, admired the admittedly over-the-top ruffles of lace that fell to the floor.

She turned to Sandro with a smile and a shake of her head. 'I can't believe you wore this.'

'If I'd been a little more self-aware at the time, I'm sure I would have been mortified.'

'Well, you were only three months old,' she teased. 'Isabella seems to like it, at any rate.'

'She's a smart girl.'

They both gazed down at their daughter, Isabella Chiara Alexa Diomedi, her eyes already turning the silver-grey of her father's, her dimpled smile reminding Liana with a bittersweet joy of her sister.

With a smile for her daughter, Liana scooped her up and held her against her shoulder, breathed in her warm baby scent.

'Careful,' Sandro warned. 'You just fed her and she likes to give a little bit of that back.' He gave a mock grimace. 'I should know. The palace dry-cleaning bill has skyrocketed since this little one's arrival.'

'I don't mind.'

There was nothing she minded about taking care of her daughter. She was just so happy, so incredulously grateful, to have the opportunity. Isabella's birth had been, in its own way, a healing; no one could replace Chiara, but her daughter's birth had eased the long-held grief of losing her sister.

A gentle knock sounded on the door, and then her mother poked her head in. 'May I come in?'

Liana felt herself tense. Her parents had arrived last night for Isabella's christening; she hadn't actually seen them save for a few formal functions since her wedding. And as usual when she saw her mother, she felt the familiar rush of guilt and regret, tempered now by Sandro's love and her daughter's presence, but still there. Already she could hear the note of apology creep into her voice.

'Of course, Mother. We're just getting Isabella ready for the ceremony.'

Gabriella Aterno stepped into the room, her features looking fragile and faded as always, her smile hesitant and somehow sad.

Sandro stepped forward. 'Would you like to hold her?'

'Oh—may I?'

'Of course,' Liana said, and, with her heart full of too many emotions to name, she handed her daughter to her mother.

Gabriella looked down into Isabella's tiny, impish face and let out a ragged little laugh. 'She has Chiara's dimples.'

Liana felt a flash of shock; her mother had not mentioned Chiara once since her sister's funeral. Twenty-one years of silence.

'She does,' she agreed quietly. 'And her smile.'

'Perhaps she'll have her dark curls.' Gently Gabriella fingered Isabella's wispy, dark hair. 'You two were always so different in looks. No one would have thought you were sisters, save for the way you loved each other.' She looked up then, her eyes shining with tears, the grief naked in her face, and Liana knew how much just those few sentences had cost her.

'Oh, Mother,' she whispered. She swallowed past the tightness in her throat. 'I'm so sorry—'

'I'm sorry Chiara isn't here to see her niece,' Gabriella said. 'But I like to think she still sees, from somewhere.'

'Me too.' Liana blinked hard, focused on her daughter in her mother's arms, and said what had been burning inside her for too many years. 'I'm sorry I didn't save her.'

Gabriella jerked her head up, her eyes wide with shock. 'Save her? Liana, you were eight years old.'

'I know, but I was there.' Liana blinked hard, but it was too late. The tears came anyway. 'I saw— I *watched*—'

'And you've blamed yourself all this time,' Gabriella said softly. 'Oh, my dear.'

'Of course I blamed myself,' Liana answered, batting uselessly at the tears that trickled down her cheeks. 'And you blamed me too, Mother, and Father as well. I'm not angry—I understand why—' She choked on the words, felt Sandro's comforting hand on her shoulder, and she pressed her cheek against it, closed her eyes against the rush of pain and tried to will the tears back.

'Liana, my dear, we blamed ourselves,' Gabriella confessed, her voice trembling with emotion. 'Of course we did—we were her parents. She was our responsibility, not yours.'

Liana opened her eyes, stared at her mother's grief-stricken face. 'But you never said anything,' she whispered. 'Father hasn't even so much as hugged me since—'

'We didn't like to talk about it,' Gabriella told her. 'As

I'm sure you realised. Not because of you, though, but because of us. We felt so wretchedly guilty. I still do.'

'Oh, Mother, no—' Impulsively and yet instinctively Liana went to put her arms around Gabriella, the baby between them.

'All three of us have been consumed by guilt, it seems,' Gabriella said with a sniff. 'And I know your father and I didn't handle it properly back then, or ever. We should have been there for you, spoken to you about it, helped you to grieve. We were too wrapped up in our own pain, and I'm sorry for that.' She shook her head slowly, her eyes still bright with tears. 'I'm sorry I didn't realise how much you blamed yourself. I just assumed—' Her mother drew in a quick breath. 'Assumed you blamed me.'

Liana shook her head. 'No, never.'

They were both silent for a moment, struggling with these new revelations and the emotions they called up. In Gabriella's arms Isabella stirred, gurgled, and then gave her grandmother a big, drooly smile.

Gabriella let out a choked cry of surprise and joy. She turned to Liana with a tear trickling down one pale cheek. 'Then maybe this is a new start for all of us, Liana,' she said, her voice wavering, and Liana nodded and smiled.

She knew there was more to be said, to be confessed and explained and forgiven, but for now she revelled in the second chance they'd all been granted. A second chance at happiness, at love, at life itself.

Gabriella handed the baby back to Sandro and slipped down to the chapel where the christening would be held. Liana gazed at her husband and daughter and felt her heart might burst with so much feeling. She felt so much now, all the emotions she'd denied herself for so long. Joy and wonder, grief and sorrow. She wouldn't keep herself from feeling any of it ever again.

'I couldn't have imagined any of this before I met you,' she said softly. 'Talking to my mother so honestly. Having a husband and child of my own. Loving someone as much as I love you. You've changed me, Sandro.'

'And you've changed me. Thank God.' He smiled wryly and then, with the expertise of a father of a baby, he shifted Isabella to his other shoulder and drew Liana towards him for a kiss. 'This really is the beginning, Liana,' he said softly as he kissed her again. 'Of everything.'

* * * * *

MARRIED FOR THE
SHEIKH'S DUTY

TARA PAMMI

CHAPTER ONE

"WHAT ARE YOUR requirements in a bride, Sheikh Al-Ghamdi?"

Sheikh Zayn Al-Ghamdi stared unseeing at the flat-screen monitor that was attached to the wall in his office. Words came to his lips and fell away.

He had known for a while now that this final step of settling down and marrying was coming at him. It had been drilled into him since childhood that he would one day marry a woman who would serve him well as a wife and his country as sheikha.

Of course she would be mostly an image that would be carefully cultivated and supervised to please the people of his country. He had also been taught, by example of his own parents, that her role even in his life would be very minor. Having his children and continuing the legacy of the Al-Ghamdi family was going to be her primary duty.

Last week when Benjamin had invited him and two other men to confab, following the exposé in *Celebrity Spy!*, he had been the one to suggest that all his problems would be solved if he married and started producing heirs.

All three men, his rivals for years, turned reluctant allies—Benjamin Carter, Dante Mancini and Xander Trakas—had looked at him as if he'd grown two horns and a tail. Until they had seen the sense in his idea after their initial grumbling and posturing.

But faced with the question asked by Ms. Young, the billionaire matchmaker recommended by Xander, he found himself bewildered.

In the little slice of his life that he was actually the master of, Zayn resented being brought to heel like a dog by some bottom-feeding, trashy tabloid.

But thanks to the dirty exposé on the four of them, his image was utterly besmirched. His parents, even though retired from public life, still had lectured him over his image, the effect of every small minutia of his life over the political climate of Khaleej. Even worse, his sister Mirah's fiancé's family was talking about canceling the match.

Conservative to the core, they didn't believe he had a right to any kind of life, much less the kind of reckless debauchery the article hinted at. But that was not acceptable.

Ten years younger than he was, his sister had been a ray of sunshine in an otherwise solitary life. From their parents' aloof, almost cold, upbringing, to the rigors of preparing for a political life, if not for Mirah, Zayn would have known no true joy. No companionship at all.

"Sheikh Al-Ghamdi?"

"My bride needs to be attractive and young. Attractive enough for me to be able to look at her for the next five decades. And healthy enough to have children. Someone not approaching or close to thirty."

Ms. Young made scrupulous notes but Zayn saw the vertical frown between her brows. "Is there a problem, Ms. Young?"

Her gaze couldn't quite hide her judgment. "Women are known to have children even at the *advanced* age of thirty, Your Highness."

"Yes, but women reaching thirty have stubbornly decided ideas, Ms. Young. They will not be malleable. I might not meet their expectations of an ideal man, either."

The woman didn't quite snort but Zayn had a feeling she wanted to. "A woman ambitious about her career will not do. She'll have to understand that her role in life is to complement me."

"So beautiful but not really smart."

"Yes. She will have to come to me as a virgin."

Outrage flared in Ms. Young's expressive eyes. "That's barbaric."

"That's the only way I can ensure there's no future scandal or shame attached to her name."

"Virginity need not be required. We check their backgrounds very thoroughly before we make matches based on your requirements."

"Ex-boyfriends and old lovers have a way of showing up in one's life to make the most trouble. I would like to avoid any future scandals concerning my Sheikha and her past. This ensures it."

"Beautiful, young, malleable, not particularly smart and a virgin. I don't know whether to say this is the easiest or the hardest match I've ever made, Your Highness."

"Are you saying you cannot find me a woman to match those requirements, Ms. Young?"

"Of course I can, Your Highness. But I just wondered if love was going to be a part of the equation."

"You run a matchmaking business for billionaires, Ms. Young. Has love ever been part of it?"

"I was curious about your opinion."

"Some foolish, fantastic notion will not make my marriage a success. I require a wife who will yield to my superior judgment in all areas of our life and be an asset to my political life."

"A kind of accessory?"

"The perfect accessory, if you will," he finished, amused at the flicker of anger in Ms. Young's eyes.

He had known for a long time that was all a wife could be for a man like him.

Two weeks later

In all her carefully mapped-out adult life, Amalia Christensen had never imagined that one bright, hot-as-Hades day she would be waiting in the administrative offices of the ruling sheikh, Zayn Al-Ghamdi. In the spectacularly grand palace of her father's homeland, Khaleej, she stared at the breathtaking domes and ornately lavish halls decorated in pure gold.

In the time that she'd lived with her mother in Scandinavia, a lot of things had changed in Khaleej, and for the better.

With infrastructure improved to rival any western nation, and its meteoric entry into the global finance world, Khaleej was now a flawless blend of artistry, tradition and technology.

If not for the constant knot of worry in her gut about her twin, Aslam, she'd have been clicking pics and Instagramming left, right and center. The rust-colored palace with its turrets and domes, sitting in the center of hundreds of acres of landscaped gardens and a golden sandy beach corralling it on one side was a visual feast.

But in all the years that she'd yearned to visit Khaleej, she hadn't imagined doing it this desperate way. The beauty of Khaleej and her reconnection with her roots was empty, meaningless, without Aslam by her side.

If only she'd visited last year; if only she'd understood how restless and angry Aslam was…

It had taken her two months after arriving in Sintar, the

capital city of Khaleej, to get this meeting with a palace official. After one short visit with Aslam, who had poured out the entire story to her in the jail; several tense, mono-syllabic conversations with her father over the phone—Amalia had no interest in addressing the decade-old silence that still stood between them—followed by end-less reaching out to friends of Aslam and learning about the instigator of the whole escapade; and finally, asking her boss Massimiliano to use his connections and arrange this meeting for her.

Massi had laughed and asked if it would bring back the best executive assistant he'd ever had to work for him. Glad that he hadn't written her off during her long-term leave, she'd promised to return soon. Much as she missed her career and cringed at the dent in her savings, she couldn't leave until Aslam was free.

The sound of the glistening blue waters of the gulf gen-tly breaking onto the pristinely white sandy beach, visible to the right of her, added a background score to the preg-nant silence of the corridor.

She'd been told the palace was usually a beehive of ac-tivity. Instead a sort of hush reigned over the scarcely oc-cupied hall.

Neither did she forget the diatribe that had flown out of the official's mouth that Amalia's appointment had been scheduled on *that particular day.*

There was hardly any staff around, either.

What was going on?

She'd never been a royalist and yet the recent exposé on the four bachelors, one of whom was Sheikh Zayn, had drawn her interest. Apparently, the sheikh led a very col-orful and inventive private life away from the highly con-servative media of the country and the grueling lifestyle of his powerful position.

Amalia had seen the numerous articles that had mush-roomed following the exposé, questioning Sheikh Zayn's dedication toward the governing of Khaleej, the conservative ideals of most of the cabinet and his very image in the eyes of his people.

She glanced at her watch one more time and stood up from the comfortable sofa. Her thighs groaned from sitting for far too long.

Gold piping in the mosaic tiles winked at her. A quick glance behind her showed no hovering security guard, and she slipped through a grand archway into a long corridor that looked like it belonged in a fantasy novel.

A blast of heat hit her and she realized that the corridor opened into a courtyard on the left. Pristine white marble gleamed for a mile or more in front of her. In a moment of uncharacteristic impulsiveness, Amalia slipped her feet out of her pumps.

With the cold marble kissing the overheated soles of her feet and a soft breeze coming in from the bay touching her cheeks, the sheer beauty of her surroundings calmed something inside her.

In the three and a half hours since the harried-looking official had asked her to wait, if you didn't count the hour she'd spent standing at the reception, waiting for the said official to appear in the first place, Amalia had begun to see a pattern emerge. Guests were being shown into this wing of the palace with the utmost secrecy and security for there would be a sudden rise in the activity around the reception area every half hour or so.

And with each group, there had been almost always one designer-clad, elegantly coiffed woman in the center, quite like a queen bee in the center of her hive.

Guests of the sheikh?

Passing a sun-dappled courtyard dotted with cool fountains and swaying palm trees on her left, she wondered why the women were being brought to the palace.

They could be applying to join the sheikh's harem, the man having decided that he needed recreational variety closer to home now that his extracurricular activities had been exposed to the world's media.

She snorted. Not even the playboy sheikh could justify a harem in this day and age. *Could he?*

What if he was building a strip club sort of thing here in the capital city of Sintar for his personal use and they were women from all over the world at the top of their career in pole dancing? A modern-day harem for one man—wasn't that pretty much what a strip club was?

Not much of a leap, given that *Celebrity Spy!* had said the sheikh's sexual appetites were voracious...

Or they could be princesses and queens and top-tier dignitaries from all over the world attending a banquet given by the royal family—hadn't she read somewhere that his sister was to be married soon?—which meant the man who'd promised to see Amalia was probably busy with the details of the banquet and not coming for hours.

The second prospect sobered her spirits. But she couldn't leave until she spoke to him about Aslam and the bogus drug charges built up against him while the real perpetrator was hiding in the lap of luxury.

The moment the palace official had agreed to see her, Amalia knew she'd been on the right path. Someone high up had to know they weren't Aslam's drugs.

She glanced behind her to the archway and realized she'd walked quite a way.

A heated conversation in the courtyard to her left lifted the hair on her neck. Alarmed, she opened the first door on her right and slipped inside.

Walking in from the bright light of the day momentarily

blinded her vision. Faltering on her feet, she reached out with her hands and found a wall.

It took her a few seconds of blinking and focusing before she could see around the room. Her stomach quivered.

The room wasn't completely dark as she'd thought first. A large skylight at the far side of the vast room cast a golden glow, showing a man sitting on a throne-like chair, complete with dark gold upholstery and clawlike feet. As if he was the king of everything he surveyed.

Shivers spewed over her spine, as if there was a predator in the room.

Light brown eyes first flicked to the pumps in her hand and then to her bare feet. "You are carrying your shoes instead of wearing them. Why?"

With a jerk, Amalia dropped the pumps and with them, *plop* went her heart.

Unlike the staff that had catered to her, the man spoke English with an aristocratic, upper-class accent. A deep baritone made the words fall over her like drops of ice-cold water over heated skin.

Without looking at him directly, she could feel the man's intense gaze on her mouth. Her lips quivered. "I…I walked out into the courtyard and I was too hot."

"I see that you are too hot." The dry statement jerked her gaze up. Intelligent and imperious, his brown eyes were wide-spaced and hooded under the dark slashes of his eyebrows. And brimming with amusement. "Why did you walk into the courtyard?"

That made her tongue come unstuck from the roof of her mouth. "I got tired of waiting. If I had to sit on my behind any longer, I'm sure it would have been flattened under me, that's how long—"

"I hope our furniture didn't cause your…posterior any lasting *harm*."

Her hand went to the particular section of her anatomy. "It's hard enough to find clothes that fit my height within a budget, so yeah, a flattened backside is not good. And nope, it's perfectly fine," she quipped. And only after she spoke the words did she realize this whole line of conversation was ridiculous.

Embarrassment sent heat flooding up her neck, blocked her throat. And she wished she had a genie in hand, like in her father's elaborate stories, to make herself disappear. Or at least, start over this whole conversation.

"I didn't mean to interrupt…"

"Apology not required," he said, and Amalia bit down on the retort that she hadn't been offering one. "The process is taking longer than it should." A hint of irritation peeked through that sentence. From anyone else, it could have been an apology. But Amalia was pretty sure he didn't intend it to be one.

She pushed her feet into the pumps. One hand went to her stomach as if to shoo away the butterflies rioting in there, and one went to her hair. She expelled a sigh of relief when she realized her tight ponytail had stayed put. Once she made sure all of her person was intact—she needed that assurance—she raised her gaze.

Between one rushing heartbeat and the next, she became aware that the man's utter dominance, over everything in the room, even over the very air she was struggling to breathe, was bred into his bones. His power clung to his skin, not his clothes or to this room or the throne.

It was centuries of legacy, she realized, a sheen of sweat covering her forehead now. He looked like a king because *he was a bloody king.* Or to use the right terminology, His Royal Highness, Sheikh Zayn Al-Ghamdi of Khaleej. Brilliant statesman, inventive playboy that *Celebrity Spy!* claimed liked fast cars, fast technology and fast women.

Her first instinct was to mumble an apology and run from the room. The element of surprise was on her side and if she just went back through the unending corridor, back to the waiting area, she could lose herself and slither out of the palace.

Poised on the balls of her feet, Amalia forced herself to calm down and reconsider.

This was the sheikh, *the man with all the power*, the man who was responsible—*fine, indirectly*—for Aslam being wrongfully imprisoned. What were the chances that she would ever get an audience with him again?

No way could she tuck her tail between her legs and run away just because the man had to be the most dominating presence she'd ever felt.

Her breath seesawed through her chest as he stood up from the recliner, prowled the width of the room and then stood, leaning against an immense white oak desk. A sitting area to the right had a chaise longue.

Although *lounging* seemed like too still an activity for him.

The energy of the man, his sheer presence, filled the room and pressed at her from all sides, as if to demand acknowledgement and acquiescence.

A shining silver tea set on the side table made her aware of her parched throat.

As if she'd voiced her request out loud, he moved to the silver service, poured a drink—mint and lemon sherbet—into a tall silver tumbler and walked over to her.

That sense of being overwhelmingly pressed on a sensory level amplified. He had a sandalwood scent. And he gave off heat like there was a furnace inside him. Or was that she who was feeling the heat when really he was giving off none?

Sensations she didn't like and couldn't control continued to pour through her and Amalia just stood there, shuddering inwardly in the wake of them.

Where was the super-stalwart Amalia that Massi depended on? Where was the woman who'd been dubbed "the calm in the storm" by colleagues and coworkers?

"Drink. Strangers to the country forget that even when they do not sweat, the heat is still unrelenting."

His command was supercilious, arrogant, exaggeratedly patient. Better if he thought her brain had short-circuited because of the heat than because of the sheer masculinity of the man.

"I'm not a stranger."

His gaze swept over her. "You do not look like a woman from my country."

She took the tumbler and drank the sherbet without pause. The liquid was a cool, refreshing breeze against her throat. Even her head felt better. Lowering the glass from her mouth, Amalia wondered if the man's theory had credit.

Really, she'd been meandering for almost twenty minutes. Was it a stretch that she had lost her composure because of the heat? Armed with that defense, she extended the glass back to him. "Thanks, I needed that."

He didn't move. He didn't take the glass she offered. He didn't speak, either.

Slowly, Amalia raised her gaze and looked at him. Really looked at what had to be the most aggressively masculine specimen on the planet.

And promptly realized all her theories about heat and dehydration messing with her composure were just those: theories with a hefty dose of self-delusion.

Tall windows above and behind her cast just the right amount of golden light onto his face as if they, too, had been beat into submission by the will of this man.

A single brow rose imperiously, his gaze very much on her face. A gesture filled with a dark sarcasm. Was it because she had given the glass back to him, as if he was a servant? Was his sense of consequence so big that he was insulted by her innocent gesture?

He had short, thick, curving eyelashes that shaded his expression—a tactic she was sure he used to intimidate people. Light turned the brown of his eyes into a hundred golden hues, the eyes of a predatory cat.

Square jaw, rough with bristles, sat below high cheekbones and a straight nose that lent his features a hardness she didn't like. His mouth was wide and thin-lipped. A mouth given to passion; the strange thought sent a shiver down her spine.

Amalia was tall, only two inches short of six feet. He topped over her easily by four or five inches. His neck was the same glistening tone as his face—a dark golden, as if he had been cast from one of those ancient metals that Khaleejians had used several centuries ago. Her father had had a small knife whose handle gleamed like his skin tone.

He propped a finger under her chin and lifted it up. All of her being seemed to concentrate on that small patch of skin. "Your appraisal is very thorough after being so flustered."

Heat poured through Amalia's cheeks. "I wasn't flustered."

"No?" The brow-rise again. "A lot of women lose their composure when they see me."

"Second of all," she continued, "you look like a man who needs to be met square in the eye, Your Highness."

Amusement filtered through the implacability in his eyes. "That is a bold statement to make. Tell me your name."

"Ms. Christensen."

"Did your parents not give you a first name?"

She didn't want to tell him her name, which was the weirdest thing Amalia had ever felt.

He waited and the silence grew. "Amalia Christensen. I was dehydrated. Now I've found my bearings again."

Taking the coward's way, Amalia stepped back from the sheer presence of the man and made a meandering path through the room.

A haunting memory of listening to one of her father's stories of ancient history of Khaleej gripped her. A traditionally designed curved dagger, almost the size of her lower arm, hung against a beige-colored rug on the wall, its metallic hilt gleaming in the afternoon light. She ran reverent fingers over the handle.

Yet, she couldn't leave the infuriating presence of the man behind. It was like trying to ignore a lion that was sitting two feet away from you and eyeing you for his next meal. Neither could she curb the rising panic that the longer she took to explain herself, the harder it was going to be to convince him to help Aslam.

The scent and heat of him rubbed up against her senses.

"This is a fifteenth-century *khanjar*, isn't it?" she said, just to puncture the building tension around them. "Men used to wear them on their belts. It was a sign of status, a sign of prowess."

"Among other things, yes," he said drily, and a fresh wave of warmth washed over her.

"A sign of their macho-ness, in modern words," she added, tongue-in-cheek.

It seemed they didn't even have to look at each other for that almost tangible quality to build up around them. Was it just awareness of each other? Attraction? Or was it her fear of the consequences of her pretense that was making her heart ratchet in her chest so violently?

"Decorative pieces now."

His surprised gaze rested on her face but Amalia looked straight ahead. She couldn't rid herself of the lingering sensation in her gut.

"You've studied the history of Khaleej in preparation for this interview?" he said, a thread of something in his tone. "I have to admit to both surprise and admiration for that. Having a knowledge of Khaleej and its customs is a huge point in your favor."

Interview? For a position with him?

For the first time in two months, luck was on her side. If it was a job among the palace staff, a position closer to the sheikh himself, much better. Maybe she wouldn't have to blurt out the truth this minute and risk getting on the wrong side of the man.

Would waiting only make it worse for Aslam? Which option was better?

"Yet, I didn't receive a file on you from Ms. Young."

Face coloring, Amalia pulled her phone out of her bag. "I can email you my résumé in a minute."

"No, that is far too…*strange*, even for me."

Now, what did he mean by that?

"Tell me about yourself. I'm curious why Ms. Young picked you to be a candidate when it's clear you don't have a royal connection or any other advantages."

Royal connection? How high up was this job that there were candidates with royal connections applying?

"I didn't actually prep for the interview," she said, deciding to dole out truth little by little and see how he reacted. She needed to get a sense of what kind of man he was—if he was fair-minded or just like his cousin.

"I was born here in Khaleej and lived here until I was thirteen. My…father is a historian at the Sintar University and an expert on antique objects. He…" The sudden lump in her throat made it hard. "My twin, Aslam, and I…it used to be our favorite pastime to sit in his study and listen to his long, rambling stories about Khaleej. He is, or used to be, a consummate storyteller." So good that she'd utterly believed him when he had said he'd send for her very soon. That had been more than a decade ago.

"Used to be?"

"I haven't seen him in a while."

"You seek to make a home in Sintar again, to reconnect with him?"

"No. And I have no intention to." He frowned and she added, "No intention to reconnect with him, I mean. I have other reasons for being here."

"But you do not have a Khaleejian name."

She shrugged. "My mother and he divorced and they split us up. She took her name back and asked me if I wanted to, as well. I said yes."

"You should have your father's name. You should have something that speaks to that part of your heritage."

"I don't really see why when he and I have had nothing to do with each other," Amalia retorted, angry with him, angry with herself for reacting at all. She was supposed to learn about his temperament, not pour out her own non-existent relationship with her father.

His frown sliced through her anger. "My point is I would be an asset in any position with my understanding of the cultural norms. My Arabic is rusty but I can polish that up, too."

He gave her one of those considering looks again. Never had she struggled so much to hold a man's gaze. "That is good but might not be completely necessary. Both parts of your heritage could be put to use. You could be the western connection that Khaleej needs."

So it was a position in close quarters with him? Excitement and alarm twisted in her stomach.

"Tell me more about yourself, Ms. Christensen," he invited in a languorous voice.

Keeping her gaze on some point left of his face, she began, "I worked for five years as an executive assistant to the CEO of a multimillion-dollar company. I'm fluent in four languages. I never lose my cool." The raised brow again, damn it. "And I work extremely well under pressure. Also, I'm very good at managing public relations and media, too."

"You sound like a paragon of hard work and efficiency, Ms. Christensen."

"You sound like it's a bad thing," she retorted.

He smiled, and Amalia for the first time understood the meaning of *knee-buckling.* Her fingers tingled to trace the grooves in his cheeks.

"I should warn you that this is unlike any job you've worked at before. What are your expectations?"

"That I would be compensated well and dealt with fairly."

He laughed then. She'd been right. Full of his own consequence he was, but he also had a sense of humor. The laugh lines around his mouth sat easily on the hard contours of his face. "Your bluntness is refreshing. You know that monetarily, you will be set up very well for the rest of your life." He sobered up. "As to being treated fairly, I always treat women well."

"Have I convinced you that I am right for this…position, then?"

"I'm holding judgment on that. As you know," a glint in his eyes made Amalia aware of her own skin, the rapid beat of her heart, the slow tingling low in her belly, "it is not a decision I can make in a half hour. But you will be glad to know, on paper, I would have rejected you immediately. I have to hand it to Ms. Young. She made a bold but different choice with you."

"You would've rejected me? When I'm supremely qualified?"

"Defiant as you are in rejecting your Khaleejian heritage, I can't believe you can be that naive about your suitability, Ms. Christensen. Khaleej is at the most troubling and exciting point in history now, straddling ancient traditions and the modern world. Everyone around me reflects on me."

Amalia prided herself on the career she'd worked so hard for. She'd dedicated years to it, had looked after her mom before she'd passed away last year, paid for her endless treatment… His dismissal of her stung. "Just tell me why," she demanded.

"A career woman full of her own ideas about independence and gender equality and with a grudge against her own father is the last thing I need on my hands."

All those fluttery, useless sensations that she was beginning to recognize died a sudden, much-appreciated death as Amalia tried to wrap her head around the sheikh's statement.

If he didn't want a professional, dedicated, experienced career woman for the position, how did he expect to get anything done? What use would a woman who couldn't think for herself be in—?

Her heart sank to the soles of her sensible pumps.

It wasn't a job he was interviewing for.

And if it was a stripper or a belly dancer she'd insanely thought, well, he'd have asked questions about that field, wouldn't he? Maybe even asked her to give a trial performance. But even that crazy idea was better.

Her pulse skidding everywhere, her eyes wide, Amalia stood rooted to the spot as the last piece of the puzzle slotted into place.

That was why the palace was mostly empty, why women had been brought in all morning. The Ms. Young he kept mentioning wasn't a headhunter but a matchmaker.

Sheikh Zayn Al-Ghamdi of Khaleej was interviewing eligible candidates for a wife, for his sheikha, and Amalia Christensen, dedicated career woman and valuer of her independence, had inadvertently applied for the position.

Her pulse skittered as fear filled her veins.

What if she had ruined Aslam's only chances for release with her dangerous charade?

CHAPTER TWO

AMALIA CHRISTENSEN WAS the kind of woman who made men grateful for being men, who brought forth all the uncivilized, rampantly aggressive instincts that men pretended they didn't feel anymore to cater to the modern feminist's sensibilities.

He had never been struck by an attraction so hard and so fast.

The way she'd been so hotly flustered when he'd let his gaze sweep over her lithe form had been incredibly interesting and stroked his masculinity in a way he hadn't needed in more than a decade.

Zayn couldn't turn his gaze away from the color seeping up her cheeks or the way her expressive eyes flashed her dismay, confusion, followed by the resolve. He could practically see her spine lock into place.

Khaleej had always been a progressive nation. Even Zayn agreed there was a place and reason for gender equality and the feminist movement.

Just not in his life. Or in his bed. He had no doubt that he, in particular, would be deemed a *male chauvinist* or an *antifeminist devil* for there was no room for another strong personality in his life, let it be a lover or a wife.

He liked and preferred women who understood and accepted that he was the dominant one in bed, that he would take care of all their needs as long as they trusted him. As long as they were equally wild as he was.

Every aspect of his life had been controlled, first by his father and then by himself, and would continue to be until he was dead. But his private life, his sex life—it was where the wildness in him ran free.

With the little time he had, contrary to the *Celebrity Spy!* lurid exposé about his alleged orgies and depraved tastes, he needed his sex life to be easy and simple, not an ongoing battle of sexes.

So Amalia Christensen—with her long, wavy, dirty-blond hair tightly pulled back in a ponytail that brought her exquisite features into stunning focus, her pillowy, lush mouth that argued that she wasn't flustered when she so obviously was and her hot little body hidden in her buttoned pencil skirt and long-sleeved top—was not the kind of woman Zayn would engage with sexually.

If she was the innocent type who couldn't even own her sexuality, he didn't have the time or patience to teach her. If that innocence was a cunning act to attract his attention, he didn't want to play that game.

Neither was her vehemence that her father's heritage had no part in her life something he liked. Clearly, she had been raised to disrespect authority figures, encouraged in her rejection of an important part of her identity. He would bet her mother, who had given her those light brown eyes and the stunning golden-blond hair, was the author of that disillusionment, too.

So Ms. Christensen was not fit to be his wife in any form or way.

Was this Ms. Young's rebellion because he had ruffled her sensibilities with his requirements in a wife? She couldn't have believed Zayn would choose this contradiction of a woman to be his sheikha in a hundred years.

But after a morning of meeting eligible candidates—all lovely virginal women with connections in high places and with a full understanding of what it meant to be the future Sheikha Al-Ghamdi, docile and respectful of his country's norms and traditions, *and* even more important, thoroughly and admittedly bowled over by what he represented—this woman was a maddening, arousing novelty. His response to her and her rough, almost insulting manner was both curious and irrational.

Because staring into those long-lashed, honey-colored eyes, he couldn't help wishing he'd met her a few months ago. Even a month ago, before the episode of *Celebrity Spy!* and ruffled sensibilities of his countrymen.

She was nothing like the women he slept with but she completely intrigued him—a novelty—and that would have made the chase and the final victory that much more exciting.

For a minute he wondered if he could give her a position in the palace and keep her close. Until he was married and Mirah was happily married and the dust settled around his image. Until he was free to pursue her... No. Even for a man who considered marriage nothing but an advantageous step in his preordered life, the idea was utterly distasteful.

He had long been resigned to the idea that, like his father, after a few years of marriage, he would find sexual satisfaction with other women. But beginning his marriage with a mistress in mind was repugnant.

He should be sending her on her way. He should think back to the women he had met this morning, make a decision and get it over with. Move on to the next task in his unending list of state duties.

"Have I insulted you by that statement, Amalia?" he said instead, using her given name on purpose.

Just as he expected, her mouth tightened. Her shoulders went back into a ramrod line, which thrust her breasts out provocatively. He had a feeling she'd never do that if she knew how alluring that gesture looked.

"I'm wondering why you're not sending me on my way if I'm such a bad candidate, Your Highness. I'm also wondering how to make the best of this situation. It seems my options are lose-lose."

Something in her eyes, a conflict, a hesitation, made him think she wasn't just sparring with him anymore. She was upset by the sure outcome of this meeting and she was mustering defenses.

Had she been so sure that she would impress him? Would this alliance mean so much to her?

Or had she conspired with Ms. Young to lure him into an alliance of a different nature? Why not? Women tried to attract his attention in every which way. He was known to be a kind and generous lover. If there was a connection he could use in high places, or a recommendation he could make to advance the current woman in his life's career in some way, he'd always been open to it.

Was this Amalia's game? Had she somehow inveigled this invite so that she could present herself as a candidate, but for something altogether different?

Doubts ensnared him.

He didn't forget that even though she'd lost her footing, she'd recovered her composure very well. She had been the most interesting woman he had met today among all the candidates. The most interesting woman he had met in a while, if truth be told. But was that interest being culti-vated and engineered with a purpose in mind?

"In your life, are there any skeletons I should know of?"

Instantly, her gaze shuttered; a paleness touched her skin. Guilt was a shining emblem on her forehead. He'd been right. The woman was here under false pretenses and convoluted motives.

Send her away, one voice inside his head said.

Play her at her own game, another said.

"You're hiding something. Or are you counting your lovers in your head?" something savage and out of control goaded him to ask.

Outrage filled her eyes. "That's none of your business. Unless you're offering to do the same count for my benefit. Will you reveal what you ask of me? Should I pull out the *Celebrity Spy!* exposé and tally your number against theirs to verify the veracity of your claim, Sheikh?"

Utter scorn, for him as a man and for his position, reverberated in her defiant question.

Instead of being infuriated, Zayn smiled. He deserved that after his probing remark. Still, he found himself unwilling to give up this sparring match with her. With every back and forth, he knew he was indulging himself in something that was fundamentally against his principles. Against the little personal respect he had put aside for his wife's position.

But the compulsion was fierce, the urge too primal to be denied. There was something about her that called to things he'd never before experienced. "It is my business if we are going to consider this, Amalia. And I will not apologize for having lovers in the past."

He hadn't decided on a candidate yet. Technically, he was still a single man. Even if that line was very thin right now. He ran the tip of his finger over her cheek. Her skin was gossamer silk under his hands. "Every past and present aspect of your life is going to be considered fair game. There has been enough scandal in my life and I do not want to deal with jealous ex-lovers."

She didn't push his hand away. A fine tension began

to vibrate from her. "That's a double standard, and you know it."

Why didn't the infuriating woman just tell him about her past? What was this curiosity that drove him to learn about a woman he could have nothing to do with? "The world is full of them."

Chin tilted at a defiant angle, she stared back at him. "So let me get this straight. If I have my hymen intact, it will give me a few more points on this list of yours?"

The fire in her eyes, the soft tremble of her lips…it made Zayn think of sultry nights and damp, tangled limbs.

"I will tell you my expectations, then. You will be given a certain amount of freedom. Your primary role will be to present an image of a healthy marriage and to give birth to our children. An affair with another man will have disastrous consequences. The media will rip us into shreds and the country will be in uproar."

"Is Your Highness promising the same fidelity in marriage, then?"

It was already a fantasy, this game they were playing with each other. This pretense they were both playing at, knowing that it was leading nowhere. Only one thing they both wanted.

She had to know that he would never marry her. He had told her that. And yet, she was still here, provoking him, luring him in for a taste. An affair with him—was that truly what she wanted, then?

Even in the charade, Zayn wouldn't lie. "On the contrary, I fully expect that within a few years, the reality of our marriage and the pressures of this life will make us, if not hateful, at least indifferent toward each other. And when that day comes, I intend to seek another woman. I'm sure you'll be glad to not have to bear my unwanted attentions. I enjoy sex and I do not intend to give it up."

"And this is your idea of marriage? This is what you've been offering all the women you've been meeting all morning?"

"No. All those women already understood these terms and accepted them. They knew even before they saw me today, that that was reality. It is only for you I see the need to set the expectation."

"Because you think I'm naive enough to believe in love? To believe that a man like you will offer fidelity and respect and love?"

The cynical light in her eyes shocked him. Why, when she was clearly here with not so pure motives… "No, I explained it all because I thought it would tell you that I'm as unsuitable a husband for you as you are a wife for me. Marriage to each other would be war, Amalia, and I have enough of them to contend with in the other areas of my life."

"Wait, you thought I'd be heartbroken that you're rejecting me for the role of your wife and this is you softening up the loss for me?"

"Yes." Before she could skitter away from him in her outrage, Zayn cupped her neck and arrested her movement. The small indent at the base of her nape was the sexiest part of a woman he had ever touched.

He swallowed his shock at how swiftly lust rose through him.

Her breath fell in rough exhales while a tight stiffness entered her body. He held her loosely enough to not threaten her, leaving it in her hands if she wanted to move away. Other hand sliding to her waist, he exerted enough pressure to bring her closer to him.

Gorgeous brown eyes widened into innocent pools. Very likely, the vulnerability in her eyes was a well-rehearsed act, but still it turned him on incredibly. Pursuing one sophisticated woman after the other, sleeping with women who knew the score, Zayn had forgotten, or maybe he had never known, how hot this kind of vulnerability was.

He wanted to kiss her. He wanted to make her all flustered again. He wanted to see if she would taste sweet as her soft sigh said or tart as her words suggested. When it came to women, Zayn had always taken what he wanted, pursued models and actresses ruthlessly. He wasn't going to let this rough-around-the-edges woman slip past him.

"I'm going to kiss you, Amalia. This is your moment to go all outraged on me and call me a savage beast."

If possible, she stiffened even more in his hold. "I… refuse to provide you with any more entertainment. I was right in thinking that you would be just as bloated and corrupt with power as—"

Whatever outrage Amalia had amassed to fight the man's autocratic ideas and her own out-of-control senses, all of it disappeared as Zayn's mouth touched hers.

The scent and taste of him was an overwhelming assault on her senses. He tasted of mint and some dark potency that stirred everything in her to waking. Heat poured through her in rivulets as he pressed one tender kiss after the other, from one corner of her mouth to the other. The softness of his mouth—who could know such a hard man could have such soft lips?—was a delicious contrast against the rough scrape of his jaw, tugging Amalia's senses this way and that.

If he had kissed her with the aggressiveness she sensed within him, or if he had employed that sensual mastery that had made him a favorite lover of women, maybe she would've resisted.

But instead the soft flick of his tongue against the seam

of her lips, the kisses punctured by the sweetest endearments in Arabic, Amalia melted like an ice cube on a hot and sultry Khaleej summer day. He tasted her as if he was dying to probe all her beguiling secrets; he kissed her as if she were a treasure he had just discovered.

This supposed connoisseur of women requested entry into her mouth as if she was the most enchanting woman he had ever met. And sensible, rational, rarely discomposed Amalia fell for it all. She eagerly opened her mouth under his questing one.

And just like that, the tenor of the kiss changed. It went from a pleasant seaside breeze to an intense scorching heat wave. His tongue swiped over the moist recesses of her mouth, teasing and taunting her tongue to play with him. The stroke of his tongue over hers released a dampness between her thighs. It was what he had done with words, too. He had somehow provoked her, called the part of her that she didn't even know existed, made her revel in the moment, made her prolong what was only a dangerous charade.

He was seducing her mind.

He was doing that now, too. It was as if he knew to soften his aggressiveness for her, to slowly draw her out instead of demand. At least until she came to him of her own volition.

With a shamefully wanton moan, she sank her fingers into his hair and pushed herself closer to him. She sucked his tongue into her mouth just as he had done with her.

Large hands roved over her body now, tracing the ridges of her shoulders, the line of her spine, setting every nerve ending on fire. Urgent and aggressive, he stroked every inch of her to the same need. Amalia had never felt like this before and she didn't know how to stop it, how to gain control over herself or this madness that had overtaken her.

All she knew was that she never wanted to stop.

Her mouth stung and her nipples peaked to tight points, grazed again and again by the hard contours of his chest. His hungry hands finally stilled on her waist and he pulled her even closer. Mouth left hers, giving her a chance to breathe. "Point proven. You can huff and puff and act outraged but truly, you want me. And you can't see how all your self-control and rules about needing respect and recognition before attraction are out the window already. That's what all this feminist bluster is about, isn't it?

"It's not about my double standards but about your own conflict in wanting me when you do not want to."

If he had slapped her, Amalia couldn't have been more shocked. It was like being drenched in an ice bath to douse her overheated senses. Still, her body throbbed in all these newly aware places, slow to cool down.

With a disgusted growl, she pushed away from him and turned around. Lungs burned as if she had run a long distance, her mind blank under the onslaught of such heady pleasure.

She rubbed her palm roughly against her stinging lips as if she could get rid of his taste. A horrified sound escaped her mouth. Dear God, she couldn't believe she'd been kissing the Sheikh of Khaleej.

The thought of her twin rotting in that jail cell while she played ridiculous games with the man who held his fate in his hand made nausea whirl up through her throat. How could she have forgotten Aslam so thoroughly?

How had she gone from asking for help to a harmless pretense to climbing all over him like a vine?

"You're offended by the kiss. But I will not apologize for doing something both of us wanted."

She whirled around, his self-assured words scraping at

her. Could she blame him for thinking she was putty in his hands? "I'm not just offended. I'm disgusted with myself."

He laughed again. And this time the sound was redolent with mockery. "Because you got what you came for? Or because you enjoyed the kiss thoroughly?"

"What I came for?"

"You and I both know that you're not suitable to be my wife in any way or form. So the only conclusion I draw from your being here is that you came seeking an affair. It is not a secret, *anymore*, that I treat my women well."

The gall of the man to think she had expressly come so that she could lure him into an affair. Was there anything bigger in the world than the man's ego? "You mean you pay them for sex?" she hurled at him.

His mouth curled, a hardness entering his eyes. "I do not like games, Ms. Christensen. I do not find affected outrage of the kind you're displaying attractive at all. If you find my conclusion that offensive, why don't you tell me why you're here?"

This was it, her opening. To prolong hiding the truth meant resigning Aslam's life to the jail cell for who knew how long. And yet, Amalia hesitated.

Something in the glittering gaze, in the sensual but hard contours of his mouth, told her he wasn't going to like it. He wasn't going to forgive her easily and then offer to help with Aslam. She might have made it worse if the sheikh thought she'd made a fool of him.

She was completely screwed.

"I did not come here hoping to marry you. In fact, I don't think there's a couple in the entire world more unsuited to each other for marriage."

His hands behind his back, he looked at her as if she was one of his subjects. "My sentiments exactly. So I see only one reason why you would be on Ms. Young's list."

"No…I'm not one of the candidates lined up for your pleasure by Ms. Young. I would never allow myself to be presented like prize cattle for viewing."

His hardened jaw told Amalia she was only making it worse, but she couldn't stop. "I figured that much, too. Which is why I have to believe that you came here seeking a different kind of alliance."

"I'm not here for an affair with you."

"No?"

"A hundred times no. I came to meet with a state official about my brother Aslam's case. I have spent two months dragging myself from one state office to the other, hoping someone would listen to me. He is in jail for—"

"Ah…so you're a family of criminals, then?" His eyes were cold, flinty, his mouth a study in utter distaste. "Brother goes to jail, and sister inveigles herself into the palace under false pretenses. Is your father really a historian? Is anything you told me the truth?"

Amalia flinched. Her credibility was zero with him and she had no one but herself to blame. She softened her tone, hoping it would appeal to his good side. If he had one. "All I did was tell a white lie. No, I didn't even do that. I just didn't clear it up. I…couldn't pass up the opportunity—"

"Opportunity to do what? To get into the sheikh's chamber? To present yourself as a temptation?"

He looked so threatening right then, Amalia could practically feel the power coming off him. Utterly different from the man who had kissed her so tenderly, even from the man who'd laughed so openly. "Of course not! I don't want to kiss you much less want an affair with you. I have a successful career and do not need any favors from a man like you, whether given freely or in exchange for something else."

She now realized how fooled she'd been by the *Celeb-*

rity Spy! Article, too. Having read about the sheikh's escapades and orgy fests, she'd decided in her head that he was someone she could persuade and plead with.

But the man who stared at her with those inscrutably brilliant eyes didn't have a soft bone in his body. The last thing he looked like right now was a self-indulgent, reckless playboy the exposé had called him.

"I intended nothing like that. I was tired of waiting and I snuck in here out of pure panic. When I realized who you were, for a few minutes, I even completely forgot..." She flicked her eyes closed for a second. Not everything had to be revealed now, even if he knew what her reaction had been to him. Opening her eyes, she willed her tone to be matter-of-fact. "Aslam has been imprisoned unfairly for something he was only a marginal part of. He was angry at life and reckless and irresponsible."

"How old are you, Ms. Christensen?"

Amalia couldn't figure out what he was getting at. "That's neither here nor there."

"I can have your entire history in my hands in ten minutes."

Domineering ass! "Twenty-six, Your Highness."

"It's a little late to be all deferential, yes?" He folded his hands and leaned against the table. The crossing of his ankles stretched the black trousers tight against the length of his thighs, and Amalia had to force herself to pull her gaze up.

When was her body going to move past the fact that the man was insanely, knee-meltingly gorgeous and a domineering, arrogant tyrant who thought every woman was out to ensnare him?

"So your brother is, too. You know what I was doing at that age, Ms. Christensen?"

Partying with your groupies, she wanted to say, but she held her tongue.

He smiled then, as if he was perfectly aware that she was biting down on her tongue. Hard. "For three decades, there have been constant skirmishes between Khaleej and our neighboring country. I was at a weeklong summit, working nights and days to sign a peace treaty that would end useless bloodshed. Once the treaty was signed, I partied, hard. Your brother is not a teenager. He has to face the consequences of his actions."

"He doesn't deserve to spend the next decade in jail when the actual perpetrator—"

"What is your twin in jail for?"

How she wished she could offer a different answer, to stop the guilty flush from climbing up her neck… "Possession of illegal substances, with intent to sell."

Instant judgment pursed his mouth tight. Her heart sank. "There's nothing I can do about it. Sentences for drug possession and distribution are meant to be harsh. He shouldn't have been using if he doesn't have the constitution for jail. And really, to send his sister to—"

Amalia covered his mouth with her hand, rage burning through her. And yet, seeing her white knuckles against his golden skin sent a shock through her, too. As did the warmth of his mouth searing through her palm. "I didn't come here to sell myself just to save my brother."

Long fingers gripped her wrist and pushed her away. "No?"

"I came hoping that your administration was a fair one. Even after I saw you and realized what you thought, I kept quiet because I thought you would be fair like you promised."

Tears threatened and Amalia pushed them back. No way was she going to cry in front of the callous man. He was picking his own damn wife from a marriage mart, like he was picking an outfit for the next week. The minute she'd realized that, she should've known he was going to have no sympathy for her case. It was clear Sheikh Zayn Al-Ghamdi had no heart. "I should've known when I spoke to your cousin that you'd be no better than him.

"Aslam is serving the sentence for what your cousin did. He took that package from him because he couldn't refuse someone 'so cool,' in his words, and yes, because my brother is a reckless, foolish idiot who didn't know who he was trusting. Your government is bloated with corruption and no wonder *Celebrity Spy!* exposed the truth of you like that.

"I wouldn't be surprised if the entire Al-Ghamdi family is a bunch of corrupt, drug-trafficking, womanizing men bloated with power."

CHAPTER THREE

"THAT IS ENOUGH, Ms. Christensen," Zayn retorted in a tone that would brook no more nonsense. "It is my family, the royal house of Al-Ghamdi that you speak of."

"And you're above law, is that it?"

"My family has its share of hangers-on and lazy fools, Ms. Christensen, like anyone else's," he added drily and had the satisfaction of seeing her flush.

He had always thought his cousin fell into that category.

A harmless one though...

No one in his entire life had spoken to Zayn like that. Even when he was learning to walk, he'd been the prince, the royal highness. Mirah had been born ten years later and though he shared an affectionate relationship with her, she'd never challenged him or provoked him.

Growing up, and even after he'd gone to university, Zayn had never really had a confidant. No one who had the guts to call him on his ego, or arrogance or his sense of importance.

Even his rivals, Xander, Benjamin and Dante, who were probably the only people on the planet who weren't intimidated by his title and all it entailed, still addressed him as Sheikh.

Infuriated as he was, he couldn't help notice one thing.

Ms. Christensen believed her brother to be innocent.

And her loyalty to said foolish, imbecile brother seemed to be absolute.

Being dedicated to his own sister's happiness, it was a trait Zayn had to admire in the woman, if nothing else.

Since his temper was dangerously close to tipping over, which was a rarity in itself, he decided he needed a breather from her. And from the annoyingly lingering taste of her.

Now that he was thinking rationally again, he realized there had been a certain lack of experience in her kiss. Dare he think that annoying innocence, that vulnerability in her glazed eyes as she looked up at him, was real?

His mind wanted to wander in too many distracting and interesting directions and Zayn curbed the urge.

A suitable wife who would fix his image in the people's eyes, that was what he needed, not a conniving waif on a wrongfully guided rescue mission.

His gaze resting on her thoughtfully, he picked up the phone on the desk. In minutes, security would guard both the entrances to the office. He didn't trust her to not escape or bamboozle some other unsuspecting man into helping her.

"You will stay in this room until I return, Ms. Christensen. If you try to leave, the guards will manhandle you to stop you and then you will cry brutality at the sheikh's hands. I would like to really not add anything more to the headache you're already causing me." Truly, his head was beginning to pound in earnest.

Damn it, he should have never kissed her. He could not show even a small weakness, could not let her have any power in the strange dynamic between them.

The woman seemed extremely resourceful when it came to cunning.

To lose his head and kiss her was one thing. But to have

not believed his own instincts that something was odd about her from the beginning, bordered on foolishness. Foolishness that could cost him another scandal that his image couldn't risk and worse, Mirah's happiness.

She sprang toward him with a jerk. Lilacs, that was what she smelled of. Zayn took a deep breath before he could restrain the foolishly indulgent impulse. "Wait, you're imprisoning me here and leaving?"

Deep satisfaction filled him at the panic in her eyes. Finally, another way to fluster Ms. Self-Sufficiency. "Nothing so dramatic, Ms. Christensen. I need to go deal capital punishment to the state official who kept you waiting and the guards who should have caught you before you snuck into my private office. Maybe I'll fire the entire incompetent staff. In the meantime, I didn't want you to escape. I still haven't decided how I'm going to punish you."

Her skin became a deathly white, her hands wringing each other. She blocked his path, her slender body radiating tension. "Capital punishment? That's barbaric. They probably were busy escorting the contingent of women you ordered to be brought here, back and forth. You probably can't see past your bloated ego but this palace is a maze and I'm sure they can't be everywhere at once and..."

Her chest fell and rose, drawing his attention to her high, deliciously full breasts molded under the soft cotton T-shirt. Her scarf that she had used to wrap loosely around her neck and upper body was trailing from her left arm, exposing what she'd been hiding all this time. Narrow waist that he could probably span with one hand gave way to full hips that made her prim pencil skirt into something altogether provocative. Tall and yet curved, the woman had a model's figure.

He waited, enjoying the gloriously outraged picture she presented.

"You tricked me!" she said in a voice full of outrage. "You purposely made me believe those men would be punished for something I did."

He laughed, surprised at finding humor in the whole farce. "You're not the only one with tricks up their sleeve, Ms. Christensen. Now stay put until I come back."

It took him twenty minutes, fifteen minutes too long in his opinion, to surmise the situation.

One of the staff members who knew someone in the legal department had scheduled a meeting with Ms. Christensen. When Zayn had questioned how the woman, a stranger to Khaleej, had known to not only contact the said official but also to arrange for a meeting with him to obtain her brother's release, his personnel had all frozen in terror.

Finally, the shaking man had come forward and said that the request for meeting had come from someone higher up in the department. Specifically on the recommendation of a Massimiliano Ricci.

It seemed at least that part of her story was true.

Zayn vaguely remembered meeting the Italian businessman, known for his cutthroat business tactics. That Amalia had gained a meeting through him did not surprise Zayn in the least.

Was she his girlfriend, then? Didn't the man know what a menace the woman was to herself? Because if she were Zayn's, he wouldn't have let her roam Sintar alone for two months, even if she had been born here.

Nor would he have let her dog the steps of the unsavory crowd that her brother seemed to keep company with. What was her father thinking?

The next thing had been to have someone find him the case file on her twin brother. Which had taken a wasted ten minutes, which he couldn't really blame on his staff.

Lost in the beguiling scent of the blasted woman, he had forgotten to ask what her brother's last name was.

Finally, he had her brother's file and a staff member finding the identity of her father. The part about her father was true, too. Professor Hadid was very well known and respected in his circle.

Drug Possession. Intent to Sell. Waiting to be sentenced.

It wouldn't be anything less than seven years, Zayn knew. He'd been one of the members on the committee who had asked for harsher sentences on drug trafficking in Khaleej.

When Zayn had tried to reach his cousin, however, he had been informed by his aunt in a vaguely roundabout way that he was out of the country. Which really didn't tell Zayn much. His cousin Karim had never amounted to any good for all his life, but could he have let an innocent man take the fall for one of his activities? It was another headache he did not need right now.

Armed with a vague sense of discontent, Zayn returned to his office.

Amalia—he couldn't refer to her as Ms. Christensen now that he knew how potent the taste of her mouth was—was standing at one of the tinted windows, looking out into the courtyard. The fading sunlight of the evening drew a provocative outline of her body.

Her shoulders were in a stiff line, her entire stance one of defense and alertness. Despite his preoccupations, Zayn couldn't stop his gaze from running down her back this time. She was fully covered up, even though that custom had more or less been banned from being required in the last decade.

And yet the flare of her hips, the curve of her bottom, made the pencil skirt the most provocative thing he had ever seen on a woman.

He had met more beautiful women, more charming ones, women who knew how to be seductive and yet feminine at once.

She was none of those things and yet he hadn't lost his mind over a woman like this in a…actually, never. He did not like anything random in his carefully controlled life and he didn't like this strange reaction to her, either.

It made his voice harsh as he said, "I have looked at your brother's file and I have spoken to the official you were supposed to meet."

She turned around. Her hands wrapped around her midriff, under her breasts, unconsciously pushing them up. "And?"

Zayn forced himself to focus on the anxiety that pinched her features. "The evidence against him is pretty tight. And this is not the first time your brother has been in trouble with the law."

"I know. But they were petty things."

"Defaming public property, heading a strike at the university, unruly behavior in a mall…it seems like he was building his repertoire since he was fourteen. I even spoke to the detective who put together this particular case and he assured me that he was thorough."

"I never said the evidence against Aslam wasn't damning. I spent two months talking to everyone connected with that arrest. I…dogged every official who was connected with it in the lightest way. Aslam took a package from your cousin minutes before the police showed up. Which, apparently, your cousin knew of."

"You talk as if you were there."

"I believe my brother. And my research was thorough. I tracked down the third friend and then fourth. Their accounts of the incident were not the same but definitely suspicious. They seemed to want to help Aslam but when

I asked them to come forward, they became slippery."
Frustration made her voice hard. "It's obvious that they
are afraid of your cousin's connections."

"Did you not think once if it would be unsafe to find and
accost these men? What is your father doing in all this?"

"He is busy with his career and his family, not that I
asked him for help. When I did ask him to talk to someone
in the palace, he told me he believed in the justice system.
And I took acquaintances with me every time I went into
new places of the city and never at night.

"I'm independent, Sheikh, not foolish. You, like a lot
of other members of your sex, seem to equate the two."

"Give me the names of these men."

She nodded, glad that finally she was getting somewhere. "If you tell me when you find them, I can persuade
them to speak out maybe. They seemed receptive to my—"

"You will stay out of this investigation and will not continue it anymore, either."

"I can help."

"Even though your accusations have no basis, I will
check with my cousin. But he is right now out of the country and there's nothing more I can do about this for the
moment."

"Can't you command him to return? You're the sheikh,
aren't you?"

Zayn threw the file on the desk and walked toward her.
"On the word of a woman who has told me nothing but
lies since I laid eyes on her? Who insists on insulting not
only me and my title and my position, but even my government and my judgment?"

Every inch of her rose to attention at his compelling
stance. "You're not being fair. My behavior toward you
should not affect Aslam's case. Not if you were truly intent on seeing justice carried out."

"That is true. But my hands are tied right now. Return to your job, or your country or wherever it is you came from. There is nothing more you can do for your brother."

"I'm willing to apologize for my deception, if that would assuage the dent to your ego."

"You offer to apologize in the same sentence as you insult me again. And there is no dent to my ego, Amalia. You are a nuisance in a very busy schedule. And now I will stop you from being one."

"You're forcing me, Your Highness."

"Into what?" He frowned, not liking the determined glint in her eyes. "I'm making it easy on you. Despite my misgivings, I gave you what you asked for. Once he returns, I will talk to my cousin, although it might be several months."

"But Aslam would have spent even more time in jail for something he didn't do," she repeated, her voice rising. Something like a growl escaped her mouth, and slowly, her breaths returned to calm. "Fine, so be it.

"But if I walk out of here, I'm going straight to the media. To a particularly nasty tabloid paper that is already very fond of you."

"And what is it you think you can offer the tabloid? How it felt to have kissed me? Will you join the ranks of my groupies, in your words? Will you tell them you tried to seduce the sheikh and failed?"

She went pale. Zayn didn't feel an ounce of regret. She was veering from nuisance to a bother now.

"No, I will tell them why I found the palace so particularly empty. I will tell them about your Ms. Young and her list of candidates.

"I will paint a very descriptive, colorful picture of what was going on here. That I saw women being brought to the palace, to be looked over by you and to be interviewed by you.

"And maybe, I will conveniently forget to mention the fact that there was a fiancé mart going on over here." She scrunched her face up, as if this was all a joke. "I don't know. I can't decide if it looks bad if I omit the fact and let them jump to all kinds of conclusions like I did or if it is worse that you are picking a wife from a list of eligible candidates."

"What conclusions did your devious mind jump to?"

"That you were building your own personal harem."

Zayn hadn't been shocked in a while, if ever. There were very few surprises in life for him. One extremely unpleasant one had been the exposé by *Celebrity Spy!* and the domino-like disasters it had started toppling in his life.

This was the second time. Of all the things in the world, the slender, pale woman to threaten him... His anger came slowly even then, like a discordant note underneath the shock coursing through him. Slowly, that shock dissipated, too, and he was thinking rationally again.

Only one course of action was suddenly visible to him.

The woman looked like an angel—all innocent outrage and yet, she had the guts to go up against him for her brother. There was no doubt. Zayn had never met a woman like her before.

"What you're saying constitutes blackmail. And the man you're blackmailing is the Sheikh of Khaleej, the most powerful man in the country. If you tangle with me, even your lofty connections in high places cannot protect you from the consequences. I could whisper a word and ruin your career prospects forever, if you do really have a career. I could make sure your father is never employed again by any university in Khaleej."

Her skin took on a pale cast, making her topaz eyes gleam like rare gems even more. "If I'm going down, I'll take you with me. But I will not let my brother rot in jail while there is still something I could do about it. I will not leave him to your tender, inconsistent mercies."

Zayn couldn't take the risk of this woman being out in the world, armed with the knowledge she had in her grip now.

He had made a bluff and she had called him on it. And at the end of it all, Mirah's wedding would be at stake, her future happiness at stake.

And there was only one way he could see out of this. He didn't like the decision one bit. He would have to put his plans on hold for a while. He would have to make do with this stubborn, irreverent, brassy woman, at least until things calmed down. Maybe even until Mirah's wedding took place and the furor about his image and his allegedly scandalous private life calmed down.

The woman had the balls to blackmail a sheikh. While she was still thoroughly unsuitable to be his mistress, much less his sheikha, she was at least equipped to carry out this pretense; she would survive in the fierce political wranglings of the palace.

"There is only one solution I see for the situation you have created, Amalia."

"Oh, I'm Amalia again?"

Now that he had come to a decision, her adversarial tone amused Zayn. He didn't trust the cunning minx one bit but he had to admit she was an entertaining diversion after the recent publicity fiasco. "Seeing that we are going to be closely involved over the next few months, maybe even years, it seems only appropriate that I call you Amalia." He took her stiff hands in his and pressed a kiss to the back of one hand. Her hand was cold and smooth against his lips, the tremor in her fingers going a long way to smooth his ire.

She jerked her hand back as if burned. Her feet stumbled

in her anxiety to get away from him and he caught her by the waist. A sudden, raw image of that indent of her waist bared naked to him came with such forceful mastery that he loosened his hold on her.

The rough rush of her breath only heightened his awareness of her, the soft but unyielding femininity in his hands. "Now who's talking crazy, Your Highness?"

"I have to insist you call me Zayn. Or else it is going to look very suspicious. Whatever our differences in private, Amalia, we have to put on a good show for the public and the media. The chemistry I feel between us should help with that."

This time she pushed away from him again, and took several steps more. He laughed and she glared at him. "And I insist that you tell me what the hell is going on in your twisted mind right now."

He made a clucking sound with his tongue. "And here I thought your intelligence might become an insurmountable barrier in our relationship."

"What relationship? And for God's sake, if you're calling me stupid, then just do it in plain words."

"Noted for future. I am telling you that I have made my choice. You are going to be my future wife for—"

She pulled her wrap around her like a weapon and headed for the door. If Zayn wasn't blocking the door, he had a feeling she would have disappeared like the morning mist against a rising sun. If it stopped there, Zayn would have gladly let her go.

But he knew, as surely as the fact that he was taking a huge risk with her, she would not simply give up on her brother because she was attracted to the sheikh. At least, keeping her close, he could mitigate the risk she presented to his plans.

"Like hell I am."

"We will have to clean up your language, *ya habibiti*. Or no one will believe that it is a love match."

"I'm not your dear or darling. You think the world is foolish enough to assume Sheikh Zayn Al-Ghamdi is capable of falling in love?"

"I like that you're able to understand me so well already. Since it will be impossible to convince anyone that marrying you is advantageous to me in any way, we have to resort to the instant-love, must-marry approach."

She came toward him then. The anxiety and panic in her eyes went a long way toward pacifying Zayn. "I cannot marry you."

"I'm not offering the option to you." He let his upper lip curl in distaste. "I stand by my word. You're thoroughly unsuitable to be my wife. But you have very cunningly made yourself into a liability for me. A liability I have to take care of, at all costs.

"If I let you loose in the world, I have no idea what that tart mouth of yours will do. If I keep you, a strange, unmarried female in the palace, there will be talk about it. So, this is the only solution that is acceptable.

"You will be my fiancée, for all intents and purposes, until I say otherwise. And you will do so with grace and sophistication, and you will do the Al-Ghamdi family and Khaleej proud. When I deem it wise to release you on the world again, you will leave Sintar and Khaleej."

"I refuse to participate in this charade."

"The other option is to imprison you, too. Maybe I can have a special cell built for you by your twin's side. Believe me, Amalia, that idea fills me with immense pleasure."

"That's blackmail."

"Quid pro quo."

"I…no one will believe that you chose me. I might choke before the first week is up. And how do you know

I won't still go to the media, that I will trust you to do the right thing?"

"You won't jeopardize his chances of release." He still could not believe that his cousin would let an innocent man take the fall like this. "I know how strong the need to ensure your sibling's happiness could be, especially if you are the stronger one."

"Aslam is not weak. He…just, he never recovered from our parents' split."

"You were just as young."

"I learned to manage."

He laughed again. *"Can respond with calm and reason in extreme situations,"* he said, mimicking her earlier tone. "Think of it as a challenge in your job."

"Fine, but only if you promise that you will look into Aslam's matter. And not after months or years, but immediately. Order your cousin home. Have my brother put in a minimum-care facility."

His face hardened. "If he is guilty, Amalia, I warn you now, nothing you do will make me help him."

"I know that he is not guilty."

Stubbornness could have been defined with this woman in mind. "Fine. I will look into it. But remember, one toe out of line in public or in front of anyone else, one small glimpse of that irreverent attitude toward me in front of anyone else, and I will make sure Aslam never sees sunlight again.

"No one should suspect that this is a farce that came about because you had the gall to blackmail the sheikh."

Eyes wide in her expressive face, she nodded. Irritated beyond measure, Zayn left the office. Before he was tempted to either kiss or kill the woman.

Neither impulse was one he could give in to, at least in the near future.

CHAPTER FOUR

"His Royal Highness Sheikh Zayn Al-Ghamdi commands your presence for dinner in his private garden…"

Amalia barely swallowed her gasp as the guard delivered his message with a straight face and left her standing in the sitting lounge of the suite she'd been shown to two evenings ago.

She hadn't been allowed to go back to her hotel to collect her things. No, she'd been marched straight here, to this wing of the palace, and her things had been brought to her so quickly that she'd barely even missed them.

And then she'd been left to stew in her doubts and anxiety for two whole days, while guards stood outside her suite. Finally, forty-eight hours later, he was deigning to see her.

Commands, not requests…not even invites… No, *commands*. How she wished to throw the sheikh's imperious command in his face and march out of the palace and straight out of Khaleej. How had she let herself be embroiled in such a crazy scheme that was worthy of… *Aslam*?

No, not even Aslam, she was sure, would have resorted to blackmailing the sheikh, of all men in the world. A twisting knot in her stomach gave her pause.

No, this crazy, out-of-control impulsive behavior was more like her mother. Every time Amalia had brought up the issue of her visiting Aslam in Khaleej, her mother had gone into one of her tantrums.

To give in to that urge and kiss him like that, to tangle recklessly with a man like the sheikh even in the most harmless way, this was a side of herself she'd never known.

Not her. Never trustworthy, reliable, calm in the storm Amalia.

But given that she'd learned what a hard man the sheikh was, she had taken the best option available to her, even though blackmail firmly put her on the other side of the law. If she had walked out at that moment, not that he'd been willing to let her go, she had no doubt that he wouldn't have wasted another minute on her or Aslam's case.

When it came to being his fiancée, she decided, looking through her meager collection of clothes, it was best to take a pragmatic, Amalia-esque approach to that, too. She would consider it the most difficult job she'd ever worked and he the most aggravating boss ever. That would define the boundaries, put all the checks in line. She had never put a toe out of line with a colleague or a boss ever, and if she thought of the sheikh that way, too, she'd be able to keep a professional distance.

She'd never done anything to jeopardize her career. Even when there had been a chance to build something. This had to be the same.

A professional fiancée, yep, that was what she had to be. Give a good grade performance and expect a raise. Well, in this case, a release.

Feeling a little more in control of herself, she did a few squats and lunges to get blood flowing. Being cooped up inside, even if she was being treated like a special guest, didn't suit her.

She finished her shower and dressed in another long-sleeved, navy blue Henley top and a long skirt, wrapped a thick colorful scarf she had bought in one of the street markets around her neck and chest and touched her mouth with lip gloss. Since the dark blue top and black pencil skirt made her look far too monochromatic, she pulled out the gold-plated jangling bracelets that Massi had given her for Christmas and wore them on her right hand. Her gold-plated watch went perfectly well with the bracelets.

A consummate professional with just a little personal flair, she felt sufficiently armored.

The welcoming table as she entered her suite with a gold-tinted tissue box, a hairbrush with a detailed design on the frame and a gleaming bronze hand mirror that looked like it was at least a hundred years old, had hit Amalia with a sudden bout of nostalgia.

It was an old Khaleej custom. A memory of her mother maintaining a table like that in her bedroom for years after they had left Khaleej came rushing at Amalia. Any doubts she had faced the last two days about contacting her father and telling him her whereabouts cleared away. Her mother had grieved over him and her love for so long, never being whole again.

And he hadn't even asked after her since Amalia had been here.

Hardening her heart, Amalia walked out into the corridor. Instantly, the guard followed her.

They walked away from the main palace and the administrative wing, through an open courtyard and a tiled path amidst a beautifully manicured garden. And with each step they took away from the palace, Amalia saw the shift in the architecture, the subtle differences even in the surroundings.

The abode they came to finally seemed to spring out of the ground.

There were no pretentious gold-plated carvings, or

heavy, outdated pieces of furniture here. It was as if she walked from an older Sintar to a new Sintar.

Now, as the guard led her toward where the sheikh waited, Amalia felt that same feeling again. Stained glass and arches, the typical elements of Khaleejian architecture, were all there but used with a modern, almost whimsical touch.

As if the architect had wanted to free himself from the constraints of tradition and yet found himself integrating them in his design anyway. What it ended up being was a flawless blend of tradition and modernity, married by impeccable design and taste.

They rounded a bend and came toward a huge, beautiful aqua-blue tiled indoor swimming pool, the bottom of which was a mosaic tile pattern that looked like a Persian rug. Moroccan-style lamps dotted the perimeter of the pool.

With a sense of wonder, Amalia realized the pool was the heart of this building, or the home.

The inner courtyard was surrounded by richly carved wood on multiple levels and hanging plants. There were cozy nooks and crannies everywhere, with built-in seating areas comfortably accessorized with pillows, carpets and planters.

The blues of the water and the greens of the plants created a beautiful slice of paradise, a private paradise, she realized with a sudden dismay.

This was the sheikh's personal space. The contrast between the hard man she'd met the other day and the cozy atmosphere of this space, made it difficult to marry the two. But she'd be willing to bet that she was the only woman who had ever been allowed in here.

The guard slipped away.

It took all of her determination to see Aslam released

to put one foot in front of the other and continue toward where the man himself waited.

He was wearing a full-sleeved, collarless shirt in a rich brown, which made his skin gleam like burnished gold. Dark blue jeans hugged his lean hips in an entirely too sexy way. Dressed down like that, he should have passed for an average man, an approachable man. But as she had already realized, the clothes or his position didn't make the man.

On the contrary, the simple clothes only accentuated the power radiating from him. Seeing him after two days, in which she had concocted a hundred different theories, all of which reduced the potent masculinity of the man to a thousandth degree, Amalia felt a fresh surge of amazement at her own daring. She must have been truly crazy to have tangled with this man and to have kissed him, to have pressed her body against the rock-hard contours of his...

He looked up and their eyes met.

Her gaze went straight to his mouth, her mind instantly supplying the taste and heat of his kiss. He had a soft mouth, the lower lip skating between hardness and passion. Both aspects controlled his life, Amalia decided with a perceptive leap.

Wasn't that what had shocked Khaleej and the world over? That the sheikh, who was supposed to rule his political life and his administration with ruthless control had such a wild, uninhibited, almost salacious private life.

Why had he kissed her like that? The question was beating a little drum inside her head. Had it been a case of proving a point, like he'd said? Or because she'd been conveniently present and men like that couldn't resist?

One kiss that lasted maybe a few minutes and she already felt as if he owned a little part of her. As though all he needed to do was look at her and she'd be reduced to a mass of sensations and feelings.

The way her lips were trembling, she knew he was looking at her mouth. And remembering the kiss, too.

Forcing herself to raise her gaze to his, she willed her body to cool down. There was not simply desire in his gaze, if it was present at all.

No, there was something more. A calculating assessment, as if he was taking her measure again. Of course, the man didn't lose his head over one kiss, like she'd been doing for two days. He probably hadn't even given her a thought considering what a busy man he was. For him, it had been a power play in that moment, a tactic to bring her into line. And she'd fallen into that kiss as if it was a lifeline.

Hands fisted by her sides, she didn't know how long she waited like that, staring at him across the pool that separated them.

"If you are thinking of jumping in the pool to cool down, I warn you, the water is very cold."

She looked to the calm blue surface jealously. "You have an indoor pool and it's not heated?"

He shrugged, raising those powerful shoulders. "This wing is not connected to any power line. It runs on a solar generator. The pool is not heated because I like a cool dip at the end of a hot day."

The wet gleam of his raven-dark hair told Amalia he'd done just that. Suddenly, the images of his leanly honed body stroking through the blue water, powerful thighs eating away the laps, made heat flush through her.

A drop of sweat ran down her back. The intense appraisal from his eyes, the hard glint of amusement, she wished she could make her gaze inscrutable as he did. "No air-conditioning? It must be hot as a furnace in the summer, then."

"The house was designed to take full advantage of the

prevailing winds in Sintar, which flow from the north and the west, to keep the air stream circulating throughout the entire house most of the year. That and the pool together, I do not miss air-conditioning."

"And if you do, it's a short walk to the palace you own. It's not like you don't have options."

He smiled, showing his teeth. The man even had perfect teeth. "Yes, something like that. What do you think of the house? You're my first official guest. Well, other than Mirah."

Instantly, an image of a gorgeous, golden-skinned beauty coiled tight around Amalia's throat. "Mirah?"

"My sister. But she prefers all the amenities and little luxuries that electricity provides so she was not impressed. She complains that her hair gets frizzy without a hair straightener every time I ask her to sleep here."

Amalia smiled, liking the sound of his sister. Good to know there was someone who wasn't bowled over by everything the sheikh did. Well, other than her. Most of the time, at least. "It's gorgeous, so light and airy. Nothing like I've ever seen in Khaleej, and yet, taking advantage of all its natural elements."

Something in his satisfied smile made Amalia look around the house again. He knew far too much about a house. Granted, he could be one of those particularly odd and grumpy sort of billionaires who needed everything just so and constantly micromanaged the people who worked for him. "Who's the architect?"

By this time, Amalia had walked around the pool. She stopped a couple of feet from him, still not prepared for that overwhelming awareness of him to flood her. He cocked his head, as if her question had taken him by surprise. "I designed the house."

Her mouth dropped open. But she'd known at some instinctive level. There was contentment, a sort of joy in him here. "You studied architecture?"

"And international finance."

"That's…*wow*. This open plan, and not using electricity, it seems you still have the Bedouin inside you."

Shock flared in his eyes. "I keep forgetting, encouraged by your looks and your attitude of course, that you're half Arab. Maybe it is the Bedouin inside me. I can't stand being walled up so much that you lose touch with nature."

"You clearly have good taste, Sheikh." She filled her words with exaggerated disbelief and had the reward of seeing him chuckle. "Have you designed anything else? You're also obviously very talented if my humble opinion amounts to anything."

A shadow flitted across his face, wiping the easy smile away. "I have no time for it. Even seeing this project to completion took me five years."

"Then why did you study it when you knew you wouldn't have time?"

"That is a very practical question, Amalia."

"I'm a very practical woman, notwithstanding my behavior the evening that I met you. But then I was desperate and it called for desperate measures."

"Now you sound just like my father." That hardness she'd sensed in him was in full force when he spoke of his father. Amalia wondered if he was aware of it. Probably not, for he seemed like a man who didn't betray himself—whether anger or any other vulnerability at all.

"You must have always known what your future was going to be."

"Since I could fathom the world around me, yes. But I have always been interested in architecture. Sintar has some extraordinary buildings, so full of stories and anecdotes. So I made a deal with my father. If he let me study architecture along with finance, I would not grumble about my duties and be a good sheikh to the people."

Amalia forced herself to smile when he glanced at her but she heard the thread of melancholy in his voice. From the moment she'd seen him, she had only seen what the world saw. A man born to extraordinary riches and incredible power, a man who enjoyed everything it entailed, and yet, that he had studied architecture knowing he would never be able to actually pursue his dream seemed like a very hard fact to digest.

A complete contradiction to the ruthless man who had cheerfully threatened to imprison her alongside her brother. Amalia wished she hadn't asked about the house. Wished she could somehow blind and mute herself and her senses to seeing him as anything but.

"Well, you have a very good career alternative to fall back on if you fail at this one." She didn't dare look into his eyes. "It seems like that exposé did a number on your... what do they call it, your job performance rating among your cabinet and your countrymen, yes? It's a sad fact of having such a public career, I guess."

The amusement in his eyes didn't hide the level look he sent her way. "*My* people, *my* country, Amalia?"

"Yes," she said without hesitating. "This has not been my home for a long time."

"And yet, here you are, fighting tooth and nail for your brother's release. How many times have you seen him in the last decade?"

"That is neither here nor there. All that matters is he needs my help."

He poured mint tea from a silver *dallah* and Amalia took a hasty sip. Refusing to look at him, she walked ahead. "What are we eating?"

"Lamb stew, chicken kebabs and wild pulao, with *bread pudding* for dessert."

Her mouth watering at the mention of an old favorite, she whirled around. "Oh, please God, don't tell me you're a fantastic cook, too, Sheikh?"

He stood before her, as if he was aware of her trick to keep a distance between them. "No, the chef just delivered it. What about you?"

"What about me?"

He took her elbow and guided her toward one of those comfortably cozy nooks. The press of her thigh against his sent her heart slamming in her rib cage. "You have a habit of getting defensive every time I ask you a personal question." He waited till she settled onto the knee-high seating and then lowered his wide frame right next to her. When Amalia tried to move to her right, he stilled her with his mouth at her ear. "Makes one wonder what big, dirty secret you're hiding."

She made the mistake of tipping her chin up, forgetting that he was right next to her. This close, she could see the golden flecks in his pupils, breathe in the scent of sandalwood that drifted from his freshly shaved cheeks. "I'm not hiding anything," she said in a croaky whisper. "I just don't think my life's been that interesting, say, compared to an illustrious person like you."

"And yet, I think you're an interesting contradiction at best."

His voice was even more potent than his words, the deep, velvety tone pulling her in. "At the worst?" she goaded him, desperate to break the spell.

"A cunning criminal, with the face of an angel," he said. He smiled when she glared at him. "You did ask."

He spread a napkin on her lap since clearly she was

acting like she was incapable of doing anything else for herself. "Eat."

Amalia picked up her fork and dutifully forked some wild pilaf into her mouth. The richly flavored rice and the nuts and raisins in it restored her balance. Without further prompting from him, she dug into the lamb. It was succulent and only then she realized how hungry she was.

A strained silence descended as they both concentrated on the delicious food. When she had finished the last morsel, she wiped her mouth and leaned back in her seat with a contented sigh.

He did the same. His gaze persistent on hers, Amalia was forced to meet it. "If I eat like that every day," she said, searching for something, anything, even if it was inane chatter, "I will need a new wardrobe."

"Speaking of wardrobes—" his gaze did a quick sweep over her body "—how many black pencil skirts and plain, long-sleeved T-shirts do you own?"

"As many as it takes to present a professional picture," she said, annoyed beyond measure. Did he have to find fault with everything related to her?

"I have a feeling you're not dressed so primly just because you were visiting your father's conservative homeland after over a decade. I think you always dress like this—all buttoned up and neatly covered away."

Amalia got up from the seat. Looking up at her from his sprawling position, he still didn't seem to be at a disadvantage. He looked like a pasha surveying gifts brought to him and disapproving them. Blasted man! "How is my wardrobe—?"

"You will choose a new one, of course." She stood there while he finished his drink. The open collar of his shirt showed a glimpse of golden-hued skin, stretched tight over lean muscles. She had a feeling her throat was always going to feel parched around him. "A stylist will meet you tomorrow. Take my advice, and let her dress you. We're going to be celebrating our engagement, not hiding from the world. My fiancée will have to be stylish, sophisticated. Not a woman who flaunts her femininity, nor one who hides it."

"I don't hide anything. I…"

In answer, he sent his gaze sweeping over her in such a thorough appraisal that every inch of her skin tingled.

"I'm dressed perfectly enough to be your fiancée or anyone else's."

"But I'm not any man. No one will believe that I would fall for a woman like you…"

"That's the second time you've said that. And I disagree. Maybe there should be a difference between the type of women you…bedded all these years and your adorable fiancée, yes? Maybe it is my rough edges that made me irresistible to your jaded palate?"

"It won't be your tart tongue. How sensually you kiss when your words are anything but." He handed out that little tidbit as if it were a survey he was filling out while even the memory of it scorched her. "Now, tell me, are there any skeletons in your closet I should know about?"

"Is Aslam a skeleton?" she quipped.

He didn't smile. "Jealous ex-lovers? Ex-fiancés? Broken-hearted boyfriends who might decide to make a sudden appearance?"

"That's none of your business."

"You will become the focus of a media frenzy within hours of appearing with me, Amalia. Either you tell me what I need to know or my advisers will find out. And believe me, reading about your current lover's unsavory past or nefarious motives is unpalatable in the extreme."

"You have the women you sleep with investigated?"

"Not if there is nothing to hide. My reputation, this charade we're beginning, is not a joke. I will not let you risk it."

"Is there anything left to besmirch?"

"What about Massimiliano Ricci?"

Amalia gritted her teeth to swallow her ire. "What about Massi?"

"You call him Massi?"

"I call him whatever the hell I want, Sheikh. My work, my life, they are not yours to dissect or to dictate."

"From now on, they are." Arrogance dripped from every pore. "That he placed such a call for you using his connections even after two months of not working says something about your relationship."

Jumping to conclusions about her seemed to be a habit of his. Or maybe that was what he did to women who didn't jump to do his bidding immediately.

The passing thought made Amalia's spine stiffer. She wished she could tell a convincing lie, wished she could feed the hateful man what he was asking for. But she had always been honest to a fault. The little white lie she had told him two days ago had to be the biggest lie she had ever told in her entire life.

"You will not understand our relationship with each other. And I will not deign to put a label on it for you." Maybe she wasn't good at telling lies, but she was getting good at hiding the truth. Some instinct inside her refused to answer what the infuriating man was asking, refused to admit that she'd never felt anything for Massi even when she'd wanted to.

His fingers loosened around her arm, thick lashes falling to hide his expression. "All I need to know is if he will create any sort of problem over the next few months, especially when he hears of our engagement."

Months in close quarters with the sheikh—battling wits with him and with her own willpower... Her heart sank to the soles of her feet. Massi's reaction to all this was the least of her worries. "Few months?"

"As long as it takes for Mirah's wedding to happen."

She frowned. "You're doing all this for your sister?"

"Yes."

"Why? What does your fiancée have to do with her wedding?"

"Her fiancé's family is very conservative. They did not like the lurid details that *Celebrity Spy!* made up about my love life. My mother heard talk of them canceling the wedding because they do not want to be connected to a family like mine."

Amalia would've enjoyed the pressure he was feeling if it didn't directly relate to her own fate. "So they dared to cut off an alliance with the ruling sheikh?"

"Her fiancé's family is old money. They care more about perception than they do about the truth."

"Then maybe Mirah is better off not marrying into such a family."

His smile dug grooves in his cheeks. "I would think the same if I didn't know that Farid's heart is true. He loves Mirah unconditionally."

"Your father has to have some power over all this, right? Why couldn't he persuade them that Mirah is not at fault for your escapades? It's not some kind of genetic defect that she might have."

"If it were up to my father, he would cut off the alliance completely. He thinks this...matter of Mirah's love is causing far too much inconvenience to me."

"Because a son ranks higher than a daughter?" she said bitterly.

"No, a sheikh's duty ranks much higher than love." The

setting sun played shadows on his face, making him look harsher. "Love has no place in any of our lives."

"But you're going to all these lengths for her?"

"Yes, because I want Mirah to have this happiness. My life should not adversely affect hers."

"I don't understand this." He called her a contradiction and here he was. His eyes softened every time he talked about his sister. "You were looking over women that this mysterious Ms. Young sent you as if you were picking up vegetables at a bazaar. And yet, you want your sister to marry for love? Something does not add up."

"My sister's life and mine are different, Amalia. They always have been."

"So all this was damage control."

"I intended to marry, yes. The exposé brought the time forward, is all. All jokes aside, you will dress the part of my fiancée. I have a two-week trip to Europe, which should work very well for our first public appearance together. You will look besotted and beautiful and convince the world that you're absolutely in love with me."

"That might be a tall order now that I know what a hard-ass you are."

"Then remember the fervor with which you were moaning when we kissed. If you want a repeat, I'm happy to oblige."

"Why can't we just announce to her family that we're engaged? Why does all this have to take months?"

"We will let ourselves be seen together. The ring on your finger and your adoring looks should prove to the world that I've fallen for your charms."

Suddenly, he produced a sheaf of documents from somewhere. "What is it?"

"It's an NDA agreement. Better late than never."

Stunned, Amalia took the documents from him. "What

will you do if I break it? Sue me? I have nothing but pencil skirts and a savings account that's dwindling by the hour."

"I will tie you to a court case in Khaleej for the rest of your lifetime."

"Then I'll tell the—"

"You seem to think we're on an even keel with each other. This meeting was about setting the rules. Just because I answered your questions and laugh at your quips does not mean I will lose sight of our objective. Do not threaten me again, Amalia.

"I have more power. I will always have more power in this relationship. Please me with your performance these next few months and I will see your brother released if he's innocent."

"You're a bully, Sheikh."

"If that's what you need to call me to understand the situation, so be it." If looks could kill, Zayn had a feeling he would be ashes now. "Did you contact your father?"

A different kind of tension filled her body, her mouth flattening into a thin line. "No."

"You do not think you should let him know some version of the truth before he sees it plastered across some social media site? You are, after all, his daughter."

"He won't care."

"I am sure he will—"

"I won't be told what to do in this, Sheikh. I don't care if you throw me in jail for the rest of my life. I'm not answerable to him. And I'm answerable to you only as long as Aslam is in jail.

"And speaking of whom, I have to see him before I leave."

"Not possible. I will not risk you leaking everything I'm trying to hold intact in an emotional moment with your brother. Believe me, Amalia, Aslam is barely suffering where he is. In fact, this might be a good lesson in growing up for your brother."

"That's not for you to decide."

"It will be precisely I who decides if your performance is not up to the mark." He tugged until she fell against him with a throaty gasp. "You should start practicing calling me Zayn. I do demand respect from my future wife. But I do not want the world to think she's terrified of me."

Outrage flashed in her eyes and her mouth curved into a snarl. "I hate you, Zayn. How does that sound?"

Letting her go, Zayn laughed. Now, all he had to remember was that Amalia was still a wild card, the wildest bet he had ever made in his life.

He didn't doubt for a minute that she would leak the entire story to a rapt news reporter in the future if she thought it to her advantage, if this whole issue of her brother's case was not resolved to her satisfaction.

The threat she represented was enough to douse Zayn's interest like a dip in that cold pool. He would have to ensure that she didn't remain a threat to his reputation, or Mirah's happiness, even Khaleej's stability.

"I think I should tell Massi the truth."

"What have you told him so far?"

"I emailed him that certain things were going out of my control. That I would not be able to return in a month."

Every time she mentioned her boss's name, he felt a tight knot in his gut. "And?"

She sighed. "And if I know Massi and I do, he's not going to like it. Neither is he going to believe that I fell in love with you so suddenly. It is better I tell him the truth—that this is nothing but a show."

"Absolutely not." Zayn moved closer to her, the tanned sheen of her smooth skin an invitation. But he resisted the urge to find out if it was as smooth as it looked. "This is between only you and me, Amalia. Not even my closest adviser is going to know that beneath your prim manner is a cunning blackmailer.

"Whatever relationship you had with Massi was finished the moment you considered blackmailing me."

Taking her to bed, much as his body was already weaving fantasies about it, was not an option.

And with the media frenzy surrounding him being what it was, he could not go near a woman until all this was wrapped up to his satisfaction.

Whether he liked it or not, celibacy, for at least a few months, seemed to be the order of the day. *Never succumb to weakness or another's will*, had been beat into him from a young age. He played hard because he needed to let loose, to cope with the pressures of his life, not because he was of weak will.

A few months with a fake, extremely annoying fiancée was a short price to pay to ensure Mirah's happiness.

CHAPTER FIVE

AMALIA TRIED TO restore some calm through her usual breathing exercises on the Al-Ghamdi private jet as she and Zayn winged their way to Paris ten days later, but the ritual that had always helped her maintain composure in the face of her mother's swinging moods and her declining health in the last two years, failed to help her at all.

She was anxious about Aslam, about the coming charade, about her attraction to the man on the opposite side of the craft and even being equipped with all the tools to face the world and the media as the playboy sheikh's adoring fiancée didn't help a bit with that anxiety.

Ten days in which a stylist and a beautician had been sent to bring her up to scratch. She wouldn't have admitted it to Zayn under the promise of death, but Amalia had loved the Parisian stylist and her chic sense of style. Instead of forcing her views on how the sheikh's supposed fiancée should look, the woman had helped Amalia choose dresses and accessories that fit her sense of style. It had been like being on one of those super-trendy makeover shows without the cringe worthy being-on-TV part.

No expense had been spared on her new wardrobe, which included only designer dresses and shoes, handbags and even hats for different occasions. It was neatly stowed away at the back of the luxurious jet. A square-cut diamond in a solitaire setting had been delivered to her suite, with the same aplomb as a non-fiction book she'd requested. Hoping that it would fit all wrong so that she could send it back, she'd been dismayed when it slid on perfectly.

Now its cold weight on her finger felt like a chain around her neck, a constant reminder that she was taking part in a dangerous charade.

Refusing to give in to Zayn's all too possessive and personal order to not cut her hair, Amalia had asked the woman if a shorter hairstyle would serve her better and had received a very stringent, almost offended reply in return.

The stylist had fingered her long locks and told her she had hair like spun gold and it would be blasphemy to the hair gods to cut it off. Instead she had cut it into layers so that the shortest framed Amalia's face. Again, Amalia couldn't ignore the fact that it had been something she had been meaning to do for years and had not gotten to it.

From then on, she had realized it was a waste of energy to protest and had thrown herself into it, at least the whipping-her-into-shape part, with proper gusto. She had been given a mud bath, a facial, a manicure and pedicure, in short, pampered from head to toe like never before.

The servants, obviously under the orders of the imperious Sheikh, packed away her work clothes. It felt as if her armor was being torn away from her. His comment that Amalia always dressed to hide herself hit her hard.

Had she been doing that? she wondered for the hundredth time.

All she'd received when she'd boarded the jet had been a cursory look from Zayn and a condescending nod as if to say he found her acceptable.

She was clearly losing her marbles because she'd been disappointed by that cursory look. Greedy for more, she had hunted down that *Celebrity Spy!* article again and apparently, Sheikh Zayn preferred sophisticated, confident women who knew all the rules of the game. Women who probably didn't run hot and cold at the idea of just one kiss, much less panicked about being his partner, even for a short while.

If Amalia had any doubts about whether he was attracted to her in any way, her meeting with his sister Mirah had put paid to that. Mirah had not just been surprised but shocked when he had introduced Amalia as his fiancée. Granted, some of it had been because of how sudden their engagement was. "You are a career woman. Wow, my brother truly does not realize what has hit him, yes? I have always felt sadness that Zayn would not even consider love as a factor into his marriage. But you…clearly, love is the only reason he chose you," she had said with a beaming smile on her face.

Just then, Amalia found herself chewing on those words. Why was it sad that Mr. Alpha Sheikh did not want love in his marriage? He probably knew any woman would run far and fast at the idea of loving him and had suitably adjusted his expectations.

As though called, pulled toward him by some invisible rope, Amalia found her gaze moving toward him. Thankfully, his dark head was bent to his laptop and she studied him greedily.

The wide breadth of his shoulders against the compact design of the jet's seat, the lean, powerful line of his thighs—Amalia got warm in her silk suit just looking at him.

The sleeves of his light blue dress shirt were rolled up to his elbows, displaying olive-skinned arms with a generous sprinkling of hair. Papers were strewn over the desk in front of him. Long fingers, fingers that had tugged at her hair, fingers that had rasped over her cheeks, tapped away at the keyboard in a somewhat stultifying way. As if he didn't quite know how to type.

The deepening scowl on his face made Amalia smile with a wicked joy. Apparently, Mr. Sheikh was not perfect at everything. She stood up from her seat and took the one opposite him. Even with the spacious seating and her adjusting her legs, her knees bumped against his. "Need a little help, Sheikh?"

He looked up, and for once his focus on her was a bit diluted. Good, she could handle him like this. "One of my PAs fell sick at the last minute and one has to stay behind in Sintar to deal with any contingencies. And the third one is useless. All she does is blush and mutter incoherently every time she lays eyes on me. I would have fired her if I hadn't been assured again and again by the rest of the staff that she's utterly efficient and hardworking in my absence."

He sounded so disgruntled but she couldn't manage a smile. "It must be a curse to be such a perfect specimen of manhood," she said a little acidly.

"You're more nuisance than a help. So return to your seat, say very little and just look perfect for the rest of the flight. Let us call it your job description for the next few months." His gaze turned away dismissively. "That pantsuit, while sufficient, is not good enough for the fundraiser."

Amalia swallowed the growl that wanted to rise from the depths of her soul. The dismissive prig! "I feel sorry for the woman who ends up marrying you, Sheikh."

"Don't. Some women like having a man who will take care of their every need."

A part of her was more than tempted to leave him to his hell, but a part of her, the part that had become extremely bored over the past ten days and the part that was acutely aware that there were six hours and eight more minutes left on the flight, and the stubborn part that wanted to prove something of herself to him said, "That software you're struggling with, we use the same program to manage Massi's schedule."

"It's not just the schedule. I need these reports sorted by urgency and importance and summarized for me. Not everything needs to end up on my desk. There are different departments that most of these requests can be routed to."

"Believe me, Sheikh, I can do all that, too."

"Why are you offering to help?"

"Even though you have been an utter a—" he raised that imperious brow again and she changed her word "—beast to me, you mean?"

"Did you talk this way to your Massi?"

She shrugged, refusing to accept or deny. Damn it, she should have never hinted as if there was more to it. "I'm offering to help because there are a million minutes to pass before we reach Paris and I've been twiddling my thumbs for ten days. Believe me, a makeover that you don't have to pay for is all well and good but I've never been this idle for so long. I'm bored to death and the guards you have on me don't even know how to play cards."

"They're not for your entertainment, Amalia." He let his gaze sweep over her face, something challenging in it. "There are all kinds of state programs here. And you did refuse to sign the NDA. How do I know you're not collecting material for your next blackmail scheme?"

Amalia didn't know why his lack of trust in her should pinch her so. Really, it seemed she was existing in some dream land. Why did she again and again find herself surprised by what a hard man he was? Why was it that she weakened with him when no other man had even come close?

She sat back in her seat, waiting for that emotional re-action to subside before she spoke. "You either trust me over the next few months, Sheikh, or you do not. Like you were so careful to point out, I have no power in this rela-tionship. And everything to lose.

"You can dress me in the fanciest clothes and threaten me with everything from jail to incarceration, but no one is going to believe this charade until you trust me. And you treat me, *no, at least pretend* like you value my place in your life."

"Of course you were feeling neglected. Once we return, I will arrange a vacation for you." Having her out of his hair, under surveillance, Zayn congratulated himself on thinking of it. It was the best way to minimize the damage she could do to the situation with her loud mouth.

That he was hiding from the problem was something Zayn refused to even consider.

"You're not packing me off to Siberia with two guard dogs. The one thing I wanted was to visit with Aslam and you vetoed it." She snorted. "I have worked for five years for a man who controls a million-dollar business. You... you pretty much run the country. I think I can imagine what a working day for you constitutes. I'm not complain-ing, just informing you."

"You are different from any woman I have ever known, Amalia."

If she had to hear that one more time, Amalia was going to scream. "So you keep reminding me, Sheikh. And the message has been noted, loud and clear. Now can we move on?"

"I will arrange for you to visit Aslam once we return to Sintar. On your word that you will not reveal anything of our agreement to him."

Now it was her turn to be shocked. "Clever move,

Sheikh. Dangle the carrot in front of the poor donkey. You're only using that to keep me in line."

"Now who has trust issues?"

The silence that descended was strained with so many things that Amalia looked away.

"Is it only me and what I provoke in you that has made you so combative, Amalia, or are you like that with all men, including your Massi?"

"He is not my Massi and I…they call me Calm in the Storm back at work. Did you know that?"

"I'd have just called you the storm. So it is me, then."

Such asinine satisfaction drawled in his words that Amalia wanted to do something violent. Which would only confirm his arrogant theory. She was a little afraid to test it, too. "We got off to the wrong start, yes. Which is why I think it is time to call truce," Amalia finished, admitting to herself that she had provoked him from the moment she had set eyes on him.

And to be brutally honest, he had behaved like a gentleman even though he had every reason to doubt her. Except the kiss. She still had no idea what that was about.

She stuck out her hand over the small table between them. "Since I'm not the type to hold a grudge, I'm waving a white flag… *Zayn*."

His name on her lips reverberated through the entire craft, as if some invisible barrier had been smashed, leaving something else in the air around them.

Amalia met his gaze and saw the infinitesimal widening of those dark eyes, before he lowered them to look at her hand. Slowly, he made contact with her right hand.

A curious swooping sensation in her gut, she suddenly wished she hadn't forced the issue. Only now when it was too late, did she realize that the sheikh and she being at each other's throats covered up a lot of things she didn't want to face.

Like her increasing attraction to him.

Suddenly, it felt like it was written all over her face and in the stilted silence between them. Just as she was about to stand up, he leaned forward in his seat, his legs bracketing hers on either side. "I do not know that I prefer my name on your lips, Amalia."

"Exactly what I was thinking. I think I'll stick to Sheikh."

Confined to her seat by his large body, Amalia shivered. Her breath was a languorous fire in her throat, her pulse skittering madly as his finger traced the veins on her wrist.

She'd never been so afraid to look into a man's eyes and see what they held, never been afraid of what was written in her own eyes.

He turned his laptop so that the screen was facing her. The software program she had claimed she was an expert on could have been written in Arabic for all she could make sense of it. "I will go through each of these and dictate notes about who should address it and the steps that need to be taken. Start typing."

She looked up then, shock stealing her words.

He raised those dark brows, the hard mouth twitching at the sides. "Problems already?"

Pulling her watch and bracelets off, Amalia put them in a corner of the desk and straightened in her seat. Tugging the rubber band she'd been playing with through her fingers, she pushed back her hair and gathered it in one hand.

A hard glitter in his eyes, the way he followed her movements, sent a pulse of longing through Amalia. It was hard to be in the company of a compellingly attractive man like the sheikh and not feel a feminine flutter. To not imagine all sorts of romantic illusions even if one tried to be sensible.

Indulging in a moment of weakness didn't mean she would pursue anything, Amalia told herself. Not that the sheikh wanted a personal anything with her. He barely trusted her, did he?

So Amalia clung to what did make sense. She opened a new Notes window and smiled at him. "I'm ready when you are, Sheikh."

CHAPTER SIX

THREE... THERE WERE three small white pearl buttons on Amalia's pink pantsuit and they were driving Zayn to distraction.

Every time she moved in her seat, which she did constantly, the thin blouse she wore under the deeply cut jacket stretched sinuously against her breasts.

It was the same every day, his awareness of her growing by the minute.

He fisted his hands by his sides, fighting the urge to fill his hands with something else. He had seen women wearing skimpily provocative clothes and still somehow look less sensual than the woman working away on his laptop, her brow tied in concentration.

Her long hair pulled into a high ponytail swung as her fingers raced over the keyboard.

The pantsuit was the height of designer chic, taking advantage of the long line of her legs. When she'd come aboard the jet, Zayn had felt a wave of startling awareness again. He'd heard reports from his senior aide and had chosen to avoid her, all the while telling himself that he was just too busy.

Now he knew why he had avoided her.

Ten days had not dimmed her appeal one bit.

From the buttons to the narrow collar to the silk that

didn't quite hug her curves, it was Amalia to a T—prim, buttoned up and yet utterly provocative.

He shouldn't be surprised by anything this woman did and yet Zayn was. He wasn't quite sure what to expect from her. What had she called the house? The perfect marriage of tradition and modernity?

Not even Mirah had seen his struggle reflected in his design. He, who prided himself on knowing himself and his mind, even he had missed it.

Her attire was the perfect blend of sophistication and the demureness that he sensed was an innate part of Amalia. That she'd managed to retain a sense of her own style and self under the obvious duress she felt at being his fiancée, at being thrust into the eye of the media from her average life, spoke to the strength of her personality.

By now, Zayn would have written off any other woman with such decidedly strong views. Yet, Amalia continued to persist in his mind and body.

Utterly covered up as every inch of her skin was, it still hadn't stopped him from losing his focus more than once. Her skin gleamed with the tan she had acquired, no doubt trudging through the city streets of Sintar and harrying unsuspecting males into answering her questions about her twin.

Even now, all he could think of was unbuttoning those buttons slowly while he kissed every inch of the silky-smooth skin he exposed.

He'd always compartmentalized his private life and his public one. Which was why everyone including his father and Farid's family had been so thoroughly shocked at some of the lurid stuff that *Celebrity Spy!* had said about him.

This had to be the same. Amalia was part of his public life, even though his reasons were personal. Ergo, he couldn't indulge in fantasies about her.

"Okay, how does this sound?" she interrupted him, her brow thoughtful. And then rattled off the press release she had volunteered to put together about a donation he was making to the Sintar General Hospital.

"It's perfect," he said, a little jolted again at the quiet efficiency with which she finished her tasks. Apparently, the woman was just as good at her job as she had claimed. Could he believe her word that he could trust her? "We'll break for lunch and start in a half hour again."

"No, I want to finish this summary for why you're denying the proposal for the Art and Education Center in downtown Sintar."

With a shrug, Zayn leaned back in his seat. He checked his watch and realized that they had been at it for three hours without a break.

Once he had realized how supremely capable she was, there had been no point in not using her abilities.

And of course, Amalia being Amalia didn't work in silence or peace. She offered opinions, sometimes in drastic opposite to his, and to their mutual shock, thoroughly agreeing with him on some foreign policy matter.

Piles of what he'd considered boring, menial tasks had been completed in a most engaging way, thanks to her efficiency and her interesting opinions.

True to her word, she hadn't even blinked at the grueling pace he had set. For a woman who wasn't aware of the intricacies of palace policy, she'd learned the administration's priorities and his personal policies on some of the administrative matters superfast. But of course, he had forgotten that she was very learned about Khaleej and its history and politics.

He wasn't fooled by her rejection of everything that was her father's heritage. Her anger only hid some deep-rooted pain but Zayn had no need to know or understand what it stemmed from. Her issues with her father were of no interest to him except for how they affected the outcome he wanted.

Amazing as it was that it had come from her, she was right. They needed to call a truce, if he wanted to pull this off. But the truce did not have to extend to exchanging their every dream and fear. She had surprised him that day in his wing but he would not veer off course again.

Zayn had never been allowed a confidant before and he was too rigid in his ways to want one now.

He ordered lunch and drinks for both of them just as Amalia finished and looked up. The little knot in her brow and the way she met his gaze head-on, he knew she was going to disagree with him again.

He had never met a more opinionated woman in his life. Raising a hand, he preempted her. The tight purse of her mouth made him smile. "I know you're about to launch into one of your lengthy opinions about what an old, dying beast Sintar and its administrative policy is, but I'm famished."

"Your country is a contradiction, Sheikh. Just like you are."

Did the woman not know her limits? Or was this her agenda, to infuriate and annoy him so much that he released her brother? "My country, Amalia?"

She raised a brow casually while her up-tilted chin betrayed her defiance. Two could play at the perception game, he decided with a smile.

"This will only take a minute, and the food is not here yet. And really, Sheikh, I didn't realize that your ego needed so much validation that you only surround yourself with yes-men."

He sighed. For all she looked like an angelic wraith, the woman was like a pit bull when she got her teeth into something. "Go ahead. You have three minutes before you lose my attention."

"That's not enough!"

"That's how long people usually have to convince me."

"You're a—"

"Two minutes and counting."

She looked down at the screen and back at him, determination written all over her face. "I don't think you should refuse to fund the Arts and Education Foundation in Sintar. Khaleej needs the kind of human development this foundation promises."

The depth of her passion reminded Zayn of himself when he had been younger and idealistic. For all she seemed self-sufficient, there was a charming naïveté to her. "Those funds will be more useful channeled toward health care. Education Reform will get its time."

"But you just signed off on what equates—" she scrunched her brow and Zayn's mouth twitched "—to ten million dollars for just the next three years toward reforms in health care."

"I just proposed it. The cabinet will still have to approve it. And the reason you're interested in that foundation is because it promises the kind of academic freedom for both sexes in all fields that is seen in the West. As progressive as my father and I have been, things move slowly here. I will alienate a bunch of cabinet members if I give the green signal on that."

"I say this threefold mission of education, scientific research and community development is just as necessary for Sintar. I've seen the development in infrastructure and health care in the two months I've been here. And I know that it is all attributable to you, Zayn, but Khaleej is going to be left behind in the global world if it does not also embrace a more global approach toward arts and education.

This wealth that Khaleej enjoys because of its oil and gas reserves is not going to last long.

"You will need an educated, qualified workforce that includes both sexes if Khaleej wants to continue its current healthy financial growth, and this center seems to be the right step in that direction."

"You are very passionate about this. Why?"

"Does there have to be a reason for pure common sense?"

"The more something is important to you, the more flippant you get. If that is your answer—"

"There is no other reason than that women should be allowed to pursue academic interests just as men do."

"Is that what your mother and father split about?" The question fell from his mouth despite his intention to stay out of her personal matters.

A bitterness he didn't like seeing at all entered her beautiful eyes. "For as long as I can remember of their marriage even before they divorced, they fought about everything. Prestige and perception was a big deal to my father and his family, and he forbade her from going back to her former profession. Her definition in life was to be a wife and mother. As long as her ambition or her dream did not interfere with those duties, she was allowed to have them."

Her placid eyes blazed when she said *forbade*. Within minutes, she transformed from an efficient PA to a tigress.

"How old were you when they divorced?"

"Thirteen."

"You were a mere child, Amalia. Things always look black-and-white. How can you be so sure why their marriage fell apart?"

"Because I was the one who lived with the fallout. For years, I listened to her while she…she grieved the loss of him."

"What was her profession?"

"She was a model at the height of her career when she met him."

"Then he was right to forbid her."

"Of all the—"

"This is not our fight, Amalia. But I'm being realistic. Professor Hadid is a venerated historian, a man with a powerful public image. Your mother would have known the sacrifices she'd have to make when she married him. I cannot see how she thought she could continue with such a controversial career and still be his wife."

"I don't think she cared so much about the modeling as much as being boxed in the little space he had for her in his life, the little he allowed her to do. That they were both strong personalities and came from different cultures, I'm sure, didn't help. It's a wonder that they fell in love at all."

"Lots of couples mistake good old lust with love. It is possible—"

Defiance radiated off her. And it was vulnerability, pain, that she hid beneath that defiance. "She never stopped loving him. Not until her last breath last year. He never once…" She closed her eyes, fighting for control over herself. "She made herself weak by loving him while he re-married and just made himself a new family."

Something in her tone broke through Zayn's hands-off policy and he clutched her hand on the desk.

The jolt from the contact was instant. Never had he felt a connection like this before. The more he tried to ignore it, the sharper his awareness of her became. Her hand was soft and slender in his big one and yet, there was strength in her grip.

Eyes wide pools in her face locked with his, brimming with emotion. The rawness of it went through Zayn like lightning shifted the entire picture of the sky. Her hand gentled in his, a little trusting, a little searching, and he felt some core of ice inside him, a place that he hadn't even known existed, thaw a little.

This new emotion that surged through him, urging him to take her in his arms...was this tenderness for her?

"Was her passing hard for you?"

She shrugged and pulled her hand from his. When she looked at him again, there was none of that vulnerability in her eyes. Curiously, Zayn felt both relief and a strange sense of loss. As if he had been granted a glimpse of something intense, something real, something he had never known before but it was taken away from him before he could fully comprehend it.

He wasn't sure he wanted to see that vulnerability in her eyes again. For it made him forget that she was not to be trusted.

"She gave up on life a long time ago." Guilt pinched her features. "Is it horrible of me to say I felt a sense of relief when the end came?"

Zayn could not answer her. Why had her father not shared this responsibility with her? If not for his wife, he still had some duty owed to his daughter. Even his parents, who were coldly practical with their own children and barely had any time or interest in parenting him or Mirah, still made sure they were taken care of by others.

He had been taught early on in life that he wasn't supposed to have any emotional vulnerability. And he completely agreed with that policy for someone in his position. Whereas Amalia, he was realizing, had seen only that in her parent.

"Just because he remarried does not mean he did not love her." He gritted his teeth hearing how sentimental he sounded.

Damn it, he had no taste for playing a hero, *her hero*,

and he was sure as the bright desert sun neither did Amalia want one.

"Whether he truly loved her at all, now that…I doubt." Challenge glimmered in her eyes. "Powerful men, men who are used to having the world at their feet, I fear, will say and do anything to have a woman they fancy. Did you know my father is a great lover of objects of beauty? I remember our home used to be littered with them, people from all over the country coming to see him. I have no doubt he thought her another collectible he should own. When she refused to sit on the shelf he provided for her, he discarded her."

And me. The unsaid words hung in the air, full of a pain she would never admit to. The more he learned of her, the more Zayn was sure that Amalia was one of those complex women he had no use for.

Still, the depth of her bitterness stunned him. "That is a twisted view to have of one's father."

"It's a realistic view of my father and what love can do when it is not returned in the same way. Don't tell me that you're a closet romantic, Sheikh. That you're privately agonizing over having to choose a docile, traditional bride." A brittle smile came to her lips, a determined glint in her eyes.

Her little remark bounced off his hide. "I heartily agree with you that the whole concept of love only complicates marriage. My parents' marriage is a success only because they had no expectations of each other. And so no complaints, either."

"What does that mean?"

"They married because it was an advantageous match for both of them. My father would get a bride from an aristocratic family and she her own sphere of powerful people to command. An heir for the country was the one common goal and once they had me, they pursued their own lives. My father had his mistress and his politics, and my mother, her own pursuits. Everything else, even Mirah, was a byproduct of the main goal of the marriage."

The look in her eyes made Zayn laugh. It was refreshing and a little addictive to see a woman not cater to his personality or his status. But he was sure it would soon lose its charm. Sooner or later, Amalia would lose her appeal to him. He was too used to docile, pleasing women who didn't question their role in his life. After all, no one woman had ever swayed his control, ever. "Why do you look so...combative even when I agree with you?"

"Because that's not what I said at all. That does not sound like marriage at all. That sounds like...a clinical agreement in a science-fiction novel. This is what you're modeling your marriage on, too, isn't it?"

"By all measures, their union continues to be a success, so why not?"

"If you don't even want your wife's companionship, why marry?"

"To produce legitimate heirs."

"And then you set the wife aside?" She didn't even wait for his nod. "Did your mother not mind it? I can't believe that any woman would willingly walk into a marriage like that."

He shrugged. "The number of women Ms. Young found for me says otherwise. As to Mother, if she didn't know it at the beginning, I'm sure she learned it soon."

"I could never marry a man like that."

"My wife will want for nothing. She will never have to work a day in her life, will be independently wealthy beyond imagination and will lead a life of globe-trotting, couture-shopping and feasting on mussels and duck confit of the highest order. And to top it all, she will have me in her bed, for as long as she wants me, to fulfill every little heated fantasy she might have ever had." Zayn had no idea why he was goading her like that, or why he wanted to hear her admit that she wanted him. Was it only a stroke to his ego as she had claimed?

Or was it all the confidences they had exchanged, this talk about marriage and love that stirred something inside him? That gave him a vague sense of disquiet in his gut?

All he knew was that he wanted to muss up Amalia's self-sufficiency, to push past the prickles and see what she was made of beneath it all.

He could see Amalia in that role, especially in that last scene. Amalia, whose heated fantasies he was making true. Amalia, who stared at him with naked longing, her long, silky limbs splayed invitingly over his bed, Amalia submitting that fiery temper and that steel core to him.

"Tell me you're not a little tempted." The hoarse need in his voice shocked him, the languorous heat flaring through him coming up against the self-control he prided himself on.

She tipped her chin, her gaze sweeping over him in a thorough appraisal that Zayn found incredibly arousing. As if she was weighing all the benefits of going to bed with him against everything else, as if she was imagining the same incredibly erotic scene… Was she so thoroughly naive that she didn't know the signals she was sending?

And yet, even as her topaz-colored eyes flared into wide pools, her sensuous lower lip trembled, she would even deny admitting it.

How thoroughly aggravating could this woman be! And yet, Zayn's awareness of her, his desire for her, only grew sharper.

He had months of this pretense, months of sparring with this woman before he would be able to remove her from his life. Before he could go back to the path that had been decided for him even before he'd been born.

Her openly hungry gaze said she was more than tempted, by him at least if not by his wealth, while her lush mouth said, "No. Not in the least bit. I have no romantic illusions, but I want a marriage between equals. I want affection, respect, a man who will deem my ambitions equally important as his own."

"That will never work in reality. Even if my duty to Khaleej didn't come before my personal desires, I would always be the aggressor in my relationship with a woman."

He saw the tremor that went through her slender shoulders, the shift to sensible reality as her gaze cleared. "Fortunately, not every man on the planet is so rampantly, aggressively masculine that he demands complete submission in every aspect of life, including…"

"Including?"

She looked at him and then away, but he caught her glance. Abashed.

The sound of his laughter reverberated in the confines of the jet. Feral satisfaction coated every breath he released as color poured into her cheeks. Her mouth pursed, her eyes flashing topaz fire at him, her lithe body radiating barely suppressed outrage, she made a delicious picture.

Zayn had never been so satisfied that his *aggressive masculinity* apparently could drive a woman nuts. Nor had the exposé been the source of anything but a headache. Until now. "So how many times did you read the part about my…voracious appetites?"

He wondered if smoke would come out of her ears if he teased her any more. "It's not a compliment, Sheikh," she offered in a dull voice. "It's more…a statement of fact."

"What will you do if you never find this ideal man?"

She shrugged, but by the little frown on her head, Zayn

knew she had never really thought about any of this. He wondered if her mother's poison had forever turned her off men, or if it was justification to never commit herself to one man. That meant she was either untouched or was one of those modern women who could have sex for the pleasure it afforded. Like he did.

Utterly hypocritical of him, but even in this indulgent speculation, Zayn found he preferred the first option far better than the second when it came to Amalia. He, who had always welcomed sophisticated and sexually mature women into his bed, women who knew what they would get from him.

What was beyond disturbing, however, was that his... *interest* in her didn't wane either way. The growing realization that Amalia might be innocent should have been a deterrent. It had been before, for he was not a man from whom women could expect flowers, or gentle kisses or wooing. Jewelry, designer clothes, the right word in a highly connected ear, and mind-blowing sex—that was more his forte. For the first time since he'd come into his own, Zayn had a sense of inadequacy, for Amalia wanted nothing he could give.

"I'm far too busy with my career right now anyway. And if I can't meet a man like that, I guess I'll stay single." Did she know how dejected she sounded at the end there? That her eyes ate him away even as she challenged him?

He leaned in, trapping her in her seat. She was forced to spread her legs to accommodate his frame, and the warmth of her body was a teasing rasp against his own. "You work all kinds of hours, you want this impossibly ideal man to marry. What will you do in the meantime?"

Her tongue snaked out and licked at that lush lower lip, while her gaze locked with his. "In the..." a little throaty rasp, "in the meantime? What does that mean?"

"What about passion, Amalia? What do you do when you get lonely at night, or when your body demands a certain kind of satisfaction that only a man can give?"

He leaned in a little more until his breath feathered over the rim of her ear. A little tremor shook her shoulders, her fingers tight over the armrest. Something she had dabbed on her pulse point in her neck floated up at the warmth of her skin, the scent incredibly arousing. God, did she smell like that all over? "Are you telling me you've never felt even a little stirring of sexual hunger? Or do you take lovers just for that purpose and discard them when you're done?"

"Passion is overrated," she whispered, and her breath caressed his cheek. In utter contrast to her words, her fingers rose to his cheeks, traced the line of his jaw. "All my life—" tips painted the palest pink now moved to the edge of his mouth and started tracing the curve of his lower lip "—I've seen the toxic effect it could have, not on one or two, but four lives."

Zayn felt like a predator caged and forced to sheath his claws while his favorite prey sniffed out around him. He wanted her hands on his hot skin, his tight muscles, those questing fingers on the part of him that was thickening in reaction to her touch. "But what about passion shared between two people who have no expectations of each other except mutual pleasure?" The question fell from his mouth before he realized he was asking it.

Naked longing swept across her face as her gaze rested on his mouth. "I've never...been tempted to throw caution to the wind."

Until now.

She didn't say the words but her rumbling breath, her trembling mouth, they spoke for her. Her chest fell and rose fast, her mouth moving closer and closer to his. Another breath and he knew he would plumb the taste of her lush mouth.

He tipped her chin up until she was looking into his eyes. Desire had darkened them; her nostrils flared. "If I kiss you now, I will not stop, Amalia. Come to me when you're ready. Come to me when you can admit that you want me."

Before he was tempted to lick the pulse that was hammering madly at her neck, Zayn got up from his seat.

His blood hummed with the thrill of the chase, his muscles tight against the heat flooding his body. He had never played at seduction this way; it had never been a chase like this where he didn't really know how it would end.

He didn't know what he wanted to do with Amalia, only that he wanted to tame that fiery spirit of hers, just a little. To possess a part of her. Maybe like his Bedouin ancestors had done with wild horses.

After all, he raised horses and he knew all too well what an edgy, risky venture it was to conquer the spirit of a high-strung filly without breaking its spirit. That it wasn't about submission but only establishing his dominance over the wild horses. Until they became one.

It was about possessing something wild for a few minutes in one's lifetime; it was about living. He was sure Amalia would club him if she knew that he had compared her to a beast. Amalia, with her stubborn notions and impossible ideals, needed to be shown how to live a little.

He had months yet with her, a devilish voice whispered in his mind but he squashed it for now. As he reached the entrance to the rear cabin, he turned.

She was still sitting in the seat, quite as he had left her, her chest still rising and falling. "Amalia?" he prompted.

"Hmm?" She looked up with a start and then blushed profusely. He let the amusement that filled him curve his lips, knowing it would aggravate her even more. Soft and vulnerable and a little too dazed to keep up her prickly defenses, he liked her like this. A lot. And from there, it was only a quick slide for his mind to imagine how she would be sated and pliable in his arms. Under his aching body. In his bed with her golden hair spread over his pillow.

"Do not forget to finish the rest of the correspondence, yes? You look a little lost there."

He didn't wait to see her expression. But he could feel her glare on his back, could imagine the steely set of her shoulders return. Zayn whistled a tune he didn't even know he'd remembered, feeling lighter than he had felt in a long time.

CHAPTER SEVEN

AMALIA HAD SPENT most of the week meeting more people than she'd ever want to meet in her entire life. The luxury hotel Zayn and she were staying at, while sharing the same suite, had views of the Seine and the Eiffel Tower on either side.

In the week since they had arrived here, they had been to a movie premiere and then reception with A-list stars, taken a quick flight to Dublin at predawn so that he could visit a stud farm on the outskirts of the city to buy a filly called Desert Night because apparently, her fiancé was not only a brilliant architect but also an expert on horse breeding and owned a world-class stud farm in Sintar, gone to a trade summit with some European leaders, and the culmination of the week was to be a charity fund-raiser at the Four Seasons in Paris again.

Of course, there was media coverage of their every movement. And the wave of news began from the fact that Amalia had been the only woman to have ever been the sheikh's partner for more than two days in a row. At the movie reception she had been called the sheikh's new arm candy. After returning from the stud farm, she'd been called his new mistress. At the trade summit, they had speculated that maybe she was the sheikh's new PA/lover.

Because of course what hardworking prince of the coun-

try didn't want to save money with a convenient woman doing double duty as both PA and lover... She'd made the tart remark thoroughly frustrated and overwhelmed by the press's interest in him and them.

"Should I be paying you double, then?" he'd said with a devilish twitch to that hard mouth that had made Amalia's knees wobble. When he smiled like that with that amused gleam in his eyes, the panorama of his entire face changed. And Amalia's resistance to him slipped a little.

Somehow she'd had enough working cells in her brain to throw a pillow at him across the room and retort, *"You don't pay me even for one role, Sheikh."*

His languid gaze had crept over her modest dressing gown that didn't cover her wobbly knees, her vanity's weakest point, and her horrible bed head until her pulse leaped into her throat. *"You'll let me know if you're interested in joining my staff or my bed, won't you, Azeezi?"*

Her heart thudding violently against her rib cage, Amalia had thrown the next thing she could find, her hairbrush, across the room. Laughing, he'd ducked in a graceful movement and said, *"You're exactly like Desert Night, Amalia. Prickly and wild-tempered."*

She had stood there a full five minutes after he'd left, the suite's silence amplifying what had to be the most absurd question she'd ever asked herself.

Had he been only joking? Did he really want her? Damn it, why wasn't she sophisticated enough to just ask?

But even the thought of showing her slowly fluttering interest in him sent Amalia into an ice-cold sweat. What if he rejected her and laughed at her? What if he was disappointed with her, the sexual sophisticate that he was?

The worst—what if he...had sex with her, was through with her the next morning and then expected her to continue their pretense like nothing intimate had happened between them?

Fortunately, she had very little time to think these roundabout, frustrating thoughts. The shock that she'd even considered it remained with her for the rest of the day.

Every movement of his and, therefore, hers, was so thoroughly followed that Amalia couldn't breathe in the whirlwind the first three days. Arrogantly ignoring her protests, Zayn had arranged for a PR and social media expert to coach her every day on how to manage her responses, on dealing with suddenly being the media's darling because apparently, only after three different appearances on Zayn's arm, her sense of style had been labeled stellar and unique, and on to how present even the best profile to the press.

Thanks to the prep and her own years of experience in dealing with a super-busy job and her mother's deteriorating health, Amalia hadn't blinked at the endless lessons in etiquette and protocol and the crash course in Khaleej's politics.

"For a woman who snuck into my office only two weeks ago, you're very good at handling this," Zayn had said, a grudging admiration in his eyes when Amalia had smoothly cut off a reporter for asking her about her fiancé's tastes for multiple bed partners.

The question had unraveled a disquiet in her gut, only she'd gotten better at hiding it. At examining it in the relative privacy of her bedroom at night, an all too familiar restlessness in her limbs.

The very idea of Zayn's colorful sexual life, the images supplied by her overactive mind, began to leave a bitter distaste in her mouth, a dark emotion whirling in her gut.

The media coverage didn't make Zayn even blink. He wouldn't have cared about the lurid exposé, either, if it hadn't affected Mirah's wedding. And if not for the pressure of the article, he would've had her thrown out of the palace and she would have missed this glimpse into his world, the different facets of the man beneath the sheikh.

Something, Amalia realized, was beginning to enthrall her more and more.

And when he wasn't attending dinners and lunches, the man worked like a demon. Of course, Amalia had known this and matched his punishing pace without a complaint.

She'd never lacked in confidence in her ability to do her job, but the respect she saw growing in such a brilliant man's eyes made Amalia feel as if she could conquer the world.

Every single night, he'd asked Amalia if she was up to working with him for a few hours. Always work with him, he'd say. He'd even started asking for her unbiased, bluntly honest opinion, as he'd taken to calling it on most matters. Those ended up being Amalia's favorite times she spent with him. For even though he was still the sheikh and she his unofficial PA, they quickly began to build a rapport with each other.

When he'd shared the blueprints for the trade and commerce center in Sintar, she'd been dazzled by the scope of it. When she'd asked him who was designing it, his expression had shuttered before he had answered that it was a firm out of London.

But it was the time when they weren't working and they weren't in the public that became the hardest. Even though those moments were few and far between.

No public declaration had been made, too tacky for the sheikh's personal team to cater to the media, she'd been told, and yet the flash of diamond on her finger after a week spent in Paris, the most romantic city in the world, and the fact that she appeared with the sheikh at every event, had done the deed.

Amalia Christensen was now the fiancée of Sheikh Zayn Al-Ghamdi. The evening when the story had hit the press, Amalia couldn't focus.

With a sigh, Zayn had looked up from his laptop after she'd asked him to repeat something a second time. Scolded herself for being so weak, after all these years. "You're restless tonight."

She shrugged, trying to make light of it. "I'm—"

Perceptive brown eyes stayed on her as Amalia tried to erect her defenses. "You expected your father to call."

"No," she retorted loudly, betraying herself anyway.

"You're determined to hate him for the rest of your life but there could be a hundred reasons he didn't contact you now. And he is a phone call away for you."

His sympathy was unbearable in the face of her foolish, childish hope that her father, at least now that she was engaged to the sheikh, would call and ask about her. The long breath she took forced the lump back down her throat. She lifted her eyes to him and her resolve almost broke at the tenderness in Zayn's. "The past week has been a crazy whirl, Zayn. Can you handle your workload without me tonight?" she forced herself to say.

If he'd forced her to confront her feelings, Amalia was sure she'd have thrown herself at him and sobbed. And the last thing she needed was to weaken, especially in front of a coldly calculating man like him. Fortunately, his answer had been a coolly delivered, "Of course."

And just as she reached the door, he said, "You called me Zayn." She heard his light footsteps on the carpet, felt the heat from his body stroke her back like an intimate caress. "But I have to admit, Amalia, never has my title sounded so good as when it falls from your impertinent mouth."

Amalia didn't turn around, an unexpected bashfulness rooting her to the floor. It seemed that the last and somehow stalwart barrier had been finally razed. He didn't know it but she knew what it signified. She'd seen the man beneath the sheikh and as much as he tried to remove the real him from the man he needed to be, she had seen him. And worse, she was beginning to like the hell out of him.

That was about the only personal exchange they'd had in the whole week.

But as the first week merged into the second and Amalia was so thoroughly integrated into every aspect of his life, a different kind of strain began to descend on her. Like a thread of silk that was stretched too tight and too far.

What the endless number of teams and strategists and PR experts hadn't taught Amalia was how to bear the little touches and intimate glances from the sheikh himself, how not to dissolve into a puddle at all the attention he showed her.

When his rock-hard thigh collided against hers, when his arm draped around her waist, becoming the center of attention for every cell in her, when he ran his shockingly abrasive fingers against her upper arm, almost without his knowledge it seemed, when she had replied to someone's question about Sintar…it was a continual onslaught on her senses.

The boundaries she'd been so sure would come to her aid were already blurring under that dark, perceptive gaze. And yet, he seemed to be utterly unperturbed by the deluge of sensations that seemed to be drowning her.

After hours of perfectly synchronizing their acts, of playing the roles of affianced lovers a bit too well, they returned to their suite, and their masks fell away.

The easy camaraderie they shared through the day disappeared instantly.

Tension corkscrewed in the air around them, and more than once, Amalia had wondered desperately if it was only she who felt it. He ignored her so thoroughly in those moments that in contrast, thoughts of him and them began to consume Amalia.

She didn't fit into his life, in any way, she kept reminding herself, but it didn't stop her from imagining them as a couple.

His comments about her appearance were always polite, impersonal, just adequate. Which perversely made her pay even more attention to her outfit and her makeup and her hair. Only to be disappointed again and again at his changing behavior toward her in the last week.

While the little bits and pieces of information she hoarded about him made her own attraction to him more and more consuming.

That he was a ruthless boss but a fair one, too.

That beneath the cloak of power he wore for Khaleej, he was at heart still a dreamer.

"Why do you think I'm in such a hurry to beget sons?" he'd said, when she'd called on his fixation with an heir. *"The moment they're ready, I will pass on the mantle of Khaleej to their capable hands and then I'm going to start my career and live my dream."*

Amalia hadn't had the heart to tell him that she couldn't imagine Zayn ever chucking that duty away, that he'd probably serve Khaleej in one way or the other until his last breath. But then she'd caught a glimpse of a faraway look in his eyes, the hard curve to his mouth as he watched the young apprentice architect describe some building design and she'd realized that he knew.

That the duty-bound, coldly powerful sheikh always, always came first and far behind was Zayn the man himself.

That if, a big *if*, he had felt any attraction to her that first day they had met, he'd have effectively killed it by now because Amalia Christensen didn't fit in to the life of Sheikh Zayn Al-Ghamdi.

It had been a painfully vulnerable moment to witness—she was sure Zayn didn't even realize how well she understood him now—a moment that defined her relationship with him for Amalia, the moment that had brought home pretty hard that at some point, Amalia had started believing in the powerful charade, that she'd passed from attraction to admiration to feeling something much more powerful and terrifying for Sheikh Zayn Al-Ghamdi, the man who found her unsuitable for everything other than posing as his fake fiancée during the day and as his efficient PA at night.

The last night of their two-week itinerary, they were attending a charity fund-raiser gala. The charity named Hope supported young professionals who came from underprivileged backgrounds. Amalia had found it really interesting that four of its most important and generous patrons were the Dirty Four exposed in the *Celebrity Spy!* Article, including Zayn.

When she'd taunted him about how he would know anything about being underprivileged, he'd given her a scathing glance.

Yes, her remark had been irreverent but Amalia's curiosity had been genuine. How could a man who had everything—power, good looks, intelligence—understand someone else? How could a mere woman hope to amount to something to a man like that?

Which was what she'd been doing. And yet, he had proved Amalia wrong.

From his discussion with the patroness to his highly detailed and involved questions about the candidate they'd chosen to receive the scholarship this year, she'd realized this wasn't an impersonal event where he showed his face and disappeared.

Only when Amalia and Zayn had been introduced to a freshly graduated architect before the evening began had she realized the importance of the event and the charity itself to Zayn. This charity was Zayn's project, not the sheikh's.

When she'd asked the thrilled protégé what he was most excited about, his answer had been the project he'd been assigned to in Sintar. Amalia had seen the bittersweet smile in Zayn's face, and for the first time, felt shame at how prejudiced she'd been. Zayn could've become bitter over what he was denied but he'd found a different way to find satisfaction.

Why hadn't her mother done the same? For so many years after they had left Khaleej, Amalia had heard from her mother about all the things her father had forbidden her to do. And yet, she had only wasted her life, filled with that bitterness.

She could have pursued all the things she complained her father hadn't let her do, she could have loved and cherished Amalia, she could have asked Aslam to visit them… instead, she had wallowed in that grief, given up interest on life.

How much of that bitterness had she passed on to Amalia herself?

She'd made so many assumptions about Zayn and he had proved her wrong every time. How many things in life had she denied herself because she had borne witness to her mother's pain and her failures?

That evening she dressed in an ice-blue fitted shift dress

that played hide-and-seek with her knees. The perfect cut made the most of the dip of her waist and the flare of her hip and her legs. It was both trendy and elegant, and Amalia never tired of that style.

Purple pumps had added a flash of color to her outfit. Her thick, wavy hair, had taken two hours to blow dry, straighten and then beat into submission into a chic chignon at the back of her head.

Unlike the last couple of weeks, she found pleasure in dressing up for the evening. Anticipation and excitement made her movements jumpy as she used the naked palettes and a black eyeliner, as the makeup artist had shown her to do, to achieve the kind of glamour she'd only seen on magazine covers before.

And when she had joined Zayn outside the banquet hall where the fund-raiser was being hosted, all of her breath had piled into her throat.

The black tux hugging his wide shoulders and tapering off, he looked like he belonged on the cover of *GQ*. Power and charm radiated from him. A frisson of knee-melting awareness snaked down her spine as he pushed off from the wall.

She was aware of a quiet hush descending around the guests that were already there. Her muscles shook all over, anticipation a bubble in her chest. Even though his gaze swept over her in a leisurely appraisal, all he said was, "You keep getting better and better at this."

Swallowing her disappointment, Amalia stared back at him. It was a wonder she could speak at all. "At what?"

"At this touch-me-not ice-princess image you project. At making me believe that this is the real you." There was a thread of something in his tone that Amalia couldn't quite pin down. At his signal, his junior aide appeared, a box in his hand.

With that arrogance that seemed to be embedded in his very blood, Zayn waited while the man opened the velvet case and extended it toward him, all the while his brown eyes cataloged every small detail about her.

Heat she couldn't fight flooded Amalia at this pointed, masculine appraisal. Her skin felt too tight, her nipples peaking to attention, and a low thrum began to beat in her lower belly. He was doing this on purpose, she realized with a horrified gasp; still, she couldn't stop her reaction.

She would be damned if he let her use her attraction to him as some kind of weapon. Chin tilted, Amalia glared back at him. "If you tell me what I have done to—"

With a flick of his fingers, Zayn dismissed the aide. In the next blink, he had his powerful arms around her and she was drenched in the musky warmth of the man.

Every inch of her skin sang as his hard chest grazed her breasts, his thighs tangled with hers. Tension was so thick around them that she shivered when his fingers rasped against her nape.

The cold slide of something against her neck brought her head down. Diamonds, enough that she couldn't even count, nestled around a delicate platinum wire settled against her heated skin. She fingered the dazzling, multifaceted stones, unable to quell the pleasure that rose through her. The gift didn't matter so much as that he'd put it on. It seemed a romantic gesture although she was the last person who'd know anything about such gestures. "Thank you. I… I'll make sure to…"

His fingers crawled up the sensitive skin of her nape and into her hair, while the other hand remained on her hip. The intimacy of his touch sent her pulse soaring. "It's yours to keep," he whispered at her ear. "I saw it and thought of you."

A sigh escaped her mouth and brought his gaze level

with hers. "You're trembling. Until this evening, I would have bet my kingdom it was me."

His cold tone sliced through the daze her senses seemed to be swimming in. Suddenly, his gift, the possessive way he'd put it on her, everything took on a different meaning. "What are you talking about?"

"Your... Massi is here."

"Here?"

"Mysteriously, yes." The tip of his finger traced the line of her jaw. "Tonight, at the exclusive fund-raiser whose guest list was decided months ago."

Massi was here? In Paris?

A smile came to Amalia's mouth, the thought of a friendly, familiar face filling her with pleasure. A smile that dominated the shock she felt. As far as she knew, Massi was not connected to the Hope charity in any way.

He was here because of her.

Which was exactly what the man in front of her was thinking. Except he'd gone two steps further and come to another conclusion, too.

He didn't come out and say it, but Amalia saw the suspicion in the granite set of his jaw, in the hard contour of his mouth. In the way his beautiful eyes glittered without any real warmth.

The whole necklace and his putting it on her, it had all been a show. The embrace and the intimacy had been his way of staking claim in front of a man he didn't even know. Hurt pinged inside Amalia's chest.

It was her own fault for giving vague answers every time he'd asked about Massi. Now she wanted him to demand answers, to demand his right in her life...

But she would forever be waiting.

Zayn thought of her as the woman who'd blackmailed him. As the woman who wasn't fit to be anything in his life. These two weeks, their exchanges, nothing had significance to the sheikh. For him, it was only a means to achieve his sister's happiness.

The cold kiss of the diamonds on her skin made nausea whirl up through her throat. "If you have something to say, Zayn, say it."

The jut of his stubborn jaw made Amalia want to growl. "No? Then please, let me go so that I can finish this damn pretense and we both can go back to our lives."

Uniformed waiters circulated through the hall, supplying unlimited glasses of champagne. Amalia had sipped a few times from her flute and then passed it back. Even though she'd been sorely tempted to get drunk for the first time in her life and make a spectacle of herself.

That would show the arrogant sheikh how unsuitable she could be.

But too many fates hung in the balance and she decided her little rebellion wouldn't be worth it.

An echo of the frisson that had shot through her when he had seen her went through her again as she looked around the banquet hall and found his dark head.

As if she'd telegraphed it, he looked straight at her and raised his champagne flute. Amalia forced a smile to her lips, a sort of sinking sensation in her stomach. Their little confrontation wasn't over. It hadn't even started, she realized.

He'd only postponed it to the privacy of the night. Because, of course, the sheikh couldn't show even a smidgen of emotion, a weakness in front of the public. Even his anger over her supposed betrayal was under his supreme control, whereas she hadn't been able to hide anything.

What would happen when they went back to the suite they shared?

CHAPTER EIGHT

"I WOULD APPRECIATE it very much if you unhand my fiancée." Zayn had no idea how he managed to make the warning sound dire when his heart was pounding in his throat. He'd spent a hellish two hours searching for Amalia on the streets of Paris, along with his security team while she…

The fist in his gut would not unclench.

He hadn't known fear like this in…*ever*. The thought of Amalia hurt or worse had consumed him.

He had sworn to fire his entire security team once she had been found. He had called himself a hundred names for not making her aware of what a target she could be to so many different factions now that she belonged to him.

And here she was…in the arms of her lover.

"Stop fondling her at the same time, before some camera crew gets a picture of it and plasters it all over social media tomorrow."

"Zayn, I wanted to…"

Her topaz gaze met his in defiance and slowly, softened. Even her temporary yielding did not calm him. Slowly, she moved in the man's embrace, trying to extricate herself from him. "Massi wanted to catch up and I thought we would have more privacy away from—"

"You will explain later, *habibti*, in the privacy of our suite." A shadow of fear he still could not subdue made his tone harsh. "I have no intention to provide your boss or some other sneaky reporter with a lovers' spat.

"You are a sheikh's fiancée, Amalia. Sneaking out with other men is exactly the kind of fodder that the media looks for."

Her chin tilted up. "Even if it's to catch up with an old—"

"Friend, or ex-lover or your boss…it doesn't matter. After the last two weeks, I thought you understood that. Come, let's return to the suite."

The man turned and looked at Zayn, the cocky tilt of his head deepening the anger in Zayn's stomach. "I'm not done ensuring that Amalia is not with you under some sort of coercion," the Italian replied, his English only slightly accented.

Amalia cringed, but the man's arm did not budge from her waist. "I have already told you the whole story. I know you mean well but Zayn is right."

A tender smile curved the man's mouth, the easy camaraderie between them too obvious to miss. "You have no one else to look after you and…"

Jealousy prowled like a monster in his blood, and it took all of Zayn's carefully cultivated control to stop from pulling Amalia from her boss's arms into his. This was how one of his barely civilized ancestors must have felt when their claim on their woman was challenged so blatantly.

Having always believed that a man could use his brains more effectively than fists, right now Zayn saw the appeal to the old approach.

"Amalia knows perfectly well what she means to me, Massimiliano. And I always take care of that which belongs to me."

Instead of backing off, the man frowned.

Amalia's laugh, forced and brittle, tinkled in the oppressive silence that was only punctured by the greeting called out by Parisians taking advantage of a beautiful night. Clearly, she didn't understand that men, arrogant, powerful men, used to getting their own way, communicated on a different level with each other.

Massimiliano wanted Amalia, was doing everything to show he knew her better than Zayn did. But it didn't matter.

Amalia was his, at least for now.

"Didn't I tell you meeting in secret like this is not the best idea, Massi?" Her topaz gaze flicked to him only for an instant. Finally, she moved toward him and Zayn felt a wild elation, a primal satisfaction as if he'd won a war.

She stood by him, even as every inch of her was stiff like a pole. Zayn thought she might shatter if he held her too hard. The smile that curved her lips had a tremble to it, as if she was working very hard to keep it together. "Zayn is a little too possessive."

"I'm aware of the sheik's personality, Amalia. And I've known you for five years. Which is why I find it hard to believe that you would fall for a man like him," Massi replied from behind her.

Something glittered in Amalia's eyes then, a shadow of vulnerability when she looked at him before she turned back to the Italian. "There's more to my fiancé than the world knows. And apparently, I'm no less susceptible than the next woman to a powerful sheikh's arrogant charm," she finished, her tone curiously flat.

But Zayn was far too angry to care what it meant.

All he could think of now was if she had betrayed their pact...she had reason to go to the press about their little deal; she had means through her champion to create a furor about Aslam and his release; she owed no loyalty to Zayn...

Why would she when Zayn didn't know how to inspire

trust in a woman? He knew how to charm, seduce and blackmail one…

And it wasn't Mirah's happiness that mattered to him in that moment. It was, he was shocked to discover, his own emotions that were blindsiding him from all sides.

The anger that burned through him was still coated with that fear, was not the cold ire that he kept a lid on. This was hot, fiery.

Zayn didn't know when his hand had descended to her waist, or that he was even keeping her by his side. Her body stiffened next to him, her mouth a flat line.

Slowly she undid his arm from around her, walked up to her boss and gave him a quick kiss on the cheek. "Massi, I'm with Zayn because I want to be." She said the words with conviction; still, a disquiet unfurled in Zayn's gut.

With mounting irritation, he realized he wanted Amalia to choose to be with him, to want to spend this time with him. To give in to the attraction that had been getting out of control over the past two weeks between them.

To choose him even though he was fully aware that he could give her nothing but a temporary affair.

A more ridiculous, nerve-racking thought, he'd never had.

With a start, he realized how used he'd become to seeing her face every morning over breakfast while his aide rattled off their schedule. Intermittently during the day when she played the part of his fiancée seamlessly and to utter perfection. And then at night, when she worked alongside him into the long hours without missing a beat.

That he'd begun to think of Amalia as his. He'd always been possessive about the women he slept with, demanding fidelity for as long as they were with him. With Amalia, that feeling went even deeper.

He'd become used to her irreverent humor, the paradox of cynicism and naïveté in her view of the world. Even the smile that broke through that reserve when he asked her opinion on something. Or the way she chewed her lower lip when she was either nervous or excited.

It was a relationship he'd never had with another woman, ever. Even the most time he'd spent with one—the deep understanding he was gaining of how her mind worked. That was all this fascination had to be. Had never waited to bed a woman he wanted…that was all this frustration, this restlessness in his blood, was.

Zayn Al-Ghamdi could not be losing his head, his cool, over a mere woman. But the statement sounded hollow to his ears and full of that arrogant confidence that riled her so much.

"I appreciate you looking out for me, Massi. You've always been a good friend," she finished with a soft smile. There was affection in her eyes, in her smile, when she looked at the Italian, and only a wary reserve when she turned to Zayn.

Of all the ridiculous things in the world to bother him…

"Should I consider this your resignation, then?" Massimiliano asked, his gaze locking with his over Amalia's head.

The slump in her slender shoulders twisted Zayn's gut. Did the man matter to Amalia or was it the job?

She squeezed Massimiliano's fingers. "We'll talk soon, and at length. Zayn is right. The media watches us relentlessly. I have to go."

The Italian kept his gaze on Zayn while he kissed her cheeks. "Remember you can count on me, Amalia. Against anyone and anything."

Amalia nodded, took Zayn's outstretched arm, her topaz eyes for once hiding her expression from him.

* * *

"Your knee is bleeding." Zayn's clipped words rang around the silent corridor. Amalia waited with bated breath as he slipped his key card into the door and opened it for her.

Feeling the sting in her knee now that he had pointed it out, she walked into the suite and shivered. The room was in a disarray, from papers strewn all over the room to several laptops and walkie-talkies sitting on every available surface. They had even set up a comm center in the suite, she thought, flushing with shame all over again.

It looked as if a storm had blown through the luxury suite in just a couple of hours.

"How did you hurt your knee? The rest of you—" his gaze swept over her with a thoroughness that made her insides melt "—looks fine."

"I slipped on the steps to the roof and slid down a couple of them. The side of the staircase where I banged my knee was rough." Guilt she didn't want to admit resonated in her tone. "I'm not used to heels."

His mouth hardened. "Were you in such a hurry to get away with your lover, then? Did I not offer enough of an…*inducement* for you to stay?" The taunt came before he left the room.

How could he sound so calm when it was clear he was ragingly furious? So cold, even? Her own emotions felt as if they were walking a tightrope to what, she had no idea. Amalia had never felt this turmoil, this feeling of standing at a fork not knowing which way her life was going.

When Massi had asked her to meet him on the roof, she'd given the slip to Zayn's security team. An overwhelming sense of guilt had pervaded her all the while.

As if she was really cheating on the man she was supposed to wed. As if speaking to a man who'd been her friend and confidant for so many years was turning her back on Zayn. The guilt had been a shock, driving the realization that she was far too involved in the charade.

Far too involved with Zayn...

So, instead of doing the sensible thing and informing his team, she had let that shock propel her into leaving with Massi. Even knowing that soon Zayn would note her missing and start looking for her.

Suddenly, standing in the middle of the banquet hall and catching Zayn's glance across the room, Amalia had felt as if she was losing herself, being swept along by a current that was changing her far too fast.

All she'd wanted was a short escape from the complex charade she was playing, a little touch with the reality of her life outside of being Zayn's fiancée. A desperate need to fight her own feelings.

A quick chat had turned into two hours of stubborn argument with Massi. An argument within herself for the loyalty she felt for Zayn.

It had been irresponsible, juvenile, even reckless, knowing how Zayn was going to react. It was the mixture of rage and fear that she had seen in Zayn's eyes that had brought something else from years ago to her mind.

Something similar that her mother had done, driving her father insane with worry. How she had forgotten that night, Amalia had no idea.

Any anger she had felt over his savage words had died an instantaneous death as shame filled her over her own behavior. Whatever her disagreement with him, she had no cause to have acted like a reckless wild child.

He had worried about her safety, she had realized belatedly, the white cast of his ferocious features making her guilty all over again.

Now she was sure she had made both men doubt her sanity.

She had alienated Massi, who had always been kind and fair to her, burned her bridges with the man who had helped her at the hardest time of her life. All for a man who had no use for her in his life…

God, she didn't like that she had lost all the credibility she had built up with him over the last month. Why his opinion mattered so much, she couldn't even pin that down in the chaos of her thoughts.

"Amalia, you look pale. Did you hit your head, too?"

It was her sense of self that felt bruised and battered, but she couldn't tell him that. She felt upside down, inside out, weak. "No."

The intensity of his gaze touched her, the warmth of his body a tantalizing caress. Amalia couldn't meet his gaze just yet. For some reason all her bluster and confidence seemed to have left her, leaving her shaking.

"That question didn't even get your standard outraged response. Either I'm losing my touch or something is really wrong with you."

The dry, sarcastic tone of his words didn't quite hide the anger beneath. "My head is fine. I just…I don't like the way you confronted Massi. Not his fault that I didn't tell the team where I was going."

"No, I recognize your little rebellion. But that confrontation was bound to happen the minute he decided to show up here and play knight to you."

"What does that mean?"

"Men have their own ways of communicating, especially over a woman they both want a claim on."

"That's ridicu…" Her heart slammed so hard against her rib cage that she was dizzy. "Massi does not want a *claim* on me any more than you do," she said, her voice catching in her throat dangerously.

His jaw went rigid, his expression exasperated fury.

Amalia had never felt more out of her depth than at the moment. No way to understand what it was that she felt. "Then you're truly naive in the ways of men."

Now what the hell did he mean by that? Why couldn't he just come out and say what he wanted of her?

She stretched her entire leg, and her knee stung again. With a sigh, she looked down and saw blood. For some reason her throat closed up and she felt like a leaf, ready to blow away at a small breeze. Or crunched beneath an arrogant, unfeeling man's foot.

Hand on her abdomen, she leaned against the wall, tried to make sense of the morass of feelings piling upon her.

It had been so easy, far too natural, to convince Massi that she had fallen in love with Zayn Al-Ghamdi. As the words had poured out of her mouth, conviction had set in. There was no act that she had put on for her friend's sake, no lie that she had spouted because she didn't want to betray Zayn.

She hadn't thought of Aslam or Mirah or anything else. *Only the glitter in Zayn's eyes when he had provoked her, the charming smile that softened his mouth when they argued, the touch of his hand at the base of her spine that made her want to melt into him...*

She had fallen in love with Sheikh Zayn Al-Ghamdi of Khaleej. If her mother's love for her father had been a mistake, Amalia's was a blunder of epic proportions.

They had spent two weeks under the same roof, working and talking and arguing and yet, today, the intimacy of their shared suite seemed to scrape her raw.

"There's a first-aid box in my bathroom," she said, not meeting his gaze. She wanted to escape his dark glare and examine her newfound feelings in the privacy of her bedroom. "I'll take care of it. Good night, Zayn."

"Sit down on that chaise." He ordered her around as if she were three years old.

Finally, it sparked her temper again. "I'm not a child."

"Then stop cowering like one. I've never hit a woman before, however furious she might make me. No, that's not true. I've never met a woman who made me this furious and worried, and I've known a few women in my life."

The last thing she wanted was to hear about the women in his life.

She pushed off from the wall, intending to reach her room come what may. "I said I'll take care of—"

In one sweeping movement, Zayn picked her up.

Amalia gasped.

His long fingers pressed into her rib cage, the knuckles grazing the underside of her breast and she lost all the will to fight in one swooping breath. His shoulders were like a wall of steel under her arm, his mouth unyielding and harsh, like the desert land of his ancestors.

Not his, *their*, ancestors. For the first time in her life, Amalia wanted to own her heritage, to belong to the same world that had made this man.

Of all the men in the world, how had she fallen for this hard, aloof man? A man who had ruthlessly decided that he would naturally take a mistress after he had sons. A man who decided that he could not open himself even to his wife.

Much as she would've preferred it otherwise, she had fallen in love with the sheikh, and Amalia knew she couldn't have just the man, Zayn.

Her fingers tightened around his nape; she hid her face in his chest. The scent of him filled her nostrils, the warmth of the man twisting the longing in her chest tighter.

The depth of her need frightened her.

He deposited her with a surprising gentleness that belied the dark scowl on his face, on the chaise longue. "If you value your independence, Amalia, you will not use that tart tongue on me today."

"Or what, you'll lock me up and ship me back to Khaleej like a disgrace? Build that jail cell for me next to Aslam's?"

Hands on his lean hips, he towered over her. Since he'd marched onto the roof, Amalia looked at him properly for the first time. Deep grooves settled on the sides of his mouth, and her heart ached.

All six foot four inches of muscle and aggression and forceful will towered over her, his battle to keep his temper under control clear in his tight mouth. And instead of being angry or afraid, her heart pumped faster, her blood sang.

Passion, she wanted his passion, too…

Just then, he hadn't sounded in control. She'd never seen him in such a dangerous mood. Was he still worried about her because he counted himself responsible for her? Or was that emotion in his tone more personal?

Before she could get her muddled thoughts under control, he returned with the first-aid box. Her breath knocked into her throat when he knelt at her feet and pulled her leg onto his muscled thigh. His black trousers pulled up, delineating the hard strength of his thighs.

She jerked at the clench of his muscle under her foot, at the sensations pouring through her at that simple contact. Hurriedly, she shuffled her toes away from reaching up toward his groin. "Zayn, I can manage this."

Thick black hair gleamed, her fingers tingling to run through it. To learn every inch of his hard body, to share an intimacy she'd never wanted before. "For both our sakes, I suggest you put away that headstrong, stubborn independence of yours for the night, Amalia. You will not find me manageable like the other men you—"

"*Suggest?* You never suggest. You command, order…

you… And just because Massi respects my opinion does not mean he's less of a man than you are, you arrogant ass."

He looked up then, a ferocious blaze in his golden-brown eyes. But instead of calling her mouth tart, or her attitude offensive, he said, "I am what I have to be, Amalia. I will never be a sensitive or a tender man, neither will I act civilized when the woman I want sneaks away to be in another man's arms."

And just like that, he stole away the ground from under her. And the breath from her lungs. And the last of her will from her.

With gentle fingers that belied his explosive mood, he pulled the offending four-inch heel off her foot. "Why do you wear them if you're not used to them? You're tall enough for me without heels anyway."

"Not everything I do or wear is to make myself perfect for you," she threw at him, fighting the little burst of pleasure in her chest.

When his fingers lifted the hem of her dress higher above her knees, Amalia froze. "What are you doing? Don't…lift my dress like that."

The broad line of his shoulders tensed. "Move forward and roll your pantyhose down slowly. The blood's already crusted and it's going to sting."

She reached for the hem of her dress and then looked at Zayn. Her breath came hard and shallow, coated with the scent of him. "Turn around."

The very devil lurked in his eyes. "I have seen women's legs and more before."

"You have not seen mine." No man had seen hers.

His head cocked, the sinful curve of his mouth a dare. "I have noticed that they go on and on and have had dreams about them. Especially how they would look and feel wrapped around my hips while I—"

Amalia rocked forward, her entire body shuddering with heat. "Please... Zayn."

Long fingers reached up to her cheek and stroked. "You're really that shy." He stated it with the confidence of a man who had known her for years. "I have not met a beautiful woman who did not know her worth or who didn't take complete advantage of her looks."

"I was taught the opposite. My mother pleaded with me relentlessly not to make much of my beauty, to make sure I found a man who didn't think of owning me as much as he loved me... That in her case, it had turned out to be a curse that attracted the wrong kind of man. She..."

He tugged her hand into his. "Amalia, you know that—"

"I know," she whispered back. "She loved me, Zayn, and she wanted me to be happy. But yes, I realize now that she probably lost all objectivity when it came to men and matters of love. But you see, I started working as soon as possible. I neither had the time nor the energy for a social life, and Massi and my mom ended up being the total of my world."

A tightness descended on his face, a dark glitter in his eyes. He looked dangerous, almost savage. "I do not want to talk about Massi anymore." His thumb traced the plump vein on her wrist. "At some point you have to move out of her shadow and begin living, Amalia."

He stood up and went to the small kitchenette the suite had while she wiggled her hands under her dress and started pulling the sheer material down.

Just as he had predicted, the material clung to her cut when it came to her knees. A small gasp fell from her mouth. Again, Zayn appeared at her knees, put one large hand on her thigh and tugged with the other hand hard.

The material came away with a tearing sound and Amalia felt the prickle of tears. She bent her head while Zayn pulled the tights all the way down. Then with gentle fingers, he cleaned the cut, dabbed antiseptic cream on.

His arrogant head bent over her in concern, a rush of emotions surged through Amalia. The gash had been pretty small in the scheme of things but it had been so long since someone had looked after her with such thoroughness. Not since she had gone to live with her mother.

It was as if that small act of tenderness had unlocked a memory she had completely blocked out.

Her father had always been protective of her, even as he'd encouraged her to be more playful and Aslam, who was the opposite to her in temperament, to employ more caution.

Overnight, Amalia had become the stable one, the parent in the relationship. She'd buried the hurt over how easily her father had abandoned her; the ache she felt to be with Aslam again erected a shell around herself so that she could move forward.

Had she stopped living that day, too?

No, she'd done that later, after seeing her mother grieve day after day, pine over her father year after year. Hardened herself so much that she'd refused to even talk to her father when Aslam nudged her. She'd done nothing that could hurt her like that, taken no chances.

But something inside her roared, *If not now, when? When would she live? Was she willing to give up this time with Zayn, knowing that she might never have another such chance?*

At that moment Amalia couldn't care less if he was right for her or not, or that he was exactly the kind of man she'd sworn she'd never fall for…or that when these few months were over, and he had no use for this charade or her, he would simply remove her from his life…or the worst, that he would just go back to his damn Ms. Young and those candidates for his brides…no future with him.

All she wanted was to feel his touch, to feel like the woman she was supposed to be, to live her life away from the shadow of her mother's own love story.

When he tried to rise, she stopped him with her hands on his shoulders. Pulling in a much-needed breath, she stole her fingers under the collar of his shirt, searching for skin.

The tendons in his neck stuck out.

His skin was like rough silk, so warm that it sent a pulse of heat straight to the core of her. How would it feel if he was naked on top of her against her own bare skin, all that fierce power and passion narrowed down to her. A pulse throbbed between her thighs, bringing fresh heat to her cheeks.

The line of his shoulders was hard, tense. He said, "I see that seeing Massi has made you emotional and perhaps nostalgic, but if you provoke me tonight, I—"

Amalia leaned forward until her face was bent over his. Fingers trembling, she pushed a lock of hair that fell forward onto his forehead. Traced the strong, proud planes of his face. The sharp hiss of his breath was the only sound. "Among those women Ms. Young sent you that day, did you pick one?"

Warning glittered in his dark eyes. "That's the last thing I want to talk about right now."

Her fingers crept under his collar again, roaming and searching, her body articulating her need before her mind could. "No, I want to know." She tried to speak past the closing of her throat. "Is there a candidate in your mind, one you decided will suit you perfectly once you dispose of me and my...situation."

"No," he said, his fingers pushing through his hair in a restless gesture she'd never seen in him. Their fingers tangled and laced, his grip fierce. "Even for the schedule

I have, I cannot just dump you and go to the next woman on the list. Right now all I care about is making sure you… Mirah weds Farid. After that…" His mouth twitched as if they were co-conspirators. "Your blackmail scheme bought me a little time. I am sure even my staunchest opponent in the cabinet and conservatives in Sintar would not expect that I marry soon after one engagement is broken."

Her breath left her in a soft exhale. As long as he hadn't given a woman a role in his life, he was hers.

And she would make most of this time with the man she loved, this opportunity at hand. She would not waste her life like her mom had done.

Anticipation and excitement twined together inside her, making her voice husky, uneven. "Zayn, will you make love to me?"

CHAPTER NINE

WILL YOU MAKE love to me?

Even as he stood under the cold shower jets, Zayn couldn't get those words out of his mind, nor get his X-rated thoughts and body to cool off.

It was the last thing he'd expected Amalia to say tonight. A taunt on his lips, he'd looked up and read the resolve in her eyes.

She wanted him.

All his life, he had surrounded himself with brazen, sophisticated women who wanted sex and mutual pleasure or women like his third PA and the candidates sent over by Ms. Young, who only saw the glitter and power of his position in the world.

Amalia fell into neither camp and yet, to both. From the time he could understand the world he'd been told that he was the prince, the future sheikh, not just Zayn. Never just Zayn.

And yet he felt different, both and neither when held by her alluring gaze, when she glared at him or argued with him even.

With a gritted jaw, he realized she might not be truly innocent, but it was clear that she was inexperienced. A woman he'd begun to understand and admire. A woman he couldn't blithely seduce and walk away from when the curtain fell on their charade.

Damn it, she had looked crushed when he'd claimed he needed a shower and left the room without acknowledging her question. As if it wasn't the hardest thing he'd ever done in his life—to walk away from the lush temptation she presented.

He stepped out of the shower and toweled himself dry.

Sharing the suite with Amalia for the duration of their stay in Paris seemed to be the worst idea he had ever had. Right in line with choosing to keep her close by parading her as his fiancée.

Knowing that she was in the next room, probably freshly showered like he was…just the passing thought sent a flurry of images through his overheated mind.

Her silky skin would be soft and damp, the towel sticking to those pouty breasts that had finally been displayed in their full glory in that dress tonight. Her long, toned legs would be bare under the towel, would be perfect wrapped around his waist as he…

Gritting his jaw, he wrapped the towel against his hips and walked out into his bedroom. The Paris skyline was a feast outside the French windows but tonight he drew no pleasure from it.

The jar of the door behind him made every muscle curl with heat and want.

He turned to find her leaning against the closed door. Her hands hung limply by her sides. A fine tension seemed to resonate from her but it was her face that arrested him.

Her face was free of even the little makeup she had worn earlier. Hair tied up in that ponytail again, pulled tautly from her forehead. She wore a knee-length robe tightly cinched at her waist.

And just as he guessed, her legs went on and on under the hem, tanned and shapely in the moonlight. Seeing a woman's bare legs for the first time had never been such an intimate act. A small gold chain hung at her neck where her pulse pounded violently, quite like his heart inside his chest.

"You're probably used to and expect all sorts of flimsy, sheer stuff—" pink scoured her cheeks here "—but I don't have any...sex clothes," she finished, and absurdly, he wanted to laugh.

She didn't wait for his answer, either. Pushing away from the door, she glanced around the room. On every third breath of his, her gaze focused back on him and then skittered away quite without landing. She halted when she came to the middle of the room, her bare toes pressing into the thick carpet.

"Amalia, I did not—"

"Lisa...the stylist, did ask me if I wanted to look at some lingerie and nightgowns, too, and I was like, *dude*... the last thing I'm going to do on this trip is have sex and she gave me this strange look, I mean, I didn't actually say it...anyway, so I only chose a couple of cute pajama sets."

She undid the sash of her silky robe and shrugged her shoulders to let it slide off.

The robe pooled at her feet and Zayn's breath slammed into his throat.

Somehow he possessed enough wits still to say, "I would not call that attire cute."

She scrunched her nose and he had the most over-whelming urge to kiss the stubborn tip of it. He had been seduced before, yes, but it had been a game he had willingly played.

This...*whatever* it was that Amalia was doing, it disarmed him on more levels than he could fathom. Resolve and innocence played in her every word, every action. Never had a woman beguiled him so thoroughly...

Navy blue silk top with thin straps bared pale skin and fluttered against her breasts. His mouth dry, he watched as her nipples pointed against the silk. He would tongue them and suck them into his mouth; he would make sure she'd never forget about him. The top left a strip of flesh at her midriff bare while her shorts barely covered her toned thighs.

He cleared his throat, his blood rushing sluggishly through every nerve ending now. "I cannot offer you anything beyond the next couple of months." Hands fisted by his sides, he saw that made no dent in the resolve in her eyes. His will against hers—tonight, Zayn realized, he was going to lose. "It is why I have been trying my best to not indulge in all the fantasies I have of you every night."

She swallowed and nodded. Every second seemed to stretch between them while his heart pounded. "You've had fantasies about me?" An edge of complaint crept into her tone. "All these days, I've been wondering, going crazy..."

"I did not think—" his skin felt tightly stretched over his hungry muscles "—it a good idea for you to know the power you could have over me."

Her face fell. "That's what this will be, too, between us, Zayn? A power struggle? An agreement?"

"No, but why tonight, Amalia? I will not be a replacement for another man."

Her head jerked up, and the breath bated in his throat. "I don't want Massi. I've never felt this way about him or any other man." The flutter of a breeze played with the hem of her top, giving him a peek of silky soft flesh and the cute indentation of her navel. Every silky inch of her— he would learn it, lick it, know it. "You were right. I have to start living my own life now and this...you and I, this is what I want."

The urge to fasten his mouth at the pulse on her neck and taste the small drop of water clinging there rode him hard. She licked that pillowy lower lip and all the blood in his body fled south. "Yet, your gaze will not land on me."

Finally, she met his gaze. Resolve laced with naked desire in her eyes razed the last bit of reason from his mind. "Put your hair down," he demanded in a rough tone, a sense of defeat in his veins making his voice harsh.

Was it defeat just because he was indulging himself? Because the lines between his private and public life were blurring?

He'd been given a respite from the marriage he had to make, so why not take it? Why shouldn't he, for once in his life, have a meaningful, if brief, relationship with a woman he admired? A woman who incited more than just lust in him?

"What?" she asked, face blazing, long lashes barely revealing her expression.

"*Your hair*…it is always tied up like that or hidden away in some elaborate style."

"It took me two hours to get it into this style," she complained.

The return of her backbone made him smile. "I hate it like that. I want to see it down." He could practically feel those silky strands wound up around his fingers as he held her still beneath him. While he plundered her mouth and filled her body.

Fever took root in his muscles. But he held the words to himself. The last thing he wanted was to scare or hurt her when she'd come to him with such artless desire.

Amalia wasn't like any other woman he bedded and not just because she was inexperienced. She was someone who should be cherished and loved and cared for. Loyal to the last, with a steely core, and beautiful on the outside and inside, such a woman deserved a man who would worship her. Not use her in a torrid affair under a pretend engagement…

But all the recriminations in the world were not going to make him turn back on tonight. There was one thing he could make sure Amalia had tonight and he would give her that—pleasure.

She set those doe eyes on him for so long that he thought she would protest. Desire clashed with anticipation inside him while he waited. Slowly, she raised her hands and tugged the band holding the tousled waves. Just as that day on the flight, the movement thrust her breasts up, and his belly tightened.

Hair that was the color of burnished gold fell down in lustrous waves, framing the delicate angles of her face. She pushed her hand into it and shook it out, an intrinsically feminine action that made his mouth dry. It fell to her waist and to her midriff in the front, covering the outline of her nipples from him.

Suddenly, the custom that the Bedouins followed, making their women cover their hair except in front of their men, seemed a very good idea. Magnificent and lustrous, he wanted no other man to see her like that...no other man to know how she would look with only her hair hiding her body from his eyes...

"It's too much to manage and takes almost an hour to wash and dry. I'm going to ask the stylist to cut off most of it. Maybe something really short and fun now that I—"

"No." His voice hadn't risen but the command in it carried around the room.

Her fingers stilled in the silky weight, her eyes wide in her face. "No what?"

"Do not cut it. And that's an order."

She laughed then, and the defiance in her eyes greeted him like an old friend.

"I mean it, Amalia. Cutting it off would be a crime."

"Zayn, you can't order me to… I want to be your lover, not your…your…"

He raised a brow and waited, his mouth twitching. "When you look at my body, which I know you've been avoiding since you entered the room, does it give you pleasure, *habibti*?"

Those long eyelashes lifted and her gaze did a sweep of his torso. Slowly and thoroughly over his naked chest and abdomen, flitted sideways to his lean hips and the towel resting there. Then stopped at the line of hair that disappeared beneath his towel.

"I don't see all of you, Sheikh," the minx demanded then, and husky laughter came from his chest. Her hand moved to her nape, a restless slither of her body that made his skin stretch taut all over him. "Drop that towel and I can tell you whether you please me or not."

He raised a brow at her saucy tone. No woman had ordered him like she did, nor demanded her due.

Chewing her lower lip between her teeth, she looked up. "What? I can't order…I mean ask my lover to—"

He dropped the towel. The air was a cool whisper against his heated skin.

Her mouth opened and a soft gasp slid out of those lush lips. That pink mouth wrapped around the head, that tongue licking the length of him…images tightened his body to near torturous arousal.

"Does my fiancée find me to her liking?"

Color made her sharp cheekbones even more pronounced. Her breath left her in a whistle, breasts rising and falling. Her hand drifted to her abdomen and Zayn smiled at how telling her gestures were. At how artlessly naive she was even when she taunted with her words.

"I wouldn't be a woman if I didn't like the look of you,

I think." She swallowed as he took a step toward her. "And I completely forgot where we were going with this."

He pulled long strands of her silky hair and wound it around his fingers, tugging her closer and closer. She came with her mouth upturned, her body thrumming lightly. "Your hair…" He traced the lush lips. "Everything about your body drives me crazy even when you hide most of it. I wouldn't want to lose that pleasure. Just as you wouldn't want me right now to cover up, yes?"

"My pleasure feeds yours and yours mine," she whispered, her words throaty.

"Yes."

She covered the last few steps between them. Hands on her shoulders, Zayn pulled her closer until the silk of her top rasped against his body. Her forehead fell against his chest, her body shaking.

"You're trembling. I would never hurt you."

Not physically, she knew. But what about her heart?

Amalia lifted her face to Zayn's and lost the ability to breathe all over again. Such a breathtaking face rendered harsh by his will, implacable by his duty…and all she could see in that moment was the desire that unfurled in it, for her.

How had she doubted whether he wanted her?

She felt as if she was suspended over a cloud of desire and need, not quite able to land her feet anywhere. As if there were a rope that was hooked into her lower belly tugging her higher and higher, amplifying every sense…

The dark gleam of desire in his eyes prodding her, she touched her lips to his. Instant heat sizzled over them as lips merged with lips, as her breasts rubbed against his hard chest. Groans rippled through the charged air, erotic sounds full of need and desperation that played over her nerves.

He took over the kiss almost instantly, none of that gentling in his caress now as that first kiss. Such harshly contoured lips could kiss so softly.

"You taste like a berry, Amalia, tart and sweet, incredibly erotic. And I'm going to taste you everywhere…"

She groaned as his legs spread and created a cradle for her own. The contrast of his body against hers sent ripple after ripple of sensation over her. They were so different in so many ways and yet it seemed their bodies were made for this, every press of their muscles, every whispered slither of skin against skin ramping up the need.

Clutching his nape, Amalia sank her fingers into his thick hair and pressed herself to him. The jut of his manhood against her lower belly, thick and hot, branded her.

Fingers held her jaw tight while he plundered her mouth. His lips devoured her upper lip, the erotic swipe of his tongue teasing her to do the same. But when she did, he backed off. Until she demurred and he started all over again.

In minutes her lips felt swollen, hot, her breasts were crushed against his hard chest, her lungs burning to keep up with her heart.

This kiss was one of possession, of primal masculinity demanding her surrender, of the wild desert heat finally claiming her for his own.

She surrendered willingly, slapping her fingers onto his bare chest.

His muscles clenched under her fingers, the fine hairs on his chest tickling her palms. Golden tanned skin stretched taut over pectorals that were defined but lean.

His tongue delved into her mouth while his hands landed on her hips. Amalia shuddered all over as his tongue called hers into a wildly erotic dance that made her toes curl into the carpet at her feet.

Oh, the press of his arousal against her lower belly…an answering ache spread low within.

When he pushed his hand under her top and branded her hot flesh with his fingers, she wanted to do the same. Her questing touch roved over his hard chest hungrily and soon she discovered that she affected him just as he did her.

Hot mouth skimmed over her jaw, the sensitive rim of her ear and then the pulse at her neck…when he dug his teeth into her skin, Amalia jerked in his arms, a jolt of heat narrowing down to her core.

So many sensitized places throbbed under his expert caresses; so many sensations battered at her that she felt her breath saw in and out of her in an unsteady rhythm.

But even under the assault, a dim sort of doubt lingered at the back of her mind. He'd done this so many times with so many women. Even if she didn't believe all the numbers that exposé had quoted, his expert caresses, the way he'd already learned how he could play her body, how to turn her on so skillfully, it spoke of what an experienced lover he was. God, already he knew her body better than she herself did.

Amalia didn't want to be another woman the playboy sheikh took to his bed to satisfy his voracious appetite. A convenient relief after the hard, relentless pressures of the last two weeks. "Zayn…" She pulled his face down to hers, breathing so hard that the sound echoed in the thick air.

His hard chest rose and fell, his hands pulling her hips flush against his.

"You didn't ask me if I betrayed our deal to Massi."

Sensuous lips pulled back to a snarl. "You're asking me this now? Now? Amalia, if your plan is to—"

"How do you know I haven't?"

Nimble fingers crawled up and up her abdomen under her top, and cupped her breasts. His fingers were abrasive, rough against her sensitive skin. A working man's hands… And then he covered the hard nubs with his palms, kneading and lifting one to his mouth.

Something harsh fell from his mouth in Arabic. In the haze of desire, she couldn't catch what it was. Every inch of her trembling, she stared as he lifted the pouty nipple to his mouth and flicked it through her top. A bolt of pure desire shot through her and Amalia arched her body into his, a pit of longing in her gut.

"Seeing you in his arms made me forget everything, *azeezi*. About Sintar, about my duty, about Mirah's happiness, about your brother and the media... I forgot everything." He punctured the words with flicks of his tongue and now he took the nipple into his mouth and sucked it. Amalia pinched her thighs together against the arrows of pleasure converging around her sex. "So you tell me now. Have you betrayed our deal, Amalia?"

She sobbed when he released her nipple with a soft plop, her entire being tense like a bow. With hands that could play her like a violin, he took the hem of her top and pulled it up over her head until her torso was bare to him.

And then his hands stroked over the flesh he had uncovered. Large hands pressed and stroked her until all she could do was give herself over. Moving to her shoulders, he kneaded her back, so aggressively male that Amalia drowned in him.

"Did you, *ya habibti*? Did seeing Massi remind you what an arrogant beast I was in comparison?"

Amalia didn't want to agree. She wanted to remind him of his tenderness when he'd thought she'd hurt herself, the concern she'd read in his eyes because he'd feared for her safety. But no sooner than the thought formed, he drove it out with his fingers plucking restlessly at her turgid nipples.

Hardly had she shaken her head before he resumed the plunder of his mouth on her other breast.

Again and again, he ministered to her breasts until the wet points were tender and sensitized, until a fever ran in her blood. Pain and pleasure seemed to coalesce and beat like one pulse all through her body.

When he stopped his caresses and moved his hands down her body, Amalia felt like her entire body was waiting for a breath, parched. Like she'd been waiting her entire life for this moment with this man. The pulse he had built to a keening pitch between her thighs dulled down. And she was desperate enough to beg. "Please, Zayn, I need—"

"Not yet, *habibti*." Dry amusement sprinkled his words. "First, I shall make sure you are ready for me, yes?"

Amalia protested with a sob. He was already holding her up, her quivering legs of no use. A hand under her knee urged it up and she locked it around his hip. The graze of his hip bone, the rough musculature against her inner thigh, sent a moan hurtling through her, the press of his shaft against the core of her sending an ache through it.

She hid her face in his chest at the way he opened up the heart of her, heat flooding her cheeks. "Zayn, that's... the bed..."

A wicked gleam in his eyes, he pressed a sizzling kiss to her damp mouth. "No, here," he whispered, before his fingers found the wet heat of her.

Amalia groaned as he pushed one, then two fingers into her core, while his thumb pressed and stroked the spot that ached for his touch.

His jaw gritted so tight to resemble a marble cast, he looked down at her. Passion pinched his features, all the hard contours of his face even more pronounced now. "You're swollen and wet for me, Amalia." When he tweaked the bud with his fingers, Amalia jerked at the wave of pleasure that claimed her. "And so violently responsive. Shall I take you like this, *latifa*?"

Amalia knew she should say something but the sight of his leanly powerful body arrested her words. While she watched with widening eyes and whistling breath, he ripped off the cover on a condom and rolled it on.

Her mouth went dry. She went willingly when he took her in his arms again and his fingers plunged into her wet core as if they belonged there. The insistent pressure and strokes of his fingers sent wave after wave of such blinding pleasure that she clung to him to ride each.

She was so close, so desperate for that peak, she dug her teeth into his flesh and panted against his skin.

In the next breath, he was lifting her as if she was a petite, fragile thing, urging her to wrap her legs around his hips. The wall kissed her bare spine, while his muscles pressed into her front. His fingers left her just as Amalia hung on the edge of her climax and then he was entering her with one hard thrust...

Stinging pain rippled through her core and Amalia tried to contain her whimper against one rock-hard shoulder. And failed. Every inch of her went rigid against the waves of pain.

This time she understood the curse words that fell from his mouth.

His fingers gentled on her hips, his breathing like bellows around her. "Damn it, Amalia...why didn't you tell me?" He sounded so utterly pained that she lifted her head and looked at him.

Such tender concern filled his gaze that the fingers of pain dulled by a deeper longing. "I should have, I know. But I did tell you that I haven't had much life beyond my mother and Massi..." Her words drifted off as she saw his jaw tighten. "You thought I had been with Massi?"

"Yes. It was clear in his eyes that he wanted more, Amalia."

"He did. We tried a couple of dates but I couldn't...I just couldn't see him as anything other than my boss. And maybe an older brother. So I told him that I didn't want to ruin what we had."

"It is clear from his gaze today that he still…" He stopped and carried her to the vast bed. He brought her to the edge of it and gently lowered her. He'd already pulled out of her and all she felt was an aching awareness, a void in her sex, just like the one in her chest.

God, she didn't want the night to end yet, not like this.

Fingers tight against his biceps, she stayed him. Pressed her face to his chest and breathed in the musky scent of him. His skin was smooth and rough at the same time, a damp sheen clinging to it. "Don't leave me, Zayn… I came to you tonight because I wanted this."

He clasped her cheek gently, his eyes full of a warmth that set her heart racing. "Hurting you physically is bad enough, Amalia. I can't justify—"

"But it is a pain I welcomed willingly," she pleaded, beyond pride or shame now.

Gentle fingers dug into her hair, molding the shape of her head. She'd never seen the conflict mirrored in his eyes as she did now. Something expanded in her chest, as if this fight he was going through between what he was supposed to be and what he wanted was a personal victory of hers. As if she had smashed through to the complex man beneath. "You know where my life is headed. If you waited this long, it should have been with someone special. I just—"

"You're special to me, Zayn." Instantly, his gaze shuttered and Amalia reached up to touch his face. "No, please don't…withdraw from me. I'm not asking for anything. I do feel…there is a connection between us, do you deny it?"

"It's attraction, Amalia. Lust at its most primal."

She swallowed away the hurt that pinched at his dismissal. "Well, you're the first man I've lusted over quite like this. So…how about you make good on your promise,

Sheikh?" She filled her tone with taunt, desperate to have him finish what he started, desperate to have that closeness with him again. "Shouldn't I get some reward for the pain I just felt? Or are you in the habit of leaving your woman unsatisfied? I wonder if that tabloid—"

"You're a stubborn, manipulative witch," he mumbled while he climbed over her onto the bed. Amalia slid up the sheets, her breath stuttering in her throat again.

His golden skin tautly stretched over a gorgeously hard body, Zayn took her breath away. He rested alongside her, his hands palms down on her body, restlessly stroking her everywhere.

Amalia closed her eyes and arched into his touch when he strummed her breasts again. Caught between the cool silk of the sheets and the heat of his knowing touches, she drowned in sensations. This time she was a little more aware of her own body's partiality and she gave in to the delirious pull at her sex.

Then she felt his mouth at her nipples, suckling and stroking, while her body climbed higher and higher. When his other hand rested on her mound again, she tensed, the reminder of that cleaving pain driving her reaction.

He kissed the upper curve of her breast, "Shh...*habibti*, just relax. You trust me, don't you, Amalia?"

Amalia opened her eyes and fell deep into his molten gaze. Her lips sought his and she moaned at how familiarly exciting he already was to her. How every inch of her recognized and thrummed for him. "I do."

"Then give yourself over, hmm?" His fingers delved into her folds again and resumed stroking her.

Amalia brought her knees up and held his shoulders as he increased the pressure. Faster and faster while his mouth tugged her nipple again. She was panting, flying, every inch of her being concentrated on the pulls of her sex. The hunger was so intense that she felt like weeping for release.

"You're a firecracker. Just listen to your body, *latifa*, and demand what you want from me," Zayn whispered in a barely recognizable husky tone. She heard the smile in his words instead of seeing it. "Like you always do."

As if that was all her body needed, she rocked into his touch, raising her hips, her fingers desperately holding on to his hard body. "Faster, Zayn, now," she demanded wantonly and had the pleasure of hearing his deep laughter. The soft graze of his teeth against the tautly aching nipple sent Amalia soaring over the edge.

Pleasure splintered and shattered her into a thousand flashes of light and even before the tremors subsided, he thrust into her in one smooth, deep stroke. The groan that fell from his mouth was drawn out, rubbing against her senses. Amplified the utter sense of completion she felt down to her bones.

Pain this time was more of a fading imprint. Utterly replete, Amalia opened her eyes as his hands held her shoulders and he settled so deeply into her that she didn't know where she ended and he began.

She ran her hands all over his hard body. His muscles clenched under her touch, a fine sheen of sweat covering his smooth skin.

"You feel incredibly good, *habibti*. I won't last long."

She loved seeing the dark desire in his eyes, the unraveling self-control. In that moment he was hers, Amalia knew. The sated languor left her body as he flipped her in a blink.

Every nerve ending felt tautly stretched as he pulled his legs forward and they were facing each other—nose to nose, lips to lips, and hips to hips. "Now, let's see if we can make you scream again," he whispered, sucking the tender flesh at her neck.

Such greedy languor spread through her lower belly that Amalia instinctively rose from his grip and then pushed herself back on him.

This time it was he who growled, his flesh pleading with her to not leave him. "Ride me, Amalia. I'm yours," he said, and it was all the encouragement she needed.

She gloried in grinding herself against him, again and again, up and down until a bone-deep pleasure spread its fingers through her sex again.

When he thrust up, a wave of such piercing pleasure splintered through her that she screamed. And then she was landing on her back again, his big body covering hers as he thrust sharper and faster, exploding her pleasure into a newer level. Amalia locked her ankles around his, urging him on shamelessly, the move as instinctual as breathing.

He took her mouth in a hard, punishing kiss as his body bucked above hers and he climaxed with a guttural growl. And his bellowing breath fell around her, and his sweat-kissed body folded over her almost crushing breath. Amalia wrapped her arms around his sinewy strength and held on.

She felt like she was reborn, renewed, part of which was the raw experience of being possessed by this arrogant man. But part of it was this amazement at herself, too, for taking a chance with him, for taking a risk with her heart.

As her breath softened and her body felt boneless, fear touched that euphoria, too. She kissed his damp shoulder, her fingers tightening around him.

Because sharing this intimacy, opening her body to him, would make it a thousand times harder when it was time to leave him. But if she was given a choice as to knowing this with Zayn and a pain-free life, she knew she would make this choice again and again.

CHAPTER TEN

"YOUR FIANCÉE IS both beautiful and smart, Your Highness."
Translation: "Did you know that she is one of those modern, independent women?"

"Your fiancée has some interesting opinions about our education reforms, Your Highness." Which actually translated to "This woman of yours thinks far too much. Control her."

"Your fiancée, Zayn, has some strange ideas about Khaleej. Tell her where her place is before she becomes a liability." This glittering warning from his father while his gaze held Zayn's in a question.

A man who didn't mince words, his advice was, "She's a PA, Zayn. You could still keep her on in whatever position you want, and marry a suitable woman."

Zayn had walked away before he could give voice to the storm brewing within him, before he forgot that this man was his father, a man who always deserved Zayn's respect and loyalty.

The thought of making Amalia his mistress while he married another, reducing their relationship to that dimension, filled him with bile. Why when he had always accepted it as part of his fate? Was a faceless woman in the future in the same role just more palatable than a woman with whom he had shared the deepest and truest parts of himself?

For that was her appeal. With Amalia, he need not be just the sheikh or just Zayn. There was no dichotomy inside himself. He could be both and neither and still be comfortable in his skin, still know that he could trust in her absolutely.

Know that she understood everything that drove him, that made him who he was.

That kind of intimacy where they learned of each other, where they realized that there was so much more to learn, was both terrifying and exciting.

And addictively immersive.

The warnings and innuendos landed on Zayn like a pelt of stones, jarring the dreamy, drugged haze he seemed to be existing in in the month since their return from Paris, stirring inside him a violent urge to pound his fists into the nearest wall.

But since he hadn't given in to that urge when he had been thirteen and his father had had his secretary transferred because the man's fourteen-year-old son, who had been Zayn's first, and probably only, best friend, was being a disrupting, corruptive influence on the prince, he didn't do it now.

He pressed a hand to the back of his head where a soft pounding was beginning and retreated to a table at the corner of the hall. The way he was feeling right now, he would probably bite the head off some poor staff member who didn't deserve his wrath. And the ones who did, the one who spoke of Amalia as if she was somehow beneath them, he could not shower his displeasure.

Signaling a passing waiter for some coffee, Zayn leaned back in his seat and closed his eyes. The fragrance of coffee that wafted toward his nostrils lightened the growing tightness he was beginning to recognize in his chest.

He picked up his cup and took a sip. Amalia had gone from complaining that the brew was too bitter and pouring coffee into the creamer than the other way, to now asking what she had to do to ensure he sent her a supply of coffee for the rest of her life when she left Khaleej.

Even as he had been beyond tempted to voice his darkest desire, he had known that it was also a reminder. A reminder that she wasn't forgetting that this was only an arrangement between them, that she knew the status quo.

That she didn't, and never would, expect more of him than he was willing to give. That she wouldn't get emotional and clingy when it was time to leave.

She gave so willingly and wantonly of herself to him in the dark of the night but Amalia also prided herself on her self-respect. She wouldn't venture where she wasn't sure of her welcome, her stubborn will her shield in so many ways.

Look how they'd been in Sintar for a month and she refused to still visit her father. Zayn knew from his aide that Professor Hadid had called her numerous times. He had even come to the palace but she bluntly refused to see him. Put him off with some excuse.

"Now he worries about where all this will end and what damage I might do to his reputation," she had said when Zayn had argued that Professor Hadid was obviously concerned.

Amalia's tough attitude hid so much hurt. Confronting her father, he knew, would break her. A vulnerable, hurting Amalia, he also knew, could become his own kryptonite.

So he let it be, even as he knew she had to face her father sooner or later.

Looking out around the vast hall where Mirah's fiancé's

family was mingling with his own relatives, he pulled in a deep breath. He needed to shake off this spiraling feeling of losing his control, of being caught in an eddy.

Everything was going according to his own plan, he reminded himself. The risk he had taken with Amalia had paid off. Even as they questioned his choice, no one had doubted his relationship with Amalia.

The palace was ringing with the groom's family and the wedding guests enjoying the lavish three-day celebrations that preceded the wedding. Even after this breakfast there were ceremonial events he had to attend as the bride's brother and the sheikh.

Mirah's *nikah* to Farid was tomorrow night and that was all that mattered, at least, for now. Not he nor Amalia or their all too real-feeling relationship.

He didn't know why the shock and taunts of his friends and guests, even his parents, was leaving such a bad taste in his mouth. It was not news to him what Amalia was or what kind of a reaction she would draw from people who called themselves his well-wishers.

All he wanted to point out was that she had been by his side constantly for six weeks now and all she'd done was carry herself out in public with grace and decorum that made her no less than any daughter of some distinguished royal house that were assembled at the wedding even now.

Even when she disagreed with people's views or faced prejudice just because she was a woman and an outsider, she did it with logic and conviction, with respect, even when she was denied it.

He also hadn't failed to notice that she had ruffled more than one conservative cabinet's feathers, and didn't limit herself to a vapid, social existence. Even in the pretense, she had already involved herself in more than a few social issues and charity boards.

It was whiplash, for his statesmen had never seen a woman get involved in so many things, never mind break so many unwritten rules.

He had just finished his coffee when he heard a wave of excitement at the entrance to the hall. Dressed in a pale cream long-sleeved dress made of the sheerest silk and lace and with thousands of dollars' worth of beadwork, Mirah walked into the hall. And next to her, dressed in a light mint-green dress was his fiancée.

Sheer sleeves covered her long arms, while lace panels covered her chest and neck. Demure and stylish, and yet utterly sensuous, she took his breath away. She smiled at female members of the groom's party while her topaz gaze searched the vast hall.

The moment it touched him, genuine pleasure touched her bow-like mouth. It knocked him like a cool breeze on a hot day, fracturing something inside him wide open. He had hardly processed his own reaction, caught the answering jolt in his chest, when his cousin appeared at his table.

"Hello, Zayn."

Zayn covered his shock at his cousin's sudden appearance. He had known he was back in Sintar but he had been avoiding Zayn. Karim had always been snakelike, elusive and sneaky, which was why he was here today of all days.

Showing his face to Zayn here when he was busy with Mirah's wedding and the guests almost guaranteed that Karim could sneak away without causing himself any problems. One look at his cousin's fake smile reminded Zayn why he had never quite liked the man, even though they were of a similar age.

Suddenly now, it seemed Karim enjoyed everything—all the perks and pleasures of belonging to the royal family without any of the responsibilities and duties. An understanding that he had never resented before and yet was never far from Zayn's mind these days...

"You arrived in Sintar ten days ago. Why take this long to show yourself?"

"I didn't realize it was the sheikh's summons," Karim whined in that nasally voice.

Zayn gritted his jaw. How had he not known Amalia was right? Of course Karim had let someone else take the fall. "You were told it was official business."

"If it is to prod me toward some state job again, I will tell you the same as I told my mother, Zayn. I'm busy with my charities and business. I do not need a job at some junior level in your administration. Neither do I—"

When his words drifted off into ether, Zayn turned to his cousin.

Karim became pale beneath his untanned skin. "What is that woman doing here?"

Zayn followed his gaze to Amalia. Who turned in their direction just then. The last fragment of doubt he'd held on to even after evidence had been found, shattered at the pale cast of his cousin's face.

"Which hole have you been hiding in, Karim? That woman is my fiancée."

The entire vista of Amalia's face changed instantly. Her smile vanished and that same combative look that she had used on him those first few days entered her eyes. Alarm and amusement vied within Zayn, rendering him incapable of action for a few minutes.

She was loyal, passionate and generous, and he no longer wondered why Massimiliano had come after her or why he'd been so protective. Even with her independence and self-sufficiency, Amalia would always have that kind of effect on a man.

He sighed as she marched through the crowd toward them, a definitive set to her shoulders.

"That woman is stubborn, argumentative and a hound dog. You must be thinking with your—"

Zayn let Karim see the full force of his fury. Pounding his fists into his cousin at Mirah's wedding, he reminded himself, was a bad idea on many levels. "Careful, Karim. She is a woman I respect and admire. Do not force me to clean up your act with my own hands."

Karim stayed mute, a sulky light in his eyes.

"Now, you have two minutes before Amalia is here and raises the valid question of why I am not having you arrested right here, right now."

His face was chalk-white. "Arrested for what?"

"For possession of drugs, which you conveniently passed off on her brother."

"That's not true. I didn't even know her brother was—"

"I found the third man, Karim. He confessed to knowing that Aslam had nothing of that sort in his backpack. That leaves you. If you confess now, you can at least stop this from becoming a ruckus right now in front of the whole family. Even—"

"You can control your woman and stop it."

"No, I can't," Zayn said, another small fissure opening up in his chest. He could not control Amalia, neither could he control this irrational, inconveniently growing attachment of his to her, it seemed.

There were too many voices crowding in his head and the fact that he wanted to smash them all into silence told him he had become far too invested in his own facade and very little in the end.

The harshness in his voice when he spoke again was self-directed as much as it was on this weak man who had brought her into Zayn's life. "Though you deserve no such concession, I cannot shame my aunt in front of others. So leave now, and I better learn from the case detective by tonight that you have confessed your role in this."

Whatever spurious righteousness Karim had drummed up for this meeting disappeared when he noted the set tilt of Zayn's mouth. With no word, Karim left in the same sneaky way.

Leaning back into his chair, Zayn studied the woman rushing toward him like a sandstorm. Nothing had stayed the same since she'd marched into his life that day. Even now he felt as though he was standing on shifting sands, everything he had known in his life so far shaking in front of his eyes.

But he was Sheikh Zayn Al-Ghamdi and he had to do what was right for Khaleej, what was his duty.

Not what felt right in his gut.

His childhood friend, a fellow architect he had admired when he had been at college, a woman with revolutionary theories in medicine he had befriended, people who could have been friends and confidants, Zayn had bid goodbye because they were not suitable company for the Sheikh of Khaleej. But in months, if not days, they had become mere memories and he had moved forward with his life.

In mere weeks, Amalia would make her exit, too.

He would move forward again and she would become one of those memories.

"You let him go." Amalia forced the words past the disappointment turning her throat raw.

She rubbed the sleeve of her dress between her fingers, her entire body restless. It felt as if she was constantly trying to slow down time with her mind and each tick of every second, every sunrise, was pulling at her, trying to break her apart.

Only one more night before Mirah was married. As if that wasn't hard enough to come to terms with. Seeing the man who was responsible for her brother's plight calmly leave the hall twisted the knot in her stomach.

A cold smile in his eyes, Zayn looked distinctly unruffled. "Good morning to you, Amalia. Is it true that you took one of Mirah's fiancé's cousins by the collar yesterday afternoon?"

"Yes."

"Why?"

"He...was mouthing off."

"About you?"

"Does it matter?"

"Yes, because I had to smooth it over with his parents and apologize on your behalf for the emotional trauma you caused the boy."

"That's...you're impossible, Zayn. You immediately assumed I was guilty. I got a little physical with him because he was saying nasty things about you and when I called him on it, he started mouthing off about our relationship. The kid was a bully in the making and really, have you seen how big he is?"

"Apparently, now the parents think he will never get over his shock that women, especially tall, beautiful, angelic-looking women, could be so...offensive."

"You're laughing at me."

"I'm amused that you think I needed your defense."

"At that time I forgot what an arrogant ass you are," she said just to say something.

Because, like every morning and every evening and pretty much every time he looked at her, Amalia's breath ballooned in her chest at how gorgeous he was.

His pristine white shirt contrasted with the burnished bronze of his skin, emphasizing the virile masculinity of the man. Flutters emanated in the depth of her lower belly. Amalia shifted her gaze from his face to his throat. The strong column of it, her fingers longed to shape it like she had done last night. To feel the muscles in his shoulders clench under her fingertips, to feel the taut pressure when he moved inside her…

Flushed with unbidden heat, she moved to the table. His long, clever fingers drummed on the table, the same fingers that had been deep inside her heat…that drove her to maddening ecstasy every night…

"As flattered as I am by that look in your eyes, you're making me very uncomfortable in a public area, in the midst of everyone, and it will be at least afternoon before I can give you what you want, *habibti*."

A furious flush claimed her, and she looked away from him. "I don't know what you're talking about. I came to talk to you about that sneaky man and Aslam, not to—"

"It's nothing to feel defensive or shamed about, *latifa*. Believe me, I know exactly how you feel."

She lifted her gaze to him, her gut folding in on itself in anticipation. "You never…you don't…"

"Do I have to speak about how crazy you drive me with need for you to know, Amalia? We have spent every night together in the last month. Every night I tell myself that one more night will end the madness between us, that one more night of taking you, of feeling you writhe under me, will be enough…but it never works."

Dark hunger made the rugged landscape of his face even more breathtaking. "You know, it is only when this fire flares between us do you let me see all of you."

"I could say the same about you," Amalia whispered, longing coursing through her very blood. She looked around her to focus on something else, anything other than the words that fought to rise to her mouth, words that would push him away from her before she was ready to let go.

It didn't help the entirety of the guests being served in the vast hall had all focused on them. If not for Aslam, if not for Mirah, Amalia would have long happily… Aslam! Damn it, how could she forget why she couldn't wait to speak to Zayn?

Her gut felt like a hard knot. "Your cousin…how could you let that man leave?"

"I let him leave only from here."

"It took all these weeks to locate him and you just—"

"I told you I will take care of it."

"And Aslam continues to be in—"

"Amalia, sit down and calm yourself. You're drawing far too much attention."

"Because I am not shutting up about you, the Sheikh of Khaleej, letting a criminal slip out because he's your family."

His lips pulled back, a hardness entering his eyes. "No, you're drawing attention because you're raising your voice at your fiancé, who is currently surrounded by his guests, some of whom are state dignitaries and a wedding party, and all of whom would like nothing better than to point out that you lack the finesse and sophistication to deal with this in a sensitive and adult manner."

Amalia swallowed her gasp, his words pinching like sharp needles. It was one thing to hear from Mirah that Zayn's family, his advisers and the entire world did not think her suitable for the sheikh, quite different when he put it that way.

Dear God, she hadn't been hoping that something would change in the last few weeks, had she?

She felt like that little girl, confused and yet somehow aware of the painful reality of life. It felt like her heart was punctured inside her chest.

But she had come too far to give up now. "I don't care what they think about me."

"I do. Care about what they will say about you."

"You do?"

"Yes. Your reputation directly affects me."

Amalia had never felt this desperate struggle inside to be something she was not. Had never dreamt that falling in love would mean finding herself so inadequate to the man she loved. Being with Zayn was cleaving her within. "God forbid the sheikh is perceived as a weak man, a man who did not control his wayward fiancée, as a man who actually paid attention to anything coming out of a woman's mouth."

His eyes darkened into hard chips, his mouth a forbidding line. "Amalia, do not turn an age-old prejudice that has nothing to do with us into our fight. Do not turn your parents' disagreement into ours. I have never treated you with anything less than the respect you deserve. You forget that I'm not your lover, Zayn, all the time. I'm the sheikh and yes, I cannot be seen as not being able to stop my unruly fiancée from turning my sister's wedding breakfast into a ruckus about the justice system of Khaleej.

"Especially men and women I've been trying to appease with this whole charade."

He was not just angry, Amalia realized, her temper slowly losing its edge. It was more than his usually amused, tolerant annoyance at one of her blunt opinions. This was different.

This felt like withdrawal. Like he was retreating behind that damned mantle of his position. Like he was using her lack of discretion this moment to remind himself how unsuitable she was for him.

She wanted to scream; she wanted to walk away and hide in the privacy of her bedroom. But she did neither.

She settled down into the chair he had pulled out for her, a morass of emotions churning through her.

Her stomach slipped to her feet at all the curious faces that were watching her and Zayn. His parents' disapproval was like a force field even across the hall. No, she wouldn't feel as if she'd done something wrong just because she had lost her temper a little.

Then she saw Mirah and Farid at the main table and the fear mixed in with shock in Mirah's face. Shame filled her then. Mirah had been nothing but affectionate and welcoming to Amalia, even as she had realized that Amalia created waves among her family, even as she learned that some of Farid's family members disapproved of her.

Whether she had a right to be angry or not was moot. This was Mirah's day, a day she'd been looking forward to for quite a while.

She forced a smile to her lips and pulled her chair closer to Zayn's. With trembling fingers, she pushed at some imaginary speck on his collar. Filled the nerve-racking silence by telling him the morning she had had with a staff member and her stylist.

If it killed her, she'd not make a spectacle of herself. And him.

"Are you planning to kill me with that uncharacteristic inane chatter?" Zayn interrupted her in a dry voice that scratched against her senses. His thumb drew circles over her wrist, spreading a soft languor through her skin to every inch of her.

"Isn't that what you wanted?" she asked with fake sweetness.

"For you to act like there's nothing but cotton wool between your ears?" He sounded distinctly put out. "For you to simper at me with that fake smile and no real warmth in your eyes, no."

She sighed. "Sometimes I don't know what you want from me. Except—"

"Except?"

"Except when we're making...when we're having sex."

Something hard glittered in his eyes. Whatever anger she'd seen in his eyes until now, it was nothing like this fiery blaze that set his gaze alight. "You were going to say making love. You changed it to sex. Has your attitude toward that intimacy changed so much? Has it become so casual, then?"

"No, of course not," she protested hotly. She sighed and hid her face in his arm. How could she be angry with him when she'd provoked him on purpose? When it was this answer that she wanted from him?

When she probed him for answers while she couldn't tell him how she felt? Her time with him was counting down, mere days now, yet all she wanted was to forget Aslam, or Mirah or their respective positions in life and just be Amalia and Zayn.

The last thing she wanted to be was clingy when it was time to leave, but she wasn't able to harden her heart, either.

"I've never been this confused in my life," she said into the stretching silence. It was not the complete truth, but it was not a lie. "All I did in the last three weeks was accompany you to all the social events you bid me to, and look at some interesting issues when people courted my interest.

"And yet I'm called opinionated and too forward-thinking. All I was doing was just being—"

"You were just being yourself," Zayn finished for her, taking her hand in his on top of the table. "That is not your fault, Amalia. You're right, you did everything that I asked you to do."

But she was never going to be the right woman for

him. In a million years, she could not change herself and become the sort of woman everyone would approve of. Was this how her mother had felt with her father? Had there been no easy way to love her father without changing who she was?

She nodded, feeling a strange gush of tears at the back of her eyes. "How can I not be furious when you let him go?"

"Do you trust me, Amalia?"

Every logical thought said she shouldn't. It had been eight weeks since she'd walked into his study and except for allowing her to visit Aslam once and now letting the real culprit go, Zayn had done nothing to help her cause.

But every instinct, every irrational impulse that had absorbed everything about the man, screamed yes. "Yes, I do," Amalia finally whispered. "I think I trusted you from the beginning, Zayn, even when you were blackmailing me."

He laughed then, a hard, but genuine sound, and Amalia gazed up at him. Once again, they drew the attention of the crowd. But this time she knew it was because they were as mesmerized at the sight of him laughing as she was.

"I owe you an apology for not trusting your word. And that you had to resort to blackmail for what was right."

His apology, the tenderness in his eyes, sparked a joy inside her. "I liked blackmailing you, Sheikh."

Wicked amusement lit his gaze. "If my calculation of my cousin's character is right, he will confess in the next day. After that it will be a matter of days before Aslam is released. Just a matter of hours before you can see him."

Amalia shivered and instantly he held her close. "I can't wait to see him, to hug him."

"He is lucky to have you for his champion. I hope he learns to not throw away his life like this again. There's so much he could do."

The wistful note in his voice shook Amalia from within, that glimpse of the dreamer within. "And your cousin? Will he go to jail?"

"I do not know."

"But we both know that he is culpable. You told me yourself that your policy is harsh against drug offenders."

"Yes, but it is not in my hands to see his punishment matches his crime. My father or someone high up will interfere, because they will fear the reputation of the royal family, and his sentence will be lesser for that fact."

"How can you be so calm about that?"

"Nothing can be achieved by raging against things that you cannot change, Amalia. It is a lesson I learned very early in life."

"So much for making me believe that you're all powerful," she snorted, even as she understood what he meant.

If she had learned anything in the last two months, it was how delicately Zayn had to balance his actions with how the populace perceived him.

He couldn't be too forward, too westernized in his thoughts, nor could he let Khaleej live in the past. Progress and tradition had to be carefully weighed in every step he took in the name of the state. She wished she didn't; she wished she could see him as a ruthless statesman, as a playboy and not as a man sometimes caught between past and future, between his own dreams and his country's needs.

Because the more she saw that, the more Amalia felt as if she belonged by his side. Instead of wanting to run away from the challenges she would face, she felt energized by them; she felt as if this was what she was supposed to do.

To love this honorable man and be his mate in everything. To embrace her culture and her roots finally because Zayn embodied the best parts of it.

Except he was like an island, believing that his duty had to be carried out without an ounce of happiness in his own life.

Didn't he need someone who would walk that delicate balance with him, someone with whom he need not be the all-powerful sheikh and just Zayn, a man with vulnerabilities?

But she lacked the defiant courage to say that to him, to put her own deep feelings into words. She'd shared the most intimate moments of her life with him, but to open her heart to him, fear and pain at the prospect of his rejection rippled through her.

A wicked smile curved his mouth. "Now you know my darkest secret, *habibti*. Maybe I should make you a lifelong prisoner so that you do not tell the world what Sheikh Zayn Al-Ghamdi is beneath what they see."

Amalia had never been so glad for being interrupted by Mirah at that minute. If Zayn had looked into her eyes, he would've known how much she wanted to be part of his life, even when it was an upward battle for her pretty much on every front.

CHAPTER ELEVEN

"WHERE ARE YOU GOING?"

Only after the question reverberated in the bedroom did Zayn realize how accusatory and childish he sounded. No, not just sounded. That was how he felt.

As if he was being pulled in polarizing directions, being split in between. As though he was being told again and again by a relentless voice that his life was different, that his life was not ordinary.

"Love is a weakness for other people, a fantasy, an indulgence we cannot afford, Zayn."

His father's derisive words were like little worms inside his head, and he took a deep breath trying to banish the turmoil he felt inside.

It was impossible that this turmoil, this constant confusion, could be love. He didn't even know what love was, truly. He didn't know how deep and abiding a connection could be between a man and a woman.

All he knew was he still hadn't quite driven out the attraction, the lust he felt for Amalia. Given that she was the first woman who had integrated into aspects of his life that had never even known a woman, it followed that he felt a connection with her.

A connection he was not prepared to sever just yet.

"I asked you something, Amalia."

Her hands stilled on the bag she was packing, but she didn't turn around instantly. He hated when she did that, when she hid her reaction from him, when she pulled some facade together so that he couldn't even guess what was going on in her mind.

In five days of the most lavish celebrations and ceremonies around Mirah's wedding, all he had seen was what the rest of the world saw.

Amalia Noor Hadid Christensen, as the Khaleej media had taken to calling her once her roots and her background had been discovered. Poised, stylish, the perfect ornament on the sheikh's arm, with a ready smile for the guests or the media. As Mirah's wedding day neared, it was as if the light had gone out from her eyes. She had retreated so far behind her mask that even Zayn began to long for her impertinent remarks and her blunt honesty.

The rip of the zipper on her bag hurtled him out of his brooding thoughts.

She finally turned around, her gaze implacable. "Mirah is having a kind of girls' night with her friends in her wing tonight. As she is leaving with her husband tomorrow." She darted from her bedroom to the open area near the pool and he prowled after her. The charge that was never far behind between them built up, even more electrifying for she was leading him on a chase.

Something savage and atavistic filled Zayn for they both knew how this was going to end, how tonight was going to play out. His pulse raced, his muscles tightening already.

"She invited me over and I thought I would make a night out of it."

"Do you have to pack all your things for one night?" he asked again, walking around the pool, following her, just as she picked up a paperback from one of the alcoves.

He closed his mind and instantly, the image of her spread out on the low divan with a book in her hand flashed. Always, he realized that image would haunt him now.

With a frown, he looked around the house he had poured all his dreams into. Every nook and cranny was now touched with memories of Amalia.

He reached her at the entrance of his own bedroom and blocked her exit. A nightgown and her iPad were in her hands this time. He had hid the iPad two nights ago when she wouldn't give him the attention he wanted.

She had squealed and tried to get away, and he had tackled her until they had both fallen to the rug in a heap. And then he had covered her body with his, desperate to possess her. The same insistent desire filled him now, blinding him to everything else.

The freedom he found with her, the ecstasy when he sank deep into her…it was a drug he would forever crave.

"I thought it a good idea to pick up my stuff. Six weeks is a long time and I have strewn small things around everywhere."

When she turned to step out, he blocked the entrance. Skin flushed, mouth trembling, she would not even meet his gaze. "Zayn—"

One arm stretched out to stop her, he leaned against the other side. "I did not think I would see the day when you would be so intimidated by me that you would not even meet my gaze, Amalia."

Shoulders went back; she glared at him. "I hope that day never comes."

His hands found her shoulders, automatically tipping her body toward his. "You've been avoiding me for the past few days. Actually, since that morning breakfast."

She didn't shy her gaze this time, but conveniently hid it in his chest. His heart rumbled against her cheek, a reaction he was used to now. "There were a lot of places I needed to be. Mirah was counting on me."

"And today?" he asked. When she would have danced away from him, he snaked both arms around her. Shaping the curve of her bottom, he pulled her flush against him. He couldn't stop touching her, couldn't stop the passion from flaring between them at a moment's notice. "Would you rather spend it with Mirah or her brother?"

Amalia knew she should say Mirah or a hundred other destinations that didn't have the man. But she was weak, irrevocably in love with him, hungry for every second she could spend with him. In his arms. Her flesh was trembling and weak after avoiding him for four days.

A gloriously savage smile curving his lips, he kissed her possessively, instantly filling her with wanton heat. One touch of those gorgeous lips was enough to ready her for his possession, enough to make her cling to him with a keening groan.

She clung to him and pressed her lips to his neck when he lifted her into his arms and carried her to the pool area. A soft gasp left her as the raw beauty of the house overwhelmed her again.

A sky dotted with silver jewel-like stars reflected in the pool below, making the surface of water ripple and glitter like a jewel itself. Moroccan lanterns around the pool provided just enough light for them to see their way. The smell of rose incense drifted from somewhere, filling the air with the voluptuous tendrils of it.

She had never imagined herself in a place such as this, true. But it was the man who had her breath fluttering in and out of her throat, her limbs liquid and aching.

Barely out of breath, he carried them to an alcove that gave the best view of the sky and the pool.

When he slid her to her feet and reached for the zipper of her dress, Amalia stayed his hand. "The staff…"

"Did you not realize that no one is allowed here, especially during the night, *habibti*?" His low whisper strummed at her nerves. Fingers danced over the skin he bared, pressing and stroking. "I did not want anyone to hear the sounds you make when you come. I could not take the chance that one of them could walk by and see your silky skin, or those pouty breasts, or the way you drape those legs around me when you sleep.

"You are mine, Amalia. Something savage awakens in me when I think of any other man even looking at your beautiful body or hearing those little whimpers you make."

Her mouth dry, Amalia stood awash in the sensations that pummeled her.

She was his. She wanted to be his in every waking moment, not just in the dark intimacy of the night.

But before she could even form the words, he rid her of her fitted sheath dress and her strapless bra, leaving her in her bikini panties. The cold breeze kissed her nudity and she shivered. Only when his own skin, heated and like rough velvet touched her, did Amalia realize that he had already shed his clothes, too.

Slowly, pockets of heat began to emerge on her cold skin, until in mere seconds, she was burning with need.

Turning her around so that she could see their outlines in the pool, he pressed his mouth into her shoulder. Rough bristles scraped against the sensitive skin. Amalia would have melted to the tiles on the floor if he wasn't holding her up.

"From the minute you walked in here that day and looked around you with such wonder, I have dreamed of taking you like this. Out in the open, with the sky and the stars witness to this magic between us…"

By the time he was rolling her nipples with his fingers, Amalia was already panting. Her flesh damp and ready for him. Melting her skin with his kisses, he brought them to the ground.

Smiling when she protested, he pulled her over on top of him, until she was straddling him. Different sensations, an even more stringent awareness, drenched Amalia.

She closed her eyes when he moved his palm from the valley between her breasts to her abdomen that clenched with need and then finally to her core. A groan ripped from her when he tested her readiness.

"You astride me, with your glorious hair falling about you, and the jeweled sky in the background. It's all the Bedouin inside me wants. Take me inside you, *ya habibti*."

Greedy for him, Amalia reached for him and guided his hot, thick erection into her. He held her hips loosely, letting her set the pace. The first slide of his turgid flesh inside her channel sent her head back.

"Tell me how it feels," he demanded, his voice thick and hoarse.

Amalia couldn't bear to move yet. Nor open her eyes and look at him. "The pleasure is intense. Zayn, you…you feel like you're everywhere inside me."

His hands slowly moved to her buttocks then and taking the cue, Amalia wiggled. Their groans ripped the silent air, the sound drifting into the sky.

She slapped her palms on his chest, tilted her body forward until he almost pulled out of her.

The tight, bruising clasp of his fingers over her, the veins stretching in his neck, told her how much he was rearing to take control. That it stretched the edges of his desire to give her the lead.

Reveling in the sheer power of rendering such a man

out of his control, Amalia straightened and moved up and down again.

Hard and filthy, his words sent a thrill through her. With every thrust, she learned what this fiercely gorgeous man wanted, learned what increased her own pleasure.

And then she set a rhythm that set all the wildness of her love that she hid free. Here, there was no distance between them. Here, she didn't fear rejection.

In that moment they were perfect for each other. Only with each other were they complete.

Sweat coated her skin. Amalia clenched her inner muscles tighter just as Zayn stroked her clit.

Throwing her head back, she cried out, tears pouring down her cheeks at the intensity of the pleasure. His hard upward thrusts filled her body, riding the wave of her orgasm. The hard slap of his thrusts chased the contractions in her muscles, making her limbs molten. His hard body jerked under her as he came with an explosive growl.

She fell on top of him, feeling as if she had broken apart into a thousand pieces.

Her panting breaths fell on his damp skin as he held her tight against him. Every time he was inside her, every time they shared this explosive fire, her defenses were shattered, too.

She closed her eyes and willed herself to remember every texture of his skin, the scent of his damp body, the clench of his muscles, the beauty of this hard man who possessed a big heart.

For it was time for her to leave.

"Zayn, we have to talk."

"No, we don't. I don't care if Mirah invited your favorite rock star, Amalia. You're not leaving my side tonight."

"I'm not talking about tonight. I want to discuss something important."

His hand slid blatantly between her thighs and already, a wanton thrill began again at her sex. She became shamelessly damp again, a groan rising out of her against her own will. Ready for him again.

If he moved that thumb that was languorously resting against the swollen bud at her sex, if he even touched those lips to her skin, Amalia knew she would not recover tonight. And another night and another night would pass on while the long days would gouge her with hope and hollow her with wanting.

Waiting to be told that their charade was over.

Waiting to be told that Zayn Al-Ghamdi did not need her anymore.

Waiting to feel her heart ripped out of her chest…

She needed to leave while she still had a little of herself intact, before he completely crushed her.

"I want to talk about us, our relationship. This can't wait till morning."

He released her so fast, all the desire disappeared from his face so quickly that Amalia would have laughed if she wasn't so close to crying again. Feeling as though more than just her body was nakedly vulnerable to him, she pulled the blanket he had covered them with earlier around her.

He obviously felt no such self-consciousness. Still, she had to have this conversation and Amalia needed it to be without an evidence of what she was walking away from. So she stood up along with her blanket, reached for another one and threw it at him.

His mouth twitched but thankfully, he said nothing about her continual shyness with him. Not that he hadn't awakened her into all kinds of wanton desires…

"Is this a discussion we have to have tonight?"

Dragging a forceful breath into her lungs, she held on to the anger that rose through her. "You need not look so alarmed. I just…I wanted to talk about our plans."

"I'm not alarmed. I am…" He clutched his nape with his hand, and the muscles in his chest shifted, tempting her. "This is the first night we have had some privacy, a little time with each other in over a week." He sounded like a little boy and Amalia stared at him in consternation.

"Zayn…"

But the moment of vulnerability was already gone. "Tell me, what is it?"

"I…need to make plans. Mirah is happily married to a man who will love her for the rest of her life, thanks to you."

"And you," he added, his mouth flattening.

She shrugged. "I heard from one of your aides today that Aslam will be released any day now. Once I make sure he is okay, I need to leave—"

"Back to Massi and your waiting life?"

"You know how I feel about him and yet you continually—"

He pulled her to him suddenly, a blaze of emotion in his eyes. "Because I'm jealous of your friendship with him. This is what you do to me, Amalia."

Her breath slammed hard into her throat. "This is about us. Now that we've accomplished both our goals, I need to go back to my life. I can't put it on hold forever. Neither for Aslam nor for you. At some point, I have to walk out of this fantasy and back into reality."

"You do not have to leave Sintar yet." *Or me.* His unsaid words fluttered in the air.

Hope fluttered in her chest like a fragile bird's tiny wings. "What…what do you mean?"

"You were right. Mirah is married and as much as a poll comes out every week about your unsuitability to be the next sheikha, Khaleej and its populace, my family, my staff, the entire world, believes we are together. That you've thoroughly enchanted me. Apparently, you are the modern-day Cinderella.

"Why ruin it when we don't have to?"

"You want me to stay in Sintar?"

"Yes. With me, here at the palace."

If her heart beat any faster, Amalia was afraid it would burst right out of her chest. "Zayn, I don't know what to—"

"Thanks to your blackmailing scheme, I do not have to worry about marriage for a little while. And I do not see why we cannot continue to enjoy each other, continue this pretense until I have to do the duty thing again."

Pain was an arrow in her chest, a knife lodged in her ribs. Words wouldn't rise to her lips past her raw throat. "You still intend to look for some suitable candidate?"

"Yes. I can indulge myself for a short while, Amalia, but in the end, I will need a sheikha…"

Amalia rose to her feet so swiftly that her head whirled for a second. She had been right. He would never see her as anything but unsuitable. Never give her a chance.

She raised her chin, draping her pride and self-respect like a blanket over her breaking heart. "As good as it is to know that you have it all worked out according to your plans and life, I'm afraid that will not work for me, Zayn."

Something hard entered his eyes at the way she had imitated his formal speech. "And why is that?"

"You see, just like you, I have some expectations for myself, if not a kingdom's. And since I joined this whole living away from the shadow of past a little too late, I intend to make up for lost time.

"A toxic relationship that's predestined to go nowhere

while I fall more and more into its depths…" Her voice wobbled here, her grief over losing him overpowering her stupid pride. "That reminds me far too much of a fate my mother lived.

"If there's one thing I have learned in these six weeks, in our torrid affair, it is that I don't have to live my life based on anyone's fears or hang-ups. And that includes you and this notion you have, this template you have of what kind of woman would suit you."

He clutched her arms, his grip painful. Tears filling her eyes, Amalia struggled to not sink into his embrace. "You have always known where this was going."

"Yes, I did. And I'm saying enough now. Before you completely break me. Before you make me into a shadow who could never recover her old self.

"Don't do that to me, Zayn. Don't make me regret knowing you. Please don't make me hate you and myself."

Such a fierce glow burned in his eyes. Amalia shivered violently, seeing the knowledge that dawned in his eyes. They both knew how powerless she was to resist him again and again… They both knew that in that minute, all he had to do was to cover the distance between their seeking mouths and she would agree to stay…

But slowly his grip on her loosened. And he walked away without a word.

Amalia crumpled to her knees on the tiles, disappointment and relief and every other emotion crushing her.

CHAPTER TWELVE

HANDS TUCKED INTO the pockets of his trousers, Zayn stood at the window of his study, looking out over the grounds that surrounded the palace. The last few weeks had been the hardest of his life. He had buried himself in work, driving himself at a relentless pace that had strained his staff to the maximum as if he could run far and fast from the desolation that seemed to be weighing him down if he took a moment to breathe.

Duty over personal happiness…it had been a tenet by which he'd lived all his life and yet, that same duty lost its satisfaction for him. The more he worked for the betterment of Khaleej, the more resentful of it he grew.

For it was a steep price he had to pay.

Amalia had shattered the cold aloofness he had built into a shell around him, reaching a part of him that he had buried deep.

He had spent all morning on his phone and still, he had no idea where she was. Morning had given way to noon, sunlight glittering over the gardens in the courtyard.

Had he drifted here because this was where he had met her first? Had she so thoroughly written him off that she had made herself so unreachable? Only one man could have helped her, and the idea of Amalia with Massi burned an acrid hole in his gut.

Regrets piled over him. He should have never let her leave him in the first place. He shouldn't have taken so long to break out of his own shell, to realize that his world was empty without her by his side, that he couldn't even stomach the idea of some faceless, docile woman... The thought that she might be permanently lost to him carved paths through him, making him utterly restless.

He had never felt so alone; never had the burden of Khaleej felt so unbearable. He didn't even want to face his father.

He had never been a gambling man and yet, he had taken this chance. Had hoped that the thought of his wedding would somehow bring Amalia back to him.

The creak of the door made him turn, his heart jumping into his chest.

He let out a harsh breath when he saw that his guest was Benjamin Carter. Newly wed and nauseatingly in love, the New York tycoon was the last man Zayn wanted to see.

At least with the rest of the palace and its staff, no one dared to point out the obvious with him. That he was to be married in hours and his bride was missing.

"It has come to my attention that you're missing a bride, Sheikh," the American drawled, a lazy twitch to his mouth. "Is it possible that our esteemed Ms. Young was unable to convince a woman to take you on?"

Zayn rolled his eyes. "Since you're my invited guest and your bride will clearly be horrified by the result, I will refrain from messing up your face, Carter. Now leave me in peace."

Any other man would have cowered at the steel in his tone. However, as he had expected, the warning barely registered on the man. His gaze, at least, lost that wicked smile. "Your staff is in uproar, your PR people don't know if they should issue a statement. This could easily become another big scandal, Sheikh. Even if your sister is happily married, your reputation could still—"

"In your slang, Carter, I don't give a damn."

"Where is the woman you're supposed to marry?"

Despite the void in his gut, Zayn found it easy to answer. Maybe because Carter was one of those few people in the world who wasn't intimidated by the mantle of power that Zayn carried. "Not supposed to, Carter. The woman I want to marry."

Carter's gaze cleared, as if the meaning was clear. "Yeah? So where is she?"

The expression on the other man's face made Zayn crack a smile. "I don't know where she is. I don't know if she will show up, either."

"But she knows that she's marrying you today, yes?" Now he sounded as if Zayn had lost his mind.

Maybe he had. Maybe waiting for a woman he hadn't even asked to marry him was foolish. But if this talk of his wedding didn't ferret Amalia out, nothing would. He would have a mess to clean up come tomorrow, but Zayn found he didn't give a damn right now.

Zayn shook his head and a filthy curse fell from Carter's mouth.

"This is not some strange custom in Khaleej, is it, Sheikh? That the groom doesn't know if the bride's going to show up?"

"I should feel insulted, I think, but I know you mean well, Carter. And no, it is no strange custom."

He had defied all customs and traditions by falling in love. He didn't think Amalia was unsuitable for him anymore. It was he that fell short of the kind of man Amalia deserved.

He had incredible power at his hands; he was probably one of the wealthiest men in the world, but he would not be able to give her unlimited time if she spent her life with him. Nor could he give her a loving, welcoming family.

Except for Mirah, he had no doubt that most of his family would give her the cold treatment. For most of her life, she would be made to feel like an outsider.

She would have to trade so many things that she could have with any other man to be with him. If he had any sense, he would just let her go.

But Zayn realized he was also selfish when it came to her. Giving up architecture, unsuitable friends, personal happiness, they were nothing when he thought of how empty his life would be without Amalia by his side.

"Then I need a drink and it's clear that you need one, too, Sheikh. So why don't you—?"

The door slammed open again and this time, Amalia stood at the threshold. Mouth trembling, chest rising and falling, she looked blazingly furious. "*You*…arrogant, heartless, cold brute. How could you?"

His heart thudded against his chest. Something twisted and settled deep in him, an overwhelming urge to take her in his arms and hide her away in the desert. Where she would never have another opportunity to escape him.

He smiled at that imagery—that would be as palatable to Amalia as him dragging her by her hair into his cave… Throat tight and air gushing from his lungs, he couldn't quite hold himself together.

His bluff had worked. But it was still a long way to go. Pride came to his rescue. "I believe heartless and cold mean the same thing, Amalia." It was the only way left to him to fight the lost feeling that had surrounded him for three weeks.

He was not good with this feeling of inadequacy, this self-doubt. He did not like that he was going to have to finesse the deal of his lifetime and he had less to offer than the other party.

Twin spots sat high on her cheeks as she curled her mouth in that threatening way of hers. "You don't want to mess with me today, Zayn. Maybe you've forgotten, but I'm very good at blackmailing, remember? And the whole world, once again, would love to hear what I have to say about His Royal Highness Sheikh Zayn Al-Ghamdi."

Shock made Zayn silent while Carter's laughter boomed in the room like the explosions of firecrackers.

She cast a glance at Benjamin, her chest falling and rising. "Can I have a few minutes with the sheikh?"

That lazy smile returning to his mouth, Carter nodded. To Zayn, he said, "I assume the wedding is on, Sheikh? Should I alert your staff to the fact?"

If there was a moment when Zayn would have happily forgotten that they were supposed to be adult men and not pummel each other, it was this. He kept his eyes on Amalia, saw the anger in hers and caught the urge. "Yes," he said irritably. He hated the weak feeling in his gut, this feeling of being out of control. Nothing in his life had prepared him for this.

"Ms. Christensen, I suppose," Carter asked and Amalia nodded. "Give him hell."

The door closed behind Carter, leaving them in a stark silence. For a few seconds all they did was stare at each other. He had faced so many daunting situations in his life—political and financial with innumerable lives in his hand, and yet, the tension that was strummed through every inch of him was a stranger.

"Amalia—"

"You said you were going to wait a few months. It's been barely a month since I left and this date... God, this was the date we told people *we* would be marrying. I just..."

She ran a trembling hand to push a lock of hair out of her eyes and that was when finally Zayn noticed it.

It felt like a punch to his gut, a slap of rejection.

She had cut her hair. Those long waves that he'd loved wrapping around his fingers, that had caressed his body with a silken touch, they caressed her face and jaw now, giving her an elfin-like look.

But since he meant to begin the way he wanted to go on, he pursed his mouth. He needed her in his life like no other but he didn't want their life to become one battle after another. There were going to be enough battles to fight together without their personal life becoming one, too.

"You cut your hair," he said, accusation high in his tone.

Her fingers drifted through her shoulder-length locks. Defiance made her eyes glimmer like precious jewels. "I wanted something different, something that didn't make me think of you every day."

Another punch, another roughly indrawn breath. "And it was as simple as cutting off your hair?" Something he had adored.

She shrugged. And when the furor in his chest calmed down, when he let instinct, the newly discovered emotions in his gut, drive him rather than plain facts and logic, Zayn remembered that she did that when she didn't want to quite tell the truth.

She was here, he reminded himself again. She had come blasting through his doors at the idea of his wedding. That was the start he had wanted.

"Where have you—"

"I didn't come here to answer your questions or to be harassed by you."

Why had he thought this was going to be easy? He had little enough experience dwelling on and talking about his feelings…only a handful of times when he had even felt such strong emotions…and this was Amalia, who turned everything into a battle. He sighed. "Why are you here, then?"

"I came to give you a piece of my mind."

"And where have you been for the last month?" The question slipped through his lips, bitter jealousy tugging at the reins of his control.

"With…" Again that infernal shrug. "That doesn't matter. I needed to come because—"

"Is Aslam in trouble again?"

"Will you stop interrupting me as if I'm one of your staff members? This is hard enough as it is," she mumbled at the end.

Only now did he realize the dark circles under her eyes, the pinched cut of her features. "I was merely curious about Aslam. I thought I would keep an eye on him for you but my staff could not even locate him."

She stared at him, as if she didn't know what to make of that. And her startled disbelief that he could care about even such a small thing as her brother's welfare made his ire rise. "Is that so hard to believe?"

"Yes. No…" Her lashes flicked down and she moved away from him. He saw her swallow forcefully before she did that. "He…is making changes in his life, the right ones. You were right. That time he spent in the jail, I think it made him see that he was heading toward utter ruin if he continued like that. He's thinking of returning to college."

"I am glad, for your sake more than his. I know how much you love him."

She shrugged, a sheen of wetness coating her eyes. The slight tremble of her mouth, the shuddering breath she drew, it hit Zayn like a blow to the chest.

"Yes, but love is not always enough, is it? I have found

out that my father loved my mother just as much as she loved him, but they could not make it work."

"You went to see him?"

She nodded, a lone tear carving a path on her cheek. "Aslam refused to let me leave. Nor would he go with me. He kept saying I belonged in Sintar with—"

"You do." His statement fell in between them like the pounding of a gavel.

"When he heard of Aslam's release, my father came to see us at the hotel…I realized I couldn't be a coward for the rest of my life. It was time to face him."

"You're the last woman on earth I would call cowardly, Amalia."

She blanched, her skin losing every ounce of color.

"Is it so hard to think that I think well of you, Amalia?"

"Whether you think I'm strong or beautiful or intelligent, it doesn't matter, does it, Zayn? Not when you think…"

Silence ensued between them again fraught with tension and their emotions, things that were rearing to break out into the open. Zayn felt as if he was going to break from the inside out.

Her shoulders shaking, Amalia looked like a slight breeze would fell her, too. Only then he realized how much it would have cost her to come here today, when she would have had to see the woman he would've chosen.

And in the face of that vulnerability, pride and self-respect and arrogance, everything dissolved. That she would take this step toward him when he'd done nothing but use her was humbling and even disconcerting. Love, it seemed, given and returned, was a roller coaster, one minute exaltation and the next, utter desperation.

"There is no bride here today."

She frowned. The tremor that went through her lithe

body was far too obvious to miss. "No bride...what does that mean?" She pushed her hair back from her face, a gesture left over even though she cut the thick waves. And it tugged at him as nothing could.

She looked toward the door, her body poised for flight and then turned toward him again. The frown deepened into a scowl. "But there are guests flying in from the neighboring countries and from your own family. There are network station crews everywhere waiting to telecast...how the hell can you not have a bride, Zayn?"

Zayn came to her and took her hands in his. Never had his heart beat so rapidly. "I forgot to ask the bride to marry me. So she doesn't know. I was just hoping against hope that she would show up. Carter thinks I've lost my mind and I believe he is right."

Comprehension dawned on her face and she jerked her hands away from him. "This was all..."

"Amalia—"

"You're a manipulative jerk!"

"Manipulative? You disappeared off the face of the earth. You would not take my calls, you cut me off from your life as thoroughly as you did your father."

"Because my heart was breaking and there was only so much of you I could resist before I weakened and stayed for as long as you wanted me."

"You do not know how much I regret putting you through that, how much I wish..." Tenderness filled his gaze, stealing what little rationality Amalia was trying to hold on to. "Will you marry me? Today?"

"Is this some kind of political face-saving?"

"No. In fact, I've had advisers continually offer infernal advice that you might not be a good candidate to be my sheikha."

"I heard enough of that while I was here. And I think

you and your damned advisers are all wrong. That's what I came to tell you."

"That's what you came to tell me…" he repeated, a little spark of hope fluttering to life inside him. Her wrist bones were delicate in his hands, almost fragile. And yet she held his happiness, his future, in her hands. "Tell me, then."

"I think your assumption that you can't have even a small flicker of happiness in your life is wrong. Your assumption that I would somehow detract you from your duty, somehow minimize your power, is even more absurd.

"I understand about duty and selflessness more than you think.

"I put my life on hold for so many years to look after my mom. And I never once weakened, or resented her for it. I would never weaken you, Zayn. How could I?

"There have been kings and presidents and heads of state all over the world throughout history who married for love, who chose to reach for a little personal happiness, too, and they have only thrived.

"If you think I would become a liability to you—" her voice caught here, her throat a mass of emotions "—then you're not the man I thought."

A gold blaze flared in his eyes, drenching her entire being in a joy that she couldn't contain. "And if I told you that I came to the same conclusion, only a little slower than you? That I could shoulder all the responsibility in the world if I have you by my side, that you make everything joyful, meaningful?"

There was no stopping her tears now. Her heart thundered into life as if all it had been doing until now was pump blood. "You tricked me! You still think this is some kind of power struggle between us. You…"

"You left me no choice but to trick you. I…could not

find you and I…went crazy imagining all kinds of scenarios."

"I was never in any kind of trouble, Zayn."

"Trouble? No." A stark need filled his eyes then. "You're the most capable woman I have ever known, Amalia. Some nights I found myself fervently wishing you weren't so strong and independent, so stubborn that—"

Throat raw, she said, "I know what you wish I was, but this is who I am."

"You misunderstand me. It took you—your strength, your spirit, your independence—all of you to unlock my heart. So much that I have this unbearable feeling inside my chest that it is I who is not enough for you. My worry was that you must have realized you deserved a man who recognized that, who loved you like you should be loved.

"I was terrified that you went back to Massi, had written me off completely."

Amalia could do nothing but stare at Zayn, at the vulnerability that punctured every word he uttered. She went to him then, any anger she'd held on to as a defense melting at the warmth in his words.

He clutched her to him hard, driving the breath out of her lungs. Hard body shuddered around her, telling her more than his words ever could. He loved her, she knew it now, even if he had yet to say it. But feelings and emotions were hard for him. He'd been trained to view them as weaknesses, trained to believe that he needed no one and nothing.

He had taken an enormous risk on her, this man who didn't put one step wrong if he thought it would hurt Khaleej and the perception about him. He had made himself vulnerable for her. And for now that had to be enough.

They all kept crowing she was far too opinionated, far too independent to be good for him, didn't they? Well, she was. And she couldn't bear for him to second-guess himself. "I've never loved and will never love a man like I love you, Zayn. What do I have to do to make you believe that?"

His fingers clasped her face, and such sheer happiness, such liquid joy, dawned in his eyes that Amalia forgot to breathe. Just that smile of his was enough to hurtle her into falling in love with him all over again. A smile, she knew, no one but she had witnessed. That was all for her, only her.

A jagged breath left him as he leaned his forehead against hers. "My heart belongs to you, *ya habibti*. This feeling, this cavernous void in my chest as if I had left an essential part of me somewhere, as if I would never feel whole again...I have never felt anything like it. I have never resented everything I have to be as I do when you're not with me.

"You've opened my heart. I love you, Amalia."

His mouth covered hers then and Amalia melted into his touch. Every cell, every inch of her, felt like it was touched with light, with a piercing sharp awareness. Lacing her fingers around his nape, she moved under his expert caresses hungrily, opening up for him, like a flower did for a sun. The fluid power of his lean body, the hard rattle of his heart against hers, she had never felt more powerful; never had she reveled so much in being alive.

A shiver danced over her spine as he widened his legs and cradled her, as his erection imprinted itself against her belly. A month of separation had only made the need to know him in that intimacy that much keener. It was fueled by fear, too, for only in bed, only when they were sharing that deepest intimacy, did Zayn open up to her.

She moved her hands to his lean hips, desperate to have him inside her again. Laughing against her mouth, he pulled back, after he drew her body into a punishingly raw response.

"I would love for nothing but to take you here, *latifa*, but…" He looked so drugged that Amalia laughed. "I remembered. Where were you, Amalia?"

"With Aslam and my father."

"I wish you had let me be there with you. I wish you had let me be your strength."

"But you made me see myself through new eyes. Made me question everything I had ever believed. I was so angry by what my father had done by sending me away with her, I clutched all my mother's complaints about him and let them feed my hatred.

"If I hated him, I would never have to face the hurt. When I left here, I was so angry with you and with him. With myself. That anger was good, positive."

"What did he say?"

"I'm still angry with him for giving up on me so easily but I understand why he did it. Mom was always prone to these periods of extreme joy, then would come volatile periods and then these deep, dark periods where nothing could jolt her out of it.

"And their differences and the pressures of marriage didn't help. When he suggested she needed to seek medical help, she flew off the handle. Even I remember that day when I blocked out everything else. He told me how he realized that life with him made everything only that much harder for her.

"It was the day she told him she wanted a divorce."

Zayn scowled. "I don't understand. He thought that she might be suffering from depression and he still let you go with her. That's the height of negligence."

She shrugged, and he knew she was still fighting the same fight. He held her in the circle of his arms, wishing he could somehow take away her pain. He wanted nothing in the world to hurt her and yet, a life with him would only be a challenge for her. But he was determined to make up for it, to love her that much more. He would never let her doubt how much he loved her, how important she was to him.

"You do not have to forgive him or give him a place in your life, *azeezi*. If it's easier for you to face it, hate him. We will never see him again."

Eyes shining with unshed tears, she looked up at him. "It hurts, but I see it, Zayn. She promised him she would seek help if he let her have one of us without contest, if he never came back into her life again.

"And he gave me to her instead of Aslam."

"Because you were the more stable one," Zayn gritted out. He looked so angry on her behalf that Amalia almost worried for her father. "He knew how much she was going to lean on you. He made you an adult long before you were one."

"He had no choice and he loved her far too much, I think. More than he loved me or Aslam. And once I left, he had his hands full with Aslam and then his new family. And although she kept her word to him and sought medical help, I think she never forgave him for giving up on her, for not fighting for her."

Hiding her face in his chest, she took a deep breath. "He…he was so upset when he learned what happened between us." Zayn stiffened around her and she hurried, "I didn't tell him about the blackmail part, just that I… fell in love with you.

"We stayed up the whole night talking. I think he was hoping that I'd walk away from you. He said he only saw problems ahead for us."

"I told him we were nothing like them but he said we have it that much harder."

"He is right, Amalia. I could not lie to you about what lies ahead for—"

It felt like the bottom fell away from under her feet. Again. "What are you saying?"

"That I love you so much that, apparently, I have to put your happiness above my own, *habibti*. A life with me will not be easy on you. A royal life is never without pressures but—"

"You think I'm not aware of it. I came fully prepared to take you on and anyone else who stood in my way, Zayn. I...I think if we love each other truly—"

"There is no *if* about it, *latifa*. I'm lost without you."

Her heart on wings, Amalia kissed him hard. "Then we should be able to conquer anything that comes our way. I know I want to be with you more than anything I have ever wanted in life."

"Will you be my wife, then, Amalia? My sheikha? Will you marry me tonight because I cannot part with you for one more night?"

Amalia nodded, and he took her mouth in a tender kiss that was a promise from the man, and surrender from the sheikh himself.

EPILOGUE

Five years later

THE STARS IN the moonlit sky shone in the dark water beneath, making it look as if they belonged on earth, in that pool, in the house where Amalia made a home with her husband, Sheikh Zayn Al-Ghamdi.

After a month tour of Europe by her husband's side, along with their son and daughter and their entourage, Amalia was glad to be home. It was hard to travel with their itinerary being so full, with kids and nannies and aides, but she wouldn't trade it for anything in this world.

She far preferred to have at least glimpses of her husband at a dinner with politicians rather than not see him for weeks on end. They argued ferociously at times, they compromised sweetly sometimes, but to be never apart more than necessary, to work out their differences and share their dreams... Amalia had never even imagined that she would love so deeply, so completely and have it in return.

It had taken five years of marriage for the media and the populace of Khaleej to finally understand that Amalia had every intention of being her husband's confidante and friend and ally and lover on top of his dutiful wife. That she went on diplomatic tours with her husband. Even when she had been pregnant with Rafiq and Lilah. That she wouldn't quietly sit in his shadow. That her husband and she shared a true marriage of hearts.

The unconventional sheikha, she'd been named. And she'd grown into it happily.

The conservatives, of course, went on a rabble every time she expressed her views but both she and Zayn had long understood that it was more out of habit and principle than any real objection to her.

With her cup of tea in hand, Amalia retreated to one of the cozy nooks. Propping her feet upon the low divan, she closed her eyes.

She loved this house as much as she loved the man who had designed it.

"I thought you would be in bed by now."

She put her cup aside and moved over as Zayn settled down next to her on the divan. "You're done for the night?"

With a chuckle, he nodded. "Is there much left of it?" He unbuttoned his shirt and pulled it out of his trousers. The power in his frame still made her breath catch. Even after five years. "I'm sorry, I know this is the first night we have had to ourselves since we returned but—"

Amalia covered his lips with her finger and pressed into him shamelessly. "You're here now."

"I missed you, *azeezi*."

His arm went around her, his large body coating hers with a warmth she could never get enough of. She turned into his touch eagerly and touched her mouth to his in a lazy kiss. His fingers crawled up her nape and into her hair, holding her still for him. Tendrils of want awoke within her, the raw possession of his touch making her desperate.

"It was nice of Aslam to take the kids," Zayn said in a voice laced with dark honey. Nimble fingers pushed away the straps of her nightdress, working their way to her breast. Her breath caught, a tight wave of pleasure claiming her lower belly.

"Zayn…" She groaned, stretching into his touch, like a cat. "I wanted to talk about the Center for Women's—"

The rest of her words morphed into a groan as her wicked husband pushed her into the divan and covered her with his hard body. Instantly, she wrapped her legs around his hips and cradled his thick erection. "Tonight I do not want the sheikha, nor the razor-sharp, wave-making power woman." He rotated his hips and her head went back at the friction on the aching bundle at her core. "Tonight I want my wife."

Amalia nodded, speech rendered impossible by the man kissing her with a drugging passion. Large hands moved up her calf, up her knee, her quivering thighs and reached her ready heat. "What is it that you want, *ya habibiti*?" he whispered against her forehead.

"You, Zayn. Always you," she managed between blistering breaths and had the reward of seeing the dazzlingly wicked smile of the man she loved, before he entered her and they danced that age-old dance of love again.

* * * * *

THE REBEL KING

MELISSA JAMES

This book is dedicated to Rachel Robinson, for going above and beyond, and for making Charlie the hero he became. Thanks to Robbie and Barb also, and to Emily Ruston for excellent revision suggestions.

PROLOGUE

Sydney, Australia

BY THE time the crew truck screeched up the footpath, the bottom storey of the house was engulfed in flame. Roof tiles at one end had already buckled and were smouldering. The wailing siren of the fire truck seemed obscenely loud over the terrified confusion of people racing around. The night sky was alight, the tinsel of the Christmas decorations in the windows had turned to blazing flame, warming the faces of the onlookers—and seeing the avid interest on so many faces didn't make things better.

That's the job. Charlie Costa faced it as he'd done for years. He'd store the jumbled mass of emotions for later.

'We have a five-to-ten-minute window. Winder, Costa, gear up and go in,' Leopard, the captain, yelled for Charlie and his partner, Toby. 'Do a sweep for any signs of life. The rest of you, douse the house and grounds, and watch those trees. We have to keep the monster from leapfrogging to the surrounding homes.'

'The monster' was the name 'firies' gave the enemy. Charlie remembered the cold shiver that had raced through him the first time he'd heard it. Now it was a battle cry against the hungry destroyer that was the fireman's daily enemy.

'Dissect your internal conundrums later, Rip,' a deep, growling voice came from beside him. 'For now, we fight the Great Destroyer.'

'I'll ask how I can do all those things you said later on, O Grizz, Lord of the Dictionary.' Charlie grinned at Toby Winder, his closest friend. The joking camaraderie they shared in life-and-death situations—such as calling Charlie 'Rip', a nickname due to his legendary temper, and Toby 'Grizz', due to his six-foot-five, muscular frame—helped to defuse the tension.

'Let's rock and roll.' Charlie threw on the mask and strapped on survival gear. Covered by the guys shooting a storm of water and fire-retardant chemicals, he and Toby charged in. They didn't use the axe to break down the door, but shut what was left of it behind them. The other guys would find and close any open windows, and board up those that had already exploded. The less oxygen in here, the better chances for any survivors of this inferno, and reports had come in that there was a young family still trapped inside.

'It's a kitchen fire,' Toby reported into the two-way radio as he bolted through the smoke-filled living room. 'It looks like the gas oven wasn't turned off. It shot straight up through the ceiling to the second floor before it took hold down here.' He wasn't spouting his favourite polysyllables now; he was too worried. 'I'll go upstairs, Rip can take downstairs.'

'No,' Charlie yelled, following Toby to the stairs. 'If anyone was downstairs they'd be outside already. We go up together, and find the kids first, parents after.'

What he didn't say was that pairs had a greater chance of survival. With the risk of the floor buckling under Toby's bigger frame, no way in hell was Charlie letting Toby go up alone. For some reason he'd never understand, his being there to balance the weight usually kept the floor from going a little longer.

They found the first survivor sprawled in the curve of the landing. A young woman, presumably the mother, her arms outstretched to the top storey. Toby did a quick ABC of her condition. 'Get the paramedics in. She's not breathing, pulse weak and thready. She's going down fast.'

Charlie doused the stairs and carpet leading to the door with flame retardant, and moved all furniture that could burn. Toby dragged in a clean breath, turned off the airflow to his mask and began artificial respiration. They couldn't chance any flow of oxygen or even tanked air on her until they were all safely out of here. She wouldn't thank them if they saved her but killed her kids in the inevitable explosion.

A sharp crack, followed by a tearing sound, came as the woman was stretchered out. 'The roof's going!'

As one, the two men bolted up the stairs. 'Send in two more guys to buy us some time!' Charlie yelled into the radio.

Leopard yelled, 'Get out, both of you, and that's an order. It's gonna go!'

Neither paid attention. Charlie took the far end of the hall without discussing it with his friend. Toby knew. He was the bigger and stronger of the two, but Charlie was leaner and faster, with a better chance of getting through any runners of flame.

Without glancing at Charlie, Toby ran into the first room to the left and Charlie immediately heard him shout a directive. 'Ladders to the top bedroom windows!'

Resigned to the inevitable, the captain gave the order. They all knew these two never left a building until the last survivors were found. The way they worked was almost uncanny, which was why the Fire Brigade had kept them together after training. Knowing each other so well could be a handicap in life-and-death situations, but with Toby and Charlie their honesty and camaraderie, their brotherly love, and the way they read each other's minds, made them the best team possible.

Crouching, Charlie ran along the sagging carpeted floor of the hall. It was ready to fall. He jumped from side to side against the walls where the floor remnants would be strongest because of the support beams. Keeping safe meant he'd make it into the room at the back of the house.

He opened the door, slipped in and shut the door behind him to cut off oxygen.

Through the haze the room took shape slowly, but moving would change the landscape, and he'd have to start focusing anew. Thirty seconds later and the picture came to his stinging eyes: a white room, pink bed-spread, a Barbie doll's house. He yelled, a weird, muffled sound through the oxygen mask, 'Is anyone in here?'

Even through the roar of the approaching monster, his trained ears heard a tiny cough.

He shut down and ripped off the mask. Talking through it scared kids, and the suit was scary enough. 'Hey, sweetie, my name's Charlie. I'm a fireman.' He choked on the smoke that filled his lungs and throat in seconds, and breathed in clean oxygen before turning off the mask. He couldn't risk feeding any starters in the room. 'Want to see your mummy?'

Another cough, weak and unformed, came from under the bed. Diving under the quilt, he saw a tiny ball of curled-up humanity. She was dark-haired and sweet-faced, about three. 'It's okay, sweetie, I've got you.' He croaked into the two-way, 'Ladder to the back room, far left! I've got a kid!'

'Forty-five seconds!' Leopard yelled.

Replacing his mask to breathe, he did a quick check on her. The child was alarmingly limp. He wrapped a rope around her fast, ready for the transfer when the guys got to the window, but she'd stop breathing any moment. He lifted her into his arms with excruciating slowness.

It was the cardinal rule: never take off your mask to give to a victim, because you can't save someone if you're dead or unconscious. Doing this would risk not only his life but the lives of his team who'd have to come in to save him, as well as the child if he passed out. But she was little more than a baby. He'd had his life—hers had barely begun.

Hoping there were no sparks in the room to feed on the oxygen, he ripped the mask off, turned the setting to 'air'—too much oxygen right now could do her more harm than good if she had smoke inhalation—and put it over her face. Then, holding his breath, he turned to get out of the door—but the paint was blistering down the edges, and peeling off the entire centre of it.

Smoke was curling off the door handle, and seeping through. An explosion came right beneath him. The house was going. The floor sagged under his left foot.

'I need a ladder to the extreme right of top floor! I've got an unconscious child. He isn't breathing!' Charlie heard Toby yell again, his voice harsh too. Obviously he didn't have his air mask on either. Time was running out fast.

The floor started buckling beneath Charlie's feet. Slowly, inch by inch, he spread his feet further apart, feeling it give way each time he moved. His feet began to burn through his boots. 'We're gonna make it out, sweetie.' Hearing a voice, even his own, gave him comfort when everything was going down. 'Our guys are the best.' He coughed. *Crouch low for air, idiot!* But he couldn't shift down; it would cave the whole place in.

He was about to choke. He couldn't risk the floor going with the motion. He must breathe now, or risk both their lives when he fell. He watched the baby breathe in, took the mask, breathed in and shoved it back on her face before she inhaled again.

No talking now. His world consisted of watching her breaths: in, take the mask and breathe, back to her, and count the seconds. Glass smashed in the room next door. The fire was in the back walls, and the window had burst. The monster was about to hit.

A whoosh of clean air filled the room. The door burst into glowing sparks as the fire leaped in to meet the oxygen. A voice screamed, 'Give her to me!'

Thank you, God! Charlie leaped for the bed where the window was. 'Take her!'

The bed sagged sideways as the floor collapsed under his weight. He passed the child over as the heat at his back seared him. The hairs on his neck withered and his skin was melting—he could actually smell his flesh cooking.

'Jump, mate!'

He could barely move; the heat, pain and lack of air had left him in a stupor. One hand gripped the window sash; the other made it. *Good. I can do this. One knee up…*

The bed lurched back into the maw where the floor had been moments before. His body jerked back, but his desperate fingers held on. 'Help,' he whispered as his hands lost strength and smoke filled his lungs, his nose and throat, his eyes…

Hands came out of the cloudy darkness, lifting him through the window into a safety harness to lower him to the ground. 'We've got you.' It was Leopard. 'You saved her, Charlie. The little girl's going to make it, and so are you.'

Charlie coughed and coughed; the fresh air hurt, because the hairs lining his airways were gone or damaged. 'Toby?'

'He's okay, he saved the boy. We've done all we can. Let's go!'

He knew by what the captain hadn't said that someone was dead.

Oh, dear God…those poor kids had lost their mother.

As he was winched to safety, he felt the flashes and glare of media cameras turned on him. He heard the words 'hero' and 'saving the lives of a family', but he couldn't answer questions or accept praise for doing his duty. He fell to his knees, coughed until he choked, then threw up: the body's instinctive way of clearing foreign objects.

The paramedics had him on a stretcher within two minutes, and he was on his way to hospital. He slipped into unconsciousness, knowing the 'what ifs' would haunt him until he died. Maybe he'd done all he could, but a woman had died today; two kids had lost their mummy before they'd been able to have memories of her—and, in his book, that meant that all he'd done hadn't been enough.

CHAPTER ONE

Sydney, three months later

'I'M THE grand what of *where*?' Charlie grinned at the grave solicitor in the panelled oak office in the heart of Sydney. 'Yeah, right, pull the other one, Jack. Now, why are we really here?'

His sister's hand crept into his and held tight. 'I think he's serious, Charlie.'

At the fear smothered beneath the shock in Lia's voice, Charlie's protective instincts roared up. Lia was pale; he could feel the tremors running through her.

He couldn't blame her. If this was on the level, this news could destroy his sister. After all these years of progress, she could slide back to anorexic behaviour to cope with the stress of what this stranger was telling them.

No way would he risk that. 'Come on, Mr Damianakis. Tell us why we're here. You're scaring my sister.'

The lawyer smiled at Lia in apology, but his

words didn't give Charlie any relief. 'I'm aware this must be a massive shock for you both. It was a surprise to us, too. The consulate contacted us after the story of your rescue of the children in the house fire.' Now the apologetic look was aimed at Charlie. 'They'd sent photos of your grandparents to every consulate around the world. You really are the image of your grandfather. The photo of you getting the medal for bravery led to an investigation which showed your grandfather's entry papers into Australia weren't on the level. The Greek records showed that the real Kyriacou Charles Konstantinos, who shared your grandfather's birth date, died in Cyprus in the second year of the Second World War, eight months before your grandfather arrived in Sydney in 1941 using the same certificate.'

'That doesn't prove anything but that Papou was an illegal alien,' Charlie argued. It was something he'd always suspected. Papou had always worked for himself, and worked for cash whenever he could.

Charlie frowned, realizing for the first time that Papou had built and paid for the house and everything in it with cash—a man who'd claimed to be the son of a humble bricklayer, and who had only ever worked as a carpenter. Where had the money come from?

'No, in itself it proves nothing—but it was a start.' Mr Damianakis shifted again in his seat, reacting to Charlie and Lia's obvious discomfort with the situation. 'Your father's name is the Marandis family name—Athanasius, like your great-grandfather, the twelfth Grand Duke. Your grandfather's medical records showed some family anomalies, such as the crooked little finger on the right hand, and the AB-negative blood type, which is usual in the male Hellenican line, but rare among Cypriots, and is not at all in the Konstantinos family.'

Lia's grip tightened on Charlie's hand, and he could think of nothing to say to comfort her. Damn, he wished Toby was here!

'And your grandmother's Italian heritage clinched it. When we contacted her family in Milan, got pictures of her at a young age and saw her resemblance to you, Miss Costa, we knew we had the right people.'

Charlie rubbed the healing skin on his neck, where the heat of the fire had gone right through the flame-retardant suit to melt the flesh. The fallout from that fire had done more damage than even he had anticipated. The media had followed him for days, trying to make him a hero. They'd followed him and Toby as they'd visited the kids in hospital, and had awkwardly tried to console the grieving father who'd lost his wife. If he hadn't been instructed by the service to do it, for the sake of donations and good political mileage…

Damn the entire brigade! Those kids had lost their mother because he hadn't been able to save her. If it weren't for the press turning him into something he wasn't, he'd still be living in happy obscurity.

Whatever happened now, he had a feeling that much was at an end.

Charlie jerked to his feet, bringing Lia with him. 'This has to be a joke. You have thirty seconds to tell us why we're really here before we walk out the door.'

'I am one hundred percent on the level, sir.' Mr Damianakis handed Charlie a document and a photograph. 'Here's the late Grand Duke's birth certificate, and his photo taken when he came of age, sir.'

Charlie looked down, fighting a spurt of irritation. No one had ever called him 'sir' in his life, and never like he was a grand 'what' of where.

It was a young Papou in the photo, no doubt of it; Charlie saw the likeness. He'd always been the image of his grandfather. His Papou, who'd always hated war and had only fought over the backgammon table, was dressed in full military getup, covered in ribbons and medals, and the legend said:

1939. The 18-year-old Marquis of Junoar at his graduation from the Hellenican Military Academy, with his parents the Grand Duke and Duchess of Malascos.

The birth certificate gave no reprieve: *Kyriacou Charles Marandis, son of His Grace, Athanasius, The Grand Duke of Malascos, and Grand Duchess Helena Marandis, née Lady Helena Doughtry, daughter of the Earl of...*

The words blurred in front of him as his head

began spinning. The birth date was right; the face was exact. And he couldn't deny the name— Kyriacou Charles. It was his name as well as his paternal grandfather's name, in the old tradition, just as Lia was Giulia Maria, named for their grandmother, their beloved Yiayia.

If all this rigmarole was true, their shy, retiring Yiayia had been a count's granddaughter, an untitled royal nanny for whom Papou had given up his position to run off and marry, if Mr Damianakis could be believed.

He was descended from dukes and earls? He was a lost heir?

'So when do the man in the iron mask and the three musketeers show up?' he asked, with a world of irony in his voice.

The lawyer gave him a wry smile in return. 'It must seem unbelievable: the runaway duke, the lost prince and princess—a massive fortune.'

Lia had read the words on the photo over Charlie's shoulder and stammered, 'It can't be Papou. You have the wrong people. Our last name is Costa. We're Greek.'

'Your grandfather took the surname and nationality he was given by the man who created his false identity, and changed Konstantinos to the simpler version—Costa,' Mr Damianakis said gravely. 'Probably to avoid media scrutiny and being followed around the world. But there is no doubt. He became the Grand Duke of Malascos at his father's death, and you became the Marquis of Junoar when your father died. Due to the tragedies in the nation in the past decade, you are no longer merely the Marquis of Junoar or Grand Duke of Malascos.'

Merely? Charlie heard his mind shout in disbelief.

'But by Hellenican law, as the last male in the direct line, you are Crown Prince, heir to the throne. And you—' he smiled at Lia '—are Her Highness Giulia Marandis, Princess Royal of Hellenia. Your great-grandfather left a massive private fortune to his lost descendants, totalling over five hundred million euros in land, gold and in bank accounts. I think he wanted his son to know he'd forgiven him.' He rushed around to Lia, who'd turned alarmingly pale. 'Please sit, my lady.'

Lia released Charlie's hand and fell into the chair, her breathing erratic. 'Don't call me that,' she said, her voice horrified.

The room swung around Charlie in slow ovals: around and up and down, like he was in a crazy ride he couldn't get off. But he was a fireman, damn it, and he didn't fall down under shock. He strode to the window, saw the limousine with diplomatic flags on it, and clenched his fists. The fairy story he wanted to laugh at was crystallising into horrifying reality. 'You said the king and my great-grandfather disinherited Papou when he married Yiayia. So what do they want with us?'

'When your grandfather was disinherited, he was

ninth in line to the throne, but there were another twenty direct members of the Marandis family to inherit,' Mr Damianakis said, in the tone of respectful gravity that killed Charlie's urge to laugh this all off. 'The past thirty years has been a tragic time in Hellenia. An attempted coup killed several members of your family. Twelve years ago rebel forces created civil war on behalf of the heir of a man in direct rivalry to the throne, named Orakis, in an attempt to reclaim it. The war lasted a decade. Thousands died, towns and villages were destroyed.'

Good God, now he'd gone from romantic legend to an item on the news networks. 'So if this Orakis guy wants the throne so much, let him have it,' he snapped. 'Then nobody else has to die.'

'Charlie,' Lia said in gentle rebuke. 'This isn't Mr Damianakis' fault.'

'Sorry,' he muttered with distinctly unroyal grace. He waved. 'Go on.'

'Not quite two years ago, the Prince Royal and his son contracted meningococcal disease and died within a day of each other, leaving only the Princess Jazmine in line for the throne. The laws of Hellenia do not allow for female inheritance if there is a direct male Marandis to take the throne. The Grand Duke of Falcandis is a descendant, but through the female line. King Angelis began a search for his first cousin, the Grand Duke of Malascos, and his descendants.'

Had they fallen down the rabbit hole? Charlie kept waiting for someone to jump out of a cupboard, yelling 'Surprise!'. 'Just call me 'Charming',' he muttered.

Lia chuckled. 'Yeah, like that's ever going to happen.'

He grinned at her.

Mr Damianakis spoke again. 'If you require further proof, sir, there's a limousine waiting outside to take you to the private jet waiting at Kingsford-Smith airport. It will fly you both to the Hellenican Embassy in Canberra. A representative of the royal family is waiting to answer any questions you have, and give you the papers you need for an immediate flight to Hellenia. His Majesty the King of Hellenia, as well as Her Royal Highness Jazmine, and the Grand Duke of Falcandis, await your arrival.'

As the lawyer said something else, Charlie's mind wandered. He shook his head, trying to clear it, to wake up and find he'd been knocked on the head. Half the time he barely felt qualified to be a fireman, and now he was…was…

Maybe he'd taken a hit by a supporting beam at that Christmas fire, or suffered brain damage with the smoke inhalation, and kept relapsing into delusions?

'Charlie…'

He turned on his heel to see his sister's cheeks holding the dreaded greenish hue. 'Lia?' He ran to her and knelt at her chair, checking her pulse automatically. 'What did you say to her?'

Damianakis licked his lips, distinctly nervous. 'You didn't hear me?'

'Would I need to ask if I had?' He heard the lash of impatient anger in his tone, felt Lia's hand press his, and tightened his lips. How many times did he have to shoot the messenger because he couldn't keep his temper under check? 'This isn't your fault. Just tell me what upset Lia.'

Damianakis shifted in his seat. 'I said you need to prepare yourselves. The ambassador thought it best that I tell you here, in a quiet environment.' As if gathering his courage, he looked up at Charlie. 'His Majesty, King Angelis, has arranged royal marriages for you both, to take place as soon as possible.'

Orakidis City, Hellenia
The next morning

The beautiful old black Rolls pulled up outside the front of the sprawling, four-winged mansion that was the royal family's summer palace, where the king was keeping residence until the main palace was fully repaired from a fire attack a few years before.

There were too many repairs still yet to make to the nation's towns, cities and homes for the royal family to think of repairing a palace as a priority.

Jazmine's heart beat hard as she stood beside Max at the foot of the stairs, four feet behind the king, as adherence to royal protocol demanded. As Princess Royal and the Grand Duke of Falcandis, they held positions the world would envy; yet here they were again, the king's dolls to rearrange as he wished. Old friends, they'd been engaged to each other until a month ago; now they were both engaged to strangers.

Was this a case of a magnificent escape for them, or being tossed from the king's frying pan into his fire?

'Courage,' the Grand Duke murmured in her ear.

She stiffened. A princess to the core, she'd had correct deportment and proper distance drilled into her since birth. 'This is my duty. I don't need courage to face what I can't change.'

His deep, smooth voice was rich with amusement. 'You're right—resignation would be more useful in our case.' He waited, but she didn't answer. 'Talk to me, Jazmine. Surely, as the most recent object of your duty, I can intrude on your pride and share our changed circumstances with someone who understands?'

She felt a tinge of heat touch her cheeks. Her grandfather, the king, had dissolved their engagement when the news of Prince Kyriacou's existence had been confirmed. His press secretary had hinted that childhood friendship made the engagement awkward: a truth His Majesty used when he found it convenient.

Jazmine smiled up at the fair, handsome face, so like his English mother. She'd been so embarrassed by her grandfather's dictum, she hadn't been able to look at him until now. 'You're right, Max. Thank you.'

'Here come our respective futures,' he murmured, smiling at her with the sibling-like affection they'd shared since she was thirteen. 'Our third or fourth cousins, or something. Almost not related at all, apart from the name.'

Thank goodness, Jazmine almost said aloud. She'd found the thought of marrying any relative revolting, but, with Prince Kyriacou's grandfather marrying an Italian count's grandchild, and his father marrying a Greek woman—a *real* commoner!—the lines had blurred. Jazmine's mother had been of the Spanish nobility—more line-blurring still. The more the better, in her opinion.

She started as the trumpets of Grandfather's private band blared the national anthem of Hellenia—*In Our Courage We Stand*—in acknowledgement of royalty's arrival. It was odd, considering that no one else was there but family and royal staff.

A young woman emerged first, wearing the tailored skirt and silk blouse Jazmine had chosen. This was Giulia, no doubt.

No doubt at all, from the moment she looked up. Though she resembled her Italian grandmother, Giulia was a complete Marandis. She had willowy curves, thick dark curls tumbling down her back, the heavy-lashed, slumberous eyes, the deliciously curved top lip. On the Marandis women, it looked like a hidden smile waiting to burst out, a wonderful secret they wouldn't tell. Tall and graceful and golden-skinned, Giulia was beautiful in the quiet, understated, Marandis way.

Then her brother emerged from the car, and

Jazmine heard the death knell of her plans before she'd even been introduced to the prince.

Oh, he was handsome—dark, lean and oozed hot sensuality. But he was no story-book prince come to win the princess's heart, and—her heart sank—she doubted he ever would be.

Thick curls cropped short, dark eyes and the regal nose. Yes, Kyriacou was as much a Marandis as his sister, but on him it didn't achieve elegance. In the charcoal Savile Row suit supplied for him on the jet, with the white shirt and sky-blue tie, he didn't look suave, he looked turbulent. Every inch of him was lean and muscled, big and fit—'buff', her friends from Oxford would have said. She might have said it herself, if she wasn't a princess.

And, if he weren't a Crown Prince, she'd call him hostile.

He looked as regal as a lion, ready to attack, as frighteningly compelling as a wind-tossed storm cloud about to unleash a torrent.

Yes, that was it exactly. God help her, she was engaged to a wild beast set to pounce. And the wind-storm was about to break right over her head.

Well, she was used to flying in storms, and flying blind. Five years ago she'd been a minor royal, then after the civil war had ended, she'd become Princess Royal. She'd become the unwanted, 'couldn't-inherit' female heiress two years before. She'd been engaged to Max until a month ago; now she was engaged to this stranger.

If she'd had a choice, she'd still have taken this fate for the sake of her country and her people. She'd make this man want to marry her, unless she wanted to create an opportunity for Markus Orakis to seize the throne.

Hellenia had seen enough of coups, civil war and murder to last ten generations. She'd do whatever it took to end the bloodshed, to help this country heal from its scars—and she'd cope with this Marandis the same way she coped with her grandfather, the king.

Keep your dignity. Don't let him walk all over you. When you give in, do so with grace. You are a princess, no man's doormat.

If only it didn't sound like a fairy tale in her own mind. No matter how much she wanted to be her own woman, she, like Max—like the new Marandis brother and sister—was a servant to the crown, here to bend to the will of king and country. If Kyriacou and Giulia Marandis didn't understand that, they soon would.

The new Crown Prince and Princess Royal walked through the line of saluting king's guards, and beneath the meet-and-kiss flags showing the royal scarlet-and-gold over deep turquoise that was the symbol of Hellenia, and the Marandis banner: the soaring royal eagle over verdant hills and valleys. A massive bouquet of white roses was thrust in Giulia's arms: the flower of peace.

Grandfather stepped forward, every inch the regal

ruler. He extended his hand towards the brother first—the expected way in this male-dominated society. 'Welcome to Hellenia, Kyriacou,' he said, using the traditional first-person version of the name Kyriacou, making it more personal, intimate. 'And to you, Giulia.' With an attention to detail he'd never lost, the king pronounced her name with beautiful precision: *Yoo-lya*. He smiled warmly. 'Welcome to our family, and to your new home.'

Neither responded for a few moments. Though she smiled, Giulia's face held a look of bewildered wonder at the change in her status. Kyriacou held his sister's arm in obvious protectiveness. He didn't move to take the king's hand, or bow in response to the traditional but sincere welcome.

'My name, *sire*,' he said clearly, 'is Charlie.'

CHAPTER TWO

STUNNED silence reigned at the flagrant breach in royal protocol.

Breach? It was more like an abyss. Nobody spoke to King Angelis like that, or refused his hand. Hadn't Eleni taught them the correct mode of address while on the jet? Jazmine had sent her own personal assistant to Australia for that sole purpose.

Giulia stepped forward with a gentle smile, placing her hand in Grandfather's. 'Thank you, your Majesty.' She dipped into a deep curtsey. 'Forgive us. We're still confused by the changes in our lives, and tired from the long flight.' She lifted her lovely face, smiling. 'We're not used to this level of fuss attached to our arriving anywhere.'

Jazmine relaxed. At that moment, she knew she'd like Giulia. She was a peacemaker who knew how to keep her dignity and courage.

It was a good thing. Marandis women needed to be strong to survive.

Seeming mollified, Grandfather smiled again.

'Well, at least you listened to the procedures for royal protocol on the flight.' The look he slanted at Giulia's brother was frost itself. Pure snow.

'Pardon me for being underwhelmed by thirty-six hours spent in lawyers' offices, limousines, consulates and jets. We were forced to leave our home and life without warning, pushed into limos and jets without consent, told we had to obey the will of a king we knew nothing about. We've been bowed and scraped to wherever we go, "Your Highnessed" to death, had "this is a royal secret" slammed into us every thirty seconds. If I was given any choice in any part of the past thirty-six hours, I might have *chosen* to listen,' Kyriacou—Charlie—snapped. 'I'm not a puppet whose strings you can pull, and it would be good for you if you remembered that... Your Majesty.'

More silence, as everyone held their collective breath, waiting for the king's reply. If Jazmine didn't have self-discipline, she'd have closed her eyes. The new Crown Prince of Hellenia was a moron, unable to follow simple instructions or to know one always respected royalty.

Grandfather's eyes narrowed. 'You will learn differently, Kyriacou. My word is law in Hellenia. I can force you to return to your obscure life without the benefit of your great-grandfather's fortune. Don't embarrass me publicly, boy, or you'll regret it.'

'With respect, Your Majesty, bring it on,' Charlie returned without a blink, or lowering his voice. 'I was enjoying my life until yesterday. Obscurity and the single life suit me right down to the ground. Maybe you should find a new heir, Your Majesty, because I'm nobody's idea of a duke, let alone a prince—and bringing me here is the furthest you'll manipulate me.'

It took all Jazmine's self-will not to gasp. Instead of being intimidated, the new heir met ice with fire—and a tiny part of her, the rebel she'd submerged years ago, wanted to cheer him on.

Maybe he wasn't as stupid as she'd feared. And maybe there were possibilities in this. If he could stand up against the old autocrat and hold his own, he could be perfect for her purpose. If she could bring him to see what he could accomplish for Hellenia…

Her brain began buzzing with plans.

A royal staffer stepped into the breach, performing his assigned duty with no sign of discomfort. Every inch the Oxford-trained gentleman. 'Your Royal Highnesses, may I introduce you to Jazmine, the Princess Royal, and Maximilian, the Grand Duke of Falcandis?'

Perfectly done. His name was not to be mentioned until the important personages were introduced. Diplomats and royal staffers knew how to blend in.

'Your Highness.' Giulia dipped into another curtsey. 'Your Grace.'

Max smiled but remained silent, waiting for the first in precedence to speak.

Jazmine smiled with genuine pleasure at Giulia.

'Please don't curtsey to me. And call me Jazmine.' She kissed Giulia's cheek with warm welcome.

Giulia smiled back. 'My father was an only child, and my mother's relatives were all still in Greece, so I've never had a cousin, Jazmine, but I've always wanted one. My brother tends to be a bit overprotective.' Those glorious eyes twinkled at her brother, who merely grinned. 'My friends call me Lia.'

It seemed their lives were more alike than Jazmine had anticipated. She too had grown up with her relatives far away; she too had lost her mother at a young age, and had longed for a friend, a confidante, who *belonged* in her life. 'Perhaps we should be thinking of each other as sisters, Lia.'

'I'd like that.' Lia's face lit, as if Jazmine had offered her a fortune.

Without warning, her throat thickened. How long had it been since she'd had a simple offer of friendship from a person she could trust? But, much as she wanted to explore a friendship with Lia, her duty wasn't complete.

With some trepidation she turned to Charlie, allowing none of her concerns to show in her face or voice. 'If you don't mind, I'd rather not think of you as a cousin, Charlie.' She held out her hand to him. 'I don't think it would bode well for the future.'

To her surprise the new prince took the extended hand, and grinned as he shook it. He drawled in a mock-Southern accent, 'Smacks too much of hillbilly movies and all them there in-breeders?'

Caught out, she did laugh this time. 'Well, we're only third cousins.'

Suddenly Jazmine needed a long, cool glass of water. Her mouth and throat had dried, watching that dark, dangerous face soften with the sexy Marandis smile. His voice was rough with the Australian twang, deep and intensely masculine. Suddenly it made the cultured accents of the men she knew sound, well, namby-pamby. And she was having the strangest reaction to the feel of his hand in hers.

For the first time in years, her self-control vanished and she had not the slightest idea what to do or say.

'Don't worry,' he whispered softly as he pretended to kiss her cheek. 'This isn't your fault. I'll find a way out of this crazy situation.'

She blinked, stared, opened her mouth and closed it. Where had her famous self-composure disappeared to when she needed it?

Max's smile told Jazmine he'd seen her reaction to the new prince. Taking the focus from her, he moved forward to meet the new arrivals, shaking hands with the right degree of friendly welcome.

'We will take tea.' The king turned towards the stately sandstone house—the Marandis summer palace since the eighteenth century—before anyone else could speak.

The smile vanished from Charlie's face. He nodded, as if his permission had been sought, and turned to walk with Lia into the house.

Despite his being a firefighter, obviously taking

orders wasn't something he enjoyed, though he seemed to know to choose his fights and bide his time.

Though that meant more work whipping him into shape, the complex nature of the new prince seemed to fit into her very personal agenda for the future of Hellenia. A modern hero with rebellious tendencies—as shown by his rescue of the children in Australia—and knowing when to keep silent, was exactly what her people needed.

She turned to follow her grandfather, taking Max's arm. Then she remembered, and turned to Charlie to walk inside first. He was Crown Prince now, and above her in station.

He took his sister's arm and stood, waiting. 'I was brought up to allow ladies—and princesses— to go first.'

The words told her more than she wanted to know. He had no intention of accepting the title, or becoming a part of the royal family. He wanted to return to Australia as soon as possible. He'd soon learn it wouldn't happen. Royal families didn't belong to themselves, or have the luxury of independence.

As Max took her arm, he whispered, 'I suspect life is about to get interesting. Our new prince is a firecracker. Good luck with that.'

She stifled a laugh. 'I suspect you're thanking the gods for your changes, now you've seen Lia.'

'She certainly is lovely,' he murmured, 'And smooths over the waves. Good manners and well brought-up. Just what every man wants in a wife.'

Jazmine caught the irony in his tone. If Max resented being a slave to royal duty, he hadn't shown any sign of it in the past few months—but then, how could he until now?

'If the sister was well brought-up, what happened to the brother?' she whispered.

'By all accounts, his grandfather never bowed to the will of the crown,' Max replied, just as softly. But as they passed through the grand double doors to the ballroom-sized chamber known as the tea room, she saw Charlie stiffen.

Max ushered her into the room. 'Well, you can't fault his hearing. You might want to keep any future liaisons—'

'I'm not biting.' She smiled sweetly at him. A prince in waiting and a gentleman to the core, Max had always enjoyed putting the cat among the pigeons.

Max grinned. 'You can't blame me for trying. It doesn't appear as if my future bride has the Marandis fighting spirit your future king has in spades. I fear she'll make me a poor opponent.'

Jazmine shook her head. Having read the investigative reports into the brother and sister, she doubted Lia lacked anything, including spirit. Her story of anorexia survival proved that, but Max would have to find out in his own time and way.

Grandfather waved them all into chairs facing him. By the way he drew himself up and refused to sit, he was about to hold court, as he called it.

She called it laying down the law.

'Tea,' he ordered a servant, who bowed and disappeared. The room emptied.

To Jazmine's surprise, Charlie took a seat beside her. He was glancing from her to Giulia—who sat on Jazmine's other side—but his expression didn't change. He still looked grim and protective.

'We will have no public displays in future of family discord, Kyriacou.'

Grandfather never descended to such terms as 'do you hear me?' As king, he could enforce his word with the full force of the law, even in the twenty-first century. He believed the Hellenican people liked it that way.

Jazmine had other ideas, but they'd remain her own until she was queen. *If* she became queen. She kept her gaze on the man who held her entire future in his hands.

Charlie was sprawled in his chair, watching her grandfather with polite interest, as if the king was an unusual exhibit at the zoo. 'It's been a long time since anyone defied you, I'd guess, Your Majesty.'

Grandfather put a hand on the back of the carved-oak chair. His brows lifted a touch. 'Certainly.'

Charlie said politely, but with finality, 'Well, here's the lowdown on *family discord*, sire. I'm not your family. I met you *five minutes* ago. I am an Australian citizen—'

The king's smile stopped him mid-sentence.

'Actually, Kyriacou, you are a Hellenican citizen,' Grandfather stated with well-bred relish.

'You are a descendant of the royal family. You have been Hellenican, subject to its laws and regulations, from the moment you stepped into the consulate in Canberra.'

The silence was absolute. Even the servants didn't breathe.

After a minute that seemed to take an hour, the king went on. 'My word is law in Hellenia. You will do as I tell you, and leave only when I allow it.' He smiled at Charlie in barely restrained triumph.

Giulia's face was pale as she turned towards her brother. Max lifted his brows.

Jazmine felt herself gulping on air. Whatever Charlie said or did, unless it was capitulation or an abject apology, would only throw a landmine into Grandfather's proud, stubborn face—and, on five minutes' acquaintance, she felt sure 'capitulation' and 'apology' were words as foreign to the prince's nature as they were to the king's.

After an interminable minute, Charlie answered without the expected fire. 'Without prior knowledge of Hellenican law, we've been subjected to false imprisonment, which is subject to international law under the terms of the Geneva Convention.' He smiled back at Grandfather, whose lined, regal face whitened. 'You made a mistake in underestimating me, Your Majesty. I will not be forcibly detained here. Nor will I allow you to force my sister or me to accept the positions. We are not political prisoners. If you make us such, I'm sure the world media would love to know about it.'

War declared—and it was about to be accepted. Before she knew it, Jazmine was on her feet, looking down at Charlie. 'May I speak with you, please, Your Highness?'

Arrested by her intervention into the hostilities, Charlie turned and looked at her. A brow lifted as he searched her eyes. Jazmine's panic grew as he seemed to be looking past her projected calm. Seeing more than she wanted him to.

'Of course, Your Highness. I'm at your service.' Just as slow, seeming almost insolent, he rose from the chair, stood and held an arm out to her as he'd seen Max do.

He was a quick learner when he wanted to be...but the challenge in his eyes told her the changes would come only in his time and way.

This man definitely had hidden depths—and, as he'd said to Grandfather, it was a mistake to underestimate him.

'Do the goons get in line every time you move?' he said in a conversational tone as they headed to a parlour, and four Secret Service people followed at a discreet distance.

'Actually, two of them are yours. They're here to protect you.' Resisting the urge to pull her arm from his—the Secret Service would report the disharmony to Grandfather—she checked his reaction.

Bad mistake. The brows were up over laughing,

derisive eyes. 'Protect me? A little, five-foot-four Miss Perfect is going to take me down? I need help handling *you*?'

She nodded at their combined minders to step outside, then closed the parlour door behind them. 'I'm five-foot three,' she retorted, intensely aware of keeping her dignity. 'And, though we both know it isn't me you need protection from, I have a green belt in karate.' She could also fly a jet and combat swim: they were basic requirements for the royal heirs of Hellenia.

She wondered if that would pique his interest; he was a man of action after all. How would he take it if he knew that both she and Max, whom he saw as pampered royals, could do all he did and then some?

Charlie grinned. 'Are you going to bring me to the mat? Want to know how many ways I could take you down, princess?'

She shook herself. This half-sexual banter put her in a ridiculous situation; it was beneath her. 'We've just come out of ten years of civil war. There were ten million people in Hellenia fifteen years ago. We're down to eight million. Lord Orakis tends to eliminate competition in violent ways, and you and I both stand in his way. The king doubled the protection of all the royal family three years ago.' *After the palace attack.* And she intended to change the over-the-top protection levels, too, if—when—she became queen. He had to listen to her. He had to.

Charlie's brows lifted again, and she guessed he

was digesting another facet to his unwanted elevation in status.

She sat down. 'We should get comfortable. There are things you need to know.'

'Shake out the list, it's miles long.' His tone was as dry as new wine as he sat opposite her. It seemed he was a man who liked his personal distance. 'We might need to ask the goons to bring in dinner and breakfast while they're out there doing nothing.'

The words made her hesitate; he was already on edge, and obviously didn't want to belong here. She abandoned her original, perhaps too harsh, words. 'Life is very different here—'

He laughed, hard-edged. Words couldn't adequately describe the wealth of half-repressed emotions it held.

Trying again, she forced herself to hold to her resolve. He'd been here less than an hour and he'd been threatened, had been given veiled bribes, and told he had no rights. A man like Charlie was bound to react badly to that. 'No doubt you've been brought up very differently to those of us within the royal family, but you're no longer in Australia.'

'Gee, thanks, Dorothy. If I could find my red shoes I'd disappear back to my life and career, and make everyone's lives easier.' He cocked his very handsome head back in the general direction of the door. 'His Furious Majesty's less than impressed with the new heir.'

Strange that his speech sounded so arrogant, yet

she heard rough exhaustion, and his acceptance that Grandfather was right to be unimpressed. 'I'm trying to help you, but you're not making it easy,' she said, repressing the urge to grit her teeth.

At once his face and deep, velvety eyes softened, and again Jazmine felt that odd loss of emotional equilibrium. She felt less princess, and more...

'I'm sorry, princess. I'm sure you're as unhappy with this situation as I am.' He swept a hand over the suit. 'Even in the borrowed threads, I'm nobody's idea of a prince. Believe me, I know. I've had enough ex-girlfriends informing me of the fact.'

Oh, but you could be, she almost said, but he was obviously uncomfortable in his new skin. Showing him possibilities, or ordering him around, it would be alienation to him.

No, just alien. He can't be expected to see life as I've been bred to do.

Charlie had grown up ignorant of his heritage, in a modest four-bedroom brick home he'd occupied with his sister and friend until two days ago. Instead of years of royal training and sterling education at an international school and Oxford, or perhaps Yale or Harvard, he'd gone to a local high-school and had gone into fireman and paramedic training. He was a Marandis only in name. No, in Charlie's mind, he was a fireman from the backblocks of Sydney. He'd had no time to adjust, saw no reason *to* adjust.

Grandfather had made a tactical error in his peremptory summons and enforced extraditions of this pair. He expected Charlie to obey orders he didn't understand, to see his expected future as an honour, and accept his position when he had no idea what that future and position entailed. He'd made a mistake in expecting Charlie to bow to the royal will without full knowledge of *why* he and Lia were so necessary to the continuation of the Marandis royal family.

And, to Jazmine's mind, wanting him to be a traditional Marandis was as impractical as it was counterproductive to the future she had planned.

'Do you mind?'

Startled out of her plans, she looked at the cause of her hope and confusion. He'd shrugged off his jacket, and was tugging at his tie.

To her surprise, she smiled. 'Only if I can take off these heels. You have no idea how much they hurt after a couple of hours' standing.'

He grinned. 'Go for it. I won't tell.' He tugged at his tie and pulled it off, then undid the top three buttons on his shirt, and rolled up his sleeves. 'Hasn't this place got air-conditioning?'

'This house is almost four hundred years old.' Charlie's untamed golden masculinity, exposed in the open column of his shirt, emptied her head of everything but the need to stare her fill; to cover her pounding heart she added with would-be calmness, 'The real palace does, but we haven't lived there in a few years. It's still being repaired.' She half-expected him to ask why it was taking so long, or make a caustic comment on spoiled royals wanting everything perfect.

Instead, he said gently, 'I'm sorry.'

Confused again, she lifted her brows in query.

He smiled at her. 'Lady Eleni told us about the palace fire-attack during the war, and your father's and brother's deaths so soon after the war ended. It's no wonder you agreed to this engagement. Security's not to be sneezed at after all you've been through.'

Moved yet unnerved by kindness from a stranger, she turned her face. 'I barely knew my father or brother.' She willed control against the vast sorrow that there wasn't time to know Father or Angelo now. She turned back, forcing a smile. 'I was sent to school in Geneva when I was eight, and then attended finishing school. I was at university in London when I became Princess Royal, and summoned home. Father was busy with his duties, as was Angelo. I'd only been back here a year or two when they—' Without warning, her throat thickened. *Control, control!*

'I see,' he said very quietly.

She closed her eyes, struggling to go on.

He leaned forward and touched her hand. 'Lia and I lost our parents when I was seventeen. We'd all lived together, all three generations, all our lives, and Yiayia and Papou were fantastic, but...' He smiled at her. 'It's okay to cry sometimes, princess. I know I did my share when I felt so alone I could scream.'

The words were beautiful and foreign to everything she'd been raised to believe. *Don't cry, Jazmine,* her father had said at Mother's funeral, when she was seven. *You are a Marandis. You are strong!*

Her spine straightened. 'I'm sure you're right.'

The kindness and warmth vanished from his face. 'Sorry; I crossed the royal line. There's proof that I'm not a real prince, and I never will be.'

'But you are,' she said softly, backtracking fast, and letting the fact click into place: *he doesn't like being locked out.* 'Like it or not, you're a Marandis, Charlie, and we need to discuss—'

'Mmm. Say my name like that, and I'll discuss whatever you want.' A smile curved his mouth. 'Char-r-r-lie,' he said, as softly as she had, but with far more sensual intent. 'I never heard the Mediterranean burr in quite that way before. Your voice is so blurry and sexy. I love listening to you, Jazmine.'

And his eyes, lingering on her face, said, *and I really like looking at you.*

He spoke her name as it had been pronounced: *Zhahz-meen.* One word, just a name she'd heard ten-thousand times, but he'd turned it into silk and shadows, with the summery sensuality of a lush Arabian night.

Without warning, a new kind of wolf had leaped from his lair; the hidden lion was pouncing. He'd spoken to her not as princess, but as man to woman. And she felt the slow melt inside, feminine liquidity racing like quicksilver through her body. He'd taken her from blue-blooded princess to red-blooded woman with just a few soft words.

She'd never met a man like him before. He was unique, an unexpected prince in a fireman's skin, all hot-blooded male. He'd never learned to hide his emotions as she had. And, by his words, the look in his eyes and the slow burn in his touch, he wanted her to know he found her attractive. He didn't play diplomatic games; he didn't know how. This golden-skinned, dark-eyed man, strong and beautiful, a hero as much as any from the pages of *The Odyssey*, found her as attractive as she found him.

'And, as regards this engagement, it's a farce. I don't want to be here, and the last thing you need is a man who'll never fit into your world. Nobody can force us into this kind of thing in the twenty-first century. I swear on my life I'll get you out of this.'

She started out of her lovely daydream as his words sank in. And her heart sank right down with it.

CHAPTER THREE

CHARLIE saw the instant distress in her eyes—the intense disappointment—before something clicked back into place, and the warm woman she'd been became the 'Mona Lisa princess' the tabloids called her: picture-perfect and smiling, comfortable in the public eye, if remote somehow. 'What makes you assume I want to get out of this?'

He stared, wondering if someone as lovely as the princess could have only half her marbles. 'It has to be obvious. Even a real-life princess must want the whole nine-yard cliché: the handsome prince, babies, a palace—and a happily-ever-after. It's only by accident of birth I'm here. I'm a Sydney boy, a rough-mannered fireman. I don't have class, I don't do "for ever"—and I'm certainly not the guy who'd make your life easier. I'm not what you'd call easy-going.'

Her smile grew, but it wasn't one he liked. It made him feel out of control, and that was a feeling with which he was neither familiar nor comfortable. 'It seems I have at least six of those yards, Your

Highness. A palace—' she waved her hand around '—and, if we married, babies would be part of the deal, I'd assume.'

His heart darkened at the thought of it. Royal children with royal minders, who'd have to bow and scrape to His Majesty's every whim? Not on his life. 'Four-and-a-half yards aren't enough for a woman like you.'

'I hadn't finished,' she said softly. 'In my opinion, I have a handsome prince, even if he's a reluctant one.' She broke the smugness with a bitten-lip grin, the woman in her peeping out for a moment, and he found himself responding in kind. 'If I must marry, I'd rather have a firecracker than a dog rolling over on order. You have a mind of your own, ideals and dreams. I respect that.'

Damn. Much as he liked her words—she'd made it obvious she found him attractive, and liked both his temper and his independence—now he had to be blunt. 'As tempting as you are, I don't want to get married, princess. I could *never* become what you'd want in a prince. I couldn't stand the constant intrusions into my life you endure from the press every day. It was bad enough after the fire a few months back, but if I had to handle it on a daily basis I'd end up hitting someone. Not very royal behaviour, is it?'

She shook her head, still smiling. 'I noticed your discomfort with the press—it was obvious in every photo. But, rest assured, we'd help you to acclimatise to that sort of thing.'

His jaw clenched tighter. 'I don't *want* to acclimatise,' he said baldly. 'I can't think of a single benefit in being here. I want to live my life without black-suited goons following me and cameras waiting for every stuff-up I make—and I *will* make them.'

Jazmine nodded, as if she'd expected him to say it. He found himself wondering what it would take to rattle her cage, to put a crack in her perfect composure. 'You do realize that the only way you can go home is by repudiating your position, which likely means your sister will go home with you?'

He shrugged. 'I don't see a problem with that. Lia likes her life at home.'

Her voice filled with gentle amusement. 'Have you asked Lia what she wants, or are you taking it for granted you can make a decision of this calibre for her?'

He felt his jaw clench. 'I know my sister. She's happy living with Toby and me, running her business and teaching the kids.' *Well, happy enough now*, he amended silently. After her failed attempt to enter the Australian Ballet on the heels of their parents' death in a car crash, it had brought on her dance with death-dealing anorexia. If it hadn't been for Toby's complete devotion to her returning to health—staying at the clinic with her day and night around their firefighting training-schedule—she might not have made it. Toby wasn't only the best friend he'd ever had, the brother he'd always wanted, he was the only person Lia trusted with her secrets.

Suddenly he wanted to hear Toby's voice saying everything would be okay, he'd be there soon, though it was sure to be said in four-syllable words he favoured. 'Lord of the Dictionary' Toby might be, but he was the staunchest, truest friend he and Lia could ever have.

There hadn't been any joking camaraderie or long words when they'd talked to him from the Consulate in Canberra. Toby's silent reaction to their sudden disappearance 'on family business', unable to say when they'd be home, unable to call again—unable even to talk it through with him as a result of the officials listening in on every word—had been an almost more frightening reality than the jet they'd been about to board. He, Lia and Toby were family. None of the three of them had ever kept secrets from each other, as far as he knew.

Now he and Lia *were* secrets. Secrets of state. And he hadn't felt this alone since his parents' death.

'You know what your sister wants without asking her. I see.' The amusement lurking in Jazmine's eyes grew to an outright twinkle. She was so pretty, with that sparkle lighting her up from within. He'd always had a thing about that rich-chestnut colour, and she had it in a double dose: her eyes and hair. No wonder she was known as the last single beautiful princess in Europe, feted and courted by all the noble bachelors within five-thousand kilometres.

I could be the one kissing her next. I could take her to bed in a matter of weeks…

And thinking about that, looking into that face, suddenly the whole prince-and-arranged-marriage gig didn't seem so bad. The perks of unexpected royalty had never come in a more tempting package than Jazmine Marandis.

He dragged himself out of those thoughts before they turned dangerous. What had she been saying? Seeing something... 'You see what?' he demanded.

'I see why you and my grandfather clash. You both believe you know what's best for others without asking what they want. You're more of a Marandis than you realize.' Jazmine's infuriating half-smile grew. 'So you know she doesn't want to be a princess, live in the palace, marry a young and handsome Grand Duke— Oh, and inherit the fifty million euros that is her inheritance and dowry from the duchy?'

Fifty million euros? Charlie felt a cold shiver run down his back. Good God. He hadn't thought about the money; he'd been too furious to think. He'd concentrated on what *he* would lose, what *he* wanted.

What about Lia? Would she want the money, the lifestyle, the whole thing? What if she was attracted to the Grand Duke? Would Charlie ruin everything for her because *he* wanted to return to his life?

As if tapping into his thoughts, Jazmine asked conversationally, 'Have you always made decisions for Lia? I hear she runs a successful ballet school. Do you decide what concerts she'll do, check the accounts, or help her run it?'

'Of course not,' he snapped, hating that she was right. He had no right to decide for Lia. And he was really irritated that the snooty princess was holding all the cards. He knew nothing of this country, his new family or the laws. The only power he had was his independence. His 'pig-headed pride', as Lia put it.

He grinned suddenly, thinking of his sister as Princess Lia. Just as well his name wasn't Luke, or this whole thing really would have been a farce.

But, much as he hated to admit it, the 'Mona-Lisa princess' sitting across from him was correct. The title suited her, he thought sourly, with her intriguing, frustrating little smile, and eyes that saw too much. He had no right to decide the future for Lia. His shy, family-loving, homebody sister might hanker after the fairy-tale ending most women dreamed of, and after everything she'd been through she deserved it.

'What do you want from me?' he growled, backed into a corner for Lia's sake.

As if knowing she'd boxed him in, her smile turned hopeful. 'I only want you to give this life a chance before you disappear. And, please, stop trying to be my white knight. If you're no prince, I'm no damsel in distress.'

He felt the flush creeping up his neck. She was right. The fireman in him had crossed the world to a new kind of burning building, ready to carry out the helpless female trapped in a situation not of her making…or liking.

The muscles on her face didn't move, but he knew she was smiling inside. That mysterious twinkle in her eyes, lurking deep, fascinated him with her unspoken secrets.

'And?' He could tell there was more.

'There's more at stake than your privacy, independence and pride, Charlie. Lives hang in the balance.' She leaned forward in earnest entreaty as she said his name again, and a hint of soft cleavage showed through the correct folds of her silky blouse.

Was her skin as silky-soft? Would she say his name with that sweet, sexy little burr as he slipped that blouse from her shoulders and down...?

Shove it, jerk. She's a princess. With her minders, there's no chance of touching her before the wedding night. And a wedding night—or a wedding—just isn't happening!

The only reason he was listening to her was because he didn't know what Lia wanted. He knew what *he* wanted. And that wasn't about to change, no matter how pretty and appealing the princess was. Because she *was* a princess, she came with her own set of royal chains, and he wasn't the guy to slip his wrists into the king's cuffs for any amount of money or power. She was bred to this life. He was here by accident of birth.

'So whose life is at stake?' He was proud of the even tone. Control established.

She frowned, her head tilting a little. 'You don't want to know what your inheritance is?'

For a moment he was tempted. Then the realization came: she'd only asked to weaken his resolve, to appeal to his greed—and when that didn't work no doubt she'd try another tack. She'd keep gently chipping away at his walls until, deprived of a safe perch, he'd fall off. And, like Humpty Dumpty, if he fell no amount of king's horses or men would put his life back the way it had been.

Surely she'd seen enough of him to know the only good he could do this place was to get back on that jet and return to his anonymous life in Sydney? If he hadn't even been able to help his own sister through anorexia, how the hell could he run a country?

'No, thanks,' he said abruptly. 'If I can't take it home with me, there's no point. So, what are the stakes? Whose lives "hang in the balance", as you put it so eloquently?'

She'd bitten her lip as he spoke—not on the outside, no, that wouldn't be classy enough for the perfect princess. But she'd worried the inside of her lip, and for some reason he couldn't fathom he found the act touching…sweet, and somehow lonely.

When she spoke, it was with a kind of desperate resolve. 'The lives and future of the people of Hellenia. Lasting peace in our nation.'

His brows lifted. 'All that depends on me?' he mocked, to cover the fact that he had the same sinking feeling in his gut he felt when he saw a fire gone beyond his ability to extinguish it.

'Yes.' Her eyes grew soft with pleading.

'Grandfather seems almost immortal, but he's eighty-two, and he's had two heart attacks already. If he dies without naming a male heir, it will mean disaster for Hellenia. It's obvious you believe you're the wrong man for the job, Charlie.' His body heated up again, hearing the blurry way she said his name. 'But don't judge Hellenia's needs or your suitability until you know our history. Being one of the few absolute monarchies left in the world—'

Before she could finish the State of the Nation address, she appeared to think better of it; her voice dropped, and turned husky with emotion. 'There's been such suffering in our country since your grandfather left. It can end with us.' Her words held entreaty and conviction—no longer the Princess dolly, but showing a bare hint of the passionate woman he'd seen before, and it fascinated him. 'This is bigger than us, what we want.'

With control still in place, his jaw didn't drop, but the shock lingered inside him, roiling his gut. 'Are you saying you *want* this crazy marriage?'

'Alliance,' she corrected, her eyes calm. 'Don't panic, Charlie; it isn't personal.' She nibbled the inside of her lip again. A subtle gesture, and one most wouldn't see, but Charlie could feel her fear, sense her worry, the loneliness of her position—and the stakes he still didn't know became more urgent, reflected in the shadows inside her eyes. Eyes that, looking more closely, he noted were more like old Irish whisky than chestnut. 'I know you care about others, or you wouldn't have risked your life for that little girl, or the dozens of others we discovered you've rescued.' Her gaze searched his in deep-hidden pleading and anxiety.

Not knowing what to say or do, he nodded, wishing he didn't have to, but her complete honesty demanded his in return.

'We need your help on a larger and more lasting scale than anyone you've saved in the past. There are five-hundred-year-old laws that need changing. Not merely that, but thousands of people lost family and homes and rights during the civil war. Some of my people have nothing. And, if you leave, they'll have nothing to look forward to. Nothing.'

Though she'd said it three times, the word still held a starkness, a rawness too strong for her to be putting on an act.

'I'm listening,' he said quietly.

Her eyes lit from within, and his body tightened in spite of the gravity of the conversation. She was so *pretty*, so certain of her convictions. 'I want to bring Hellenia into the modern world, but with the way the law currently stands I can't do it alone. If you renounce your position, I lose my chance. According to laws in place since we took power in the 1700s, there must be an heir from the male Marandis line, or the crown reverts to a direct descendant of the royal family that was forcibly removed in the 1700s. The Orakis family was deposed by the people for their selfish and immoral ways. The head of the rebel force—a national hero, Angelis Marandis—was asked to become king. Marandis didn't want to take the crown, but he did, for the sake of his people.'

Charlie nodded again, feeling an unwanted kinship with this long-dead relative. He'd heard most of this from the ambassador in Canberra, but it was obvious she had something to say, and interrupting her would break her train of thought.

The princess sighed. 'The Orakis family never left. They've started civil wars, fomented unrest in troubled times—such as during World War Two, when our ally Greece was overrun. The troubles in Albania have given the Orakis supporters the opportunity to try to regain power in secret during the last twenty years.' She stopped, nibbling her lip again. Looking almost adorably lost.

Trying with all his might not to respond to her plea, to touch her, he nodded. 'Lady Eleni told us all that in Canberra.'

She smiled at his awkward attempt to comfort her. 'Sorry if I appear to be going over old ground, but you need to understand why your decision is important to far more people than you and Lia. Markus Orakis is an autocrat in the old mould, believing in his right to rule. Orakis's father spent twenty years trying to reclaim the throne.' She blinked once, twice, but the suspicious sheen turned her eyes into beautiful mirror-pools of the suffering she saw in her people's future. She looked up, those mysterious eyes shimmering with emotion, drenching his soul with her courage and her selfless duty.

'It's not that he's a terrorist—he's not. He just wouldn't *change* anything. He'd keep Hellenia in the seventeenth century to keep the monarchy absolute and unchallenged. He'd put his family and followers in strategic positions to consolidate his power, and destroy anyone who threatened him.' She sighed. 'You've watched the international news, right? This isn't melodrama. It's what this kind of man *does*. They start with good intentions, doing good to the nation, then power goes to their heads and they justify any act of violence. He's already that way with the following he has.'

Again, Charlie nodded. Anyone who watched the news could name the dictators who'd done exactly as Jazmine was predicting Orakis would do. 'Go on.'

She touched his hand, and he could feel her trembling as she delivered her final words with the subtlety of a battle axe to his skull. 'Ask yourself—if he could have returned, would your grandfather have done so? For his people, the people he loved? And, now he can't, wouldn't he want you and Lia to try?'

Ah, hell…

Click: a tiny sound in his brain, but deadly. It was the sound of manacles around his wrists. She'd found the key to his capitulation, and turned it without hesitation.

If he could have, Papou *would* have come back. He'd have urged Charlie to try to help if he could—

and, despite his denial, he knew Lia's answer. In all her life she'd never let anyone down, never said no if she was in a position to help. To her, the suffering in Hellenia would make this choice a sacred commission, the chance to put right Papou's wrong in choosing love over duty.

An hour into their relationship, and she'd put his wrists in cuffs. For the sake of the Hellenican people: Papou's people; her people. And for *her* sake, because it seemed the perfect princess did need a hero after all.

The perfect shell of the mysterious princess was a fragile illusion that, when shattered, couldn't be reinstated. Those private, proud eyes had cried for him, and if he turned his back now he'd regret it for the rest of his life.

'Enough, Your Highness.' His tone froze even him, but he was losing the freedom he treasured. He might have to accept it, but he didn't have to like it. 'I'll go back in there and behave. I gather that's what you want?'

The appealing loveliness of her vanished as if it had never been. 'There will be much more than that, Your Highness—but let's take on one obstacle at a time.'

She was every inch the princess, cool and detached. But the woman of passion and commitment lingered like a super-imposition; her warm and vital heart beat beneath the icy layer she projected. He saw the princess, but heard the woman within. He saw her, beautiful and so earnest, pleading with him to stay. She'd stripped her defences, not for herself, but for the sake of her people.

He wondered why, when she could have used other cool, level-headed arguments, she'd chosen to show her real, hidden self to him.

'Time to bow to the old dragon,' he said, not without ruefulness. He didn't want to, but he'd given his word. He put the choking tie back in place as she slipped her feet back into the heels that were way too high for so small a woman. 'See, princess, I can pretend to be civilized every now and then.'

The smile she gave in return seemed remote, yet the super-imposition remained. As if she stood in a mirror, he could see the reflection of her uncertainty beneath—and it was that hidden woman under the princess's surface face he couldn't make himself reject.

He held out his arm to her. He'd have liked a more intimate touch. Holding hands would tell him if the simmering fascination he was feeling for her was returned, or if it was all duty on her side.

But the minders waited on the other side of the door. And two stood in strategic positions outside on the terrace. When it came to private matters, he'd never been one to put on a show.

Jazmine rose gracefully to her feet and slipped her arm through his. 'Think of it as a game,' she suggested. 'You say yes, you capitulate—for now—and you make plans. When it's your turn, you can change what you like, from law, protection levels and privacy, to the rate of taxes.'

He felt his brows lift. 'Very clever, Your Highness.'

She inclined her head, but not before he caught the twitching grin, the tiny quiver of a half-dimple at the side of her mouth, and the lurking mischief in her eyes.

He knew he'd remember her face, caught in that moment in time, for the rest of his life. The superior Mona Lisa: dutiful princess, a passionate, committed woman and a sweet tease all in one. And she was beautiful like this, so beautiful.

The door opened as they approached. He flicked a glance around, and saw the security cameras in every corner.

Strangers had been watching his every move, listening to every private word between himself and Jazmine. Like it or not, he *had* been putting on a show.

It would be that way for the rest of his life, if he took this on. There would be no treasured private moments between husband and wife. Every sound would be noted by the security outside, even if there were no hidden cameras.

This wasn't the start of something between a man and a woman, it was a farce, a half-tragic sitcom for the edification of a legion of strangers.

He wanted to puke, to bolt back to that big silver jet and head back to a life where he didn't have people watching, a king telling him what to do, and a princess who made him feel like a jerk and a hero at the same time.

'I know this life is difficult, but I have one tenet I live by: nobody can take away my dignity—not a camera, a king, or a nation,' she whispered, close to his ear, so the minders wouldn't hear. 'Only I can do that…if I allow it.'

Her breath touched his ear, fluttered over the skin of his neck. His sense of danger went on full alert. Her Royal Highness Princess Jazmine was like no woman he'd ever known. Beneath the cool, sweet smile he'd seen in a hundred captions, she was her own woman, unique and private.

She hadn't been forced to give a treasured part of herself to him; she'd come willingly, warm as summer, and then as cool as an autumn breeze.

Who was this woman? It wasn't her beauty drawing him, though heaven knew her face haunted him already. Something in her called him. He knew whatever came, if he walked, she wouldn't be a bland memory. She was light and dark, heaven and hell, and had made him feel all of them at once in a half-hour time period.

All the passion beneath the smiling façade, the un-ashamed love for others, the devotion to duty, found an echo inside his soul.

He wanted to help her—he wanted to see that impish grin, the shimmering glow in her eyes. He wanted to be the hero she needed. He wanted… Oh, damn, he just *wanted*—and that scared the living daylights out of him. Even with the protection and cameras and media speculation, Jazmine wasn't a woman a man could walk away from—and he didn't mean the princess. Would she be the one he'd never forget…or always regret? Or the price he'd have to pay for wanting to play the hero?

CHAPTER FOUR

'You want me to *what*? No. Absolutely not.'

Oh, help…

Until now, Charlie had behaved impeccably with
the king. He'd apologized for his earlier rudeness,
and had listened to the old man's dictums with surprising patience, asking intelligent questions,
showing a willingness to think about the sudden
one-eighty his life had taken, and the reasons why
he should try 'this prince caper', as he'd called it.

Jazmine stifled a grin at the memory of the king's
thinly disguised shock at the terminology this irreverent royal had used.

'The rumours are already circulating, Kyriacou,'
the king replied to Charlie's flat refusal with a calm
Jazmine knew he was far from feeling. 'We need to
make an announcement to the press regarding your
presence here. We need to introduce you to the
media, and your future people, as soon as possible.'

'And make another one when I humiliate the
royal family, or the press-chases freak me out to the

point where I decide not to take it on?' Charlie's voice was rich with a delicious kind of self-irony. 'You wouldn't make a fool of yourself and your government that way.'

'Not if you stay—and not if you take the lessons you'll receive to heart.'

Charlie's brow lifted at the command in the king's tone. 'Whether I do either will remain my choice, with all due respect, sire. I won't agree to anything until I have full knowledge of what life will be like for Lia and myself as...*royals*.'

The distaste in the emphasis he used couldn't be missed. The truth was obvious to everyone: he was here only under sufferance.

His sufferance, or hers?

Jazmine worried the inside of her cheek. Had she gone too far with her plea? Until now, she'd been prepared to do whatever it took to make him stay— but Charlie was no tame canary who'd enjoy the press attention and all the trappings of this life. They might be surrounded by luxury, but all Charlie saw was the cage beneath the shining gold...and that perception was something only he could change, because, no matter how she painted it, he was right: the cage existed.

She'd had no choice but to make him aware that the stakes were higher than he knew, but if she was forcing him into life here—a life that included *her*—by guilt...

Faced with the handsome, freedom-loving reality

of the new prince, Jazmine's songs of noble self-sacrifice had had a background melody of hand-cuffs and chains. But the consequences of his possible desertion were too devastating—both to the nation and to the woman.

'Sire, if I might speak, Charlie and I both are coming to know what's at stake. We've listened to you, and we understand why our decision is so important,' Lia said, looking earnestly into the king's eyes. 'Charlie's never walked away from something he believed to be his duty, or refused to help when he could. Papou followed the news here. I believe he saw this day coming. He taught us that it's a sacred duty to help others whenever we can.'

She smiled at Charlie. Jazmine saw his face turn wry with self-mockery, and the loving resignation that, yes, she'd painted their grandfather with a perfect brush. And she found that fascinating. Why had the Grand Duke trained his grandchildren for royal life, but never returned himself?

'Yeah, but *he* didn't come back and do the job he'd been trained for, did he?' Charlie muttered, echoing Jazmine's thoughts so perfectly she felt as if he'd reached in and plucked them from her head.

'Maybe he felt he was no longer worthy enough—or wouldn't be welcome,' she suggested softly, and Charlie winced.

After checking to see if Jazmine had any more to say, Lia continued speaking to the king. 'There's a lot of what ifs and maybes in this for us all, sire. We need to know if we can handle our duties, and you need to know that too. So you must allow us both some time to make the right decision—both for the nation, and for us.'

'There's no *must* about it, girl,' the king snapped, but his eyes were soft with an affection Lia seemed to inspire in everyone she met, even in crabbed old men used to their own way.

Jazmine looked at Lia through new eyes. Yes, she'd be perfect here. A sleepy-eyed beauty with an obvious sense of duty, integrity, natural humility and the adorable factor: Lia had the potential to become a magnificent princess, beloved by the people, the press and the family.

Jazmine's belief in her was proven moments later, by Grandfather's warm, almost loving words— spoken with a feeling *she'd* often wished to receive from him. 'You're right, Giulia. I need to know you're able to handle your responsibilities with the necessary dignity and courage. So far I have little doubt about you.' His tossed glance at Charlie made him look far colder than he really was. 'I agree your brother needs time—and training.'

Jazmine wondered about the hidden family dynamics that had led to Grandfather's judging Charlie so harshly, based on Charlie's natural enough reluctance to change his life without warning, but had given in so freely to Lia…

'At least we agree on something.' Charlie moved as if to rise, then seemed to think better of it. 'Your

Majesty, I came off a four-day shift to this news, and flew straight here. I never sleep well on planes, even first-class jets.' With an effort, he smiled. 'I assume you've had rooms prepared for us?'

'Of course, Kyriacou.' The effort to smile back was palpable, but Grandfather did it. 'Jazmine will show you to your rooms in the east wing. Giulia, I assume you would also like to rest? Max will show you the way to your rooms. They're in the west wing.'

For the first time, Lia frowned. 'Sire, I prefer to have rooms close to Charlie.'

The king stared at her from behind his glasses. 'That's not possible.'

Charlie put an arm around Lia's shoulder. 'You're the king, aren't you? Make it possible,' he said with blunt aggression.

'You don't understand. Segregation of the sexes is an accepted fact for royalty unless it's a married couple. It's been this way for centuries. The people expect it.'

Charlie hugged Lia closer. 'No, *you* don't understand. Lia and I aren't royal—yet—and if you don't make this happen we never will be.'

'No, it's all right, Charlie. I'm sorry to have started this fuss.' Lia hugged Charlie before stepping away from him, standing with quiet pride as she smiled at the king. 'We've always lived together, and he's all the family I have left.'

Jazmine saw a shadow pass in Charlie's self-contained eyes, and, having read the files on their past, realized why he'd untied the fragile accord between himself and the king. But Lia had shown a quiet strength that made Jazmine want to hug her, to cheer. Yes, she'd be a magnificent princess…if the life didn't send her screaming for home.

The realization made her speak. 'The people couldn't possibly be offended at a brother and sister being close, Grandfather. If I give my room to Charlie, no one needs to know. Nobody else shares my wing, and none of the staff would dare gossip if you endorsed the order.' She saw the ire in her grandfather's wily eyes, and knew she'd be hearing his opinion on her rebellion later. And that was fine with her. She had some questions for him, too. 'My room's beside yours,' she said, turning to smile at Lia. 'I can move into the suite a floor up.'

'Thank you for the offer, Jazmine. But, truly, I'll be fine. Living next to you will be fun.' Gratitude and impish fun shimmered in Lia's slumberous eyes, and Jazmine knew she'd made a friend for life.

Charlie didn't speak, just smiled at Jazmine—and the power of his deep-hidden relief and warm gratitude made her feel as if she'd tumbled down a flight of stairs: winded, unsure of her standing and her dignity.

Inexplicably she wanted to see it again, to see the warm approval and thanks in those liquid dark eyes, even if she did find it hard to breathe. Even if she did fall.

'I'll show you to your rooms.' *Charlie's room.* She

found herself blushing, which was ridiculous. Lia had risen to the occasion—it wasn't as if he was going to…

Sleep in my bed.

The thought leaped into his eyes at the same moment. Fire met heat in eyes unable to look away from each other. Her throat closed up, her pulse pounded.

Oh, could she be any more pathetic? A quick glance showed Max and Lia studiously weren't looking, Grandfather's face was smug…and Charlie was hiding a grin. Why didn't she make a formal press release? *I find the new Crown Prince of Hellenia more than passingly attractive.*

Charlie swept his free hand out. 'Lead the way, princess. Feel free to come along, Your Grace,' he added to Max, with the mocking note that told Jazmine Charlie wouldn't consider belonging here.

'Lia, will you walk with me?' she offered on impulse. Brother and sister were obviously an unbreakable entity—but Lia had proved to have a stronger will than Charlie suspected. If she could get to know Lia, to make her see the importance of their decision, how much she could do for this country and the people.

Lia smiled. 'I'd love to.' She gently detached herself from Charlie's grip, and slipped her arm through Jazmine's. 'I don't suppose we can order hot chocolate and popcorn? I'd love to have a really good "getting to know you" talk.'

Remembering the blip in Lia's past, and the hard

anxiety in Charlie's eyes whenever he spoke of or for his sister, Jazmine grinned. 'I've been outnumbered by the men for far too long. Some fun food and cosy girl-talk is exactly what I need.'

Though she wasn't looking at him, she felt the tension in Charlie's body unwind, like a taut spring held too long. She felt the warmth of his unspoken gratitude touching her right down to her soul.

She just…felt him.

'It seems the girls will have their way.' The king chuckled and rose to his feet. 'Max, you might want to take Kyriacou to his room. Maybe after a few hours' rest, you'll be ready for a tour of the house and gardens, or the city. It's a beautiful place, truly medieval in places.' He waved at Max and Jazmine. 'The cars along with drivers, or walking in the grounds and the forest, are at your disposal whenever you wish it.'

For the first time, Charlie smiled without restraint at Grandfather. 'Thank you, Your Majesty.' Jazmine could almost hear the unspoken question hovering on his lips: *if everyone's segregated, why are you asking Jazmine to show me to my room?*

The answer was embarrassing, no matter which way you looked at it. She wasn't about to volunteer the information. She'd never been one to thrust her head in a noose.

Jazmine walked with her arm in Lia's and chatted about the portraits of their ancestors and the paintings lining the walls, from Constable to Pollock. She led the procession towards the stairs to the west wing with all her usual grace, and hoped no one else could see the unsteadiness in her legs, the trembling of her fingers. He was too close. Too hot-tempered. Too—just *too*. Too, too much.

Oh, why hadn't deportment lessons included ways to hide your emotions when you feel a sudden burst of desire as real and strong as this?

So the pretty princess did know he was a man, after all.

Remembering the blush, the half-hidden look in her eyes as she'd realized he could have been sleeping in her bed, Charlie grinned. Who'd have thought a guy from the backblocks of Ryde would get a hot look from royalty?

The answer was right in front of him, but he wouldn't look at it. He was Charlie Costa, the grand fighter of fires, the prince of rebels. Anything else was still too ridiculous to contemplate.

She was being so kind to Lia. She knew about the anorexia, and she seemed to be handling Lia almost as well as Toby could. Lia had been the one to ask about hot chocolate just when he'd started to worry. She hadn't had more than a cup of tea since arriving at the palace. Stressing inevitably led to a loss of appetite.

But Lia had asked for food, for girl-talk, was happy to be rooming beside Jazmine—Lia, who rarely spoke to strangers—and the warmth in the princess's answers made him remember the odd look of loneliness he'd seen earlier. Maybe Jazmine needed a friend as much as Lia did.

'Do you get the feeling we've been locked out?'

Hearing the vein of amusement in the Grand Duke's voice, Charlie grinned at him. 'Girls do that. It's part of their mystery and charm.'

'Yes, but two such handsome and refined personages as ourselves?'

He chuckled. 'You might be refined, Your Grace. I'm nothing of the kind.'

The Grand Duke smiled. 'Call me Max. We're cousins, even if it's rather distant…Charlie.'

He put out his hand. 'Don't you have a good Hellenican name like the rest of us?'

Max's eyes twinkled. 'I do, but if I told you then I'd have to kill you.'

Disarmed, Charlie laughed. 'It seems the men in this family have a thing about using their given names—*Max*.'

'And showing the truth inside their personalities.' Max shook his hand. 'You're a firecracker, but you're not half as vulgar as you'd like us to think you are.'

'Told you they'd see through it, Charlie,' Lia commented from ten feet ahead of them, her voice filled with laughter. 'You really don't scare anybody.'

'Speak for yourself,' Jazmine retorted. 'He makes *me* nervous.'

Lia chuckled. 'I don't blame you. I love my

brother, but I wouldn't want to have to even *think* about marrying him.'

Jazmine gasped, and a smothered giggle emerged.

Max chuckled. 'Never assume a woman isn't listening, even when she's talking.'

'Damn multi-tasking,' Charlie grumbled, and the women laughed again as he'd hoped they would.

It was a sound he hadn't heard enough of from his sister in the past decade, unless she'd been with Toby. His sister was so private, too self-contained. She'd been that way since their parents had died. She must really have connected to Jazmine.

But Lia had constantly amazed him since this nightmare had begun. She'd handled their sudden elevation in life and crossing the world, the shocking proposition before them, living at the other end of this massive palace from her only family, with more courage and good sense than even he'd expected from her. She'd shown only strength and grace in the past thirty hours, while he was still reeling.

Yet he couldn't help worrying. If she became stressed, she'd stop eating. It was her measure of control when her world spun out of reach…and if that happened he wouldn't know what to do. He'd totally lost it when she'd collapsed.

Man, he wished Toby was here.

The Costas had never been the average Greek family, reliant on the wider Greek community for companionship and marriage mates. Now he knew why. Papou must have been worried his accent or something about him would lead to his being recognized.

So, while they'd had friends, both Greek and Australian, they'd mostly kept to themselves. They'd forged a tight little family unit—Mum and Dad, Yiayia and Papou, Lia, Charlie, and Toby, when a mutual fascination with firefighting cemented a careless acquaintance into unbreakable friendship. Toby's friendship had seen him through the worst years of his life.

Toby had a way with Lia too. He *knew* Lia, from her guarded heart to her deepest soul. Charlie's instinctive protectiveness was less comforting to Lia than Toby's cheerful grin, his careless hug or the suggestion that they bake something ridiculous or impossible. And, if that didn't work, he'd take her a ride on his motorbike into their beloved mountains for one of their four-hour hikes. She always came home happy, at peace with herself.

The princess opened a door, and motioned for Lia to precede her.

Another reason for Toby to be here was that then Charlie might find time to pursue the princess's budding interest in him. Though he'd been popular with the opposite sex since he was sixteen and had begun body training for entry into the Fire Brigade, there was something about Princess Jazmine he couldn't define—a deeper, elusive quality that told him she wasn't as she appeared.

'I know,' Max said softly.

Charlie started, realizing he'd been staring at Jazmine's swaying walk, her lovely peach of a bottom beneath the crisp linen skirt. He swung round to stare Max out.

Unintimidated, Max grinned. 'She doesn't know she does it to a man, but she does. The way she walks, she laughs— Well, all I can say is you're a lucky man.'

Charlie swung around fast, fists clenched. 'Then why the hell didn't you marry her while you could?' he said in an undertone.

Max shrugged. 'I've known her since she was a skinny stick with her hair in plaits, and she's known me since before my first pimple. We're like brother and sister. The engagement was hard on us both. The thought of taking her to bed just wasn't...' He grinned down at Charlie's fists. 'I beg your pardon for intruding.'

'You didn't intrude on anything except a dog-tired guy on shift too long.' He uncurled his hands, feeling like a jerk. 'Just show me to my room.'

Then Lia cried, 'Charlie!'

The utter delight in Lia's voice didn't stop the rush to her side, the panic that she'd get sick again if he wasn't there to protect her day and night. 'What is it, Lia?'

Lia was gazing around her new suite, her eyes wide. '*Oraio,*' she whispered: *superb, beautiful.* '*Now* I feel like a princess.'

Pulled outside his habitual worry, Charlie looked

and blinked. *'Kita politeria,'* he muttered, using Papou's old expression of disgust: *is this where our taxes go?*

Jazmine laughed. 'You think this is luxurious? Wait until the palace renovations are complete. Then you'll have something to gape at. We each have our own wing there.'

'You're joking, right?' Charlie frowned, not least because the rippling sound of her laugh still resonated inside him, like the echo of a distant memory, sweet and haunting. 'This one suite's already as big as the house Lia and I have at home.'

For answer she winked, her dark lashed, malt-whisky eyes shimmering with humour. 'Gotcha.' Her tongue appeared between her teeth, not quite poking out, just enough to be a cheeky challenge. The half-dimple south-west of her mouth quivered.

Whatever else he'd expected of her, it wasn't inoffensive jokes at his expense. He hadn't known royals *could* tease.

A goddess in a silky, laughing package of woman; Princess Jazmine was a bundle of sweet contradictions. Nothing about her was as he'd expected, apart from the lovely face he'd seen on magazine covers. And everything he hadn't expected her to be was all the things he'd always liked in a woman.

A bolt of lust shot right through him, so strong it was almost painful—

And in front of his sister! His blood was so hot

it almost boiled, and for the one woman it shouldn't, because, no matter how she twisted his guts, he couldn't have her. She came with a price tag way beyond anything he was willing to pay. He was a fireman, not a prince, and that was how it was going to stay.

Lust passed. Regrets didn't.

He wheeled around. 'Show me my room, will you, Max?'

He stalked through the door before the Grand Duke could answer.

What more could an ordinary guy want from life?

But as much as he wanted to he said nothing, because again Lia was eating. She was basking in the king's grandfatherly attention and affection— the kind she'd missed so much since Papou had passed away last year. She was glowing under his tutelage, seeming to know instinctively which fork to use, how much wine to drink.

Unlike him. The king had snapped orders at him every thirty seconds, so many his fogged brain couldn't take them all in: "Sit up straight, Kyriacou… Smaller portions on the fork, boy… If you eat correctly there is no need to lean over your plate… You cannot leave the carrots uneaten; that is what children do, and will inspire no respect for you… One eats all the salad that is on the plate… One must *never* mash food together in that manner. It's what commoners do, not princes of the blood!"

I am a commoner, he'd wanted to retort. But for the sake of his promise to Jazmine he sat straight, ate smaller portions and filled his mouth with the despised carrots, without lettuce or cucumber with dressing to make them bearable. He chewed and swallowed over and over, hating the burst of fresh flavour every time he put another forkful in.

'You must show self-control. A royal personage must keep his head,' the king reproved coolly when he called for and received a second glass of dinner wine.

He counted to ten, tried to take another delicate mouthful of the sorbet, but he really couldn't repress it any longer. 'You mean the guillotine's still reserved for royals who don't pass the ceremonial-ritual meal test without using the wrong fork or running for the nearest anaesthetic?' he asked in tones of mock-horror, replacing the glass on the snowy tablecloth with unseemly haste.

He winked at Lia, who was trying hard not to laugh. He noticed Jazmine's pressed lips and dancing eyes, and Max's shoulders shaking, though his face was deadpan.

The king frowned. 'I am prepared to make allowances for your ignorance with the ways of royalty, Kyriacou, but if Giulia can manage with ease surely you can too? And there's no need to be facetious about instructions you certainly need.'

His fogged brain saw red at the deliberate rudeness, not even masked in humour. 'Believe me, Your Majesty, there is a need. If I don't laugh, I might end up jumping off the nearest balcony out of sheer boredom or fainting from hunger waiting to be fed,' he retorted, with a kind of weary politeness that sent the other three into fresh spasms of repressed laughter. 'I lost my appetite after the second round of green-and-white stuff. Where we come from, sorbet or ice cream is served as dessert, not after soup.'

The king sighed harshly. 'The *palate refresher* ensures you enjoy your meal.' The implication was clear: *and if you had any class, you'd know it*.

Charlie clamped his jaw shut.

'So tell us about your life in Australia,' Jazmine said in a gentle voice that in no way sounded like the intervention it was. 'It must be exciting to be a firefighter.'

'The sooner he forgets about that part of his life, the better,' the king decreed, his voice hard as ice.

The smile died on Charlie's face. He forgot why he was trying his best to keep quiet as his famous temper flashed to the surface. 'If yelling at me, illegally imprisoning me and forcing me to suffer through three-hour meals is the alternative you're offering to my life, Your Majesty, you'd better find a way to give me a dose of amnesia, because it's the only way I'll find living in Hellenia more attractive. My name is Charlie Costa, I am Australian, and I don't eat, walk or talk like one of you. If that's what you expect of me, you're going to fail.'

Something cold and dangerous glittered in the king's dark eyes. 'I do not fail, Kyriacou—and, from now on, you will not either.'

Charlie burst into laughter. 'You can't stop me, Your Majesty. I am who I am. You want Kyriacou Marandis, but I'm Charlie Costa, Australian firefighter, and there's nothing you can do to change it.'

Dead silence met his words. No one spoke for a full minute.

Then half a dozen servants entered the formal dining room with antique silver platters laden with all kinds of meats and vegetables.

Slowly he pushed his chair back. 'If you'll excuse

me, I seem to be feeling nauseous. Must be the jet lag. I'm sure I'll be better able to face a twelve-course breakfast after a good night's sleep.'

Before the king could speak, Jazmine jumped in. If she didn't broker some form of peace between these two, the Costas would be gone before a week was out. *Why* was Grandfather being so hard on Charlie? He already seemed to dote on Lia. 'It's fine, Charlie. The past two days have been over-whelming, and you're exhausted.'

Even with the dark shadows beneath his eyes, the power of his smile knocked her sideways... Um, what had she been saying?

Lia said quietly, 'Thank you, Jazmine. I don't think either of us slept this afternoon. If you'll excuse us...'

The king inclined his head with a smile. 'Of course, my dear. I should have thought of that. Sleep well.' He even flicked a small, tight smile Charlie's way. 'Good night, Kyriacou.'

As a concession, it was grudging; even to Jazmine it felt more like the Christmas détente on the Western Front than a cessation of hostilities. But, even exhausted, Charlie wasn't one to ignore a chal-lenge. 'Good night, sire.' Spoken with respect, but he was standing his ground. Jazmine found her respect for him deepening.

Lia smiled and quietly left the room. Max was chatting to her as he accompanied her to her wing. Which left Charlie to Jazmine, as Max had no doubt intended. Was he playing matchmaker, or throwing the fluttering pigeon to the dark, sleek, rebellious cat?

If she thought about it, she'd blush and stammer at all the stupid things she'd done this afternoon. She'd already embarrassed herself enough. She was supposed to be the one with poise and dignity.

'I'll show you to your room. It can be confusing for the first day or two.'

The look in his eyes told her she wasn't fooling anyone, and, despite her will, that ridiculous blush was returning.

Once in the main hall, she turned to the silent minders. 'We don't need you now, thank you. We're not leaving the house.' They bowed and scattered.

Charlie's brows rose. 'You can do that?'

Still lost in her embarrassment, she answered honestly. 'I can when we're here, safe. In public I can direct them to certain tasks.'

'*You* can? Does that mean I can't wave my goons off?'

Jazmine wanted to sigh. What was it about this man that made her say more than she needed to? She'd always been so discreet…until this day of blunders and blurting. 'You will be able to once you've accepted your position.' She tried to say it calmly, with a positive direction. 'Once you've been trained to recognize the dangers and know when it's safe to be alone.'

'I've had years of that kind of training, princess. It's ingrained in me.'

'Right now you only know physical dangers, Charlie—a fire, falling roofs and walls, and the like. You haven't been through civil war, or lived in the crosshairs of a sniper's rifle.'

Finally Jazmine *did* close her eyes. Could she have said anything more calculated to send this over-protective brother straight back to safe Sydney?

'Things have been that bad here? For you, I mean?' he asked quietly.

Startled, she swung around to look at him. How did she balance truth with not scaring him all the way back Down Under? 'It's not only here in Hellenia, Charlie. Even peaceful nations surround their leaders with security. Every nation, every monarchy, democracy and totalitarian state has its enemies, and those who believe they should rule instead. We live in dangerous times, where "innocent until proven guilty" can mean people aren't held accountable for their actions, and weapons are freely available on the Internet.' She shrugged a little. 'When people think of royalty, they think of riches and limos, jets and tiaras, waving to an adoring crowd, and living in a palace. While we do have all that, the reality is far more complex.'

Even as she heard herself speak, she wanted to turn and thump her head against the wall. Could she have put it any worse? Did she *want* him to grab Lia and bolt to that jet as fast as he could?

'As the sole heir until now, you must have been surrounded by bullet-proof glass.'

It was said tentatively, like a question. She nodded, relieved he'd looked at it from an outsider's point of view. For the first time she was glad he didn't see himself as royal. 'It has been rather restrictive since…' Again the unexpected lump rose in her throat. *Since I've been completely alone, apart from Grandfather, who expects duty and gives little or no affection…except to Lia.*

'I'm sorry, princess.' His voice was warm with compassion. 'I didn't mean to remind you of your loss.'

He touched her arm in awkward comfort. The strangest feeling streaked through her, like warm chills racing just under her skin, and then fear ran alongside those goosebumpy chills. If she reacted so strongly to one simple touch, she'd make a complete fool of herself if she ever found herself in his big, muscled, firefighter's arms.

'Thank you.' Two words, not quite clipped, but not letting him in. She had to find some distance from this man who'd turned her life upside down and inside out in a matter of hours.

The tenderness on his face vanished, and a tiny part of her rejoiced, because she'd seen that look on his face for Lia. Whatever else she was, she was *not* prepared for him to see her as a sister. 'I know my way from here, princess. Thanks for the guide.'

Now she really wanted to hit something. Where had the inborn diplomat in her gone? She'd always trodden the waters of people's emotions, walking the tightrope of royal distance and approachable warmth without sinking, but with Charlie she always seemed to overbalance. 'We need to talk.'

His brow lifted. 'No offence, princess, but I've been here eight hours, and in that time you've given me more than enough to think about. If you give me more, the silicon chip in my head will hit "overload".'

She couldn't blame him. Obviously it was time to back off a little, to give him space. 'I understand that, Charlie. But your lessons in royal behaviour and protocol will begin tomorrow.'

His laugh was filled with disbelief. 'You people really don't understand the meaning of the term jet lag, do you? I just finished a four-day shift with about a three-hour daily-sleep average. I fought five fires in that time, two of them major stuff. Two of my good friends are being treated in hospital. Do you think I'm always as reactive and rude as I've been today? Why do you think Lia's covering for me? I'm *tired*, princess.'

You think you're tired? Try living a week as the only royal in a country torn by war and not enough funds to repair everything, travelling from one end of the nation to the other, meeting officials from everywhere to beg or borrow funds, and see how tired you are then!

She had to grit her teeth again, and remind herself Charlie's reaction was normal, given that until yesterday he'd been a normal man. 'Of course, they'll start once you've slept,' she said, with a smile. That was it—show him some gracious capitulation while still making the boundaries clear, and maintain distance. Because, even though he was exhausted and halfway into shutdown, the dark heat of him, the fire he was keeping banked, was making the woman in her wake up.

All her life she'd been cool, reasoned, gentle and generous—everything she'd been expected to be. No man had given her more than an hour or two of wondering what it would be like to step outside her duty and become a real woman. She'd thought herself immune from physical desire, above what she'd been taught to believe was a mere human weakness. All her life she'd put her country first, as she ought to do.

All it had taken was one smile from a real man, one touch, to show her how human and utterly feminine she really was.

And how big-mouthed. Again. 'Grandfather and I decided that it's best for now, given that you don't want to make any announcements, if I become your sole tutor in protocol for the next two or three weeks.'

Charlie turned at that, his brows furrowed in a deep frown. 'Protocol or seduction, Your Highness?' he drawled, the banked fury flaring up. 'Are all bets off here? Is this "let's get Charlie to agree at any cost"?'

She felt herself blushing. It was as if he'd been a fly on the wall in Grandfather's private rooms: *He might hate me, but I've seen the way he's looking at you, girl. Do the come-hither dance with him. Don't let him touch you, but make him think he could…* 'I'm to make certain you're ready for anything, from meeting the press to foreign diplomats, as well as basic flight-training.' It took a massive effort to speak as if he'd been wrong. 'There's a lot more to this job than you think.'

One of those frowning brows lifted. 'Flight training?'

She nodded, relieved he'd taken the bait. 'Once you've decided to stay—' *That's it, Jazmine, sound calm and positive* '—you'll have a captain of our air force to take over your training, as well as a naval diver to teach you combat swimming. It's important that you learn to—'

'Um, right.' Now both brows were up. 'Care to tell me why this is an important part of my training?'

'As king, you'll be head of the armed forces. Defence is vital to Hellenia—so it's crucial that you understand some of what they do.'

'So when does the army make its appearance?'

'You'll receive weekend-reserve training for three months before coronation.'

He groaned and shook his head. 'Why do I feel a Village People song coming on? When does the YMCA join in?'

Relieved he was taking it so well—she'd feared he'd get all caustic about the restrictions of everything he was expected to do—she laughed. 'So long as you don't invite Rasputin along, it will be fine.'

'That was Boney M, princess.' He chuckled when she made a rueful face. 'It was way before our time—and I don't suppose you attended many school dances.'

'Make that none. It's not in the required protocol, and created a security problem as well as the fear that I might—shock, horror—kiss an unsuitable local lad.' She sighed. 'I remember hating my entire family when the girls at boarding school put on their silky dresses, make-up and heels, and I was stuck in the dorm studying or reading.'

'Is the required protocol for everyone in the royal family, even extended members?'

'Only since someone took a potshot at my uncle when I was a child, and called us the offshoot of lowly soldiers.' She grinned wryly. 'Grandfather laid down new rules to protect us and keep us alive. I hated him for it for a long time. I didn't feel protected, I felt like—a freak.'

Strangely enough, Charlie didn't back off; his eyes were dark with empathy. 'I didn't grow up royal, but, especially in the past fifteen years, Papou separated us from things he felt were beneath us, especially Lia…' He started to say something else, frowned and closed his mouth—not shutting her out, but thinking.

Well, he has a lot to think over, she thought. *He hasn't even been here a day…he has to be on information-overload by this point.*

On *everything* overload, thanks to those fires he'd

fought, the jet lag he was suffering, her blurting mouth and Grandfather's attacks.

'I'll leave you to sleep,' she said with a smile she hoped was encouraging, kind—all the things Grandfather hadn't been since Charlie's first words. And she was about to find out why. 'I'll make certain nobody bothers you until you come down for breakfast—lunch—whatever time it is.'

Charlie's face warmed as he smiled down at her. 'Thanks, princess. I'll be more human by then.' It wasn't a hopeful sentence, it was a vow. He was a man who knew himself, had mastery of his body…unless he was thrust into a new life without warning.

'Today's been enough to unsettle anyone.' She thrust out her hand.

'Thanks for understanding.' Ignoring the outstretched hand, he bent and kissed her cheek. It wasn't sexual, didn't linger, and yet she knew she'd feel it for hours…

'Good night.' She turned and walked down the hall with a slow, measured tread. She could show she was in control too.

And right now she needed control. She was about to rattle the cage of a king.

She stalked down the stairs and into the dining room, prepared for battle. 'What was that, Grandfather? Why are you attacking Charlie all the time? What's going on in your head, to push away our only and brightest hope for the future after a few hours?'

* * *

'I just wanted to make sure you're okay,' Charlie said awkwardly into the phone.

It was weird, to say the least. Though they were in the same place, he had to call his own sister because they were so far apart. It reminded him of the time she'd been in the clinic, and he'd *hated* that. He never wanted to feel as lost and helpless again.

'I'm fine,' Lia said, on a yawn. 'A bit wired, that's all. I'm finding it hard to sleep. I think I'll see if they have a gym or a place I can dance off the jet lag.'

'You don't have your points,' he said, angry again. Why wouldn't they at least let them go home to pack?

His sister laughed. 'Check your cupboards, Charlie. They obviously have complete dossiers on us, what we like and how we work off stress. I have new points, a CD player and no less than four workout-suits.'

Charlie took the cordless phone over to the wall-length wardrobe. Besides the required suits, there was running gear and a choice of three of his favoured shoes, as well as a complete golf set— Taylor, no less.

It filled him with fury to have his privacy thus invaded—but obviously it didn't bother Lia. She didn't need to talk out her fears and emotions with him; she just wanted to dance. But when had she ever talked out her closest feelings with him? It was always Toby she turned to, and Toby wasn't here. What would happen when she did fall and Toby couldn't pick her up?

It's not Lia falling at the moment, is it? It's you, and you're the one who seems to want help.

He said goodnight, wished her happy dancing and hung up grimly, his heart hurting as he realized for the first time that, much as he loved his sister, she was as distant as starlight sometimes. She did keep her secrets.

It must run in the blood. No wonder she and Jazmine had become friends so fast.

Jazmine. Even her name got him all hot and bothered. Why couldn't she be Jane or Sally, a name that didn't roll off his tongue or his mind with a lush, silken sensuality reminiscent of seven veils? He'd have to keep calling her princess, or he might end up doing something he'd regret. For life.

Damn Papou for putting him in this position! Damn her, too, for showing him that Papou had by his training prepared Charlie to come here. Damn his own conscience for forcing him to keep to his word, for seeing the work to be done in this shattered place.

He had to stay the month out, or be tortured by his conscience the rest of his life.

He wouldn't sleep yet. He jerked on one of those immaculate tracksuits and new shoes, left his room, stalked back down the hall, down the stairs and out through the tea room to the balcony and gardens. He needed air, and space.

As soon as he was free of the beautiful sandstone walls and pink granite balconies, he broke into a run. It had only been two days since he'd discovered his heritage, and he'd already blown it more times than he could count. How many mistakes would he make in a month, let alone a lifetime?

Oh, please, God, take me back three days in time so I can disappear…

Exhausted from his run through the forest behind the gardens, embarrassed by having to ask the damn goons the way back, Charlie stalked down the hall, past his silent minders into his room, his thoughts still in a jumble, filled with worry, stress and—

No! He had to stop thinking about Jazmine. Even her name turned him on!

But it was hard to not think about her when inside the locked suite, with cameras and security everywhere, sat the object of his lust, smiling at him.

My forbidden *lust. Never forget that. Remember the price tag.*

But she was there on the exquisite ivory-and-gold *chaise longue*, her bare feet tucked beneath her. And, though she was in the formal attire the king had demanded they wear for dinner, she'd undone a few buttons, shrugged off the jacket and she'd let her hair down. *Where's a fire when you need to run?* Soft, tumbling loose curls of silky brown, framing her face like lush, dark silken veils… And that tiny, curving quarter-smile that said, 'I know you want me, but can you afford me?'

No, no, *no*. Not now and not ever.

Taking a chair opposite, he sprawled in inelegant abandon. 'So, wassup, princess?' he drawled with deliberate crudeness, flicking his fingers, watching them instead of her.

He didn't need to look. Her face was laser-burned into his memory, etched in his mind in every bright spot and hidden corner.

'Must be important for you to break protocol and risk the sensibilities of the goons outside,' he went on before she could speak. 'How'd you get around them?'

Her smile was as beautiful as sunlight on snow and as deadly as an ice pick, chipping away at his self-control smile by smile, hit by hit. 'There's a secret passage that runs from behind this room to the library.' The smile grew a touch. *Chink...touch her. Chink again, kiss her; just kiss her.* 'My brother Angelo and I found it when we were children. There're twelve passages going to a major passage leading to about a mile from here, in the forest. One leads from every royal suite. This house used to belong to the Orakis family, you see. They needed a series of escape routes for when their enemies attacked, or the people rose up in revolution...again.'

His brows lifted. Despite himself, he felt the intrigue growing. 'How many years did you spend looking for them?' he asked, to banish his interest in Hellenican history and all its attendant dangers. But the curiosity remained, and was growing hourly.

You can help the people on a far more lasting scale…

Her rogue dimple came and went; her eyes held that lurking twinkle. 'Who says I've stopped looking? Nothing beats the secret thrill of sneaking outside the palace walls at night with nobody the wiser.' She winked.

He grinned outright now. Man, this girl was charming, right at the moment when he wanted her to be…

No, he just *wanted*.

She was too dangerous by half, this Da Vinci darling. And didn't she know it, despite what Max thought? The look in her eyes said it all.

'So are you going to tell me why you're here, princess, or will we continue playing twenty-questions for a while?'

She was silent for a moment. 'If we are, I believe it's my turn. Why do you become so rude every time you feel threatened? Is it exhaustion, a defence mechanism you've used for a long time, or only against my family?'

Taken aback by her perspicacity, yet enjoying the game she'd begun, he said, 'Oh, your family is reason enough for rudeness, princess.'

Her brow lifted now. 'As an entity, or as royalty?'

He shrugged. 'Either will do, or both. Take your pick.'

'It won't work with us,' she said, her eyes soft-shimmering again. 'We're used to the stories made up by paparazzi, the encroaching attitude of the wannabe's, you name it. People of all walks of life feel they have the right to say what they like to us, or intrude on our privacy. We're used to it.'

'I'm not.' His enjoyment of the game they'd been playing faded abruptly. 'And it isn't something I *want* to become used to, princess.'

'Ah, you have your armour on again. You're calling me princess, locking me out. I understand. You've had a hard few days, and this must rank as the most overwhelming day anyone ever went through.' She rose to her feet and headed for the back wall. She looked at him over her shoulder, and the little, maddening smile told him she saw right through him.

Well, two could play at that game.

'You opened the door, princess,' he said lazily. 'I just didn't step through it at call. I've never been a "here, boy" kind of guy.'

The smile vanished. Her eyes grew wary, but she turned back around to face him. 'You have something to say.' She wasn't backing down.

He shrugged. 'I've said it already. I'm not into repeating myself. I like my life at home. I enjoy playing the field.' He looked her over. 'I'd ask you to dinner under different circumstances.'

'Which circumstances—my position, or the press?'

'Again, take your pick.' He continued making the words slow, lazy. As if he didn't care—because he didn't.

Liar. You care, or you wouldn't be here. And Her Royal Pain in the Butt knows it as well as you do.

'As I told you before, this isn't about me,' she said, with penetrating insight. 'For you, it's about going home and returning to your life. For me, it's about eight million lives that could become much better or worse, depending on your decision.'

Though his jaw clenched, hating the thought that he could hurt anyone by simply going home, he clapped once, twice. 'Good one, princess. That's the spirit. If you can't win me over with bribes, your looks and bedroom visits, by all means try the guilt trip. It's guaranteed to work on the average Greek boy.'

'Or Hellenican,' she smiled, though her cheeks tinged pink in acknowledgement of his shot. 'We are related to the ousted Greek royal family, though distantly.'

'It's working,' he said bluntly. In truth, he hadn't even been here a day and he felt the tug of duty clinking the iron collar gently around his neck. 'But there are some things I don't understand.'

He saw the tender fire leap into her eyes—at the thought of his agreeing to help her beloved people. He'd never met a woman so turned on by the notions of duty. 'What's that? Anything I can do to help…'

Though part of him didn't want to alienate her, he made himself say it. 'Can I still become king if I remain single? Do I lose it all if I refuse to marry you? In other words, is the whole shebang at the king's discretion?'

She'd stiffened before he finished speaking. Her face was white, her eyes holding shadows, but still she answered honestly. 'The position is yours to take, but the choice on marriage is yours to make—so long as she's of the right connections and power. In short, she must be someone the people and press will accept, and is in a position to help Hellenia. Grandfather will press you on the matter: I'm the best qualified to be your helpmate in making the best decisions for the nation. And the people will expect it.'

So, in other words, it was 'marry me or some other royal', but that was the limit of his choices, he thought grimly. And how many single princesses were there in Europe?

'What about Lia? What's the truth about her choices?' he asked, hating the look on her face—the same kind of mute suffering he'd seen on the Save the Children posters that had made him support three villages. She was no royal spoiled-brat in designer clothes and limos; she really *cared* about her people. 'If I refuse to take the position, can Lia choose to take it? Can she marry Max…or not? Is her position dependent on my decision, or her marriage to him?'

She was watching the slow-setting sun through his western-facing window. 'She doesn't *have* to marry Max, but he's the only man remotely suitable for the hand of a princess in Hellenia, besides you. As the law stands, she can't marry below the rank of Grand Duke—and, if she tries, there will be anarchy again. Our people have…expectations of us. *Strong* expectations. It's not Grandfather alone, though he has the ultimate power.'

'But the king likes her,' Charlie said slowly. 'Better than he likes me.'

Her hands balled into fists. 'Who wouldn't like her? Lia will make a magnificent princess. She was born for the role. I think Grandfather would still do his best to push her into a marriage with Max. There's nothing to dislike with him, is there?' She looked at him, with a deep keenness. 'Unless…is there a prior attachment? Is she in love?'

'No.' He frowned again as he thought of it. Lia was twenty-six, and she'd never fallen in love.

He shook himself, coming back to the present conversation. Despite doing his best to alienate Jazmine—and he believed he had—he couldn't restrain the admiration, looking at the upright figure, the quiet strength and dignity in every line of her. Even at the thought of losing the only thing she wanted, she still told the truth. He was sure the king would want her head for it, too.

Jazmine Marandis was a woman of integrity and courage.

'Thank you for your honesty.' What else was there to say? Reassurance was ridiculous at this point; he didn't know her well enough. He wasn't a man to her; he was a means to an end. She might find him as attractive as he found her, but that wasn't enough to base a lifetime of sacrifice on.

Not for him, anyway. It seemed she'd take him on, but the thought of her taking him as a noble sacrifice turned his stomach, no matter how attracted she was to him.

'You'd better go before your guys come looking,' he said.

At that, the glimmering smile returned. 'What, the big tough fireman's afraid I'll create a scandal to force a wedding?'

'I don't know about you, but, from what I've seen of the old guy, I have no doubt he'd do it,' he retorted, laughing despite himself.

The dimple peeped out as she grinned. 'I wouldn't put it past him at all.'

He said abruptly, 'He doesn't think I'm good enough to be prince.'

At the abrupt words, she leaned forward. 'He's set in his ways, Charlie. Just because he's a king doesn't make him less human—a crabby old man with gout and a heart reliant on a battery of pills, morning and night. He's used to clicking his fingers and having exactly what he wants.' She lifted her hands in an elegant kind of shrug. 'He doesn't want to understand that, without the training and all the years spent at Eton and Oxford, you couldn't be another Max.'

He felt the lines of his body relax. 'I understand that. Papou adored us, but it didn't stop him yelling at us on his bad days, or grunting at us on his good days.'

She chuckled softly. 'Just remember, Charlie, the decision is yours, not his. Old people don't like change, don't like being defied or criticized. He wants someone to carry on life as he did. Though he knows it won't happen, he doesn't have to be happy about it, just as his father was unhappy with him.' Her eyes shimmered with sweet mirth. 'Don't let him fool you; he was a rebel with a temper in his time.'

It took a few moments to digest the vision of the regal old boy in a leather jacket on a bike, upsetting the king before him. When he looked again, the princess was moving like shadows in the dusk to the back wall. 'Don't tell anyone about the passages.'

'It's our secret,' he returned as softly. She'd given him a gift tonight. He could at least try to return it.

He watched her as she ran her hand along the panelling in the wall, and a door appeared. She turned to him for a moment, with a look compounded of mischief, sadness, and something almost like regret. Then she was gone, and only the soft breeze from the passageway lingered: a faint scent of pine-forest and loam. And then, carried on the breeze, was a touch of roses, vanilla and woman… And, just like this afternoon, the thought and scent of her inspired tossing and turning and very little sleep.

CHAPTER SIX

Ten days later

FRESH back from an hour with Lia, seeing her delightful enthusiasm at trying each of her new duties, and her graceful dancer's ability to get so much right so quickly, Jazmine returned to her lessons with Charlie.

'I can manage a simple handwriting session alone, princess,' he'd drawled, and she'd sensed he needed time on his own.

But it was obvious it wasn't so simple for him. He was sitting on the high-backed chair with tight spine and straight shoulders, trying to turn his left-handed scrawl into the elegant, flowing script Grandfather demanded. He barely moved, apart from his arm and shoulder, but his hand looked awkward, curved over itself as he tried to write sitting like a statue. Though he said nothing, she sensed his discomfort and sense of failure.

He'd put up with the long list of 'must haves'

with stoic silence and taut-jawed acceptance: 'Straight shoulders, Charlie… Your signature must be legible, with the Marandis elegance… You aren't rushing to a fire; you are His Royal Highness, Prince Kyriacou… Slow down the stride. Make it formal and deliberate, but with all your innate strength… Your tie must be straight when in public, meeting officials or at a press conference… Your chin should be half an inch higher—no, not an inch. It is that half-inch that separates regal pride from haughty indifference.'

As well as reading the Australian newspapers daily to keep up with home news, he read the classics and European news—in both Hellenican and Greek. He was also learning French, German and Italian: an hour's lesson for each language each day.

On Charlie, his silent stoicism was more frightening than his outbursts. His self-control sat on him like the suits he was forced to wear: *this isn't me*.

Hours of this every day would be enough to break anyone's spirit. Grandfather had decreed nine to ten hours a day, every day, for the month. *He has to know what he's in for, girl.*

Jazmine had always hated her lessons in royal behaviour and protocol, and she'd only endured four hours three times a week. She'd had years to get it right, not a few weeks—and she felt miserable and confused that *she* was holding the whip over his head.

Lia's intensive lessons were at a far easier pace, her 'royal list' far shorter.

Charlie seemed to be good at waiting, for a man with a temper. The paradox confused her. All her life—the people she'd known, the world she inhabited—had been about self-control…but not Charlie's kind. The self-control was real, living side by side with a volcanic temper and a brotherly love that never reproved but only gave.

She'd never known a man like him, had never seen family love as Lia and Charlie shared—and often lately she'd found herself wishing Grandfather had been the one to abdicate and run away to the other end of the planet.

As she watched him—she could barely take her eyes off him these days, so deep had her fascination become—Charlie's mouth turned right and grim as he tried again for an elegant signature. His knuckles were white.

'That's enough for now,' she heard herself say as she crossed the room to him.

He looked up at her, frowning. 'It's not even time for afternoon tea.'

She repressed the grin. He'd worked out Grandfather's habits, all right. Work only stopped at meal or tea times. 'Your hand's cramping,' she pointed out gently. 'And don't argue with me, please. I am the teacher, and I say enough. How about we take a walk in the gardens to relax, or spend some time in the gym?'

'Don't let me off the hook, princess.' His voice was tight now. 'It's not as if you have pure gold here.

There's a lot of dirt to wash away, and not much time to do it.'

She shook her head. 'You don't have to be perfect, Charlie. As I told you, Grandfather wants you to be just like him, to carry on the life and traditions he began, and that won't work in the twenty-first century.'

'You think mine will work?' he asked dryly. 'The Crown Prince's pub diet: instigate beer after work, meat pie and chips Monday, fish and chips Friday?'

'A rough diamond?' she suggested with a smile. 'It might be a refreshing change for all of us.'

He shrugged, an eloquent movement that indicated his comfort with whom he was. 'Problem is, princess, I can pretend to be what I'm not; I might even convince some people I'm okay at it. But the man I am is obviously not acceptable.'

'To whom?' she retorted, feeling uncharacteristically heated. 'I told you, the king has no jurisdiction here. *You* are the heir, and the changes we're working on are mainly cosmetic.' To her inner shock, she realized how true it was. She didn't *want* to change the man he was inside. She liked him—more than liked him—just as he was.

'He's right, princess,' he said quietly. 'We both know this is only the start. I have to know what the world's doing and its relation to Hellenia, how each country interacts with us, and what problem we have with them. The cosmetic stuff will only get me to the photo shoots. If I don't win the respect of other rulers and diplomats—'

'Don't quote Grandfather to me!' she snapped. 'He had *years* to get this right, and even then he rebelled. He has no right to treat you as he does—and I don't know why he does it. I have never heard him speak to a member of the royal family with such—'

'Disrespect, bordering on contempt?' he put in, when she broke off. 'Water off a duck's back, princess. What I learn from him is more important than how he does it.'

She stared at him. 'He didn't offend you with his attitude?' He'd certainly offended her.

Charlie shrugged. 'He might have, if I didn't understand why he's doing it. It's for Hellenia, and he's got to push me. It's good practice, anyway. If I take this on, I'm going to get plenty of disapproval and disrespect. If I let one opinion break me, how will I handle the press and the people?' He saw her frown at him, and grinned. 'Do you think I *need* to waste time worrying about the opinion of people I don't know or care about?'

The moment of fragile understanding and accord vanished; all of a sudden the gap between them broke wide apart, like an earthquake fissure. 'You'll *have* to care when they can sell the story and it will go worldwide. It will humiliate our people, and they've been through enough.'

The grin faded. 'That's the king's point, princess. So let's stop tap-dancing and tell it like it is.'

'Yes, let's.' She turned away, unable to stand it when his turbulent male beauty turned so self-mocking, wry with knowledge. It drew her like a lasso, dragging her to him. The only option was *not* to look. 'You've been learning for ten days what we've been learning from birth, and we still get it wrong. So, I repeat, he is too harsh on you—and you're way too hard on yourself. You're doing just fine.'

'If that's true, why aren't you looking at me when you say it?'

The blush crept up her cheek, but she turned to him and said, 'I'm not used to teaching anyone, Charlie. I don't know how to say things—and when I look at you…'

'Yes?' He moved closer, until the fire inside him reached out and burned beneath her skin. 'When you look at me?'

His gaze mesmerized her, drew truth from her prim, proper training and scared little-girl's soul. 'When I look at you, I forget what I want to say.'

His eyes darkened; a finger touched her cheek. 'It's all new for you, isn't it, this wanting?' he whispered. 'Poor little princess wasn't given any armour for this fight.'

Her entire body quivered under the single touch; she melted beneath the untamed heat of him. He'd come to her—and, right now, despite his irreverent use of her title, he wasn't seeing her as a princess, but a woman. And having a man see her as something apart from her position was a rare event in her life. 'Yes,' she whispered. 'Um…I…I mean, no.'

His eyes darkened. 'If you keep looking at me

like that, princess, you're going to get yourself thoroughly kissed by a rough commoner from Sydney.'

'You're not a commoner, and maybe I want to be kissed—*thoroughly kissed*—Charlie,' she whispered, couldn't bear to break the languid, sensual warmth floating between their bodies, their mouths, saying his name with the husky, blurry sound she knew made him hot for her.

His gaze dropped to her mouth with smouldering heat. 'For the first time, I'm sympathizing with arsonists,' he murmured, coming closer millimetre by delicious millimetre. 'I suspect a single kiss will turn into spontaneous and unstoppable combustion.'

'Charlie,' she breathed, her eyes fluttering shut as she leaned into him.

A gentle cough from the doorway of the private study that was their sanctum made them spring apart. 'Your Highnesses, the king requests your presence at your earliest convenience.'

'What is it?' Charlie snapped with obvious irritation at the interruption, and Jazmine wanted to smile.

The servant looked scared and backed out of the room without answering—and suddenly Jazmine thought she knew exactly why.

Without bothering to ask further, Charlie took her hand. 'Come on, princess.' He walked out of the room, but his stalking gait slowed when he noticed Jazmine rushing along in her high heels, half-afraid of stumbling. 'Sorry' was all he said, with the private smile that told her he hadn't forgotten the kiss they'd almost shared.

She almost pooled into a puddle of melted femininity at his feet.

Grandfather was lying on his recliner in the corner of his private reading-room, having a nap. He started to half-wakefulness when they entered. 'What is the meaning of this intrusion?' he barked, obviously to cover the embarrassment at being caught napping like any other elderly man.

'You tell us, sire,' Charlie said with cool respect, still holding her hand. 'We were told you wanted to see us immediately.'

Jazmine noted with sadness that, while Lia had progressed within days to calling the king Theo Angelis, and hugging him on greeting and goodnight, Charlie remained on the most formal of terms with him.

A crafty look crossed her grandfather's face, and she knew she'd been right. The wily old fox. What was he up to? 'I see. I'm afraid I can't quite remember.'

At that, Jazmine lost it. 'Yes, you do. You gave specific orders for the servants to interrupt us if they saw us getting too close.'

Charlie turned to her, his face startled. Then, to her shock, he grinned and slowly started laughing— and kept laughing until he released her hand, doubling over.

That got Grandfather's full attention. He sat up straight, and asked in his frostiest tone, 'What is so funny about that, Kyriacou?'

Charlie kept chuckling. 'You only make me cross the world to marry her, and then you want to stop us kissing? I'm obviously missing something here.'

Grandfather frowned, but before he could speak Jazmine spoke. 'You broke your promise, Grandfather. You told me you wouldn't interfere for the month.'

His brows rose. 'Have I interfered with his royal training in any way?'

'Apart from the mile-long list of do's and don'ts, and setting servants to watch us?' she retorted, exasperated. 'I'm not sure. You tell me!'

Grandfather put on his haughtiest look. 'You are a princess of the blood, Jazmine. You will not behave in a common manner.'

'So she can't get it on with a commoner?' Charlie interrupted in a tone of mild query—deliberately drawing Grandfather's fire, she suspected. 'I thought that was the whole point of my coming here—to create satisfactorily royal offspring. The theory being that, though I was raised as a commoner, if I bleed it'll come out blue. But, hey, what do I know? I'm just a fireman with the necessary ancestry, right?'

Charlie grinned at her, and Jazmine felt her lips twitching; she felt furious and hilarious and touched. Nobody besides Max had stuck up for her for the longest time. But Charlie knew, had seemed to know from the first day, how to make her laugh. He could poke fun both at himself and at tradition and belief that, through a stranger's eyes, didn't seem so sacred—or so scary to change. And, oh, how she wanted to kiss him right now. Deep, long and hot. She wanted the kiss she'd been denied only minutes ago, to touch his skin like a lover, to trust him to show her the way. She'd been a porcelain piece kept on the shelf too long: 'look but don't touch; admire me from afar, because you can't afford me'.

But she'd come alive with one look at her turbulent prince; the princess had become a woman, and she didn't want to return to her starved, duty-only existence.

'You will withdraw the surveillance, Grandfather, and allow Charlie and me to bond in our time and way. You will also stop treating Charlie like the enemy. It's as if you're trying to force him to leave. He is *not* his grandfather, and *I* am his teacher, not you. I'm asking you to keep your promise to stay out of our personal business.'

A tiny shock ran through her as the look on her grandfather's face changed, and became tinged with something almost like respect overlaid with embarrassment. Jazmine flicked a glance at Charlie; it told her all she didn't want to know.

Charlie knew, or had at least suspected the source of the rudeness.

Grandfather *had* set him up to fail—and Charlie continued to meet each challenge with ice-cold control and stoic silence. He'd refused to let the old man beat him.

The fury she'd felt in the ballroom was now double-pronged. Was everything between these two a game?

Her mouth tightened. She waved an irritable hand, and turned on her heel. 'Do as you will; you both appear to be enjoying your games. You have my apologies for my interruption into your little "who's going to break first?" contest!'

The measured tread she used could in no way have been called storming out. If they wanted to win so badly, so be it. All she knew was that neither of them would be allowed to beat her down. And they could both grow up!

Charlie gave her half an hour before he went looking.

He finally ran her to ground in the gym. She was on the walking machine, but she wasn't walking.

'You'll break it, at the rate you're pounding on this thing. You must be doing fourteen kilometres an hour,' he said, but she didn't answer.

He saw the MP3 player at her waist, the earpieces in her ears, and, with a grin, walked around so she'd see him.

She started and made a mis-step—and, at the speed she was running, it could have been lethal. He leaped toward her, arms extended so her torso would land into his arms, hips and waist; but before he touched her she'd grabbed the handrails, and after a couple of stumbles she was on track again. And she kept running as if he didn't exist.

She still hadn't got all her anger out. His grin grew. She must be really mad.

He turned and walked into the male dressing-rooms. He changed into designer running trousers and a tank top, and found his trusty old trainers, refusing the top brand waiting for him.

Within minutes he was walking beside her, building up to a run. He'd prefer to be pounding the pavement, but the security issue would create a nightmare for the Secret Service, so he had to settle for what the secure gym could offer.

Jazmine kept running, looking straight ahead. The only things she seemed to notice were her water bottle and towel.

He'd never seen a more sensual sight than that water going down her throat, or seeing the towel grow damp from the perspiration she wiped from her forehead, throat, and chest. He was even turned on by her bouncing ponytail, the way some curls escaped from the band and grew wet against her nape and throat.

Man; he really had it bad.

How he could, he had no idea. Everything between them was prim, proper and correct. And, yet, he kept seeing her in his room, lying on the *chaise*, like the naughtiest invitation he'd never accepted…and wished he had.

So many layers to her; so many super-impositions, every one real and true. She wasn't acting with any of them, except perhaps 'the proper princess'. And every layer fascinated him—perhaps because the complexity made her less royal, more human.

No matter which layer she showed at the time, he wanted her more.

He wasn't stupid. He couldn't have her. She was too high, too clean, too *pure* for him. Despite the heated looks she gave him, he knew she was innocent: she didn't know she was looking at him like that. The sweet surprise in her eyes told him he was the first man to awaken her to the fact that she was a woman. She didn't want to make love; not yet. She wanted to feel pretty and feminine, to have flowers and go dancing, and all the things a normal girl had. But Jazmine wasn't normal, never had been and never would be—at least, not his version of normality.

Again he saw the parallels to Lia, to her life. No wonder they'd taken so well to each other. They were sisters under the skin, girls raised in opposite ivory-towers. Papou had protected Lia as well as King Angelis had protected Jazmine.

But now, Jazmine was cool and distant. Even after she'd made him reach flashpoint by caring about him, she'd done that incomprehensible woman thing and had turned into the ice maiden for no good reason he could see.

He'd put a crack in her composure again.

If he had to change his entire life to get this prince gig right, she could drop a few of her little mysteries, let go a little. If she wanted him for her future king, she could be more than that intriguing and lovely Mona Lisa. She'd be that stuttering, blushing, real woman she'd been when she'd admitted she wanted him.

The challenge was on: the royal and the ordinary Joe. Let the best player win.

So he kept running, using the water bottle and towel as she had, but letting the sweat rest on his skin a little longer than he ought to.

She never turned her head once.

After a twenty-minute run, he saw she was out of water. He took the bottle and refilled it for her while he refilled his.

She kept running; didn't even nod in thanks or acknowledgement. Charlie's grin grew. Missing her manners, was she?

He strolled over to the weights area, lay on the mat and began his crunches: a hundred of each, including cross-waist. He did them far more slowly than he would normally do. Why not? It was better for his body, and until she remembered the lessons he had a little free time. And he wasn't in her direct line of sight. Behind the chest-wall hydraulic machine, she'd have to crane her head to see him.

And she would—oh, she would. He'd knock the invisible tiara right off her head with a little street smartness…

He didn't bother with the 'show off in the gym' stuff so many guys did—the kind of women he liked rarely fell for the obvious. They usually gave those guys a contemptuous smile and avoided them. When he finished his sit-ups, he moved to the corner of the room, out of her range of sight, where she'd have to actually turn her head to see him—she'd have to *want* to look.

And he began his favourite workout: chin-ups over the high bar.

It wasn't a show-off measure, either. A lot of his job entailed lifting himself into inaccessible places. He had to keep his fitness levels up. Could he help it if it showcased the muscles of his arms, shoulders and chest with every movement?

When he was done, he turned his head to look for her—and she was right behind him. Was the flush from the exercise, fury…or was she just a little excited?

'Princess,' he greeted her gravely.

'I have a name, firefighter,' she countered, with mirror-like composure, her eyes challenging.

His heart was still hammering, and from more than the exercise. 'Jazmine.'

Slow and deliberate, she ran her gaze over his body, flushed and sheened with sweat. 'Have you finished your silent "how to" lesson in gaining muscle without bulk?'

Caught out—and willing, *glad*, to admit it—he nodded. Her lovely, curvy body was luminescent, shimmering. He wanted to rub himself over her skin like that towel…

The game was on. Both aroused, willing to show it—wanting so much more than just to look.

'Good,' she said softly. 'So tell me why Grandfather's riding you, and why you're letting him do it.'

The look in her big, angelic whisky-eyes was ir-refutable. This adorable, hot and sweaty, kiss-me woman was setting boundaries at the moment his body began to scream. She'd pinned him to the mat when he'd least expected it—but her demand was honest. Even now she didn't know how to turn games to her advantage, and he liked that. Wanting a woman was natural to him; liking her was a bonus. *Respecting* her as deeply as he did Jazmine turned desire imperative.

Telling her wouldn't take the edge off—might even lend some piquant spice to the contest—and the victory.

'He doesn't hate my grandfather for his disap-pearance alone. He was angry about that, but hated him for who he took with him.'

Her eyes grew; her lush mouth fell open. 'Oh. So the woman he loved and lost was your grandmother?'

Touch her, touch her, touch her... He pulled himself together, tearing his gaze from her ready lips. 'He adored her, but she loved my grandfather. I look like Papou, have his name and his temper. Lia has Yiayia's name and her personality—her gentle ways, her way of defusing tension, and her smile.'

'It makes sense.' She nodded, looking so sweet and delightful with that little crinkling frown he ached, hard all over with the need to kiss her. 'And you don't mind that he so obviously favours Lia?' She peeped at him through her lashes.

Gone, gone; he was *so* gone. Unable to stop the surging king-tide taking over his body, he leaned forward, his mouth hovering near hers. 'It's not the old guy's favour I want,' he whispered against her mouth. 'I want you, Jazmine, I want you.'

A tiny moan escaped her throat, sexy and husky and *needing*. 'Char-r-r-lie…'

Absolutely and totally gone. He pulled her against him, loving the hot, slippery feel of her. The sweat made her human, a woman who wanted him and didn't know any games to put him off or make him wait. Her desire was clear to read in every look of those wide, new-woman's eyes, in the way she swayed into him, the aching yearning in the way she said his name.

But, as he was about to kiss her, she put a hand on his chest. 'The cameras. Tonight, Charlie…tonight. The secret passage,' she whispered.

Liking, lust, respect and a touch of the forbidden; how could he resist? He moved just a touch, so his mouth brushed hers with every movement. 'Tonight.'

CHAPTER SEVEN

SHE was floating around the room. One moment she was sweetly smiling on that *chaise*, wearing something filmy and soft, her hair a silky cloud around her face and throat, the next she was coming to him through the closed balcony window, wearing only the most feminine of perfume. Driving him crazy, trying to catch her. Always beckoning to him with that tiny princess-wave he'd seen in photos: try to get close, I dare you…

Though he wanted to be strong, to resist her game, she'd whisper, 'Char-r-rlie,' with that incredibly arousing accent, and all his good resolutions crumbled to show the raw, elemental man beneath. Night and day, no matter what he was doing, she was there, in his mind if not in person. Making him ache for her simply by breathing.

'Jazmine,' he growled, and reached for her, but his arms found only cold air. He shivered, and in that instant she had vanished again, back to the land of impossible dreams and fairy tales. And he had what he wanted—he was just a normal guy, back in Sydney and in uniform, fighting a fire.

But the fire was in him. Toby was dousing Charlie in water and chemicals, but nothing put it out. He needed *her*—only she could make him stop burning and live...

He sat up abruptly in bed, amazed to find he wasn't soaked in sweat from the heat of the dream. The rose-and-vanilla scent of her filled his head; the ghost-lights from the garden and the silver half-moon flooded the night with unearthly radiance, illuminating the trailing clouds and the slender statue of a goddess on the edge of his balcony.

It looked like Jazmine, with that maddening half-smile she threw at him as she glanced over her shoulder. No wonder he couldn't stop dreaming about her.

Knowing he wouldn't sleep again for at least an hour, he got to his feet and threw open the balcony door, taking deep breaths of the sweet, fragrant summer air.

As if on cue, he saw a small, upright figure wandering amid the rose garden below his room, not wearing the shimmering, filmy thing from his dream, but, in a simple blue summer-dress and peasant sandals, her hair unbound, she'd walked right into it.

So he wasn't the only one losing sleep. Why hadn't she come to him as she'd promised?

As if sensing him, she turned. Her eyes met his,

limpid shadows in the deeper dark, her hair touched with gilt by the lights above. She took a step towards him.

It was a tiny movement. Then Charlie saw the minders behind, and remembered the one always out on his balcony, watching. He waved, as if that was all either of them had intended, when they both knew.

Her chin lifted—a small, haughty nod for the sake of their unwanted audience—then she allowed her face to come into the light. Her eyes asked the question.

Heart pounding in anticipation, he nodded. He watched as she turned to the path leading back to the palace, then he returned to his room and closed the doors.

Waiting.

He sat in the warm, silvered dark for almost fifteen minutes before the quiet clicking sound came, and she slid in from the secret passage. Her eyes were shining. 'Come with me,' she whispered. Her hand made the little gesture that always seemed to say—to him at least—'come and get me'.

Unable to deny that he'd go wherever she beckoned, he followed her.

Within moments they were plunged together into soft, welcoming darkness. Every sense was heightened; he was aware of everything he couldn't see. A warm hand slipped into his. He felt her rise up on her toes, angling towards him. Warm breath touched his ear. 'There are light- and movement-sensors above the ceiling—not close, but not that far. We can't make any sudden movement, or any noise above a mouse.'

He shuddered with the rush of hot desire. Her touch, her whispered words, roared to life in him. His fingers closed around hers with a caressing motion. He moved his face until cheek touched cheek, and he nodded. 'Let's go,' he whispered, and felt her shiver.

He didn't ask where, and she didn't ask if he wanted to know. She led and he followed, and they both knew: what was here.

What was coming.

There was a peculiar intimacy in the tunnel. Holding hands, they moved foot by foot, free hands touching the wall. It was like connection, as if the tunnel was a friend, as if they were friends.

Were they? He didn't know, didn't know if being with her now was a good thing or a disastrous thing. All he knew was she'd shimmered into his soul with the sheerness of a gossamer dream, seducing him with her courage and strength, her honesty and sweetness and big-eyed prettiness…and he trusted her.

She should be the enemy. God knew she represented everything he wanted to run from. But it was as if he stood in sinking mud and couldn't move from her. Because of her, he couldn't run, couldn't hide, he could only be himself—do his best to jump all the hurdles set for him, and hope what he offered was good enough.

Good enough for the Hellenican people, and good enough for her. He'd run from responsibility for others all his life, even from Lia's illness. It was always Toby who'd done the hard work—the emotional stuff—with his sister.

He wasn't going anywhere, not yet. He wouldn't shirk his responsibility. He couldn't—no, he wouldn't—leave Jazmine in the lurch.

Jazmine. The name was a drumbeat in his blood.

He bumped into her when she turned to the left. About to mouth an apology, he felt her turn and touch her finger to his lips.

A finger. Such a little thing to send a furnace rip-roaring through him. It was too late now, too late for talk, too late to wait. Jazmine, Jazmine; *I have to have her; I have to have her; I've got to.*

Using his free hand, he touched her waist, asking, not commanding. Not because she was a princess, because she was a woman with too few choices in her life. He let it rest for a moment while he waited for her answer, and his blood thudded in his ears and pounded in his head and he hoped.

Her soft intake of breath, a gentle move closer, was all the answer he needed. He bent—such a small woman to hold all that courage and self-sacrifice—and kissed her.

He missed. He could hear the sensuality in her quiet laugh as she wound her hands into his hair—she missed first time, too—and brought him in the right direction.

Almost.

Laughing without sound, bumping noses, their bodies moving to crowd into each other, they both whispered at the same time, 'Let's go outside.'

She took his hand again, and the rightness of it flooded his entire being. He didn't question it. He'd second-guessed too much lately. He wanted her, was with her, was touching her… and it was enough.

Something about that thought haunted him, something he ought to connect.

'The exit's just ahead,' she murmured as the passage began sloping up, and they stepped out into a wider cavern with filtered moonlight illuminating small patches. There were niches in the walls, the sites of old religious rituals. He stepped into an indent in the floor, and almost tripped over the rocks filling it. It looked, felt, smelled, incredibly ancient. He could see Greeks and Hellenicans of olden times living, working here, hiding their beliefs from those threatened by it.

Hellenicans sneaking into and out of a palace for lovers' trysts, for political meetings or sacred rites— running for their lives. This cave was silent witness to the rise and fall of kings, including his ancestors, and he could be the next to rise.

Somehow it felt right to be here with Jazmine.

He inhaled the scent of loam before Jazmine pushed aside a mess of bracken and vines covering the exit cave, and he knew where they were. Still clasping her hand, he looked around at the cool, dark forest surrounding them. 'Somehow I knew you weren't taking me into your bedroom.'

She laughed, low and sweet. 'The lack of stairs was probably your first clue.' Her face lifted to his, eyes glowing, lips curved in that secret woman-smile that made a man's heart yank from his chest and want to do a primitive victory-dance with it. 'No one can see us now,' she whispered, and added, 'And we can see each other.'

'It helps.' He smiled and drew her close, going slow, wanting to drag her to him and devour her, but the moment felt too important to rush it.

He didn't know what he'd expected when they kissed—fireworks, fire, or at least an explosion of passion. What he hadn't expected was this, a soft, dreaming adagio of innocence. A slightly clumsy, laughing, joining of their souls.

The missing kisses in the passage, the bumping of noses, had been a prelude to the real thing. A shivering rapture, yet tender as a moth's wings touching him. Her skin was silk, her mouth honey, her smile, even as they kissed, magic.

The bungee-jumping in the dark that had been his life since he'd found out he was the 'grand what of where?' felt worth it when he touched Jazmine. Everything that scared him most came with touching this woman—and, yet, she was everything he'd ever wanted. He wanted to bolt, yet at the same time he wanted to live for her, and her alone.

Just as the laughter and rippling sweetness of a

hidden waterfall refreshed the heart and soul, so did holding Jazmine in his arms, kissing her smiling mouth, feeling her cool, gentle fingers exploring his skin. So innocent, yet it was *him* trembling like a virgin. He felt like he had when he'd kissed his first girl on her front doorstep: like he was jumping the moon, and expecting a shotgun to his head when her dad busted them.

The shotgun was already there with Jazmine; he hadn't forgotten the price that came with having her. But he couldn't make himself care, not now, not when with a simple moving of mouth on mouth it felt as if he held the beauty of misted moonlight in his arms, the untouchable magic of laced fairy-ice in the forest above him.

He almost laughed aloud. How ironic that, after all these practical years, he'd turned into some sixteenth-century poet. How Toby would laugh at him, and call it 'poetic justice'! But it was what he felt, and he couldn't stop kissing her. He couldn't.

'We need to talk, Charlie,' she said softly against his mouth minutes, hours, later. He didn't know.

'Yeah.' He kissed her again. 'Soon…'

Having her against him, fluid and feminine, and *Jazmine*, made him feel…

It was stupid, ridiculous, but there was no other word for it: *complete*. Like two jigsaw pieces he'd spent a lifetime trying to find a fit; like jagged shards of porcelain that came together to make something exquisite. That was Jazmine in his arms.

Questioning 'why' would destroy it, so he didn't. He held her and kissed her and ignored the moments becoming minutes.

'Charlie...'

'Jazmine...' He touched his forehead to hers, aching to kiss her again, but knew her determination. 'If we have to talk, *loulouthaki*, then talk.'

He had no idea why he'd called her 'little flower', but, again, it fit. Perhaps it was her name, which meant 'star flower'; perhaps it was because, like little flowers that grew in inaccessible hills and rocks, she clung: to life, to hope, to doing what was right.

A smile flitted across her face at the nickname. Then slowly, as if she ached too, she nodded and pulled away from him to a rock near the cave entrance, and sat looking at her hands. Perhaps that was because she dared not look up into his tense face, his aroused male body. 'I couldn't come earlier. Grandfather...'

'I thought so,' he said quietly. 'Crazy, isn't it? He wants us to marry, but doesn't want it to be anything but a business arrangement.'

'It's what he had with my grandmother,' she sighed.

Charlie frowned. 'So?'

'So it's all he understands, Charlie. "Duty is its own reward" is his motto.'

'He loved Yiayia.'

'And never had her to lose. He had women. We all knew about his women. But none were her, you see, so they were just...' She shrugged. 'It's said the

Marandis men only love once, and for ever. That he was stuck with the duty while your grandfather had the happiness? It's no wonder he turned duty into a sacred privilege.'

'And no wonder he takes it out on me. I came here mocking all he holds dear, all he knows.' He came to her. Something in her body said 'don't touch me', so he sat beside her on the rock. The size of it precluded personal space, which was fine with him, but she moved. An inch had never seemed so wide as now, when she wouldn't bridge it. 'I can handle it, Jazmine. Because he's determined to beat me, the old guy's got more energy than I think he has had in a long time.' He grinned. 'I wouldn't mind betting he and Papou were friends and competitors at one time.'

She sighed and nodded. 'You're right—he has been enjoying it. It isn't that.' She sounded odd; haunted. 'But he had chest pain again tonight. His lips turned blue.'

Knowing how quickly Papou had gone downhill with his heart, he didn't need a lesson in colour-by-numbers. 'How long do you think we have before the press gets wind of his illness, and the fact that I'm here?'

She shifted another inch, until she was almost falling off the rock. 'A few days. Somebody's bound to tell, no matter how many confidentiality contracts we have signed. Charlie…' She closed her eyes and spoke in a tone reminiscent of the pain in ripping off a plaster. 'I need to know what you're feeling about it.'

Again, he didn't pretend to misunderstand. He frowned and looked away, to the ghostly shapes of the trees outlined by the slow-dipping moon, wishing they were still kissing. This use of their mouths seemed a damned pointless exercise. 'Hell if I know, princess.'

She rose to her feet and walked over to the curtain of bracken and thorns. She fingered them as if blinded and finding her way by touch. 'We have to be ready.'

'How am I supposed to know, Jazmine? I'm locked in a room with you. And, while you're telling me how to walk, talk, sit, stand, write, and how to wear suits that would cost me a month's wages back home, I'm thinking about making love to you.'

Her breath hitched so fast she hiccupped. 'I—' *Hiccup.* 'Char—' *Hiccup.*

He smiled, satisfied she was still thinking about it as much as he was. 'But while all that's important, what has it got to do with the real job? What good does looking and sounding like Australia's answer to Prince Charming do me in making a decision that changes more lives than just mine?'

Her fingers stilled over a thorn; she obviously dug in too deep, and she made an impatient noise and popped her finger into her mouth. And he wished he was that finger, warm and cocooned by her lips.

'Again, you're right,' she said quietly. 'You need to know what you're facing—politically, socially and intellectually—to—to see.'

'To see if I can fill your grandfather's shoes, or if I'll end up letting the country and family down, and taking off like my grandfather,' he filled in grimly. 'That's what worries the old guy most, isn't it—that I'm so much like Papou?'

She sighed and nodded.

He hadn't noticed that he'd made fists of his hands until he scraped them against the rock. 'It seems to me the Danes had it right when they got their Australian import: they took her to the palace and gave her a few years to see if she could handle the life.'

'They're lucky enough to be a constitutional monarchy,' Jazmine said quietly. 'Hellenia isn't yet—and Denmark doesn't have a man like Orakis waiting in the wings to take over, should you—I mean we—'

She bit her lip.

'I think the word you're looking for is "fail".'

She turned to him, her eyes limpid in the darkness, lovely—and worried. 'That's not what I believe, Charlie.'

'That makes one of us, at least.' He couldn't help the harshness in his voice—and she had to know it wasn't aimed at her.

At that, she came back to where he sat, sat beside him, and took his hand in hers. 'There are worse things than making mistakes, such as never trying.'

He turned to look at her, at that pretty face so mysterious and so giving at once. 'You're the one who said eight million lives depend on my getting it right.'

'No, I didn't. I said those lives depend on your *decision*.'

'Same thing, isn't it?'

'No.' She squeezed the hand she held. 'It's completely different. Whatever you decide affects my people. Your mistakes will affect them, too, but they'd forgive you, Charlie. Don't you see?' Her voice turned husky with passionate conviction. 'You'll make mistakes, I will too.'

He gave a short, derisive laugh. 'I don't believe that any more than you do. You know exactly what to do at any given moment, and everyone loves you for it.'

She stilled again, as if he'd really said something she didn't know. Then her hands curled over, the free hand into a fist, the other squeezing his fingers. 'If that was true, I'd know what to say to you to make you see what I see in you,' she mumbled.

He felt the burning urge to ask her what she meant, but it wasn't time for personal declarations, not when he didn't have a clue how *he* felt. This, tonight, was too momentous. He settled for saying, 'You're eloquent enough when you want to be.'

She sighed and fiddled with his fingers, sending a rush of scalding desire through his veins—and she wasn't even thinking about it. 'As I said, we'll both make mistakes—but they won't be mistakes that will see villages burned and people homeless. You'll never make mistakes from lack of caring.'

The words tapped into a core of something deep inside him. He didn't know exactly what, but, while what she'd said felt incredibly reassuring, it held the sense of putting his hand into a snake hole. Trusting her belief in him was beautiful and deadly—deadly dangerous to those who'd depend on him to get it right.

'Until I see the country for myself, and know what's going on and what's needed, I'll keep feeling like I'm walking blind in a minefield,' he said curtly, hiding the welter of confused, struggling emotions.

She nodded. 'Let's suspend lessons for now. We have decisions to make—me as well as you.'

He grinned. 'And it's hard to do that with the goon squad and Candid Camera watching our every move.'

She smiled and relaxed visibly. 'I'm due to meet with Lord Vedali, the Spanish ambassador, tomorrow, to discuss some vital matters of trade. Grandfather has been handing these meetings to me for the past year or more. I'd like you to come with me. In fact, I think you should take the meeting. He's a man of integrity as well as good sense, so we can rely on his discretion.'

Touched by her obvious faith, he smiled at her. 'I'll do my best.'

She glowed as if he'd handed her a diamond. Maybe he had. 'Thank you. It's tomorrow morning at ten.'

He checked his watch and grinned. 'I think you mean today, princess.'

'And didn't you enjoy telling me I'd gotten something wrong?' she retorted with a return smile. 'See, I'm not perfect.'

He laughed. 'Just ninety-nine percent?'

Instead of laughing at his joke, she frowned. 'Perfection is a real issue with you. If you don't do everything right first time, you think you're not good enough.'

A vision of Lia, collapsed on the ground, fainting from lack of food—and he hadn't even noticed until then—walked side by side with another: a young wife and mother dead, because he hadn't been there on time or done enough to save her.

And the biggest one of all…

No, damn it, I won't go there again!

He couldn't allow himself to even think about it. That way led to destruction, and he had Lia to care for. And, possibly, a whole damned country to run because the other candidate was a madman in a designer suit.

The fragile accord he'd been feeling with her, the gossamer beauty of their kiss, splintered and shattered as if it had never been. He stood up and yawned. 'It's time for sleep, if I'm going to take this meeting. I can barely think.'

'Yes,' she agreed. Her voice was quiet—too quiet.

He led the way in. When she tried to protest, he whispered coolly, 'If I take on the job, Your Highness, I just might need to know how to get out quick one day. It seems to be the way of this people.'

Very softly, she answered, 'If you won't believe in yourself and your ability to rule Hellenia, Charlie, then I'll have to believe for both of us.'

And he had no answer for her. He told himself he didn't want one.

As the silence dragged, she pulled him to a stop and went up on tiptoes. His heart knocked against his ribs, but she merely murmured in his ear, 'You don't know our ways, but you care—you want to do what's right. I believe that will carry you through the times you get things wrong—and the times I'll get it wrong as well. Even if I'm ninety-nine percent perfect, Charlie, that means I will still make mistakes some of the time.'

The way she said his name, a soft purr in his ear, heated his blood to boiling point—but he wasn't going down that path again. Not tonight.

He led the way back to his room in silence.

CHAPTER EIGHT

WHY, *why*, had he eaten so much breakfast?

Stomach churning as he walked beside Jazmine through the ruined village, Charlie felt sick. He couldn't think of her as a princess, not with the sick baby in her arms and the tears in her eyes as she greeted people with so much caring.

Though Helmanus had a similar beautiful forest-setting to others they'd passed this morning, with rolling verdant hills and trees abounding, and there was the scent of sage and lemongrass and soft loam everywhere, not one house was whole. Each house had a part that had been burned or blasted away. The street had dark patches on the stones that cried out their memories of suffering. The graveyard had more fresh headstones than the village had people.

Widows and orphans were everywhere, and elderly folk who had made shrines to sons and daughters who'd died trying to preserve their way of life...or had died just because they'd been there. He couldn't believe he'd ever thought he'd be worse than Orakis as a guardian over the Hellenican people. He'd been so focused on going home, and so appalled about the intrusions of the press, and feeling trapped by living in a palace with minders, when these people had so little…

Nothing.

No, they had Jazmine. Right now, nobody could throw the 'Mona Lisa' taunt at her. She held the baby with such tenderness, not seeming to care that his wet nappy and less-than-pristine baby clothes were soiling her designer suit. She spoke to the people about their needs, about what had been done and what was coming next, with thorough knowledge and complete empathy. She ignored the flashing of the cameras, refusing to answer questions on her clothing or love life, but answering the questions on conditions here with passion, conviction and vision. Her eyes still kept her secrets, but, standing close in his minder's role, Charlie could see the stress beneath, the burdens she'd chosen to take upon herself.

A tug at his trouser leg made Charlie look down. A child stood there, her hair neatly plaited and her dress a touch too tight for her. Her sandals were broken.

She smiled as she held out her hand to him.

The confidence in her eyes shook Charlie to the core. The child expected him to give to her because he was with Jazmine. Jazmine, who was quietly pressing money into people's hands with no fanfare. Jazmine, who'd arranged for the cars in their retinue to be filled with food. The security men were handing out flour, oil, fruit and vegetables, care packs hidden in hemp sacks.

'Do it,' Jazmine whispered through lips barely moving, moving the baby up to her shoulder to cover her words to him. 'Behave as the others do, or the press will wonder why you're different.'

At that moment, Charlie knew why she'd insisted he wear the anonymous dark suit and sunglasses of the Secret Service. In this disguise, he was invisible to the press.

Though she needed his cooperation to ensure the ongoing wellbeing of these desperate people, or even to become queen, Jazmine protected his privacy. She respected his right to choose his future.

Was there no one whose welfare this woman didn't place before her own?

He handed out coins and sacks of food. As he looked around to find more in need, trucks began arriving. When the drivers unloaded, the people cried aloud in joy.

Building materials. Tiles for roofing. Bricks to fill holes in walls. Glass panes and shutters to replace those in splinters. Mats for floors.

And bags and bags of warm clothing and shoes against the forthcoming winter.

Some of it was second-hand clothing, it was obvious by the worn look of it, and the uneven heels of the shoes. But, new or old, to the people of Helmanus it was a gift direct from God.

And Jazmine was their guardian angel, no matter whose money was being spent.

As he handed Jazmine back into the car, the press took shots of him.

He knew that, if they reached Australian shores, his anonymity would soon end. Even in the dark suit and sunglasses, somebody would be bound to make the connection.

It was time to make the decision—and, damn it, after today it shouldn't be so hard. Didn't he *want* to help these people? Of course he did.

But I want it to be as it's always been. I want to help in the disguise of a uniform, take my orders and then disappear with my friends to the pub. I don't want to have to wear a crown to help.

He hated the selfishness that still lived in him even after facing the magnificent self-sacrifice that was Jazmine. But he couldn't deny that, while the woman was all he'd ever dreamed of, the princess in the public eye was his worst nightmare, and the deep-hidden core of truth he didn't want to look at, because it hurt too much. Because it would always be there, every day of his life, haunting him like the words he'd said at seventeen that had changed his world for ever.

I don't want to make a stuff-up that could make things so much worse for these people. I couldn't stand to kill anyone else.

'That photo will blow my privacy,' he said as they took off, and she was resting back against the leather with a sigh he couldn't interpret.

She didn't deny it. 'Given your recent fame, it probably will. If the Australian press connects you to the fireman hero, they'll start digging—and the Consulate's "no comment" will only make things worse. Prepare yourself. The story will probably leak within the next couple of days.'

He digested it for a few moments. 'You knew this would happen.'

Her eyes were still heavy from the tears she'd tried all morning to hide, combined with the tiredness of being in the forest with him last night. 'I thought it might.'

'Forcing the decision, princess?' he asked, with milder sarcasm than he'd have shown two weeks ago.

She didn't even look at him. 'You didn't have to be the one to help me into the car. You could have chosen to fade into the background.' A tired hand passed over her eyes. 'Ask yourself who is forcing the pace here, Charlie. Ask yourself who is the one who's changing.'

He didn't want to think about it, didn't want to see the truth in her assertion; but he couldn't help looking at her. She was pale, her lashes fluttering over closed eyes. 'Come here.' He wrapped an arm around her shoulder, and pulled her close enough to remove the pins from her hair, the silk scarf from her throat. 'Better?' he asked quietly.

With a weary sigh, her head rested against his shoulder. 'Much.'

The mumble was so tired. They'd left for the village

before seven, and it was after two now. She'd eaten with the villagers at their invitation, but she hadn't eaten much, refusing to take food from their mouths.

It didn't hurt to help her out after all she'd been through today. He moved slowly back until they were against the leather. 'You did good today, princess.'

'So did you. I knew you would.' She sighed, halfway to sleep. 'And the money is better spent here than lying useless in a Swiss bank account.'

He blinked and made the connection in an instant. 'Whose money did you spend today, Jazmine?'

A tiny smile. 'I like it when you say my name: *Zhahz-meen*. You make it sound so lovely. I feel pretty when you say it.'

Despite his recent fears, he couldn't help but grin at the sleepy confession. The woman hiding beneath the picture-perfect princess peeked outside whenever they were alone—and she was too tired for the words to be practised.

She wanted him; she'd proven it too often to count. And the way she snuggled against him now was far more womanlike than childlike. 'Whose money did you spend today, Jazmine?'

Even the lifted hand couldn't cover the massive yawn. 'Don't worry, Your Cranky Highness, it wasn't your future I gave away. Grandfather and I have a private account we started after Orakis's last attempt to kill us. It's our own money that we use when we run out of government funds.' She kicked off her hated shoes as she spoke; her legs curled up on the seat and her head fell to his chest, breathing slow and even.

She gave away her own money to help others— as did the old man he'd thought of as an autocrat, someone who lived the palace life while others suffered.

Obviously, his first impressions had been far from right.

He used to think of himself as a pretty decent guy— but he'd never known himself until the past two weeks.

She felt like a trusting kitten, curled up against him. He watched her sleep, with curious warmth in his chest. He hadn't had this feeling with a woman before. He liked women, had been entertained by them, wanted them, made love if they were willing. He'd even flirted with the notion of being in love once or twice, but he'd always run from the notion of permanence. It was always a 'one day' proposition, a 'when the right one comes I'll know' belief.

Now 'one day' was here—but whether Jazmine was the right one or not didn't matter. This was his future; *she* was his future. It was take on the job or live with the regret that he could have helped change the world for the better, could have improved the lives of millions of people, and hadn't.

Jazmine's choice, or Hobson's, it had become his own. And with this complex and fascinating woman curled up in his arms and over his body, with one gentle kiss that hadn't even deepened to passion, he knew he'd found, if not the right one for him, then the unforgettable one.

When she moved against him, seeming uncomfortable, he pulled her onto his lap, cradling her. Just to let her sleep. Nobody needed to know.

She sighed and snuggled against his chest.

It had been a long, emotional day, and he still had his meeting with the king, to discuss his impressions of the day and what needed to be done. His eyes drifted shut, thinking of possibilities, dreaming of a future for the brave and strong people he'd just left, feeling the warmth of a woman's sleeping trust, believing in his honour and strength.

A passing rider on a motorbike lifted his digital camera and snapped a shot.

'Jobs, education, wealth—the words are used like political footballs these days. Jazmine says the other villages she's been to are much like Helmanus—in desperate need of something more immediate.' Charlie was pacing the room as he tossed his opinions at Grandfather like little bombs. 'The people I saw today are villagers living a traditional life. They don't *want* Western notions of what's best.'

'You know this, because…?' the king asked, far more delicately than Jazmine would have believed only yesterday.

'I speak Hellenican Greek, sire. Not quite the type they do near the Albanian border, but we communicated well enough,' Charlie replied, with respect tempered by leashed impatience. 'They want what they've always had: autonomy. Self-determination under the umbrella of the monarchy.'

'Which means?' Grandfather's voice was rich with hidden amusement, seeing what Jazmine did: that Charlie, in his pacing, was talking as if to himself and making plans in front of them for the well-being of her people.

Were they becoming his people too?

'Their own carpenter, plumber, cobbler and dressmaker. Their own water supply—and they need electricity reinstalled, stat. Running their own farms with their own sheep, goats and chickens, and eggs and fresh milk—growing their food the traditional way, not buying it at a supermarket. And they definitely need firefighting materials and a resident firefighter as well as a policeman.'

'How are we to accomplish this?'

Jazmine noted Grandfather had not called Charlie by his royal name, Kyriacou, once during this conversation. He'd done nothing to jerk Charlie from his thoughts and plans for Hellenia, just as he hadn't after Charlie had reported on his meeting with the Spanish ambassador—a meeting where he'd stunned Jazmine with his grasp on international affairs and his ability to stop the diplomatic tap-dance with words to get to the heart of the matter. She'd seen the ambassador's respect for Charlie deepen with every passing minute as well.

Jazmine smiled, watching him. Charlie was earning his own respect, forging his own path, his way.

'The village tradesmen are worn out, working day and night for little pay to make the houses liveable. They need apprentices for all trades, but can't afford to pay them, and the young men and women who want to learn can't afford to do so for nothing. They're the ones leaving the villages under Orakis's promise of something to do, right? I was thinking, if there was a government-run apprenticeship scheme—such as they have in Australia but on a bigger scale—it would bring wealth to the villages faster, it would mean extra hands for the needed work and keep the young people home.'

'Jobs, education and wealth,' Grandfather said softly, with a smile.

Arrested by the words, Charlie swung around to face the king…and slowly grinned. 'I suppose so, sire.'

'Within the boundaries of what my people are comfortable with. You're right. However, the cost of such a scheme—'

'If we start with what the nation can afford, sire—instigate the scheme in a few villages until they're autonomous or on the way to it—their taxes could be reinstated and used to fund the next few villages. And, as for the firefighting, we have a resident on tap. I could advise on what to buy, what buildings to use, even run classes if that's allowed.'

Grandfather blinked, his brows lifted. 'A fireman and closet economist at once?'

Jazmine kept her mouth closed. If Grandfather wanted to praise Charlie, she wasn't about to interfere.

Charlie's grin grew, but he wasn't accepting the praise. 'I always liked maths and economics at school. Their problems have simple solutions; it's just following the equations.' He shrugged. 'People have always been the harder thing to understand.'

'You've shown little hesitancy and great decision on how to help the people of Hellenia today.'

Charlie waved it off. 'Problems to do with money usually have an easy solution—if you have the funds for it?' He gave the king an enquiring look.

Grandfather bowed his head. 'I was wondering when you'd reach this point.'

They discussed the economy, the funds available and where to start. Charlie discussed how much it would cost with great vigour, but backed off from decisions on where to instigate the scheme first, claiming the king would know far better than he in which village or area they ought to begin.

At the innate respect it implied, Grandfather smiled at Charlie and gave the regal nod of approval. His covert glance at Jazmine also held approval—and a touch of relief.

Jazmine felt a warm glow. Her grandfather was too ill to hold the reins of government much longer. If he could hand over some of the heavier burdens to them this way, one at a time, Grandfather could rest easier with less on his mind. And Charlie, with his compassion, his mathematician's brain and eye for detail, would take on those jobs. He'd become a regent without even realizing it.

'Very well,' Grandfather decreed. 'I'll call a meeting of my ministers for tomorrow. You both are invited to attend. Thank you, Kyriacou.'

'I've suspended his classes for the next week or more, Grandfather.' Jazmine spoke for the first time. 'Charlie needs to know about Hellenia and its needs far more than the other education, which he can learn in time.'

'Well done, Jazmine.' Grandfather smiled at her. Ecstatic, she felt a silly grin curving her mouth.

Then she saw Charlie's eyes narrow as he stood silently, watching them.

With awareness of undercurrents that had always made him hard to deceive, Grandfather looked at them both and spoke regally. 'You are both excused.'

In an accord with Charlie she was far from feeling, she dipped down to a curtsey at the same moment he bowed. She felt the irony in both.

'He never gives a reason for sending anyone away, does he?' Charlie asked, almost conversationally; but she knew better, could feel the tension in his body, the heat of hidden anger.

'He doesn't need to. Why are you angry?' she asked bluntly.

He gave a swift glance around to the line-up behind them. 'We want to spend time in the gym.

Sweep it now, and then turn off the intercom system. Don't turn it back on unless there's an emergency.'

'Certainly, Your Highness.' The minders turned and, speaking into their mouth-mikes, discreetly vanished.

'I don't do public scenes,' he informed her shortly when they had all gone.

She bit her lip over a smile she couldn't hold in.

She felt the slight relaxing of his muscles, the anger dissipating just a little. 'Okay. I *rarely* do public scenes,' he allowed with a reluctant grin. 'Wait until Candid Camera's switched off downstairs.'

He didn't touch her as they walked together, but she felt the heat, the intensity of him, as if he'd run his fingers over her skin. Everything felt sensitized, alive, tingling with awareness. After the kiss last night—this morning—she'd been aware of everything he did today, his every movement and nuance of feeling. When he'd lifted her into his lap, light and warmth had filled her, even in all those hidden places inside she'd thought would always be dark and cold.

He'd cuddled her. Not sexually, not aroused— just *holding* her.

They reached the gym, and Charlie smiled and swept his hand to the doors. Within moments, the room was empty of everyone but the two of them. 'So.' His arms folded over his chest. It would have been intimidating but for the memory of this afternoon: her head resting there, awaking to the reassuring warmth of his skin, the soft thud of his heart beneath her ear. She'd felt so *safe*. Just as she'd felt when they'd kissed. Instead of devouring her, he'd *cherished* her.

Jazmine had had visions of their first kiss, and he'd shattered them all. Expecting him to take her body and soul by storm, he'd crept quietly into her heart and taken it.

Just like that. She'd felt like Sleeping Beauty, waking up after a long sleep. She'd come to life, for the first time in so long she could barely remember.

There was such tenderness hidden beneath the shell of this reluctant prince who wanted to appear hard and uncompromising.

'What's the deal, princess?'

Lost in the gentle memory of his tenderness, she started at the harshness of the question, but clicked right back into action. Harshness and demand she was used to; she had armour against that. 'I don't understand.'

He sighed. 'Let's not play games. I'm too tired.' When she didn't answer, his face turned cold. 'The looks. The grins I saw just now. You and the old guy are up to something. I want to know what it is.'

'Oh.' Hot colour flooded her face; she could feel it running rampant across her skin, and ducked down a little, trying to hide it. 'That.'

'Yes, *that*.' He angled his face so she had to look at him again.

Humiliation crept over her soul. She turned away again. 'It was…private.'

'So you're saying it had nothing to do with me?'

The blush grew furious, and, with it, anger to match his. 'Not everything is about you,' she snapped.

'Attack is the best form of defence, they say. Good show, princess.' He took her arm—so tenderly, she barely felt it, it wasn't force—and turned her back to face him. 'A shame it's not convincing me.'

'I don't have to convince you,' she mumbled. *Oh, treacherous body, rebel heart!* One touch and she was trembling, melting, turning from princess to woman...

'Jazmine.' The name was beautiful as ever on his lips, those wonderful 'kiss me' lips. 'That's not the best start for us, if we're going to spend our lives together.'

And he drew her against him. Winning by dangling what she needed most before her, and by the most tender of seductions.

Even knowing it, still her head touched his chest, and she breathed him in: heated, spicy male. Still her hands touched his waist.

Still she melted.

'Cheat,' she whispered, breathing in and out. Breathing him.

He chuckled, and dropped a kiss on her hair. 'Street smarts, *loulouthaki.*'

Though it was nearly dark, summer light and warmth flooded her being with the nickname.

'Tell me, Jazmine. Trust me, *loulouthaki mou,*' he whispered into her hair. She shivered to her soul: *my little flower.*

'He...he smiled at me, Charlie,' she murmured

into his skin. Afraid to look up as she bared that shivering soul. 'He hasn't smiled at me like that, since…'

There was a long, gentle silence while he waited, and she gulped and tried so hard not to let her eyes sting.

'Since I survived the meningococcus and Father and Angelo didn't. Since he lost his heirs and was stuck with only me,' she finished in a tired whisper. 'He's all I have. And today, he—he *smiled* at me.' She gulped again. 'He hasn't been proud of me from that day until today.'

And then years of repressed emotion broke open, and she cried. Cried on that sturdy warm chest with the heart beating as steady as his nature. He didn't speak, didn't pull away, just held her, releasing her hair from its confines and caressing the curls.

When she slowed to a series of most ungraceful hiccups, he lifted her face and wiped her tears with his sleeve because, being Charlie, he could carry her from a burning building or choke while he gave a child his air, but he didn't carry a handkerchief.

She sniffed and smiled up at him through the awkward actions of his arm, and wondered if there hadn't been a day in her life when she hadn't been waiting for him.

Though she'd denied it to him at first, she knew the truth. Throughout her lonely childhood and the most turbulent days of her life, she *had* pictured a prince coming along: a man willing to share her starved and smothered life and make her happy. She'd pictured him rich and handsome, a suave dancer and popular with everyone, knowing her world and able to overcome any obstacle with grace and style.

She'd been a silly, ignorant girl with all her imaginings, because she hadn't known better. Her visions of perfection were too much, and yet so much less than she needed, because they had never been of Charlie—her rough-diamond action-hero prince with a foul temper and a heart of pure gold.

'You know, when Lia feels down she and Toby always bake something.' He bent and kissed her nose, and it melted her heart more than any passionate merging of lips could have—though she wanted that, ached for it. But this tenderness from a man like Charlie undid her.

She smiled, feeling like an idiot but unable to stop. 'I think the chefs would have a fit if we went in and made a mess in their domain.'

He shrugged. 'So we wash up and put away. They won't know a thing.'

She stared at him, wondering if her jaw had dropped.

A chuckle burst from him. 'Don't tell me, princess, you've never washed a dish in your life?'

Embarrassed, she shrugged. She'd boarded at the best houses during her school years, with a companion, a bodyguard and a maid. She'd never made a bed, or washed or folded anything. Even minor royals in Hellenia had fully-equipped houses with an artillery of servants to see to their every need. It was generational employment; her servants' parents had served her parents, and so on. They were part of the family.

But what they did for her, and how they did the same work day after day, had always been as much a mystery to her as running the nation would be to them.

'Then it's my turn to teach you something.' With another laugh at her obvious disbelief that he wanted to teach her to wash up, he murmured against her mouth, 'Don't worry, *loulouthaki*, it's not rocket science. I'll be with you through the ordeal. You'll see—it'll be fun, just you and me, cooking, feeding each other…'

Mesmerized by the picture he painted by his touch, she nodded. She didn't pretend to herself that when he spoke so caressingly, touching her mouth with his, she wouldn't go to the ends of the earth with him.

'I'll meet you there tonight, when everyone's asleep.'

A late-night assignation with her prince… How could she resist? 'I'll make sure the cameras are turned off.'

His face didn't darken at the mention of the intrusions into their private life. He grinned and drew a finger down her nose, and her whole body heated in reaction. 'It's a date.' He winked at her, and strolled away. 'Oh, and wear something you can make a mess in, because I plan to muss you up good.'

Warmth filled her entire being at the words she'd

never heard before. He was like sunlight and rain to her dried, parched soul, lost too many years in rules and appearances.

It was time she was just a normal woman.

CHAPTER NINE

CHARLIE and Jazmine surveyed the steaming, lumpy disaster in front of them with varying amusement and disgust.

'Is that how it's supposed to look?' Jazmine asked dubiously.

He made a rueful face. 'It never looks like that when Lia and Toby do it. They've had years' more practice, I guess.' Until now, he'd merely watched sport and waited, or watched them cook with a grin. They did it so flawlessly—except when Toby tossed a bit of flour in Lia's hair, and she'd rub something else in Toby's hair...

Hmm; smearing cake on Jazmine's mouth, and kissing it off... What a glorious vision.

'So we made all this mess—' she swept her hand around the assembled riot of egg shells, cocoa and sugar, spilled milk and flour '—for nothing?'

'Never!' Determined now, he grabbed a spoon and dug it into the dark confection. 'Get the ice cream, princess.'

'So I'm "princess" again now?' She twisted her face to grin at him. 'What did I do to deserve that slam?'

He stared at her, unable to suppress the grin. 'Nothing; you're right. Your hair's a mess, your poor old Oxford T-shirt is covered in flour, and you have a big smudge of mixture on your cheek.'

'I do?' She began scrubbing at her face.

He laughed then. 'Three or four smudges, actually. I should know—I put 'em there.' *With his hands, while kissing her.*

'Well, take a look at yourself!' she retorted, pointing to a mirror in the hallway just outside the kitchens. 'Your shirt's half-undone, you've got stuff in your face *and* your hair, and you have smudge on your…'

Her blush delighted him. 'On my what?' he whispered near her ear.

She was all rosy now, and barefoot, with her ratty old T-shirt hanging over her silky tracksuit pants, and her hair carelessly pulled back with a few pins with chocolate and flour all over, she looked adorable.

How had he ever thought of her as untouchable? He could barely keep his hands off her. And she loved every touch. They'd kissed every thirty seconds while cooking—which had been the cause of this cake mess. He'd been too busy kissing her to put on the timer, and, when he'd finally remembered, he'd had to guess.

'On your chest…and stomach. There.' She pointed to a half-dried gloop of mixture across his shirt.

'Ah, that explains the smudge on your shirt, just a few inches higher.' He nodded wisely as he pulled her towards him. 'Ah, see? A perfect match. You think you gave it to me, or me to you? Because that last kiss got pretty—'

'Ice cream,' she interrupted in a laughing, would-be firm voice, and she slipped out from under his arms to run to the freezer. 'Here we go,' she announced as she took another spoon and scooped ice-cream on their messy attempt at cake. 'A veritable feast!' Grinning, she lifted the spoon he'd stuck in the cake and handed it to him. It had slimy bits of uncooked cake on it. 'Lucky it has loads of sugar.' She took a scoop into her mouth. 'Mmm…taste it, it's good.' She beamed at him. 'My first cake!'

He couldn't move. He didn't want cake, he wanted her. She was small and sweetly delectable, his own private feast, and he wanted to dine on her night and day, day and night, until he was ready to move on.

Oh, yeah, and when's that going to be? Face it, Costa—you're hooked.

He ignored the voice in his head. He'd fancied himself in love before and had tired of the girl or woman in question usually within a few weeks. This wasn't love, it was infatuation with the kind of woman every man fantasized about but knew was out of his reach. He had a little time left to get her out of his system.

If it's going to happen, the voice taunted him, es-

pecially since you're not leaving, and you know it. Jazmine is your future.

'Charlie?'

Char-rr-liee. Ah, he was addicted to the way she said his name. Whenever she said it, he had to kiss her.

'I'd rather taste you,' he said huskily, and bent to take smears of the confection from her mouth with his tongue. 'Mmm, delicious,' he murmured, and kissed her again, deep and warm and getting hotter by the moment.

'Ah, Charlie, *Charlie*,' she murmured between kisses more delicious than any food could be—the touch of her hands roaming his body, the sweetest thing he'd ever known. 'Ah, what you do to me…'

'*Loulouthaki*,' he muttered back, kissing her over and over, shaping her form with his hands so their bodies fit perfectly together. 'I can't stop. Not touching you, not thinking about you. I've got to be with you.' Roughly, he whispered in her ear, 'In my bed, Jazmine. I want to make love to you so much I'm burning inside.'

'Me, too, Charlie, me too.' She kissed his throat, and he shuddered with need, longing, whatever the hell it was that made him feel scorched from the inside out when she wanted him this way—when she only looked at him like that, his shining-eyed, dishevelled angel. From the cool, mysterious Mona Lisa she'd become a flower with her face to the sun, and it happened when she was near him.

'She comes alive when she sees you, Charlie,' Lia

had said last night, in their usual fifteen-minute talking ritual before bed. And she'd gone on, 'And so do you.'

Alive? More like *burning* alive, and never more so than right now.

'Let's go,' he whispered, cupping her breast with his palm, feeling her shiver and arch up to him.

The sweet fire in her eyes became urgent. 'Where? Where can we go, Charlie?'

And just like that reality returned. There was nowhere. He couldn't make love to her in his room or hers without the entire palace knowing; he couldn't take her to the forest. She deserved better than a tumble in the grass, and not because of her title.

He swore to himself, and blew out a sigh. 'Sorry, *loulouthaki*.' He gathered her close, stroking her hair. 'I shouldn't have let things go so far.'

Breathing harshly with as-yet uncontrolled desire, she nodded against his chest. 'I wish—I wish things were easy for us, Charlie.'

He heard the welter of emotions in her voice—the yearning, the regret—and, though he was aching too, wishing they could just have the right to choose to be lovers without consequences of international proportions, he forced himself to say, 'The things most worth having don't come easy.'

She smiled up at him as though he'd said something wonderful, as though *he* was wonderful, and his heart pumped so hard he was finding it hard to breathe. 'You think we're like that? We're "something worth having"?'

Oh, those shimmering eyes, they'd cast some sort of enchantment over him. Her sweet, sweet face, and the lips he couldn't resist! They were arranged against him now in a mysterious woman's battle-formation, and he didn't have the weapons for the fight. He couldn't take that glow from her eyes, coming straight from a heart as beautiful as it was, denied the simple things that made her so happy.

'I think we could be, Jazmine. I do.' Unable to stop himself, he kissed her once, twice, tasting light and magic. 'If everything else weren't in the way.'

She pulled away then, the light in her eyes dimmed. 'Yes.' The word was thick, forced. 'Everything else.' She turned to the counter. 'The ice cream's melted into the cake. It's inedible now.' She turned back to him with a would-be smile. 'So, now are you going to show me how to clean up as expertly as you taught me to bake a cake?'

The pain he'd tried so hard to avoid was there in her stiff stance, in the way she wouldn't look at him as she smiled. 'Would you rather I lied to you?'

After a moment, she said huskily, 'No. Would you rather I cried on you again, or begged you to stay to take on a country still in turmoil for my sake?'

Honesty forced him to admit it. 'No.'

She nodded, as if she'd expected it. 'Then leave it. We had a good time—now let's clean the mess we've made.'

He had the feeling she wasn't talking about the dishes.

Defeated, he turned to the sink and took their ruined cake, scraping it into the bin. It seemed symbolic. 'I'll rinse everything before putting it in the dishwasher. You want to clean down the counters and put the food away while I stack up?'

When she nodded, he handed her a clean cloth and a bottle of anti-bacterial spray he'd found in a cupboard earlier. She took them with quiet thanks: the perfect princess covering the hurting woman.

Hurting meant she liked him...had feelings for him.

He'd been so stupid. The protected princess—always accompanied, always in an emotional ivory-tower where everything she did and said was right—knew so much more about running a country than he did. She knew about pain and loss, protocol and manners, what to give to people, and when. But, when it came to the kind of world he'd lived in, she was completely innocent. She didn't know *how* to play the field and walk away afterwards with a smiling goodbye, lying if necessary to keep pride intact. She'd been too busy all these years doing the right thing for her family, for her people.

And he'd played with her, teased her, flirted with her; had touched and kissed her when she'd been receptive.

But he'd forgotten the essential difference between Jazmine and those women: they knew the game. If they got hurt, they went home, ate chocolates and bitched to their girlfriends, hated him for a while, then met someone else. They moved on.

Jazmine couldn't move anywhere. She couldn't eat chocolate for long without the press making a fuss about her weight or zit-outbreak. She couldn't play around with a guy or get dumped without it making international headlines. And, if Charlie was her type of guy, how was she going to meet another one? It wasn't as if he could get one of his firie mates over here and set her up.

Bloody hell. He'd stuffed it up again. He had to fix this somehow.

She wouldn't look at him, and answered his comments so briefly he gave up after a while. But the silence in which they worked, after the teasing, laughing and kissing before, grew unbearable. Damn it; how could he miss her when she was right here?

'I'm going to bed,' she said when they were done. 'Thank you for coming with me today, for letting me sleep…and for the cooking lesson.' A smile flitted across her face and was gone.

She was looking at him, but not *at* him—as if he'd turned transparent, and she was seeing through him.

He couldn't let her go like this. As she passed, he grabbed her arm. 'Jazmine…'

She didn't struggle or ask him to let go, as most women he'd known would have. She simply turned and looked at him, her smile remote.

A hurting Mona Lisa, trying to hide her pain but not knowing how, apart from resorting to the disguise she'd always used. But now he could see through it, see to her clear, sweet heart and soul.

'Hell, princess, I'm sorry,' he grated through an aching throat. 'I've been here two weeks and I've failed you.' He swore, feeling more of a jerk than he ever had before. 'I don't know what it is—wrong timing, wrong guy— Well, hell, we all know that,' he admitted with a strange, bittersweet tang. 'You're not to blame, you're perfect.'

'Stop it!' she cried, wrenching her arm from his grasp. Startled, he looked at her, and saw tears splashing on her cheeks, dashed away. 'You think *you're* a failure after two weeks? I've failed all my life! I've spent my life at boarding schools, finishing schools and top universities—places I didn't want to be, studying subjects pertaining to a job I never thought I'd have. I wasn't allowed to cry at my mother's funeral because of the stupid cameras. I was *seven*. I couldn't cry when Father and Angelo died. I've never been allowed to swear or yell, or say anything out of place. And, now I'm Princess Royal, I work fourteen- to sixteen-hour days, and am expected to look perfect the next day when I rarely get more than four hours' sleep a night. I don't want this job, either, Charlie!'

Her voice wobbled as she dashed at her eyes again. 'But, if I don't do it, who will? Can you blame me for hoping you'd want to share the job, make the best of it together? Now that's gone too, and I *hate* you for it!'

Shocked into silence before her first sentence was complete, Charlie dropped his hands and stared at her—all of her. Finally the composure had, not cracked, but broken; the real woman stood before him. He'd never heard her use so many words about herself; it had always been as if she didn't matter compared to the needs of others. He'd felt so inadequate in his selfish wish for a private life. She'd seemed so…perfect.

Now he knew the truth, and— Ah, hell, he admired her more than ever for being human, imperfect and fragile beneath the flawless façade, and doing her best anyway. Liked her, admired her, wanted her, and it was all woven together in a tangled thread.

And, like the woman of courage and integrity she was, she didn't run off but stood in front of him, panting a little, and waited for him to answer.

If only he knew what to say. If he banged his thick skull against the wall, would the right words come?

He had to say something, anything. Eventually he gave up and let words come whether they were right or wrong. 'Yeah, thank God, she's human after all.'

Could he have said anything worse? Was he so determined to destroy this? In two minutes he'd turned a peaceful, happy situation to crisis point with his stupid mouth.

She was staring at him as if half his brain had wandered off without his noticing. 'Is that all you can say? I said I hate you!'

'I want to kiss your tears away,' he blurted, and wanted to run off to find wherever his brain had disappeared. He closed his eyes. 'Sorry. I don't know what to say, except thank you for trusting me with your secrets, *loulouthaki mou.*'

'But I'm not your little flower, Mr Costa. I'm not anything of yours at all.'

The words were cool and distant. He opened his eyes to see her opening the door to the long hall and stairs to the main quarters. 'Jazmine!'

Being Jazmine, of course, she turned back. That was his *loulouthaki*, so strong, so beautiful, he ached. She said nothing, just waited.

Words came from nowhere, words he didn't know were in him until they'd reached her. 'Don't give up on me. This is a hell of a decision and I can't make it based on the fact that I like you, that I respect you, can't stop wanting to touch you, or wanting to be with you. That kind of thing doesn't always last a lifetime.'

'It doesn't always end in disaster, either,' she said quietly. 'And it isn't me giving up on you, Charlie. You're giving up on yourself.' She looked in his eyes as she threw her bomb in exchange for his. 'I suspect you've been giving up on yourself from the time Lia got sick until now.'

Now he was truly stunned. *She knew he'd let Lia down when she'd needed him most.*

He felt disaster coming and didn't have a clue how to stop it. He was unable to retaliate because he knew she fought her weaknesses, this woman who was every inch the princess, even with her shirt hanging out, chocolate smears on her face and lips thoroughly kissed.

'You know it's true.' She looked deep into his eyes as she kept tearing apart the fabric of his self-delusion—that beneath the hero there was a sham who hadn't been able to save his parents or his sister. 'Something tells me that if you give up on yourself this time, whether you decide to be Charlie Costa, fireman, or Kyriacou Charles Costa Marandis, you'll regret it for life.'

The rightness of what she said was like an electrical current racing through him, and still he couldn't move.

'I'm not giving up on you, Charlie, because I believe in you. I believe you can do anything you put your heart and soul into. I believe you can do this. And, if you end up leaving, I'll believe Hellenia has lost the best king she could have had.'

And then she was gone, and the passionate conviction of true belief hung in the air behind her.

She knew—knew almost the worst of him—and she still believed.

He strode down the long hall and up the stairs after her, taking three at a time to reach her; but this time he didn't have to grab her or call. She heard him coming and turned back, on the second-to-top stair. Still. Waiting.

'That's not it,' he grated harshly, hating himself, hating her for making him say the words he'd kept dammed up for eleven years, words he'd never told Papou or Yiayia, words he hadn't even slurred to Toby on their drunkest nights. 'You don't know it all.'

Her eyes gentled, for no cause he could find. 'Then tell me, Charlie. Make me understand why you're so sure you'll fail me and fail my country.'

He didn't stop to move or think; he had to say it now, or he'd take off and never come back. 'You seem to think I'm some paragon because I happened to be in a position to save a child—'

'Don't forget the other fifty-three people you saved too,' she said softly, those eyes shimmering again.

He had to stop it!

'Yes. I hate myself because I let Lia down,' he snapped as if it was her fault. 'She collapsed and I freaked out. I didn't know what to do if I couldn't force feed her. All I could see was my sister dying in front of me, that she had been for months, and I hadn't even *noticed*.'

DEFCON 4. Sirens were screaming in his head: *Stop; stop here*! But he couldn't.

'This within a year of your parents' death and in your first year as a fireman?'

He waved that off; it was no excuse. 'Do you have any idea how much I love her? She's my sister, my family, she's everything—and I didn't know what to do. Toby took over, did everything that was my place to do. He was with her day and night around his schedules. They let him stay because he was healing her. I just made her feel worse about being so sick, for scaring me like that. I hated my sister because she might die and leave me alone!'

There; surely she'd hate him now for being the selfish jerk he was—and if she left now, he wouldn't have to.

'So you understood why I said I hated you.' Her voice was so gentle, so filled with sympathy, he felt sick.

He couldn't look at her as he conceded, 'Maybe—but we've known each other two weeks. You can hate me for life and it doesn't matter if I'm not here. Lia is my sister, my *family*, and I hated her until the day she came out of the clinic!'

Surely it was over now? *Please, please just be disgusted and leave now...*

After a long silence, she said, a wealth of understanding in her voice, 'Was it Lia you hated, Charlie? Or was it the fear that your beautiful, wise, lovable sister might die and leave you alone in the world? So, being only eighteen, you ran away whenever you could—and now you think it's inevitable. Your Papou ran away too—it has to be genetic. The men in your family can't measure up.'

Click.

CHAPTER TEN

As IF she'd flicked on a switch inside him, he felt the defusion of all his anger in an instant. She'd found the truth without ten years of searching for it. How did she do it?

He didn't answer. He couldn't. Couldn't she see the truth—that he wasn't worthy, no matter what she hoped? But she was still here, still fighting for something only one of them believed in.

'That's still not it.' God help him, he felt his voice going; he had to force the ending out. The words to destroy her sweet faith, and make her see the man he really was. 'The night my parents died, I was supposed to pick them up from a party. I said, sure, I'll come for you—but I was on a date with the girl I'd liked for months, and turned off my phone. I didn't want any interruptions. I figured they'd get a taxi if Dad had been drinking.'

He couldn't go on. He was shaking and cold, so cold, going back to the night that had defined his life, a night he'd buried in the blackness of a memory he couldn't bear to revisit. He only did so now because eight million lives were at stake…and the happiness of one special princess.

'Charlie…'

He felt her coming down the final two stairs to him, her hands reaching out to him. His eyes snapped open. 'Don't touch me.' *I don't deserve it.*

Her hands fell. 'Go on, then,' she said quietly.

'When I didn't show up they did get a taxi—and they were hit by a drunk driver.' Stark as it was, he couldn't stop there. 'They took hours to die, Jazmine. *Hours.* And because my phone was off Toby, Lia, Papou and Yiayia had to go to the hospital without me. It broke them. Yiayia never got over it. She got sick and died two years later. Papou went away inside. And Lia—' he looked at her, waiting for the disgust, the hate without flinching '—just stopped eating.'

This was it—disaster. The end of all things for them.

After a minute, maybe two, she asked, 'Did you get to the hospital…in time?'

He sighed and turned away. 'In time to hear my father tell me it wasn't my fault, and—and to look after the family. Mum—was gone.'

And he broke.

By the time the third gasping sob was torn from him, her arms were around him, drawing him to sit on the stair, and she sat on the one above, holding him, rocking him. She crooned nonsense words and held him and rocked him while eleven years of unspoken grief escaped from its cage, having held him hostage inside a half-life. He'd saved other peoples' loved ones because he hadn't been able to save the ones he loved. He'd spent years hiding from anything permanent or good because he believed he didn't deserve it.

He still didn't. But goodness and sweetness had come to him whether he was worthy or not, by the autocratic will of an old man who needed an heir, and a brave, stubborn little flower who believed in him no matter what he did or said, or how many times he failed.

'So that's why you ran from Lia's illness,' she whispered eventually, kissing his forehead, his hair. 'You were afraid you'd make her worse. It wasn't because you hated her. You loved her too much.'

Recognizing a truth he hadn't seen until she said it, he nodded. He was so tired, too tired even to ask the obvious question.

He didn't need her answer. It was clear she didn't hate him. But why she cared at all, why she was even still here, he had no idea. The inexhaustible forgiveness that seemed to live inside her would forever be a mystery to him. He sure as hell couldn't find a way to forgive himself.

She said nothing else, and he was relieved. Relieved she didn't give him the platitudes he'd half-expected, the reassurances he wouldn't have accepted. Strange that, after so little time together, she knew him so well, better than anyone, even Lia or Toby.

They sat there a long time, until he felt something approaching peace.

Relief, and peace. They were emotions foreign to him for so long he'd forgotten how uplifting they felt…and he'd found them from a source he'd least expected.

'Come,' she said gently, after a minute or an hour had passed on that stair. She dropped down to whisper in his ear, 'I don't know about you, guv'nor, but my bum's numb. Ain't got enough fat to cover it.'

He choked on unexpected laughter at her off cockney accent. 'Where did you get that from?'

She grinned at him, proud. 'British soaps. I went to Oxford, remember. I lived in England for three years. Did history, philosophy, religious studies and political science. Very boring stuff.' She yawned hugely, theatrically, making him almost want to laugh again. When he didn't, she smiled and tugged at him until he stood.

He did so more to please her than anything else.

He let her lead him, not knowing where they went and not caring. He'd go where she wanted, would do what she asked… so long as it didn't involve destroying eight million lives and ruining hers.

When they reached his room, she opened the door and turned to the night sentries. 'This will not be reported to my grandfather. Not our time in the kitchen, nor anything you heard, nor my whereabouts for the rest of this night. Tonight remains between the four of us, or you will regret it. Is that clear?'

Despite feeling so numb, Charlie felt a brow lift. She was every inch the future queen, all five-feet-three of her the protective lioness. She was protecting *him*—and strangely, after eleven years of running a family, career and being his own man, it felt good to have someone take charge for a little while.

He wasn't surprised when the security pair nodded after hesitating a moment. 'Yes, Your Highness,' they both said, and bowed.

Jazmine flicked on the lights and walked into the suite with a regal step, a barefoot Queen of Sheba.

Enchanted by her in any mode, he followed and closed the door.

She'd closed the heavy curtains, shutting them off from security, from cameras and movement-sensors. Then she padded over to him, went up on tiptoe and kissed him softly. 'Charlie,' she whispered, her eyes shimmering, and pulled off her shirt, offering herself to him without constraints.

He'd thought his heart couldn't burst any further. He looked down at her in tracksuit pants and lacy bra, and her chocolate smears, moved beyond bearing because he knew it wasn't pity, tempted beyond almost all reason.

He forced a smile. 'You're beautiful, *loulouthaki*, and I want you so much…but tonight…' He turned slightly away so she wouldn't see the evidence that he was lying, lying for her sake, because he couldn't take this final gift from her. 'After all the confessions and crying—I don't think I can.'

It was the only excuse that had a hope of working.

When the silence stretched out and he felt her hurt, he gave her what he could, because touching her right now might have broken his will. 'I've never told anyone what I told you tonight, Jazmine. Eleven years…' His voice cracked; he made it happen. Even though what he said was truth, he needed to convince her, because one more moment and he wouldn't be able to say no. Aching and burning for her, his blood on fire and his mind and body screaming, he made himself stay still. For her sake.

'I'm so stupid.' He heard the rustling sound as she slipped on the shirt, and his body flayed his mind for holding onto its last principle. Then he felt her arms around his waist, her head resting on his arm. 'Let me stay until you're asleep,' she whispered, caressing his stomach until he was so brittle he thought he'd shatter.

With all his will, with everything he had, he nodded and forced a yawn.

His mother or Yiayia would have had a fit if they'd seen him fall to the bed still fully clothed; it was almost a cardinal sin in the family. But it was too dangerous to undress when his self-control was hanging by a thread and his lovely princess watched him with such tender hunger. What did she see in him? God help him, help them both, because this *had* to be all wrong, but it felt so damn right…

He felt her climb onto the bed beside him. He knew she'd take him in her arms before she did it.

He didn't dare protest or move; he had to lie limp and pliant. One move and she'd feel his full-to-bursting arousal. The woman of his dreams was holding him in her arms and he could do nothing about it, because she was the one woman he could never have, could never deserve.

Eventually the peace he'd felt on the stairs returned, stealing into his soul, and he slid towards sleep; it robbed him of his will. He'd never remember what he said later.

'I think I'd have married you if you weren't a princess,' he mumbled.

Her tender laugh slipped inside his half-dreaming state, bound as he was by the impossible magic of being in her arms after all he'd told her. 'I think you will anyway, *prinkipas mou, vasilias mou.*'

My prince. My king.

And in that twilight between waking and sleeping—when anything could be possible, believing he was sleeping and it would all slip away in the realm of the unbelievable tomorrow—he believed her.

CHAPTER ELEVEN

A Fairy tale Come to Life: The Lost Prince and Princess Found!
The Hero Who Won a Crown: From Fire-Retardant Suit to Savile Row. Can He Save Hellenia from the Flames of War and Win the Heart of the Princess?

FOLLOWED closely by his distraught sister, Charlie stalked into the morning room and threw down the wad of newspapers on the breakfast table. 'Did you do this?' he barked at the king, who was placidly eating a boiled egg, fresh toast and tea. Max sat beside him.

The king looked up, seeming pained. 'Must you begin the day with dramatic demands? I'm an old man. The heart isn't what it once was.'

Charlie picked up one of the tabloids and waved it in the king's face. 'These were outside my room this morning. Our lives have hit world headlines, from Sydney to London and New York. There isn't a single paper or magazine that doesn't have our faces on it!'

The king shrugged with nonchalant elegance—a man who'd got his way. 'It had to happen, Kyriacou.'

'Not without help!'

'You're right.' The king smiled up at him. 'Your own. I merely provided details. By handing Jazmine into the car with that, uh, affectionate look on your face, and by allowing her to sleep in your lap in the car as you did, you started the fire.'

Dumbfounded, he stared at the king. 'What did you say?'

With a smile, the king said, 'It was very romantic, I must say, but with the press around it was rather foolish if you wanted to continue remaining a royal mystery. A passing photographer snapped the shot and began digging. It didn't take long. I hear he got half a million for the story.'

Goaded by the self-satisfied look on the king's face, Charlie snapped, 'You don't have to be so damned smug about it. I can still renounce the title.'

'Theo Angelis,' Lia intervened, in soft rebuke. 'This has rightfully hurt and upset us. We've been trying our best to do everything you've asked, and now we feel as if you've repaid us with betrayal. Can you please tell us what happened?'

The lined old face softened, as it always did for Lia. 'I never betrayed you, Giulia. We knew nothing until the calls began coming in two days ago, asking for confirmation. When we were shown the shots, and told the captions—"love with the help"—our only option was damage control. We had to make the announcement of who you are, and announce the royal engagements, unless you both wished to be flooded with unwanted suitors from all over the world within days.'

'*We?*' Charlie asked, softly, dangerously, ignoring all the more noble reasons for the leak, and his own part in his downfall. He'd deal with that later. 'Two days ago?'

'The other person Grandfather means would be me.'

Charlie swung around to face the woman who'd so recently been in his bed almost all night. 'You did this? Two days ago?'

Seeming totally calm, Jazmine nodded. 'Yes, I did.'

He felt a muscle twitch in his jaw. 'Without telling me?'

'Yes.' Not a muscle moved in her face. Not a shred of guilt in her lovely eyes.

'Am I permitted to ask, Your Royal Highness, why neither of us were told about it? Why did Lia and I have to see these to find out what was going on in our own lives?' His voice dripped with anger and bitterness.

At that, Jazmine flicked a glance at his sister with a touch of anxiety. 'Lia, if we could have told you, warned you… I'm sorry. The story was going to come out, and—and Charlie, well—'

'Yes, we all know you weren't about to let me

handle it, right? The back streets prince would have hit somebody or done something to embarrass the royal family.'

She looked at him and lifted a brow. 'We judged that you weren't ready to deal with the press frenzy at this point, Charlie.'

He snatched a tabloid at random and waved it in her face. 'Well, whether or not I'm ready, it's already here. If I'm not ready, I'll renounce the position. Orakis will be happy to take my place. He's probably getting the party ready as we speak.'

Jazmine whitened so fast he forgot why he was so angry. He dropped the paper, and took her by the shoulders to hold her up.

At the sweet magic of a single touch, the fury flooded right back. She'd kissed him, touched him, listened to his darkest secrets and slept in his bed, in his arms, when she'd already *betrayed* him?

Still, he marched her to a chair and forced her down into it. 'Head between your knees, princess. You look like you're about to faint.'

She kept her gaze on him, dark, wounded. 'Are you going to renounce the title and position?' She spoke barely above a whisper.

'You betrayed me!' he shot right back. 'You kissed me and slept in my bed, knowing you'd betrayed me and forced me into this!'

'She did *what*?' the king roared.

Ignoring her grandfather, keeping her gaze trained on Charlie alone, she nodded. 'It wasn't planned that way. That night was so—so perfect…' She sighed. 'Believe me, I am sorry for it, Charlie—but I had no choice. There was no other way.'

'There certainly is no other way now,' the king snapped. 'You will marry her, Kyriacou, and take the position, if you have had your way with her!'

Charlie, too, ignored the king; this wasn't his place or decision. 'Then I'm sorry too, princess.' He turned to the king then who, despite his anger, looked grey again, and older than his years. 'How long do I have before I have to make an announcement?'

The wrinkled old hands gripped the edge of the table. 'The press, the people, and Orakis will expect an announcement within a day or two, or our silence will confirm your position for you. And, if you agree to make the announcement, you must be trained with the correct words, either of acceptance or renunciation. The announcements on your weddings must come at the same time. Speculation's already rife, and we need heirs. If one isn't already on the way,' he added, with a touch of acid.

Ignoring that too, Charlie gave the king a curt nod. 'Then Lia and I have a lot of thinking to do. We need peace and space.'

'Weddings? Heirs?' A tiny, wobbling whisper sounded from behind him. 'No, oh no…'

Max came round to her and whispered something—probably, knowing Max, some reassurance that he was happy to wait—but this time it didn't work. Lia stared at Charlie, and he knew what he had to do.

He wasn't letting his sister down again. Ever.

'I want a phone, sire. My best friend's like family to us. He must be pretty cut up, finding out about us through the tabloids. We need to talk to him.'

'If you mean the Winder boy, he knows,' the king said curtly. 'He's quoted as saying "no comment" in seven publications.'

Holding Lia's hand, Charlie met the old man's eyes and waited. He'd stated his needs. Repetition was a sign of weakness he refused to indulge in at this point.

Lia looked up at the king. 'I won't be rushed into marriage and babies with a near stranger to please you,' she said with quiet dignity. 'This is too big a decision for either of us to make without talking to the only person left in the world we consider family. So bring Toby here—or we'll go home to him.'

The king flinched at Lia's distant tone, which bordered on ice after over two weeks of warm wisdom and ready affection. After perhaps thirty seconds, he barked at a servant to bring a phone. 'I assume you both wish to discuss your pending decision with your friend?'

Charlie felt Lia nod at the same time he did.

'We can't risk your giving sensitive information over the phone. We've been betrayed that way in the past.'

'Find a way,' Charlie said, with that same soft danger. Not asking—telling. Demanding the king find a way to let them speak to Toby.

'This is the boy who helped Lia through the anorexia ten or eleven years ago,' the king mused. 'He obviously knows how to be discreet.'

Again, they nodded.

'Call in Genevieve,' the king barked.

When the elegant, middle-aged senior attaché arrived in the room, the king snapped, 'Contact the embassy in Canberra. Have the prince and princess's dear friend Toby Winder flown here on the fastest possible jet, with no red tape. If anyone has a problem, refer them directly to me.'

'Yes, Your Majesty.' Genevieve turned and left, already dialling on her phone.

Charlie half-expected Lia to run to the king and hug him, but she remained by his side. 'Thank you. Toby's all we have. I won't do this without him.'

Tenderness filled the rheumy old brown eyes. 'Believe me, Giulia, no matter what your decision is, you'll never be alone again. You will always have us.'

Charlie felt an abrupt movement and turned. Jazmine was leaving the room, her pace slow, measured, which meant she'd lost her inner equilibrium.

Without thinking it through, he strode to her and took her arm. 'What's wrong? Besides everything that's already happened today, I mean,' he added, mouth twisted.

Great, dark eyes looked up at him, lost. 'Please don't ask me. I can't tell you.'

She was shaking and trying so hard to hide it. Worried, he whispered, 'Come here.' He drew her close, holding her. 'Tell me, *loulouthaki*.'

He felt the negative shake of her head against his chest, almost infinitesimal. 'I—I can't. It wouldn't be fair.'

'To whom?'

'You,' she whispered. 'You've been forced into too much already.'

Moved despite his recent anger, he touched her hair and felt her shiver. 'So brave for such a small woman,' he murmured, tangled inside a web of tenderness, sweetness, honour, courage and sweet yearning—hers and his. 'Why isn't it fair to me?'

She looked up. Tears were shimmering in those haunting, haunted eyes. 'I've put you in enough chains. You—you might hate me, but you'd do the right, the honourable, thing. I—I can't do it to you.' Suddenly she went up on tiptoes, reached up and pulled him down to her, heedless of their watchers, and kissed him, quick and fierce. Fire flashed through him, but she pulled away before he could respond. 'I won't cry; I won't.'

She broke away from him and walked past the security detail to the stairs, still slow and measured. Still lost and *broken*.

A single hand lifted when he moved to follow her, asking him to leave her be.

She'd locked him out, for his sake. He didn't have a clue what to do about it. He had a massive decision to make, and Jazmine's presence clouded his head and made him want what he still believed was unattainable.

Filled with a tempest of frustration, anger, sadness and something like regret, he turned back to the breakfast room. Max was talking softly to Lia, who had that distant-as-starlight look on her face again. She was withdrawing into herself.

Who did he rescue—Jazmine or Lia?

Lia looked at him and shook her head. She didn't want or need him to smother her. *Toby will be here tomorrow*, he thought to himself. *Toby always makes it right for her*.

He walked over to the king and said, 'Tell me what frightened her so much about my renouncing my title.'

Jazmine's grandfather searched his face for long moments.

'I need to know. She believes it will influence my decision, but make me hate her.' He waited, but the king didn't speak. 'Sire, I've been locked out of too many decisions regarding my life. If this affects me…'

'It doesn't affect you at all, if you renounce your position. It affects Jazmine only,' the king said slowly. 'That's what terrifies her.'

Lia broke away from Max and stood beside Charlie. 'Charlie's right. We need all the facts. We both care about Jazmine. Let us make the best decision for us all.'

After a moment, the king nodded. 'Spoken with your usual wisdom, my dear.' His eyes, when they turned to Charlie, were dark with the same kind of shot-fawn pain that had been in Jazmine's moments before. 'We forced the issue on you, and I'm sorry in one way. But it hasn't been just about naming a successor, or about royal weddings or heirs, or even settling the nation before I die—as important as all those things are.'

'Then what is it about?' Charlie asked quietly, dread creeping into his gut and making it churn. It was how he'd felt as he'd entered the burning house where the young mother had died: that somehow, no matter what he did, it wouldn't be enough.

The king took his glasses off and wiped them before he spoke. 'If you renounce your position, not only will Orakis take the throne when I die, the people will want a joining of both dynasties.' He replaced the glasses and met his eyes with a strange, dead look in them. 'Jazmine will be expected to become his queen, the mother of his children.'

Hot bile flew up from Charlie's gut without warning. Dear God. Jazmine… But Orakis wouldn't have her, not if he was alive to stop it.

There was only way he could stop it.

'Oh, can this farce get any worse?' he muttered to himself, turned on his heel and strode, not just out of the breakfast room, but right out of the summer palace.

He snarled and swore at the security detail that followed him. 'Get away from me. I'm not your prince…yet,' he added, the bitterness filling his entire soul.

Yet.

It was going to happen. *The unfit prince—step up to the podium, please, and do your duty…and try not to stuff it up again…*

If Jazmine had no choice, neither did he. If she was what she was, so was he. She was a princess, born and bred—and he was a stupid bloody hero-wannabe, a rough-edged, hot-tempered Joe from the back streets of Sydney who'd destroyed his own family. How the hell was he going to run an entire nation, and one already devastated by war?

He was going to fail; he had no doubt—but he could no more leave a woman as beautiful and brave as Jazmine, with all the ability to shatter she kept hidden from the world, to Orakis's tender mercies, than he could have left that little girl to die.

Jazmine; lovely, courageous Jazmine had refused to tell him. She'd have gone to Orakis's bed rather than force Charlie to take a crown, a nation, and a wife.

He had no choice. If he walked away, Jazmine's fate would haunt him until the day he died.

Long, furious strides took him into the small, cool forest behind the palace grounds. He knew there were at least a dozen suits surrounding him as he walked, with their sunglasses, their earpieces and their guns.

Protecting their future prince, their future king. He knew it, and he knew they knew it. Everyone had known it all this time but him.

He turned and slammed his fist into a tree.

And, while Charlie accepted the inevitable and faced his future, King Angelis had his third heart attack in six months.

CHAPTER TWELVE

The next morning

THIS time the royal family waited behind the protection of the massive oak doors of the country palace while the next enforced visitor from Australia arrived. The unofficial royals waited outside to greet Toby. They were dressed casually in designer jeans, Charlie in a polo shirt, Lia in a plain shift-top of creamy-lemon linen.

There was no fanfare for this arrival, no anthem or flag waving—and no privacy. At least forty cameras were trained through the gates to where the Rolls swept in.

From behind the long French windows leading to the balcony, Jazmine saw a massive bear of a man emerge from the Rolls, looking as raw and masculine as the man he claimed as best friend and brother. Toby Winder was all man from head to foot, with bronzed Aussie skin, streaky dark-and-gold hair, and eyes like the Aegean Sea she could even see from this distance, they were so bright. A handsome face, bordering on craggy, with deeply grooved dimples she suspected many women would find irresistible.

He wasn't smiling now. He greeted his old friends from ten feet away, with a barely hidden hostility. Charlie and Lia moved towards him, slowly, as if pulled by magnets. Toby stared at them, every line of his face and body screaming silent betrayal.

Lia murmured something, ran to him, her arms open. His face softened; he opened his arms in turn, and she flung herself in, wrapping her arms tight around him.

After a moment's hesitation, Charlie took another step, and another. Toby Winder said something; Charlie grinned and gave him a rough hug and back thump.

And she'd thought brother and sister an unbreakable entity. This was a threefold cord she suspected no man could break.

Jazmine found herself biting her lip, worrying it on the inside.

'Don't worry,' Max said softly. 'He'll love you, Jazmine. Everyone does.'

She glanced at him, unable to hide her fear. Charlie hadn't spoken to her since she'd run off yesterday. He'd been avoiding everyone but Lia. 'If he doesn't— He's Charlie's best friend. What if he talks him—them—into going home?'

'Then we take off to Majorca and marry without

permission. We'll find a way to make the people accept me as a suitable replacement—all we'd have to do is have a baby fast.' He tipped her chin up, making her look at him again. 'I know I'm not Charlie, but you really didn't think I'd leave you to Orakis, did you?'

Something inside her went mushy, filled with Max's caring and comfort. 'You're the best friend a girl could have.' She smiled at him, her eyes misty, but knowing it wouldn't happen. Orakis's growing support would make certain of it.

'The offer's only open, of course, if the firecracker prince doesn't come up to scratch—but I've seen the way he looks at you. I think *you're* his itch, and he definitely wants to scratch.' As she blushed, Max grinned at her. 'And you've become more than just a princess since he came. You're alive, and thinking of more than your duty. You're crazy about him, aren't you?'

She turned away. The words should be spoken to Charlie first…if he ever wanted to hear them.

Max squeezed her shoulder. 'Just remember, there's someone in your corner.'

Moved, she hugged his arm. 'I know, Max.' She should always have known.

She didn't ask about his relationship with Lia; she didn't have to. Charlie was right. There was a sweet unconsciousness in Lia's eyes, no hint of the woman, when she looked at Max.

But there were worse fates than marrying a friend.

Lia had squealed something and run to the Rolls, emerging with a scruffy wad of fur…a dog? She was petting it awkwardly with the hand that held it, while hanging onto Toby. She wouldn't let her friend go for a moment. And Toby seemed to be making his friends smile and laugh—but he kept swinging his gaze from brother to sister with a half-hidden intensity Jazmine sensed wasn't normal to his nature, which showed how much these two meant to him.

Charlie, with a caution that sat foreign on his shoulders, glanced at the eager press and said something quietly to his friend. Toby nodded.

As one, the trio moved towards the house, walking like a single entity.

They were up against a force to be reckoned with. The rebel prince with a conscience and the sweet, strong-willed princess had been challenge enough when they'd joined forces—but with Toby Winder in the equation they looked unbreakable.

Grandfather, still in bed after the minor attack—he'd be in bed for at least a week, and possibly would never leave that bed—would soon see what Jazmine did. She had to think of a way to make Toby see how much they needed Charlie and Lia to stay. She had to make him realize the stakes for her people.

No, the truth was that if she wanted Charlie and Lia to stay she'd have to give Toby Winder a reason to want to stay here in Hellenia—and she sensed that he was more like Charlie than he appeared. Toby

Winder would give her yet another challenge, when she was already facing the challenge of her life.

'Your Majesty. It is an honour to meet you.' Toby bowed to the king, with the correct degree of respect.

The old king, with the back of the bed lifted so he appeared to be sitting—it helped his breathing as well as giving him an illusion of control—smiled and took Toby's hand. 'Welcome to Hellenia, Mr Winder, and to our home.'

'Please, call me Toby, Your Majesty. Nobody but banks and credit-collectors have ever called me Mr Winder.'

'Toby, then,' the king conceded. 'I hope you can convince your friend to do the right thing for this country, and its people.'

'Lady Eleni told me what's at stake on the trip over—and why Charlie and Giulia could tell me nothing, Your Majesty.' Toby drew out Lia's real name with a perfect Mediterranean inflection—*Yoolya*—that made it sound almost as exotic and beautiful as Jazmine's. He'd always called her that, and he was one of a handful Lia would accept the name from. 'I hope I can be of help not just to my friends, but to you, and the country as well, sir. Hellenia's been through too much in the past five decades since Papou—eh, His Grace—left for Australia.'

Charlie watched the wily old fox melt under the sincerity in Toby's twinkling eyes and dimpled grin, and had to hold in the laugh. His friend always could charm the birds from the trees. Big and strong, safe and dependable, and a man of action, he still had the knack of making people believe everything he said. And, because he was dead honest and completely loyal, they were never let down either.

No man on earth had a friend like his. Toby was a man in a million.

Why hadn't it been Toby who'd fallen into this accident of birth? He'd make a brilliant king.

It was easy to see the king was thinking the same thing. Toby was a man secure in his place in the world. Everyone was smiling at him within a minute. Everyone loved Toby, always had and always would.

But then Lia's stupid mutt Puck escaped her half-hearted hold and began bolting, as was his wont. The crazy dog was marking new territory, and in the chase to catch him Charlie saw the king motion Toby over.

The look on his face when Toby answered whatever he was asked was grim and cold, and Toby looked quietly determined.

What on earth was going on?

Finally a servant grabbed Puck and took him outside to the royal kennels with the other dogs, and peace was restored…a smelly peace. A peace fraught with unexpected enmity between his best friend and the king.

Toby turned to meet Jazmine and Max. A tiny dart of darkness speared through his gut, watching Jazmine smiling at his best friend without the shadows he saw

in her eyes when she looked at him. The doubt, the uncertainty, did not exist for her with Toby, and he had
no idea if that was a good or bad thing.

He glanced at his sister. She was pale, looking at
her feet. He wondered what was going through her
mind. Probably the magnitude of their decision, and
what they could say to Toby when they were finally
alone and in private.

As ever, his friend's uncanny attuning to Lia came
to the fore. He turned from Jazmine with a smile,
managing to accomplish turning his back on a
princess without any lack of manners. 'Giulia, my
beloved, to put it without any overkill, even jet food
sucks. I've missed both you and your cooking like
hell the past weeks. Therefore, I opine, it's way past
the hour when we disappear to discover the royal
kitchens and make some of your unbelievably delicious moussaka, and those decadent mud-muffins
the way only you can make them…and we can talk.'

His sister really had changed. She took at least
twenty seconds to look up, to smile—and, when
she did, her eyes were filled with shadows.

Charlie had seen that look on her face before, but
he'd never understood what it was. Not until he
realized it was the same way Jazmine looked at him…

It struck him in the gut. Finally he knew Lia's
secret, and only because he'd caught a single look,
a moment. For the first time, he realized his sister
was more than his little sister. She was a woman—
a woman really stuck in a hellhole.

She was all but engaged to a stranger she liked—but the man she wanted was her best friend: a man whose birth completely precluded marriage to a princess.

Shocked at the thought of his sister as a sexual being in any way, he swung his gaze from her—and caught the expression on the king's face. The look he gave Toby was suddenly harder, more calculating. 'I think it's time we allowed these three to catch up.'

Charlie caught the look the king flashed at Jazmine and Max, who both nodded. 'We'll leave you,' Max said with a smile. Charlie stared at his new friend, narrow-eyed, but the look Max returned was bland.

'No, we'll go to my room,' Lia said, her voice a touch wobbly. 'No cameras.'

'That wouldn't be appropriate for a princess, my dear,' the king said, gently but with finality. 'Even such an old friend as Toby cannot enter your room.'

'I'll make sure the cameras are turned off in the tea room, and nobody will be at the balconies,' Jazmine said quietly. 'They can wait at the base of the stairs.'

The king nodded, looking exhausted by the five-minute audience. 'Well thought of, my dear.' He waved them all out.

The five young people left the king's sitting-room. When they reached the tea room, Jazmine and Max stayed only a minute to be certain orders had been followed. Then they wished them happy conversation, and moved to leave.

'Wait.'

At the command that sounded anything but pe-remptory—Charlie wished *he* had the knack of it—Jazmine turned back. 'Yes, Toby?'

'I won't be here under false pretences.' Not a muscle moved on Toby's face for a few moments. Everyone waited in silence, watching him, seeing the titanic struggle taking place inside the clearness of his eyes. 'Are the rumours true about the royal marriages for you—for all of you?' He stared hard at Max.

Taken aback by the directness of the attack from a man who'd been exquisitely polite and warm until now, Max nodded. 'It's the way things are done here. The king can't enforce it, but we all know we must do what's right for the country.'

'Then you need to know the true reason I'm here, besides advising my friends on what is best, not just for Hellenia but for them.' With the lightning-fast reflexes that made the big man such an amazing firefighter, Toby pulled Lia to him and kissed her. It was a bare moment's meeting of lips, but Lia's hand fluttered up to his chest and she kissed him back.

Charlie groaned. Hell, didn't he have enough to cope with without this? What the hell was Grizz up to?

Toby's eyes met Max's, filled with steely deter-mination and open defiance. 'Whatever Charlie decides, I'll be doing my dead-level best to make Giulia choose to come home—with me. To become an ordinary firefighter's wife instead of making an alliance with you for the sake of power and wealth.' He stared at each of them in turn, keeping Lia in the curve of his arm. 'Nobody knows how to care for her and cherish her as I do. She's mine.'

Everyone in the room stood stock-still and gaped. Including the woman still lying in his arms.

Then with a gasped, *'How could you, Toby?'* Lia broke free of him and ran from the room.

'Giulia, wait!' Toby started after her.

But Jazmine grabbed his arm. 'No, don't. I'll go. You've done enough, Toby.' She ran after Lia.

And, while Max looked grim, Toby's bronzed face whitened.

'What the *hell* was that, Grizz?' Charlie demanded as soon as they were alone—after Max had followed the women in grim silence.

Toby's chin was still up, his eyes still glittering with fierce determination. *'That,* my friend, was a declaration of hostilities. The Winder version of rage against the machine—or, in this case, rage against royal power and privilege.' He sighed and muttered, 'More likely it's the rage against my own stupidity in not acting years ago.'

'English—preferably words of one or two syllables,' Charlie snapped. 'Look, mate, I know you don't want to lose us, I know you adore Lia—'

'No, you don't. You never knew.' Toby snarled right over him, startling him out of his attack. 'When it came to the relationship between Giulia and me, you've only ever seen what you wanted to see.'

Totally taken aback by Toby's unaccustomed ferocity, Charlie said quietly, 'So tell me what I haven't seen.'

Toby was pacing the room, his hands making a total mess of his thick hair. 'You might always have known I adore Giulia—but you've never known that I *adore* her.'

'Since when?' he gasped, stunned by what the words implied.

'Since we almost lost her,' Toby replied quietly. 'The day she collapsed, I knew she was my life.'

'But—but that was over ten years ago!' he gasped, unable to take it in.

Toby's mouth twisted wryly. 'Tell me about it.'

Charlie blinked again, unable to assimilate how little he knew of those he loved best. 'Ten years? *Ten years*, and you never once tell me you're nuts about my sister?'

His dearest friend in the world shrugged. 'It's the hardest place in the world to be, Rip. My best mate and his sister accepting me as family—and I couldn't look at her without...' He sighed, and grinned at Charlie a little ruefully. 'I don't suppose you want to hear that part.'

He'd barely heard it as it was. He still couldn't get over the sudden indigestion of information. 'Have you ever hit on her?' he demanded, wondering why it would bother him if Toby and Lia had ever got it on, or even if they did now.

Now, he thought wryly, *is the worst possible*

*timing, worse even than mine and Jazmine's. At
least I have the pedigree, some blue blood somewhere. Toby has nothing to offer against Hellenia's
need, and Max's bloodline is impeccable.*

As if he'd heard Charlie's thought, Toby made a
low, frustrated sound and looked out the window.
'No. There was a good reason—a damned good
one—but now I wish to God I had…then I wouldn't
be in this mess. I wouldn't be fighting a multi-mil-
lionaire duke, a king and a country—not to mention
the carrot of fifty million euros—to keep the love
of my life with me.'

A world of love and pain filled his dearest
friend's voice. He hadn't even used the correct
grammar, and Charlie, amazed as he was, couldn't
help but respond. He put a hand on Toby's muscular
shoulder with a rush of wordless empathy. The two
friends stood that way for a few minutes, seeing the
mirror of each other's lives in their situation. Both
facing a battle beyond their ability and control,
fighting uphill—Charlie to save a nation and a
princess, Toby for the woman he loved.

Suddenly he wondered about the look on Lia's
face—the same look he'd seen on Jazmine's. Did
that mean…?

He shoved the thought aside. Even though he
only had hours until he must make his announcement, right now wasn't about him. *Besides*, he
added to himself, *I have no decision left to make*.

Eventually he said, 'You couldn't have had worse

timing on this. The king had a heart attack last night. You can't make your intentions public. If you did, and anything happened to him, Lia would never forgive you. She loves him like she loved Papou.'

Toby sighed, his eyes bleak. 'You've changed—both of you. Coming here has done something to you.'

Charlie shrugged. 'It had to happen—but Lia likes the changes, Grizz. She's slipped into the role of princess as if she was born here. You should hear her talk about her pet interests—the laws on divorce, and the needs of widows and orphans. You'll have a hell of a job convincing her to go home. She's needed here.'

'I can see that.' Toby spoke with the restrained quiet that told Charlie how much he was hurting. 'I know she loves me more than any human being on the planet, even you. I know how much it hurt her not to tell me about coming here, and her title. I know she missed me like hell.' He shook his head. 'But what I don't know is if that will counterbalance her sense of duty and everything this life can offer her. And I don't even know if she sees me as anything but her best friend and big brother. I've tried to tell her how I feel so many times, but if she doesn't want me... I couldn't stand to lose her.' Another sound came from him, like he'd been wounded. 'But now it seems I'll lose her because I've said nothing.'

Charlie shook his head. So many years of painful secrets. He'd been so blind. Blind to Lia's emergence into womanhood; blind to his dearest friend's heart. The blinkers had been ripped away, and he was seeing more than he was ready to know. And the worst part was he had no idea how to help the two people he loved most in the world.

'You'll never lose her altogether, no matter what she decides,' he said, patting Toby's shoulder with awkward male affection. 'She loves you too much.'

'Too much and not enough.' Stark words. 'I couldn't do it, Rip. I've handled it all these years because she needed me, because I was first in her life. But I couldn't stand to be the platonic friend of a princess, knowing she was— Oh, God, if I knew she was in bed with another man…'

A sudden vision filled Charlie's head: the sickening rage he'd felt at the thought of Orakis touching Jazmine, and even his overreaction to Max's innocent comment on Jazmine's beauty. 'So it seems your coming, far from simplifying our impossible decisions, has added extra spice to the pot.'

With clear reluctance and an effort, Toby grinned. 'I do beg Your Royal Pardon for intruding my emotional turmoil into the heart of your current dilemmas, Rip, my friend.'

Relieved, he slapped Toby on the back. 'That's better. When I can't understand a damn word you say, I know you're back, and the world makes sense again.'

'Again I must beg Your Royal Pardon, Your Bad-Tempered Highness, but I must find Giulia. I understood why she needed to be alone. I know she needed time to assimilate what I said.'

'I bet she did,' Charlie said, his tone dry. 'I'd give her a bit more time with Jazmine. She'll need some girl-time.'

'She does girl-time now?'

At the clear shock on Toby's face, Charlie grinned and nodded. 'The two of them are like sisters; have been from the first day.'

'It seems she's changing, no matter what I do.' Toby's face set hard. 'And—the Grand Duke? What's he to her?'

A sharp knock on the door was followed by a cool voice devoid of humanity. 'Your Highness, your presence is requested in the press-room instantly.'

He mock-sighed as he strode to the door. 'Ain't royal life grand? You don't belong to yourself any more, but to king and country.'

'Keep going, my friend. Tell me it all,' Toby said as Charlie led the way to the press-room. 'The more negatives I know, the more ammunition in my fight.'

'Well, if you want to pile on the kilos, there's the twelve-course dinners, and—' He opened the door and stopped in shock.

The previously always-empty press room was now filled to overflowing with journalists, photographers and staff. Flashes were going off every second, taking shots of a frozen-faced Lia, of a grim Max who stood beside her shielding her from the worst of the attention—and of Jazmine, who stood on the podium trying to answer questions being fired at her every ten seconds.

Jazmine, who for the first time was looking far from the cool-as-ice, touch-me-not princess as she spoke. He could see her shaking.

He began moving through the crowd to her. He had to go to her.

CHAPTER THIRTEEN

'DOES Hellenia have a new Crown Prince?' someone shouted.

To Charlie's anxious eyes, Jazmine looked small, weary, defenceless, as she spoke, and so *alone* as she faced the constant barrage of questions. Where was the king? 'There has been no decision made by the either the brother or sister as yet—'

Someone else yelled, 'What do you believe his decision will be?'

She didn't move, didn't change expression. 'I have no right to speak for him, on that or any other issue.'

'Do you like him, princess?' a woman yelled over the hubbub.

'Does his Australian upbringing make him unsuitable for the role of future king?' someone else cried almost instantly afterwards.

Her jaw set. 'I have no comment to make on his fitness for the position.'

'But do you like him?' the woman persisted.

Charlie began making his way towards her,

elbowing past minders and staff with quiet 'excuse me's' and grim determination.

'Princess Giulia, have you any comment on your decision?'

'When's the wedding, Giulia?'

Lia closed her eyes and shook her head. Being trained thoroughly for this day hadn't prepared her for the sudden, terrifying reality of a press conference. At least Charlie had one advantage, thanks to that fire and the ensuing media circus. He'd been there, done that.

He strode to the platform with all the haughty command his handlers had told him worked from male sovereigns here, and excused himself to Jazmine.

She smiled at him in pure relief. Behind the podium, her hand found his. So cold, so unsure, and she was still here, fighting alone. He wouldn't let her down now.

A quick glance at his sister: there was a final moment to return to obscurity, if she chose. Lia smiled and nodded; her hand moved, a tiny sweep: *do it*. Her strength and courage was back. She was with him. Jazmine was with him.

Time to rise to the occasion, to be worthy of his wonderful, giving sister and his beautiful, brave princess.

He turned at the podium and said briskly in the Greek Papou had taught them—a relative of the old Koi Greek that was uniquely Hellenican, 'Good morning, ladies and gentlemen of the press. I am

Kyriacou Charles Marandis, grandson of the thirteenth Grand Duke of Malascos, son of Athanasius, Marquis of Junoar, and as such the Australian-raised Crown Prince of Hellenia.' He inclined his head as he'd seen the king do to servants and other lesser beings, with the barest hint of a smile. 'I am happy to answer any questions you may have regarding my right to be standing here today.'

As Jazmine gasped and clutched at the hand he held, he repeated the words in English and bowed again.

Strong and clean, Charlie, combining your birth and breeding with your laid-back Australian accessibility. The press will go wild.

He was better prepared for the multitude of flashes this time. He stood beside Jazmine, smiling, caressing her cold hand where it couldn't be seen. He allowed the din to die down before he spoke again. 'If you'll pardon me, I'm still not used to so much noise at once. If you could raise your hands…'

All of them rose at once.

'Grey suit, red tie,' Jazmine whispered.

He nodded at that man. 'You, sir.'

'So this means you're definitely taking the position of Crown Prince?'

Charlie inclined his head. 'That's so.' He indicated the next person, after Jazmine had whispered the description.

'Does that mean there will be a royal wedding soon?' the woman asked eagerly.

This was it. Feeling like second-rate goods but unable to show it, he turned to smile down at Jazmine. 'Yes, it does…if she'll have me.'

She covered the microphone for a moment as she looked up at him, her face reflecting the uncertainty. 'Are you sure, Charlie?'

The moment to turn back had come and gone. Now there was only forward. 'I just told the world, didn't I, *loulouthaki*?'

Jazmine's smile was radiant, probably sick with relief that she was free of the worst threat. She must have been feeling like a contestant on the world's worst game-show: *pick Door One—the twice-your-age, twice-married autocrat, Orakis. Pick Door Two: your childhood friend, almost a brother. And Door Three: the crude fireman.*

Well, Door Three it was. 'It seems appropriate to kiss about now,' he murmured, and at her tiny nod he bent, took her in his arms and kissed her.

He'd never tasted a kiss filled with such relief— and he felt the heady rush that came with knowing he'd done the right thing. He'd saved her.

The press went wild. The flashes were constant for the next minute.

Then the questions resumed, one after the other, blurring into a vague, shadowed memory. He'd never remember what they said, what he said—until a left-field question came from the back corner, a loud, hard bark from a man with a Hellenican accent.

'How do you feel about the allegations that you're

unfit to take the throne because of your Italian and Greek commoner's blood, and your total ignorance about the life and ways of our people? How do you feel about your constant failures to do anything right during the past weeks of tutorials?'

Simultaneous gasps filled the room, for which Charlie was grateful. It gave him a few moments to gather his thoughts from every corner of his mind and scramble them back into coherence somehow. To his amazement, he didn't feel the familiar rush of hot-blooded fury. The guy was probably an Orakis supporter, or just doing his job.

The people had the right to know who he was.

As he hesitated Jazmine moved forward, but, with a gentle touch, he stopped her. This had to be his answer.

'As I remember, there have been some comments along these lines for other commoners who became royalty,' he said, with a smile he hoped didn't look forced. 'I had an Italian grandmother, and a Greek mother. I'm not ashamed of it, nor do I think it lessens who I am. My grandmother was a gentle, loving woman who gave up her position amid the Italian nobility to marry my grandfather, and, if my mother was a commoner, she was also—extraordinary. They were the people who defined my life with their kindness, goodness and unselfish giving to others. They made me the person I am, as much as my father or grandfather, and my sister.'

'But that's why the king isn't here today, isn't it?'

the man said, his voice deadly cold. 'Can you confirm that the king neither likes nor approves of you as Crown Prince?'

Startled, Charlie answered the first part with truth. 'King Angelis is unwell.'

'My grandfather is confined to a bed at the moment,' Jazmine said quietly into the microphone. 'His doctors are attending to him.'

There followed a few minutes of questions then, on the king's state of health.

Then the man at the back repeated his question, 'Isn't it true, *Prince Kyriacou*, that the king neither likes you nor thinks you worthy of the position you claim as yours?'

'I heard you the first time, sir. I felt the questions on the king's state of health more important to answer first.' He held up a hand as the man began repeating his question. 'Please give me a moment.'

It was obvious to him now what was going on here. *This was a test*. Orakis had sent this man to try to force him to make a mistake, to become a fool in the eyes of the world.

Why that strengthened him, he had no idea. But the words came to him easily.

'I think we all know that if King Angelis disapproved of me I wouldn't be standing here today— Lord Orakis would. I have tripped over on some of the tests set for me. I don't deny it. But, if I'd failed completely, His Majesty would have put me on the first plane back to Sydney.'

Most heads nodded in agreement. He drew a breath of relief before continuing. Funny how he'd only just seen the truth of what he'd said just now. It did his self-confidence a great deal of good to realize the wily old fox hadn't hated him as much as he'd thought.

'In my view, it's not always people of birth and breeding that have changed the world. Ordinary people have taken key roles, have stepped forward with something to give the world. Some of the world's best-loved people were and are commoners. So, no, I don't think my Italian or Greek blood weakens my position. I hope I have something to give to Hellenia—and I believe the input of my mother and grandmother will help me as future king, to rule with compassion and an understanding of the common people, and to be able to dust myself off and try again when I do fail.' He smiled down at Jazmine, whose face was aglow with pride as she smiled back. 'And, with an extraordinary woman like Princess Jazmine at my side, the failures won't be too often, I'm sure.'

The press went wild again for a few minutes.

'Princess Jazmine!' The same man's deep, harsh voice called over the noise. 'I know for a fact that the man beside you, a common fireman, has failed at the most basic of royal expectations and protocols. No matter what face he puts on it, it's well known that he's been a disappointment to King Angelis from the start. How do you feel about that, since you'll be the one who will have to cover his every mistake?'

Jazmine was leaning into the microphone before the man had finished. She listened to his every word in icy silence. 'Are you finished?'

The man, unintimidated, nodded.

'Then, before all these people, I choose this man for my consort, my husband, whether or not he takes the crown,' she said coolly. Charlie wondered if anyone else heard the unsteady note in her voice as she bared her soul. 'I might have considered Lord Orakis if he had ever saved fifty-four lives or crossed the world to help others, instead of thinking only of his own advantage.'

The murmurs among the press began to swell.

'But that isn't the reason I'm standing here now beside my fiancé.' Her gaze swept the crowd, proud, disdainful, yet still smiling. Regal to her fingertips, his *loulouthaki*, her abundance of passion and fire stoked and slumbering by sheer force of her will. 'I am more committed to my country and my people than ever in their time of need—but this is no morganatic alliance. Common fireman or Crown Prince, I love him for the man he is, not for the compassion and stability he can give my people.'

As she kissed him again, Charlie froze. His brain switched off the lights and went on holiday without leaving a note. He broke out in a cold sweat, his pulse hammered and his lungs stopped working. And the seconds ticked on. He heard each one—tick, tick—coming closer and closer to the moment Jazmine stopped kissing him and he'd have to answer, and it would be time to face his reckoning.

Because he had absolutely no idea what to say.

Finally she ended the kiss; God knew, he couldn't have, would gladly have kissed her for ever rather than face this moment. Someone yelled, 'Prince Kyriacou, how do you feel about that? Are you in love with the princess?'

God help me, was all he could think as he kept staring at Jazmine, watching the radiant certainty fade from her face. Beneath the confident smile and proud eyes she reserved for the press, he saw the dread of knowledge touch her. Why he was here.

Tick, tick…

'Charlie?' she whispered, too softly for the press to hear. Her face super-imposed again: the Mona-Lisa princess and the gentle woman who'd bared her soul for his sake, who deserved a true prince and was now stuck with the toad before her.

He coughed and turned to the microphone. 'I beg your pardon. I think my fiancée just melted my brain. The woman's kiss is hotter than any fire I've fought.'

Laughter filled the room. From the side, where his impossible escape-hatch lured him like a siren's call, Toby grinned and gave him a discreet thumbs-up.

But, though she didn't move away, Jazmine's hand released his.

He threw up another frantic prayer, but nothing

came. He was on his own. Inane jokes wouldn't help him any more.

A quick glance at Lia showed him she was as scared as him. She knew him too well, knew what was coming.

Toby had his fists in front of him, pumping, up down, up down, in the old fire station signal: get on with it! Get to work!

Nope—still blank. So he settled for truth. It was all he had.

'I'm not a man who talks about private matters in public,' he said quietly. 'Those kinds of words belong to husband and wife alone. I can say, however, that I am deeply committed to the future. I'm committed to my future as Crown Prince, as the heir to the throne—to this nation—and as a husband to my wife. Hellenia needs healing, and my wife-to-be and I are as one in a commitment to helping our country to achieve that aim. And I am completely and totally committed to my bride-to-be. I'm in this for life.'

He knew he ought to kiss Jazmine yet again, but something in her eyes held him off. So he looked around for a moment, testing the reaction to his speech.

He saw Orakis's man slide out of the room, his face dark and thunderous.

He saw Toby grin and nod.

Lia's gaze was trained on Jazmine, with that secret 'girl's together' look on her face.

Not knowing what else to do, he kissed Jazmine's cold, unresponsive lips for a fourth time, and the flashes popped and the cheers were spontaneous.

It seemed there were only two people he hadn't fooled: the two women who meant the most to him.

He'd screwed it up again. He'd given all he could, yet he'd failed Jazmine. Again.

CHAPTER FOURTEEN

FINALLY she was alone.

In the suite that wasn't hers, in a place that had never felt like home, Jazmine kicked off the four-inch heels she'd been told gave her dignity and sat on the bed. It seemed a pathetic kind of borrowed dignity, a disguise, a mask of pretence, being someone she wasn't.

She had no dignity left; she had no pretence to hide behind, no pride. And the worst part was she couldn't blame anyone but herself. She'd risked it all, she'd bared her soul to the world, showed her heart for all to see, and he'd been *kind*.

Fourteen minutes. It was all she had before she had to face him again, and she had nothing. No story to tell, no lie to cover it over. She could try to laugh it off, use Orakis as an excuse—whatever rids us of his threat, right?—but she'd stripped off her mask for good. He knew the truth—and he'd been kind…

If she'd eaten anything at all in the past eight hours,

she'd have wanted to throw up. She wished she could. Her stomach seemed to be churning on air.

She couldn't do it, couldn't face him, not when he was making a sacrifice for her and she couldn't say no, couldn't stop him. She'd rather he'd lost it and yelled at her than pitied her.

The door burst open without warning, and he stood there in the entry, chest heaving, his eyes black with fury. 'Get away from here' was all he said.

The security detail behind him backed off to a discreet distance.

Jazmine sat on the bed, too tired to move, and watched him slam the door shut and stride to her, his face like a thunderclap about to burst open and pour over her.

The firecracker was back, she noted with an odd relief. Explosions she knew, she could cope with. Not *kindness*. She waited for him to start.

'I can't apologize for what I said, Jazmine. I was honest with you.'

She blinked. His face was dark with fury; why was he speaking so quietly, with such strange control? 'All right.' She couldn't think of anything else to say.

'I have enough changes to cope with. I'm learning protocol, politics, religion, how to walk, talk, bow and smile, and the titles and history of noble families around the world. Next week I start learning to fly planes and jumping out of choppers into the ocean, for crying out loud. I have to learn in a few months what you learned in a lifetime. If I'm going to become the kind of prince Hellenia needs, I can't deal with *feelings*, too.'

He seemed to wait for her to say something. 'I see.'

Her compliance seemed to confuse him; he began pacing, as if she'd argued. 'Toby's coming has only made more mess, but he's my brother, and he's in pain. He'd be there for me, the way he was for Lia. He stood by us after everything eleven years ago.'

'Of course,' she said, feeling oddly numb and stupid.

The glance became a narrow-eyed assessment. 'I saved you from Orakis. I agreed to be your prince. What more do you want from me?'

Light dawned on her. He'd given her everything he had, and he felt guilty he couldn't give more? 'Nothing,' she said softly.

He went on as if he hadn't heard. 'I swear I'll be faithful, Jazmine. I'll be the best husband I know how.'

He waited again. Her cue. 'I know you will.'

'I don't know how to be a prince or a king, but my father and grandfather were excellent husbands. I can do it.'

How could she want to smile when she hurt so much? 'I believe you.'

'But that's all I've got.' His eyes burned into hers now. 'Do you understand? I'll be your prince. I'll do my best to be king when the time comes. I'll be a faithful and honest husband. I'll be a good father to our kids. But that's all, Jazmine.'

Her cue again. 'I understand.'

And she did. He wanted her to back off, to give him space. Two weeks after coming here, he had truly done all she'd expected of him in the beginning, and he'd brought heart, thought and kindness to the role. He was already a prince, without the coronation; he was committed to Hellenia. He'd brought passion and laughter to her life, and had shared more of his secret self than she'd dreamed in the beginning.

She was being unfair in expecting more.

'It's all right, Charlie,' she said softly. 'I do understand—and thank you. Thank you for saving me, for saving Hellenia, and for salvaging my pride today.'

He shifted back, looking as if she'd impaled him instead of letting him off the hook. 'I do like you, okay? But I don't—'

'I said, it's all right.' She spoke over him before he could say the rest. Unable to bear hearing what she already knew. 'You don't have to explain any more. I understand. Princess and prince, queen and king, wife and husband; they're our roles. And parents, when the time comes. I'm a princess; controlling my emotions was drilled into me from birth. You won't have any tragic scenes to endure. We'll be excellent friends who happen to be married.' She lifted her chin and smiled at him. 'Now, if you'll excuse me, it's time for dinner. I need to change.'

She padded to the dressing room without looking back. If she did, he'd see how she'd repaid his honesty with lies. For his sake.

Six weeks later

'That was a productive day.' Jazmine sighed, closed her eyes and rested against the leather seating of the car as they left the third village at the day. She'd always refused to take limousines to the ravaged villages—she'd said it was like rubbing the differences between them in their faces. But the king insisted on their taking security cars with bullet-proof glass. Charlie called them their 'Pope mobiles'.

'Yeah—yes,' Charlie replied, watching her with a hunger he could barely rein in. It had been two days since he'd last kissed her.

'The apprenticeship scheme seems to be taking off everywhere we've instigated it.' She tugged at the shirt she wore; it was touched with perspiration.

'Yes, it has.' His gaze roamed her lovely form, damp and gently lush.

'I think we'll be able to initiate the scheme in another six villages within a few months. Wealth certainly seems to be begetting prosperity.' She smiled lazily. 'Your first decision for the crown and country was inspired. And your second really made the people love you—importing retired firefighters from Australia under Toby's direction, teaching the volunteers via interpreters. The Malascos fortune is certainly being put to good use, building fire stations, preventing fire and repairing damage.'

Did he say, 'Uh-huh?' He had no idea; he was lost in watching her lips move.

'The press and the people are lapping it up. They already adore you and Lia both, thanks to her ideas to help widows, orphans and divorced women. The flood of disaffected youth heading to Orakis's army has stopped and come back to us, because you're saving their villages and bringing in good changes, while preserving their way of life. You'll soon be a legend, you know. Statues and parks in your name.'

'Thanks,' he croaked, his desire fast reaching physical agony. He felt like a pervert of the worst kind.

It was always the same when they were alone together. He wanted and ached and burned…and always had to make the first move. It was becoming embarrassing—downright humiliating, actually—as if he was lusting after his best friend.

Not that she ever repulsed him. She welcomed his touch with a smile, and gave kiss for kiss. She just didn't *look* at him that way any more. She didn't say Char-r-liee, with that husky, blurry voice that drove him over the edge, or wind her fingers through his hair, or come to his room for late-night talks or walks through secret passages—or to hold him until he slept. No radiant smiles. No shimmering eyes as she smiled at him. She'd become exactly what she'd promised—an excellent friend and helpmate.

She was there, and yet she wasn't. It was driving him demented.

During the past six weeks Jazmine had kept her word as perfectly as she did everything else. No scenes; no tears or demands to endure. She was there beside him as she'd always been, teaching, guiding, encouraging him. She showed the way to lead her country by just being Jazmine. She smiled at him, she talked to him.

When he touched her, when he kissed her, she never rejected him or made excuses. The sweet fire he loved was in her response, if not quite the same. Something was missing; he just couldn't define what. But at least he had no need to worry she'd be a sulky wife who'd blackmail him before he could gain access to her bed.

Charlie was relieved about it. Of course he was. She was strong, she was a survivor, and it wasn't as if he was anything special; he was just another guy.

Okay, so she couldn't move on with him in her life, but she'd survived far worse. She'd shown her strength constantly during the past six weeks—when they'd been through the coronation and the engagement party, a zillion wedding shoots and interviews—and she'd been radiant and smiling through each one. And the moment their audiences had disappeared the loving fiancée had become the friend, keeping her distance unless the screaming need to touch her overwhelmed him. And when the kisses ended she walked away with a smile. No demands, no tears.

She didn't seem to be pining for what he couldn't give her. She had the palace, the prince, the crown, and the kids yet to come. She had a magnificent wedding gown, and a ring they'd chosen together from samples sent by the best jewellers in Europe. She seemed contented enough.

So why did he feel so bad?

And why did he miss her so much, when she was right there with him?

Her voice drifted into his tortured thoughts with the soft huskiness of sleep; the same huskiness she used to have when she wanted him. 'So tomorrow, when the—'

'Not now,' he growled, put up the shield so the driver couldn't see, and dragged her against him.

She smiled, her eyes pleasant—half-empty, half-full; half-*something*—and lifted her face for his kiss. *Passive.*

He pushed an errant curl from her face with some kind of fever. 'Kiss *me* this time, *loulouthaki.*' His voice was guttural with need, calling her by her nickname for the first time in weeks. Trying to push her—into what, he didn't know.

Her smile changed, became bittersweet, touched, tanged with loss, but she kissed him. She kissed him as an old friend would on seeing him again, and he couldn't handle it. Furious at her for being so obedient when she never had been before, he moulded her against him. 'No, *loulouthaki—kiss me*. Kiss me like you used to.'

She did as he asked, kissing him with her lips soft and parted and her ready passion coming to life; but still the gentle shell surrounding her didn't break. Even in the middle of a kiss that fried his brain, he felt her reserve enveloping her, impenetrable. Giving of her body, but protecting her heart. Keeping her real self in hiding.

Passion without feelings. Wanting him without caring.

God help him, it was everything he'd asked from her. It was the meaningless kind of relationship he was used to with women.

Except this was Jazmine. The woman who saw right through to his heart, and gave him what he asked for without taking in return. The woman with whom he would exchange vows before God and his people in a few weeks was treating him like a friend when he wanted a friend, and acted as a good-time guy when all he wanted to do was touch her. Easy, uncomplicated, fun.

But this was Jazmine, who was anything but those things. His honest Jazmine was living a lie, and he was making her do it.

What fool had said, 'you can't always get what you want'? He had it now, in his arms and his life, and right now he'd exchange the lot of it for an hour—a *minute*—of the fascinating, frustrating, adorable Jazmine he'd had at the beginning. With her emotional withdrawal, the sunshine and laughter had gone missing. No warmth or caring, no holding him, no sweetness and light, no addictive whispers of his name…no lifting onto tiptoes to kiss him, no innocent hands exploring him with ardent eagerness.

He was fast learning the truth of the saying, 'be careful what you wish for'.

God forgive him for his stupidity, he had it all right.

He hated himself for pushing her into becoming someone who smiled and kissed him on cue because she needed him to stay but no longer wanted it, no longer wanted *him*. He ended the kiss that disgusted him, because he couldn't stop trying to make her be what she'd been before becoming this obedient robot. 'It's all right,' he said dully. 'Go to sleep.'

She frowned as she moved back to her corner, her gaze searching his with hidden anxiety—the look he called the 'door one' option, if he left. 'Charlie—'

'No, don't,' he said roughly. 'It's not your fault, and you know it. I'm not going anywhere, Jazmine; I wouldn't leave you to Orakis, so stop being so compliant!'

As if he'd waved a magic wand over her, the fear vanished. She sat back against the seat, her head tilted in an intelligent, enquiring look. 'You're not happy.'

'Would you be?' he snapped.

A brow lifted as her head tilted more, searching out secrets he couldn't recognize. 'So what's wrong?'

Goaded by her calmness, he grabbed her by the shoulders. 'You tell me. It's like you've gone away and only your body's here.'

She lifted her hands in that elegant shrug of hers. 'Isn't that what you asked for?'

'Yeah, well, I don't like it,' he muttered, knowing he was being a hypocrite, but he didn't care.

Slowly, she nodded, her mouth slightly pursed. 'If you don't want me like this, what is it you *do* want from me, Charlie?'

How could he say it, after pushing her into becoming this? 'What do you think I want?'

Suddenly her chin lifted, her eyes sparked with life and fire, and the emotionless, compliant Jazmine slipped from her like an unwanted skin. The real woman sat beside him, complex, fascinating and adorable, all in an instant: the Jazmine he couldn't resist. 'Is this what you want—the woman I was before?'

He'd dragged her back to him before she finished speaking, his mouth on hers, and she moaned and thrust her hands into his hair, exploring him with a hunger to match his. She pulled him down on top of her, thrusting her hips against his. Taking charge with touch and kiss, using lips and tongue and soft, shuddering breaths to sensual advantage. Moaning and whispering tiny gasps: his name, just his name. *'Char-r-liee...'*

'Loulouthaki mou. Ah, yeah, ah... I've missed you so bad,' he mumbled between kisses. 'The real you. Stay with me. Just the way you are.'

She held him off, looking into his eyes. 'The trouble with this woman is she doesn't turn on and off on demand. This woman, the woman you want, has needs, has demands of her own.'

'Thank God for it.' He kissed her throat and felt her shiver. Yes, that was it. Ah, so good to have her back where she belonged…

She trailed her fingers down his neck and back, and he groaned. 'Sorry, Charlie,' the soft, relentless voice continued—and she pushed him off her. 'This woman comes complete with the things you demanded I leave out of our relationship.'

How could she be all rosy and warm with passion, so beautiful and alive, yet so cool and clear-headed at the same time? His head was spinning, and his body still pounded with the painful 'got to have her now' feeling she could inspire in him with a touch.

'This woman lives and breathes and wants and aches, Charlie.' The softest kiss on his neck made him groan out loud, dying for more. 'I laugh and cry. Sometimes I yell.' Tender, clinging kisses, once, twice on his aching mouth. 'And I *hurt*, too. You don't want the guilt that goes with that, remember?'

Only half the words went into his muddled brain and stayed. He was still locked into what he'd been aching to have for weeks, and he couldn't believe she was doing this to him now! It was like she was Salome, dancing before him, slowly stripping off the veils of pliancy covering the woman he wanted, needed, had to have, while his head was on a plate. At this moment he was almost willing to give anything to have her.

Damn women and their multi-tasking.

'And the trouble is, Charlie, that's me. This is who

I am, and my feelings are part of the deal. If you push that part of me away, you push all of me away.'

Suddenly his brain came back to clarity and focus—fear had a way of doing that to a man. He stilled, and stared down at her. 'So we're back to that.'

She met his gaze, fearless and honest. 'This is by your choice, Charlie. You're the one who wants the real woman.'

He moved to his side of the car, putting space between them. He had to think with his brain, not the parts of him screaming, 'do it, do anything to have her…' 'You're trapping me.' He heard the bitterness in his voice.

'And you think that's unfair? You think you're the only one? *You* took on the job. *You* made the choice. Nobody forced you.'

That wasn't true. Circumstances—Orakis—had forced his hand; even Jazmine had, by being who she was. But none of it was her fault. She'd done her best to give him freedom to choose. But because she was who she was, her own courageous, wonderful self, she'd forced him—forced him to *want* to live up to her standard, to be a better man.

But how could he say it? It probably made no sense to anyone but him.

'If it makes you feel better, you've trapped me too. You have from the start,' she said, her voice flat. 'You rode into my palace, the brave fireman into the burning building, and, no matter how many times I warned you, you kept saving me.' Her defiant gaze

held pride and unashamed pain. 'Even telling me
your secrets was for me, wasn't it? You had to save
me from you, but you never thought of the consequences.' She sighed and fiddled with the cup
holder built into the car door. 'That's your problem,
Charlie. You like to save people on a one-time-only
basis, to go home to your quiet, safe world alone,
because you don't want to feel. And you don't want
others to feel. Well, life isn't black and white. You
can't tailor the world to your wants or needs. Like
the rest of us, you have to live in a real world where
people do make mistakes—all of us—and we do get
hurt. You became my hero once too often, and I'm
in love with you.'

Strange that she could say 'I love you' with such
quiet loathing, as if she hated him. Even stranger
that he was hurting too, and feeling, and wishing…

Finally she let his gaze go, and he almost gasped
with relief; he'd felt like a pinned butterfly, a
specimen she was tearing apart piece by piece.
When she released him, he tried to snap back to the
person he'd always been, but something had
changed and he didn't know what.

'So take the woman with feelings, or without.'
She turned her head, looking out her side of the car
window. 'Make your choice and live with it,
Charlie. I have to.'

His head was banging every which way now. She
could do this to him, turn him inside out, make him
feel heaven and hell at once, make him live.

And leave him with utterly no idea what to say until he blurted out things he didn't know he was thinking or feeling until he said them. She dragged truth from him because she made him feel like the world's worst coward. He could rescue kids from burning buildings, but he couldn't allow himself to care. He knew how to risk his life, but didn't know how to take chances with his heart.

As the car passed the gates of the summer palace, he knew he had to say something or she'd know him for the pathetic, terrified man he was, a man who could take on a country but couldn't handle one five-foot-three woman he—he *what*…?

'I think—I think I love you.'

And he gasped. Had he really said that? And how could he feel so liberated, when his throat had closed up and his heart had become twice its normal size, suffocating him? He was going to die, to die.

He had his last, panicked thought: *at least she'll be happy now. She won. I loved her for all of a minute.*

The shocking sting of her palm hitting his cheek snapped his body back to its normal pace and rhythm. Thank God; she'd seen his panic attack and had saved his life.

Then he gasped again. He'd be willing to bet she'd never called any man *that* word before.

'How could you, Charlie? *How could you?*' she cried, her face pale and her eyes dark with devastation. She scrambled out of the car with utterly no grace, and bolted for the doors.

CHAPTER FIFTEEN

Four days later
The forty-fifth anniversary of King Angelis's reign

CHARLIE and Toby sat on their favourite stools at the bar in a quiet corner of the summer palace's ballroom. Charlie had circulated the room, spoken to dignitaries and assisted the elderly. Now he was enjoying a quiet beer with Toby, waiting for the call to dinner.

Five hundred noble guests from around the world had come to celebrate this milestone—and, given the king's increasingly frail state of health, it seemed it would be the last.

Charlie's gaze tracked Jazmine's graceful progress around the room. She ought to be here laughing with him, relaxing at this special party, not having to deal with the guy from the *Hellenican Observer*. Didn't the guy know her grandfather's health was more than a political issue to her? Couldn't the man see the sheen in her eyes, the sadness in her smile? It was visible to him even from this distance. It was all he could do to keep sitting there. If he thought she'd welcome him…

'Why doesn't this place have a pool table?' he snapped for no good reason.

'Two or three pool tables, and a few dartboards,' Toby agreed in a growl. Max had just joined Lia, who was surrounded by a group of international admirers.

Charlie picked up his beer and swilled it down with no appreciation for its import costs, imagining Jazmine lying beside him with that slow, sleepy smile that made him forget titles and duty and everything but her.

Jazmine had extricated herself from the journalist and had stationed herself beside the king, who was having difficulty speaking to his guests. He would be returning to his bed as soon as dinner was over.

Charlie half-lifted from the stool, ready to help. Jazmine caught his eye and looked away, making the crowd around her grandfather laugh at something she said. She didn't want or need him; she was coping alone. She didn't want him.

'Why is it I can run a bloody country, I can make eight million people happy, and I can't tell a woman I love her without her hitting me?' he muttered.

Jazmine had been immersed in the final details of this celebration dinner since she'd slapped him. Since it was all prearranged, he couldn't accuse her of avoiding him, but she'd had no time to hear him or sort things out. All he wanted was for things to be as they'd been between them—but, like everything else in his life, he'd woken up too late.

Toby shrugged, his gaze riveted on Lia, whose arm had slipped through Max's as they shared a smile about something. 'It's the way God made us. We're the bigger and stronger, we can build things and fight fires, but women run circles around us in emotions or argument. They crush us to dust every time. We never win.' Toby downed his beer.

Charlie tried for a third time to catch Jazmine's eye, but she turned obliquely so she was at a ninety-degree angle from him. Her unspoken 'don't touch me, don't come near me' was so loud she might as well have screamed it across the room.

'What did I do that was so wrong?' Charlie demanded, thudding his glass down so hard the beer sloshed over onto the beautiful polished mahogany, and some dignitary or other who'd been approaching him scuttled away. 'I *told* her, Grizz. Wasn't that what she wanted?'

Toby shrugged again. 'Don't ask me. I don't have a clue… obviously.'

Charlie shook the beer off his hand, but grabbed the washcloth from the bartender when he started to clean the mess. 'My mess. My job.' He wiped down the counter, and handed it back. 'Sorry,' he said gruffly.

Slowly, the bartender smiled. 'It's fine, Your Highness. And, if I may say so, I think you're doing Hellenia, and the royal family a great deal of good.'

Charlie frowned, arrested by the words for no reason he could fathom. 'Why?'

The older man smiled. 'Change at this time in Hellenia's history is good, sir. After the war and suffering, you've come in and done the things we believe Princess Jazmine would do if she was a man. They like having a man of action in the palace.'

If she was a man... The words ping-ponged around in his brain. There was something there—something significant, profound.

During dinner, he watched Jazmine take care of the frail king without taking away the old man's dignity. He watched her direct the staff when they came to her with questions. He watched her discreetly listening to the conversation around her and join in when appropriate, murmuring to her grandfather when his voice was needed.

Lia walked round her chair to Jazmine's and said something. Jazmine murmured to a member of staff, who spoke to someone else, who delivered no more wine to a bordering-on-belligerent dignitary who'd had a bit much to drink. Lia and Jazmine worked together beautifully, seamlessly, to ensure the night's success—but it was Jazmine who directed it all, Jazmine whom everyone trusted to get it right.

Everyone trusted Jazmine every time—the king, the diplomatic staff, servants, the people, the media. She did everything in the best interests of others.

If she was a man.

That was it. That was it!

The next day

The press-room was filled to overflowing again for the new Crown Prince's first self-called press conference.

Cameras began rolling from every TV station or affiliate in Europe the moment Charlie walked in from the huge corner-door. Flashes popped. Security men flanked him and stood in every row, armed and dangerous. Every member of the press had been searched for weapons.

But, because no one had a clue why Charlie had called the conference, they waited for him to start.

She wasn't here. He'd asked her to come, but she'd claimed royal duties.

It didn't matter. He knew her well enough to be sure that she'd come once she knew what he intended. Lia would be right behind her.

Once again, he strode to the podium with the regal bearing he'd been taught. Once again, he gave the flawless introduction.

And then he got to the point.

'Ladies and gentlemen of Hellenia, and the press— I am a modern man, as you all know. My Hellenican family was traditional enough to believe a man is the head of the house. But my father and grandfather taught me deep respect for women and their right to have a place in the world—and a say in their future. My past career as a firefighter, and my immersion into Australian culture, only reinforced that belief.

'I fought fires the same way I intend to fight for

what is best for this, my new country. Hellenia is a beautiful country, with people who want a life that blends the best of their ancient traditions with modern life. She has her own statutes and laws, as do all nations. I fully intend to uphold those traditions when they are best for my people.

'King Angelis has been a magnificent monarch during these uncertain times. But for every nation there comes time to change—and I believe it's time to make a change.'

He looked around the room. He could probably have heard a pin drop. They were waiting for the announcement.

He glanced to the right, to the door reserved for royalty's entrance. Toby, stationed by the door, shrugged. Jazmine still wasn't here.

So he went on with the speech he'd stayed up all night to write.

'During my last press conference, one of you made a very good point. I'm new to this country. I come from common stock as well as noble. I grew up completely ignorant of this nation. And, though I'm doing my best to rectify this ignorance, it's clear that I *will* make mistakes, will judge the people by the standards in which I was raised, by the only life I've known until now. I also know that many of my people are relying on the excellent guidance I have behind me to do what's best for Hellenia, to be the best king I can be.

'However, I am not so certain this is the right

way. I *am* a stranger. I *am* ignorant. It's only by accident of birth that I'm here now—a fact of which I'm very well aware. If the laws didn't state that a male must take the throne unless there are no male-line descendants left, I wouldn't be standing here— likely, I'd be standing at a pub in Sydney.' He grinned, let them laugh, and added, 'Princess Jazmine would be standing here instead, as the person with the greatest right to rule this country.'

The murmurs began; they whispered questions among themselves.

He cleared his throat of the nerves filling it, and continued. 'When I thought of that, I realized that she ought to be here now, today, as your future ruler. Princess Jazmine has devoted her life to this country and its people. She is a strong, intelligent and courageous woman who has put her own safety on the line time after time to help her people. If the laws were different, you would have the ruler you deserve.'

He paused to let that sink in.

'This is the change I will propose at the next meeting of the king and ministers: this five-hundred-year-old law needs to be revoked. The most direct descendant of the last ruler, be they male or female, should take the throne. I propose that when our strong and excellent King Angelis passes away, or decides to abdicate, Hellenia should enjoy the rule of the best person they could have on the throne: Princess Jazmine.'

The room erupted into a cacophony of light and sound: strobe-flashing and yelled questions.

'So does this mean you're stepping down as Crown Prince, Your Highness?'

'Are you returning to Australia?'

'Did you and the princess break up?'

Charlie allowed the questions to keep coming thick and fast as he summoned his thoughts, ready to answer each question with all the patience he could muster. Willing himself with all the self-control at his command not to keep looking at the door. Looking for Jazmine couldn't help now. She was already filling his head too much.

Come to me, loulouthaki. *Tell me that, for once, I got it right. Give me that shimmering look and tell me you've forgiven me for being so slow and stupid, not knowing how much I love you. Kiss me and tell me you still love me.*

But even if she didn't come, if she couldn't forgive him, he knew in his heart and soul that he'd done the right thing, both for Hellenia and the woman he loved.

He was still amazed he hadn't thought of it within days of arriving here. He'd known he was the wrong person for the job, and Jazmine was utterly right to rule; but he hadn't seen until last night that, if he had the power to take the title or walk away, he had the power to propose change.

But he needed to effect change. And that was why he'd called a press conference first, instead of using the privacy of a session of the lords who pretended to help the king run the country.

If the people were behind him in this, the press would know.

A small commotion to his right made him want to smile. She was here.

Moments later an exquisitely dressed Jazmine was beside him on the podium, her lovely face filled with a confusion and fury she couldn't even hide for the cameras. Without even looking at the assembled press, she dragged him to the absolute back of the room, away from microphones but not from speculation. '*What* do you think you're doing, you idiot?'

Relief flooded him. He could handle anything, even her abuse, if she was talking to him. If she was here with him, he could do anything. 'Ah, so it only takes giving up a kingdom to make you take the time to talk to me? You set your asking price too low, princess,' he said softly, smiling down at her.

She looked shaken. 'You called a press conference and gave up your position to make me *talk to you*?' she whispered incredulously.

'Well, that, and one small fact: you're the best person for the job. I don't know why I didn't see it before.' He kept smiling. He probably looked like a dork, but he didn't care. He'd missed her so badly and she was here.

'You're an *idiot*,' she repeated for his ears alone. 'You've made such a mess and now I have to fix it!'

His brows lifted. 'A mess, princess? Look out there.' He waved a hand to the rest of the room.

Taken aback by his confidence, she turned... and saw the standing ovation, heard the calls of her name.

She blinked. 'It—it can't happen, Charlie. The ruler must be male.'

Loving her sweet confusion, wanting to believe but not daring, he took her hand in his and smiled for the barrage of cameras. 'Smile and agree, and bide your time,' he whispered in her ear, quoting her words back to him. 'This is the time, Jazmine. If we wait until the king dies, I'm automatically king—and then it's too late.'

She turned to him, her face stricken. 'You're leaving?'

The roars for attention from the press grew louder. It wasn't time for personal declarations, unless he combined the best of both.

He drew her forward to the microphone. 'Ladies and gentlemen of the press, I give you the person I believe will be the best future ruler you could have—my future wife, the woman I love, Jazmine Marandis.' Knowing now the power of the press could be turned his way, he thought of kneeling but rejected it as too dramatic, so he turned her around to him, took both hands in his, and looked deeply in her eyes. Speaking too low for the microphone, he murmured, 'That is, if you still want to marry me after I threw a surprise of this magnitude into your lap.'

Slowly, she looked down and back up. Her hands trembled. 'Charlie…'

'I didn't do this to prove I love you, *loulouthaki*,' he whispered. 'I believe you were born for this. I believe I finally got something right here. Nothing ever felt so right before. I believe this is right for Hellenia, not just right for you. And I'll be at your side whenever you need me. I'm not going anywhere—for the rest of our lives.'

Her eyes shimmered as her smile slowly came to life. 'I'll always need you.'

He'd never wanted to kiss her more than now. But she'd already turned to the press, who'd been following the quiet drama with avid interest. 'Ladies and gentlemen of the press, please be seated.'

Her tone brooked no denial, no argument or question. She had something to say.

'I can honestly say Prince Kyriacou didn't shock *you* alone. I knew he'd called a conference, but had no inkling of his intention until I heard his announcement. That's obvious, I suppose, by my reaction.' She smiled and did the hand-shrug thing he loved, and everyone laughed. 'Unfortunately, as much as his gesture touches me, I believe Hellenia isn't ready just yet for change of such magnitude.'

Charlie's heart hit his gut. No, no, he couldn't be wrong this time! Not when it felt so right. She couldn't do this. But he had to trust her now. If he took over, it would look as though he didn't think she could handle the job already.

When the hubbub died down, Jazmine spoke again. 'I do believe Prince Kyriacou has it right; it's time for change.' Smiling, she turned and reached for his hand. He came forward at her tugging. 'I believe that, with the blessing of my grandfather and the House of Hereditary Lords, the next rulership could become a joint one. A co-rulership would bring the energy, fresh direction and knowledge of the common people that is Prince Kyriacou's greatest strength, and my knowledge of Hellenican people and history.'

This time the room didn't erupt, it exploded, as the press surged to their feet, cheering and asking questions.

And Charlie, stunned yet not surprised, looked at her. 'I should have known you'd one-up me, princess. You get it right every time.'

She smiled up at him. 'Only when my wonderful prince gives me the incredible, new and fresh ideas I can find ways to improve on. I'd never have thought of this on my own, Charlie. And I'd never have thought of going public with it, to strengthen our position with the people's approval.' The eyes he loved so much shimmered—not with tears, but with love. 'We're going to make such a wonderful team, *eros mou*.'

My love.

And she turned back to the press, answering questions as if she hadn't just made all his dreams come true.

But then, that was the woman he loved: his courageous, strong little flower.

After ten interminable minutes of answering questions, his hand caressed hers behind the cover of the podium with the Hellenican crest. 'How soon can we get out of here? I've got to kiss you soon. I've got to touch you, *loulouthaki*, or I'll hit something,' he growled in her ear.

A small smile curved her mouth. Her eyes danced. 'Such is the life of royalty. You have to learn to wait, from bathroom visits to making love,' she whispered back...but her thumb moved from its linked position and softly stroked his palm. 'But I promise I'll make it worth the wait.'

His heart and body went into fast meltdown. 'Something tells me you'll always make the wait worthwhile.'

They smiled at each other, warm, tender, intimate—and, too late, they both realized they'd totally missed the most recent question.

'AND now, I'd like to ask the bride and groom to take the floor for the traditional bridal waltz. Prince Kyriacou personally chose the song, and wishes to dedicate it to his bride.' Toby, in his combined role of best man and master of ceremonies, smiled and made a sweeping motion with his hand.

Charlie got to his feet, and, keeping Jazmine's hand in his, kissed it softly as he led her to the perfectly polished floor of the state ballroom. 'Mine at last,' he murmured in her ear.

Jazmine's heart skipped a beat at the look in his eyes, at his touch. In the past few weeks, they'd come so close to making love, over and over—but, no matter how many times she'd begged him, no matter how many times she got him close to nakedness and madness, he'd refused to cross the line.

'You deserve the perfect prince and courtship, *loulouthaki*. But, since you're stuck with me, you'll at least get this much: the most perfect wedding night I can give you,' he'd tell her every time. 'Not much longer to wait.'

Tonight was finally the night.

Once on the floor, Charlie didn't sweep her into the dance they'd been practising for weeks. The orchestra stumbled to a halt as he knelt at her feet—and, startled, she watched him gently lift one throbbing foot and remove the four-inch heel from it.

Then he did the same for the other foot. He winked at her and tossed them over to Toby, who caught them with the air of a plan fulfilled.

'But Charlie—'

'The cameras are gone now.' That had been the deal—their reception was theirs alone after weeks of giving of themselves to the people and press. Their honeymoon, on the traditional Aegean island owned by the ruling family, would be totally private and completely protected.

She nibbled at her inside lip. Oh, he knew her too well—he knew her love-hate relationship with heels, and she'd been standing for hours for the photo shoots. Even though they'd since had dinner, her feet still throbbed. 'But everyone else…'

He grinned at her. 'What, you can turn history on its ear by becoming the first co-ruling queen, but you can't shock a few old stick-in-the-muds at our wedding?'

She had to laugh. It was true—the coronation date was set for six weeks' time.

Grandfather had told them both a week ago that he

was ready to abdicate, due to failing health. He'd kissed Jazmine's cheek, and said with the approval of the people and House of Hereditary Lords the five-hundred-year-old law of succession would change. She'd proven herself worthy to be co-ruling queen. And Charlie, he said, was ready to be a king in the best mixture of modern ideas and respect for tradition. Charlie had almost fallen off his seat, hearing Grandfather calling him by his preferred name.

Approval for them both at last—and Jazmine would treasure the words for ever. She was going to be queen, with the king she adored at her side. Her laughing, heroic, unconventional Charlie, who thought it appropriate for a princess to go barefoot at her own wedding.

As if walking into her thoughts, he winked again. 'You know you want to.'

She bit her lip, but the grin peeped out. 'I hate you sometimes, you know that?'

He brushed his cheek against hers. 'We belong to the world, but today it's just us, Jazmine. Our wedding, our dance. Just you and me.' He smiled into her eyes, and she melted, as she always did for him.

He lifted her onto his shod feet. 'I won't make any mistakes if I have you right here.' Gently, he kissed her.

The orchestra struck up the song again—and they danced an inch or two closer than protocol demanded, and just a beat slower than they ought. And she loved every romantic moment of it. Even when the floor became crowded with guests, she couldn't see them. All she felt was Charlie. All she wanted, all she needed, was right here in her arms.

Then the song the orchestra played sank into her consciousness, and Toby's words: *Unforgettable.* 'Oh.' Tears rushed to her eyes. 'Oh, Charlie…'

'If you weren't unforgettable, I'd have disappeared long ago.' He smiled and touched his forehead to hers. 'As much as I'd like to believe I stayed, that I took on the job, for all the right reasons—the people, my heroic nobility—the simple truth is, I couldn't leave. I couldn't leave *you.*'

'You're making me cry,' she whispered.

But the tears had been there from the moment she'd awoken this morning.

The room filled with roses had been traditional and expected; but the funny card he'd sent with them—hand-drawn, with a small, white flower sticking stubbornly to a weed wearing a crown— was so uniquely Charlie, she'd felt she'd burst with love. The inside had held only five words: thank you for being you.

She'd cherish the card all her life.

Then he'd replaced her bridal bouquet of white roses and hothouse flowers. The flowers he'd sent her were unfamiliar, like small, white stars.

'His Highness had them imported from Austria,' Charlie's new personal assistant had told her when he'd delivered them.

Jazmine frowned. 'Don't you mean Australia?'

He'd shaken his head and smiled. 'Edelweiss is

an Austrian flower, Your Highness. Prince Kyriacou asked that you read the card.'

Confused, wondering why he'd send these instead of an Australian flower which might mean something to him, she'd opened the envelope.

He'd drawn some musical notes, a rough map of Hellenia, and had written one line: *bless my homeland for ever.*

Her maid and Lia, maid of honour, had had to reapply her make-up after that.

She'd walked down the aisle to him on Grandfather's arm—he'd practised walking, using a cane, right up until today. And, though Charlie hadn't seemed to take his eyes from her, when Grandfather had faltered he'd nodded. Max had quietly come up behind the ailing king, and, without touching him or lessening his pride, had let Grandfather know he was there.

And then, during the traditional wedding, he'd asked to say something. The priest seemed to have expected it, and nodded.

Charlie had turned to Grandfather, and bowed with the deepest respect. Jazmine had seen Grandfather's eyes mist up, and he smiled.

Then Charlie had said, 'People have called me a hero, in the past and now. But in history the real heroes have risen because of one thing, and fallen by it also: the strength of home and love, and the kind of faith only the right woman can give. I had none of those, Jazmine, until you. So from my heart, my princess bride, I thank you for choosing me. I thank you for making me the man I've always wanted to become.'

It was a good thing Lia had brought spare make-up for the photo shoots…

'Uh-oh. Look at that.'

Startled from her thoughts by Charlie's murmur in her ear, she looked to where he indicated. 'Oh, dear.'

The best man and maid of honour were dancing as tradition dictated, but, like Charlie and Jazmine, Toby and Lia were an inch or two closer than necessary…and swaying into each other. Toby dipped Lia with consummate grace—apparently he'd done ballroom lessons with Lia years before—but brought her back to his lips. And despite the public scrutiny Lia swayed into Toby with a dreaming look on her face, closed her eyes and kissed him.

Charlie sighed. 'We're going to have to do something about that.'

'After coronation,' she agreed.

'After our honeymoon,' he corrected, his eyes filled with meaning. 'We need it sorted—but not until then.' He gave a low growl as he saw Max heading towards them. 'Max is coming. More royal waiting-time before I can touch you again.'

She laughed, a soft, rippling sound, and caressed the base of his neck beneath his collar with slow, sensual fingers. 'The helicopter will be waiting for us in exactly ninety minutes—and we'll be on our own. No one can interrupt us tonight. You're finally mine, Charlie Marandis—all of you. All mine.'

At the thought of the night, their eyes took fire, and they kissed with slow passion. Biding their time. Because it would come. And, from four feet away, Max smiled at the very private moment and turned away, as Jazmine had known he would.

Tonight was *not* royal time. Tonight they were just a man and woman in love, a groom and bride like any other. Tonight belonged to them alone, her wonderful firefighter lover and his little flower.

For the rest of her life, the world would have Kyriacou and Jazmine—but she'd have Charlie, and he'd have his *loulouthaki*.

For ever.

JOIN THE
MILLS & BOON
BOOKCLUB

- ✸ **FREE** delivery direct to your door
- ✸ **EXCLUSIVE** offers every month
- ✸ **EXCITING** rewards programme

50% OFF
YOUR FIRST
PARCEL

Join today at
Millsandboon.co.uk/Bookclub

MILLS & BOON
True Love

Romance from the Heart

Celebrate true love with tender stories of heartfelt romance, from the rush of falling in love to the joy a new baby can bring, and a focus on the emotional heart of a relationship.

MILLS & BOON

MODERN

Power and Passion

Prepare to be swept off your feet by
sophisticated, sexy and seductive heroes, in
some of the world's most glamourous and
romantic locations, where power and
passion collide.

LET'S TALK
Romance

For exclusive extracts, competitions and special offers, find us online:

f facebook.com/millsandboon

🐦 @MillsandBoon

📷 @MillsandBoonUK

Get in touch on 01413 063232

For all the latest titles coming soon, visit
millsandboon.co.uk/nextmonth